W9-DFK-009

MIDNIGHT RENDEZVOUS

"Oh, but that's right," Drew continued as he came nearer, his blue eyes glinting like forged steel. "You probably can't remember. You and your convenient amnesia."

He stopped, his gaze holding her in place. Daunted by his nearness, Monica felt her throat go tight, her heart begin to race. "It's not convenient," was all she could think of to say.

He loomed before her, tall and so overpoweringly male. "No? Then how is it you can forget your son has nightmares, yet have no trouble remembering one hell of a lot about you and me?"

Monica shook her head vehemently, half-wanting to back away, half-hoping he'd kiss her.

"How could you know what we did in this room?" He moved closer yet, angrily grabbing her arms. "I heard your laugh just now—I saw your face."

Monica could barely breathe. All she knew was that her treacherous new body wanted to be driven back to the table. *Take me,* her mind was repeating. *Now.*

"You and your damned deceits," he hissed, his grip tightening on her arms. "Did you come here to seduce me? Or were you hoping to find someone else?"

"No." The denial was the merest whisper.

His eyes searched hers, even as his lips sought her mouth. He was so close she could feel his heat, could just about hear his heartbeat pounding the same accelerated rhythm as her own.

His kiss was electric, a jolt of pleasure that went shooting through her veins. It set off a hunger so strong she forgot everything and dug her fingers into his hair to pull him closer.

BARBARA BENEDICT

A TASTE OF HEAVEN

ZEBRA BOOKS
KENSINGTON PUBLISHING CORP.

ZEBRA BOOKS are published by

Kensington Publishing Corp.
475 Park Avenue South
New York, NY 10016

First Printing: September, 1993

Printed in the United States of America

To Vickie Bashor, Maryann O'Brien
and Angie Ray
for all your advice,

To the Literary Elite—
Dorsey "Kelley" Adams, June O'Connell,
Win "Witton" Smith, and Maralys Wills
for cheering me on,

And to Scott,
for always being there.

Monique

March 28, 1855:

Monique Antoinette de Vereaux—one day soon, my name shall be spoken in every elegant salon in New Orleans.

Normally, I am not one for the tame business of penning a daily journal, but I fear if I don't write about what I am about to do, I shall burst with the excitement.

How can I talk to parents about the glittering future I've planned? They expect me to accompany them home at the end of the month so I might wed a dull, elderly neighbor and provide scores of grandchildren to run through the hallowed de Vereaux halls.

Too soon, they shall learn that growing old on their isolated sugar plantation is not in my plans. I want—*non,* I need—the assemblies and balls and entertainments; I want to see the world and I want the world to see me!

Why, this one time, must my parents deny me what I want? They say I am too young and beautiful to be out on my own, but what they truly mean is I am too female. A woman needs a man to look after her, Papa insists, which he can ill afford to do when it is long since time he returned home for the planting.

While I am woefully aware that it takes a man to open the doors of opportunity in this world, Papa is not the only man available. If he will not get me what I wish, I shall find someone else.

I spoke of this to my new American friend, Sarah Jane Hawkins. If it is protection I need, I said, hoping to shock her, perhaps I should become some man's mistress. In truth, though, I see no sense in basing my future welfare on some man's whim. Especially when Papa would only kill him and still take me home.

No, I suppose I must agree with Sarah Jane that my only hope is to find a husband. What will she say, I wonder, when she learns who the lucky man is to be?

Not that she can change my mind. Robert Sumner is the ideal candidate, handsome enough to turn any girl's head and more than capable on the dance floor. My parents will not be displeased, for he is well-mannered, highly-connected, and obscenely rich. Indeed, the only drawback I can see is that the man has been courting Sarah Jane Hawkins for years.

In all honesty, it is a waste, linking Robert Sumner with a mouse like Sarah Jane. She herself will tell you she is pale and lifeless beside my dark, vibrant beauty. I could easily win him away from her, had I the time, but not when my foolish parents insist upon dragging me home.

My only remaining hope lies in Rachel.

I smile at this, for I can hear my slave in the other room, chanting softly as she lights her candles and prepares her potions. I will happily draw my own bedcovers this once, if it leaves Rachel free to weave her enchantments.

And tomorrow, when Sarah Jane brings her beau for tea, I shall serve Robert Sumner a cup laced with the potion that shall change all our lives forever.

Mark my words, and mark them well—before the year is out, Monique Antoinette de Vereaux shall be the belle of New Orleans.

One

"This is it, ma'am. River's Edge. Want me to drive through the gate?"

Shaking her head, Monica Ryan found now that she was actually here, she was in no hurry to answer this latest summons from her aunt.

Glancing at the driver, she thought of the cabbies in New York, as sharp and intense as the city they served. How easily this man's drawl banished the skyscrapers and bustling sidewalks, gently reminding that this was Louisiana, where life was softer, slower, the very air seemed to soothe you. Where little moved unless the breeze stirred it, from the Spanish moss draping the oak-lined drive to the lethargic frog croaking in the nearby swamp. It all came rushing back, a warm bath of memories—all those hot, lazy summers she'd pined and whined away her teens.

Would Derek Sumner be here? she wondered, her heart skipping crazily.

In her mind, she could see her aunt's stepson, coaxing Judith to sell his father's estate. He'd be smiling—always smiling—making a girl want to believe every word he said.

Shutting off such thoughts firmly, Monica dug in her purse for some bills. These were secret dreams, private agonies; and, besides, who liked to admit they were shallow enough to fall for a grin?

Stuffing the money in the driver's hand, she avoided his eyes in the rear-view mirror. "Thanks," she muttered. "I can walk from here."

"That's a long driveway, ma'am. And seeing's how much you've paid, I owe you the extra distance."

"It's okay," she insisted as she fumbled for the door handle. She'd always found tipping an awkward process, both in the giving and receiving. "I need the exercise anyway."

She winced, wishing she hadn't said that. Flaunt the weight you've lost, her dietician advised; don't call attention to how much you have yet to go.

Especially considering what she wore. Frumpy thriftshop stuff, Judith would call the pleated skirt and plain cotton blouse; but it was all Monica could manage on a teacher's salary. And at least they were her own clothes, bought with her own money.

"Come home," Judith would nonetheless add with a patronizing smile. "You need me to take care of you."

Would her aunt ever understand that no matter how much scrimping and saving it took, Monica was determined to stand on her own?

It seemed unlikely. Though only fifteen years older, Judith enjoyed playing the matriarch, intent upon running Monica's life forever—choosing clothes, boarding schools, friends—all done with a smile, an I-know-what's-best-for-you complacency that Monica inevitably seemed unable to fight.

As it did each time she thought about confronting her aunt, Monica's stomach growled. *I'm too stuffed to eat,* she chanted. Her dietician maintained that she ate to fill in the empty places, using food as a substitute for acceptance and love, but Monica often wondered if eating was just the only avenue of expression Judith had left her.

Climbing out of the cab and slamming the door, she vowed there would be no vacillating. This time, she would stand up to the woman and tell her no.

As if doubting this, the driver gave her a quick, concerned glance. "Y'all take care now," he said with that same concern before driving off.

Simple words, "take care," one person being polite to another; yet, despite the midday heat, Monica shivered.

As if called there, her gaze went to the swampy area beyond the house. In the past, she'd avoided it, happy to obey Judith's orders to stay out; yet today she found herself stepping closer. It was as if something reached into her chest and gave a hearty yank. She still stood on the road, but she could feel the heavy, dank air close around her, redolent with rotting vegetation, teeming with an unearthly quiet that blanketed the soul.

A sudden honk banished the sensation. Whirling, Monica saw the cab skid as a rabbit darted up and over the twenty-foot levee. How silly she felt, as scared as the rabbit. Two seconds more and she'd have been running down the road, pleading with the driver to take her back to New York.

Forget the swamp, she told herself as she turned to the house. Concentrate instead on the peaceful beauty, on this alley of live oaks lining the drive. It wasn't the swamp that caused her sudden stage fright, she knew. Any decent therapist would insist that if she were afraid, the cause was most likely Judith.

"Come home," the woman had pleaded during yesterday's phone conversation. "Come help me save River's Edge."

Typically, she'd refused to say more until Monica answered her summons, but you couldn't live all these years with the woman and not sense when Judith was laying a trap.

No, that was unfair. It was true that her aunt could be selfish, uncaring, and sometimes even cruel; but in the end, Judith invariably managed to find a way to atone. They were family, she'd remind with a hug—the only real family either of them had.

And if they shared one thing, it was a love for River's Edge.

Monica stopped to gaze up at the stately antebellum mansion, feeling the old familiar longing well up inside, swamping her, drowning her hard-won resolve. God, how she loved this place.

Built off the ground to safeguard against floods, the house rose up two stories to a peaked roof, its long windows and wide French doors lending an open, welcoming countenance. Tall, elegant columns flanked the broad porch steps, with others standing guard at strategic locations along the wide, wrap-around porch. Judith's friends called it a showcase of the more graceful days; but to Monica, it was a place in which to raise a family, a home meant for laughter and love.

It was her Achilles' heel, River's Edge; and, unfortunately, Judith knew it.

The only time she'd ever dared argue with her aunt was over its restoration. Barely had Judith's husband George been laid in the Sumner crypt than her aunt was out here to bully the army of workers. In no time, Judith had every shutter replaced, the gorgeous oak floors covered with marble tile, and the garden and neglected gazebo torn up to build her swimming pool and spa.

To Judith, the place was a status symbol, a showcase of her achievements; and, as a result, she'd become as tacked-on as her improvements. Judith Sumner didn't belong here, any more than her five-car garage.

For while it was now beautifully restored, River's Edge seemed as empty and unfulfilled as the rainy day Monica had first gazed upon it. It haunted her; its air of loneliness made her feel somehow responsible for bringing laughter and life back into its halls. It didn't need Italian marble or treasures imported from around the globe, it seemed to tell her; it just wanted to be someone's home.

Her home. Every dream she'd ever had revolved around River's Edge. In them, she'd picture her children, lots of children, climbing like monkeys on the porch railing. And a husband, waiting atop the broad, porch steps, his handsome face breaking into a smile of welcome as she approached.

Her own smile faded as she realized where her thoughts were leading. She had no hope of ever living her dream. Judith would pass the property on to her dead husband's son; and, no matter what Monica dreamed or hoped or did, River's Edge would belong to Derek.

"Cuz? Is that you?"

Looking up, Monica felt as if she'd taken a blow

to the chest. Dark blond hair brushed back from his face, Derek stood in the doorway, hands in his baggy shorts, his lean, muscled frame accentuated by a neon, printed tank shirt. As always, he was smiling, making her feel as if he'd been waiting there forever just to welcome her home.

"Why, look at you," he drawled as he ambled down the steps to take her hands. "You look great."

Delighted by his words, she fought the urge to twirl like Vivian Leigh's Scarlett. At five-nine with thirty extra pounds, she was hardly a southern belle, and Derek's tanned good looks were more California surfer than any Rhett Butler.

"I kept hoping you'd come." He squeezed her hands for emphasis, the action as polished as his drawl. "Ah, darlin', you've been away so long."

Flirting was like breathing to Derek. He called everyone darling; she'd be a fool to take him seriously. Monica knew this, had always known that he breezed through life with his easy charm and devilish grin; yet when he leaned down to kiss her cheek, she could no more stop the flush of pleasure than she could make herself pull away.

He was the one to do so, his expression oddly solemn. Running a harried hand through his sun-streaked hair, he glanced over his shoulder at the house. "I wish it didn't have to be me, but I guess someone's got to warn you."

"Judith hasn't decided to sell River's Edge?"

He shook his head. "She's sick. Real sick."

"With what? Her do-as-I-want-or-you'll-be-sorry flu?"

He looked at her hard, his expression double grim. "Not this time. It's lung cancer."

She knew a spike of fear, then a flood of denial.

Impossible. Not Judith. The woman was too bull-headed to succumb to something as mundane as cancer. "Who says—Doc Munson? We'll get a second opinion. They have cures now, all kinds of treatments."

"She's seen them all, and they all say the same. She has a month, at best." Derek shrugged, turning away to climb the porch stairs. "At worst, maybe a week."

All those cigarettes, Monica thought in a daze. People had always cautioned her aunt to quit. "Doesn't matter," Judith would say with an aristocratic wave of the wrist. "I'll find a new body. God knows I'm rich enough."

"You'd better go up and see her," Derek said from the doorway as he held it open. "She's been waiting for you."

"Waiting? But I told her I wouldn't come."

"You're here, aren't you?" His voice sounded hollow, oddly so.

Looking up into his eyes as she neared, she realized she had no idea what went on behind that pale blue reflection. Who lives inside you? she found herself wondering.

Her gaze slid down his tanned face, past the aquiline nose and clean-shaven chin to the pleasing strength of his neck. She could feel his breath feather her cheek, and for one wild moment, she imagined him pulling her closer, into his strong, broad chest.

He smiled. Jolted, she realized just how close she now stood to him, how she hovered there like a moth around a welcoming porch light. With a tight smile of her own, she went past him into the entrance hall.

A large expanse, it opened into the rooms for

entertaining, with the hallway on the far wall leading to the kitchens and servants' quarters. Commanding attention in the center, a wide, winding staircase showed the way to the upstairs bedrooms.

Here, Judith's decorative style showed the most. The oak floor was hidden by white marble tile, and the gorgeous cypress bannister now gleamed with several layers of white enamel. Overhead, a chandelier had been added, an obscene display of glittering crystal more at home in a Mediterranean villa than a southern plantation. Judith had been to Europe again, Monica groaned to herself, and then felt instantly guilty. What did it matter what Judith did to her house? The woman was dying of cancer.

"Do you know why she called me here?" she asked Derek, her voice seeming to echo in the wide, empty hallway.

"Why not go on up and ask?" Lounging against the door frame, Derek nodded at the stairs. "Get it over with, and then come to me. It's time we had our own little chat."

He turned on the charm then, smiling at her until she feared her limbs might melt. Lord alone knew what idiocy she might have committed had Amy Piersoll, her aunt's personal secretary, not appeared that moment on the stairs.

"Where the hell have you been?" Amy snapped at Derek. "Do you know what that old . . ."

She started as she noticed Monica. "Oh, why Miss Ryan, I didn't know you were here."

Obviously. Monica stifled a smile. It wasn't often she saw Amy Piersoll lose her poise.

The moment didn't last long. Gliding down the stairs like Miss America, Amy was everything most girls wanted to be. Her pink linen suit managed to be professional, yet sexy at the same time; and though her soft blond hair danced gaily on her shoulders, it never lost its perfect form. Heels clicking, she crossed the floor to stop beside Monica, the placement as deliberate as the smile pasted on her face. Next to petite Amy, Monica felt like a moose.

"What a pleasant surprise," Amy purred. "But shame on you, monopolizing Mr. Sumner when we've business to discuss. I'm afraid I simply must steal him away." She flashed a smile, all perfect teeth, as she slipped her arm in his.

"I'm just here to see my aunt," Monica blurted, turning quickly. "I was going anyway."

She fled up the staircase, hearing their whispers and hating herself. What a worm she was; she should have stayed and proved to Amy—and maybe even herself—that mere good looks couldn't intimidate, or even impress her. She was twice as witty and three times as smart; she should have shown Derek that sometimes beauty was only skin deep.

I should have stayed in New York, she thought as she stood before her aunt's door. Deep in her gut, she could feel her stomach rumbling. "I'm too stuffed to eat," she chanted as she knocked on the door.

She had to tap several times before a middle-aged woman in a white uniform and cap answered. Militantly obstinate, the nurse made Monica give her name twice before allowing entry. "Mrs. Sumner needs her rest," she muttered with a scowl, "not this constant traffic in and out."

"Oh, go eat lunch, Fergie," her aunt grumbled from the bedroom beyond, her husky voice barely a rasp. "I'm tired of your hovering. Go on, get out of here. Go away!"

The nurse's lips puckered with hostility as she stomped off. Alone in the small sitting room, Monica could almost taste the over-ripe floral arrangements, so heavy and cloying in the humid air. Inhaling, she thought back to the day she had viewed her parents' open caskets.

Barely eleven, she'd trudged up the interminable aisle, prodded by Judith's pinches. Staring down at the white, frozen faces, Monica had balked at touching them. There was no way those strangers could have been her mama and daddy.

"Kiss them goodbye," Judith had insisted, pushing her head down. Nausea bubbling to the surface, Monica wrenched free to go vomit outside in the bushes.

Yet it was Judith who brought the damp cloth to wipe her face. "Don't be afraid, baby," her aunt had crooned, rocking Monica in her arms. "Death doesn't always get to win."

I hope you were right, Monica thought to herself now, for the stench of death was all over the room.

Trying to ignore it, knowing she must be strong for Judith's sake, Monica forced herself into her aunt's bedroom. She stopped at the doorway, caught off guard by the change in decor. Gone was all trace of French Provincial. Functional steel supplanted the ornate brass bed-frame; a console on a nearby chrome stand controlled its various moving parts.

Both bed and windows were draped in white, the heavy brocade discarded in favor of a more readily sanitized cotton. In the corner, an oxygen tank stood at attention, armed and ready to spring into action, while several silver implements waited on a glass-enclosed tray, equally prepared for instant duty. Throat tightening, Monica realized how near that moment must actually be.

But if Judith were concerned with her mortality, she didn't show it. Propped on her pillows, she remained the queen holding court, motioning for her niece to come closer.

Automatically obeying the beckoning hand, Monica cringed at how dramatically Judith had aged, looking sixty instead of her actual thirty-nine. Appallingly gaunt, her oft-praised cheekbones were skeletal, the skin stretched over them sallow and paper-thin.

Yet for all the outer frailty, a spark of willfulness glittered in her dark brown eyes. "Quick, the top drawer," Judith rasped out, pointing toward a dresser in the corner. "Get me my cigarette case before that old worrywart returns."

"Cigarettes? You shouldn't be smoking."

"Because they're bad for my health? Don't be an ass. Just get me the damn case and be quick about it."

Monica might have argued, but how much damage could be done at this stage? Besides, knowing Judith, she would just find someone else to get them for her.

Digging through the drawer, Monica saw a leather-bound book, its faded black surface embossed with the letters M.A.V. It looked like a diary, or some personal ledger, but whatever might have once been inside was now gone. Mildly curious, she reached for it, but as her fingers brushed the leather, they tingled uncomfortably. She recoiled in alarm.

"What the devil are you doing?" Judith barked

out behind her. "Growing the tobacco?"

"I-I can't find . . . oh, here they are," Monica babbled, unnerved by the jolt she'd received by touching the book. It had felt almost electric, yet unbelievably cold. Shaken, but determined not to let her aunt see it, she turned to face Judith with an Amy Piersoll smile. "They were under some scarves," she lied, fighting to compose herself as she neared the bed. "Your nurse must have tried to hide them from you."

"Give me one, quick. You have the lighter?"

When the cigarette was lit, Judith sank back, grinning with rare contentment as she brought it to her lips. Yet after one inhalation, she began to cough, a dry, futile hacking that caused the cigarette to slip from her fingers and drop to the bed.

Monica grabbed the thing, stabbing it out on a place on the bedside table, and patting at whatever ashes remained on the blankets.

"Stop fussing," Judith barked between spasms. "For God's sake, must you always be such a clumsy oaf? You're going to break my leg."

The words were cruel, yet completely Judith. Their very familiarity might have soothed Monica, if not for the emaciated hand closing around her wrist.

For on that hand, she saw the two antique silver snakes, twining around each other, meeting fang to fang. More than Judith's touch caused her trepidation; it was the ring—always the ring—which started this awful dread.

She hated it. From the first time she'd seen Judith's engagement ring at a young and very sheltered ten, she'd found nothing but evil in those sly, serpentine features.

Judith had been *Judy* then, living with them until she married George Sumner, seeming more an adored older sister than aunt. As was her habit, Monica had barged into Judy's room without knocking; but this time, Judy had screeched at her to get out, twisting the strange ring on her hand.

When the screeching continued, they'd taken Judy away to a hospital, but it was *Judith* who had later returned. "A breakdown," people whispered; and even now, Monica felt that whatever had been broken had never quite been fixed.

"I want you to have it," Judith said suddenly.

Startled, Monica looked up at her aunt's enigmatic smile. Judith needs me, she told herself sternly, quelling the urge to run away. I'm the only family she has.

"Here, put it on."

To her dismay, she realized Judith was offering the ring. "No!" Monica cried out, barely restraining herself from slapping the hand away. "I mean, I-I couldn't. I can't possibly take something so valuable."

"Don't be an ass, take it!" Judith's eyes were intense. "I insist," she added more graciously. "Come on, I want to see how it looks on you."

Monica forced a laugh, hiding her hands behind her back. "You know I don't wear rings—I've never cared much for jewelry. Besides, it's yours. Keep it, at least until . . ."

"I die?" Judith began to cackle. "But that's why I'm giving it to you. It's family custom to pass it down. You don't want to break tradition, do you?"

"No, of course not," she said distractedly. George Sumner had given it as an engagement ring—wasn't it Derek's family heirloom, not theirs? "But—but there's plenty of time to worry about passing it down."

"Plenty of time?" Judith looked ready to explode. "Have you shared that rare bit of insight with my doctors?"

Monica cringed. Cancer would be hard enough on anyone, but for Judith, long accustomed to running every show, being helplessly ill must be a nightmare. "When the time comes, I promise I'll wear your ring," she offered, not bothering to add that she would not do so for more than the obligatory second. "But right now, it just seems so—so morbid."

Judith looked at her, long and hard, before replacing the ring on her bony finger. "All right, have it your way," she said wearily, closing her eyes.

Monica felt a spurt of guilt, that nagging sense that once again she'd let her aunt down, but even as her stomach started rumbling, Judith switched direction. "It's time we talked," she said suddenly. "Made plans for the future."

Monica stiffened. "My plans are already made. I've told you this. I worked hard to get my education. My job is important to me. I'm not about to give it up."

"Of course you worked hard." Judith smiled, patting her hand. "But tell me, are you happy taking care of someone else's brats? Don't you ever wake in the mornings and wish for your own?"

What is she fishing for? Monica wondered as she looked away, not wanting Judith to see the doubt and confusion in her eyes. Her aunt could read her like a book as it was.

Judith's tone went soft, cajoling. "I know you, girl, I know you'd give anything to own River's Edge. Look at me and tell me I'm wrong."

Monica did look; she couldn't help herself. "What are you getting at?"

Judith smiled, her face triumphant. She was fishing all right, and River's Edge was the bait with which she would reel Monica in. "I could leave it to you, you know."

Monica found it hard to breathe. "What about Derek?" she asked, thinking aloud. "Won't he have something to say about this?"

"I imagine he will." Judith chuckled. "Especially since he'll be your husband."

"My what?"

"Husband. Father of all those brats you think you want. You know, all your dreams come true?"

Monica felt the cold flash of humiliation. "You bought him for me?"

"Don't be so melodramatic. The bulb's not always lit in Derek's head, but even he's smart enough to see the benefits of this merger."

"I'm not some business deal, Judith. I won't be 'merged' on some whim of yours."

"Whim?" Judith grabbed her hand, squeezing it tight. "I've worked too damned hard to let Derek turn this place into some country club and golf course. I know you'll fight tooth and nail to keep River's Edge safe for me."

"For you?"

Judith looked away, her voice small and distant. "For my memory. Is that too much to ask?"

Monica felt her throat go tight as she realized that too soon that was all her aunt would be—a memory.

"Besides," Judith went on, "what does it matter? You'll get everything you've ever wanted—this house, a husband, kids. A family, Monica. Is your lousy job worth all that?"

Monica could feel herself weaken. Her teaching position at a private school was not ideal; but giving it up now, saying yes to the promising future Judith offered, wouldn't that be a little like selling her soul? The least she should expect from marriage was love.

She made the mistake of saying this aloud, and Judith predictably laughed. "How did you get to be twenty-four and stay so naive? Love! As if it has anything to do with it. Just give the guy a few good rolls in the hay, and he'll stick around. That's all you really need anyway."

Monica felt the color rise to her cheeks. Did her aunt have any idea of how she'd dreamed of "rolling in the hay" with Derek? Her heart skipped a beat as she thought of coming home to his handsome face, of always being welcomed by that limb-melting smile.

"The wedding will take place Saturday," Judith went on, giving her no time to think. "I want to see you married before I . . ." she hesitated as if stumbling over the words, ". . . before I pass on. I've made arrangements for Father Doring to come at six."

"But I haven't said yes."

"You will." Slumping back against the pillow, Judith sighed, closing her eyes as if the effort to keep them open was beyond her. "Leave me now," she whispered, giving Monica no chance to argue. "I need to rest."

Dazed, Monica slipped out of the room, the words, "you will," echoing in her brain. She tried to focus on her New York apartment, her friends and students there; but Derek was waiting in the hallway when she opened the door. One look at his boyish grin and Monica knew she was lost.

She made a great deal of closing the door behind her, hoping to compose herself, but Derek swung her to face him. "Don't keep me in suspense," he said, his eyes probing hers. "Tell me you said yes, that you'll soon be my wife."

It sounded good coming off his lips, almost possible. "It's true?" she heard herself ask. "You actually want to marry me?"

Laughing, he gently brushed her cheek with his hand. "Silly girl, what did you think was going on this past year? I don't write letters to just anyone, you know."

There had been nothing in his two letters to even hint at this. "But you never. . . . Judith was the one to ask me."

His hand dropped and he looked away. "She told me to wait. She warned that you'd never believe I really cared. That you'd think I only wanted the estate."

She blushed.

"Ah, cuz, you've got to know I don't give two beans about this place. I started loving you long before I knew Judith would die. Stupid me, I wanted to do it right, ease into things; but then she got sick and was determined to marry you off, and I knew I couldn't afford to wait." He held out his hands and when she took them, he pulled her close. "I've never been good with words. Maybe I should just show you how I feel."

Monica's breath held as he leaned down to kiss her. Yet though she had dreamed of this moment for so long, she felt nothing—no sparks of passion, no desperate aching for more.

Must be the shock, she thought unhappily—too much happening far too fast.

He flashed a reassuring smile. "We'll be great

together, cuz. Trust me, this is just the beginning."

Why this hesitation? Wasn't this all she had ever wanted from life? "Yeah," she found herself saying, "I guess so. I mean, yes. Of course I'll marry you."

He leaned down to kiss her again, with a tenderness that should have made her cry. "I'm going in to tell Judith," he said, breaking away. "I want her to know you've made me the happiest man on earth."

Great together? Happiest man on earth? Watching him go into the room, she wondered just when Derek had begun talking in clichés.

Deep inside, her stomach began to rumble.

They were rushing things; what was the hurry? Her aunt was sick, yes, but she seemed as strong-willed as ever. If anyone could beat this disease, it had to be Judith.

Time was what they all needed—lots of time—for Judith to get well, for her and Derek to get to know each other better. When he came out, she'd tell him so.

Smiling, feeling as if a burden had been lifted from her shoulders, Monica turned for the stairs. As she did, the door swung open behind her.

"Quick, get the doctor," Derek shouted. "Judith is dying!"

Two

"Sorry I'm calling so late, Geralyn." Monica gripped the phone, distracted. She kept thinking about her aunt, hacking away her life in the bedroom upstairs. Judith hadn't died in the attack two days ago; but she'd had several more since, each worse than the last, and the doctors doubted she'd last the week. "I know I said the wedding would be Saturday," Monica went on, "but we had to change the date. Can you be here tomorrow?"

The groan was answer enough, but she already knew her best friend wouldn't come. Teachers couldn't take off at a moment's notice; there were lesson plans and unfinished projects to tie them to their desks—not to mention the prohibitive air-fare.

Still, she heard herself pleading. "I'll make the arrangements, pay for your ticket. I want you here, Ger. It won't be the same without you."

Geralyn hesitated, no doubt hearing her panic and not knowing how to react. "You know I'd give anything to be your maid of honor," she said at last, "but I've worked on this Easter play for months—I can't abandon the kids now. Why tomorrow—what happened to Saturday?"

Monica also paused, avoiding the truth. She didn't like to talk about Judith's illness; it made it too real. "My aunt is getting frantic," she said instead. "She wants to see me married."

Monica could picture her—calm, practical Geralyn—twirling her hair as she wondered whether or not to speak her mind. It had been Geralyn who'd suggested an apartment of her own, a job of her own, and a dietician to help take control of her weight. This was more than just wanting Geralyn to be with her—she needed her friend here.

Yet thinking of her aunt in that cold, sterile room, she knew Judith needed her more.

"Isn't this *your* wedding, Monica?" Typically, Geralyn had decided in favor of speaking out. "Shouldn't it be your decision? You said you were going there to tell your aunt no, yet all I hear is 'Judith wants this' and 'Judith wants that.' What about what *you* want?"

"You know how I feel about Derek."

"Then why don't you sound like a happy, blushing bride?"

Geralyn always did see too much.

"I've a lot on my mind. It's worse here than I thought."

"She's using you, Monica. Just as she's always done. She's sucking you back into the life she wants you to lead and you're letting her do it."

"You don't understand. Judith is ill."

"You're always making excuses for that woman. That's the trouble with you—you're too nice. You think just because you're good and kind and generous, others must be, too. Well, take it from me, there are some real stinkers out there, people who care only about what they want, and they don't give a damn about who they have to hurt to get it."

"I'm not being hurt—I'm about to marry the man I love. Ah, Ger, just be happy for me."

"I want to be happy, but doesn't this sound too fairy tale-ish to you? I mean, one wave of the wicked stepmother's wand and all Cinderella's wishes come true? What's wrong with stepping back a bit? For heaven's sake, take some time. It's a drastic decision."

"I don't need time to know how much I love Derek."

"Derek? Or your precious house?"

"Judith has lung cancer," Monica broke in firmly, stopping Geralyn before she put too many angry words between them. "We don't expect her to live out the week."

There was silence on the other end.

"I know you mean well," Monica added softly, "but try to understand. Maybe Judith is sometimes more wicked stepmother than loving aunt, but she's the only family I have. Getting married now, while she can watch, seems the least I can do."

"Cancer?" Geralyn gasped. "Jeez, me and my big mouth."

"I've got to do this, Ger."

"I know. It might not sound like it, but I have faith in you, Monica. Whatever happens, deep down you've got what it takes to make the best of things." She sighed. "So just forget what I said, okay? I'm a selfish brat, and I'm going to miss you. Muriel Crichton's Academy for Young Ladies won't ever be the same."

Nothing would be the same, Monica thought

uneasily. No faculty room gossip, no more holiday plays, or tearful June partings; from now on, her life would revolve around Derek.

All her wishes came true. So why did her mind keep repeating *Be careful what you wish for?*

She longed to reach through the wires, to anchor herself to Geralyn and her common sense, but her friend was already making those see-ya-bye sounds, until with a final "take care," all that seemed sane and logical was gone with an audible click.

As Monica slowly replaced the receiver, she realized it was the second time recently she'd been warned to "take care." The cab driver had vanished from her life for good; would it now be the same with Geralyn?

She looked around her, disliking the black and white and chrome with which Judith had designed the kitchen. Oh, how she missed her one-room apartment, despite its silly gingham curtains and mud-yellow walls. I will just have to make this my house, she insisted. It should be easy enough to redecorate, once Judith was . . . when she was . . .

She couldn't bring herself to think it. Lord, she was hungry. Ravenous. As her gaze fell upon the triple-layer fudge cake she'd refused at dinner, her hands went into action. Cutting herself a slice, she didn't bother with a plate or fork.

"Do you really need that?"

She jumped, color rising in her cheeks, and she dropped the cake to the table as if it had burned her fingers.

Derek came up behind her, but she stood frozen, too embarrassed to turn and face him. "That's my girl," he said into her ear.

Monica felt a flash of resentment. As she

remembered, he hadn't deprived himself of dessert.

But was it so unreasonable for a great-looking guy to ask his wife to be thin? He did say he only wanted the best for her.

He spun her around, forcing her to look at him, his smile melting any lingering doubt. "I overheard your phone conversation. Your friend can't come?"

Monica shook her head. "We had a promise, Geralyn and I. Come hell or high water, we swore we wouldn't get married if the other couldn't be there."

Derek put a finger under her chin. "That's too bad, though I can't honestly say I'm sorry. Sure didn't sound like she approved. Another couple minutes and she'd have talked you out of marrying me."

"It wasn't like that."

He shrugged, as if knowing better. "I gotta say it made me feel good to hear you stand up for me. Especially that part about how much you 'love Derek.' You've never actually said the words, you know. Not to me."

Monica looked down, partly because she felt flustered, but also because of her doubt. She tried to say the words, but she burst into tears instead. "Geralyn thinks it's too sudden, and isn't it, Derek? I mean, a few days ago, you and I lived in different worlds. How are we ever going to make this work?"

Derek pulled back, his mouth a tight line. "I thought you loved me."

"I do. You know I do." As he moved further away, her hand unconsciously reached out for him.

He looked at her then, his expression boyish in

its confusion and hurt. "Then how about a little trust?"

Monica felt awful. "Oh, Derek, of course I trust you. It's just—I don't know—maybe I'm having wedding-night jitters. I've never been about-to-get-married before."

His quick, easy smile was worth the effort. He came back to her, taking her in his arms. "Ah, honey, I know, and here I am making things worse. A girl would have to love me to put up with getting married in Judith's sickroom, having no one to stand up for her. Well, don't you worry about a maid of honor. If I have to go down to New Orleans and buy you one, I'll make sure you have the very best there is. Nothing's too good for my girl."

She smiled; she couldn't stop herself. "There's no need to go to the city. Judith's nurse can do the job."

"Fergie?" He pretended to shudder. "No, leave this to me. Trust me, cuz. I'm gonna take such good care of you, you won't ever have to cry again."

She let her hand slide through his hair, feeling soft and loving, knowing that despite his good intentions, it was more likely she would be taking care of him. "Oh, Derek, I don't deserve you."

"No, you don't," he said with a grin, gently removing her hands. "Not if you don't go on upstairs like a good girl and get to bed. You sleep the night away, y'hear? That way, the morning will come that much faster."

"I'd rather be with you."

"All night? As tempting as it sounds, I'd be a lowlife creep to take you up on that." His smile went rueful. "We can't be jinxing things, here on our wedding eve." Kissing her softly on the forehead, he pulled back and away. "Besides, I promised Hartley I'd pick him up at the airport at ten. Can't have both our best friends gone missing tomorrow, can we?"

Monica tried not to frown. She had never much liked Hartley Buford—she thought him spoiled, weak, and selfish—but he was Derek's long-time friend. He and old Hartley had practically been born together, Derek once told her, and he expected they would die at the same time, too.

"I'll go up to bed in a minute," she told him, shooing him off to the airport. "I just want to tidy up the mess I made here in the kitchen."

He hesitated at the door, looking at her oddly. She thought he might offer to help, but she should have known better. Derek was proud of his lack of domestic skill.

With a shrug, he reminded her not to take too long. She smiled, said yes, of course; but the moment he left the room, she snatched the piece of cake and gobbled it down.

"We are gathered here in the presence of God to join . . ."

Listening to Father Doring drone on, Monica wished her things had arrived from New York or that there had been time to drive into the city to buy a dress. Washing and pressing her only clothes had done little to revive them; her brown skirt and beige blouse seemed a dreary start to married life.

Whenever she'd pictured her wedding day, she'd dreamed of organ music and happy sighs from kith and kin, yet the only sound in the room today—apart from the priest's monotonous droning—was the wheeze of Judith's oxygen tank.

The wedding party huddled around the bed, trying to ignore the I.V. bottles and grim-faced medical staff in the shadows. Father Doring read from his prepared text as if he held weddings here every day, while Hartley Buford teetered at the priest's side, reeking of champagne and pointedly staring at the maid of honor's chest.

Not that Monica could blame Hartley, considering the daring neckline of Miss Piersoll's pale pink sheath. Curving suggestively over Amy's slim hips, the dress made Monica's outfit look like a grocery sack.

She'd agreed to Derek's substitute in the interest of speed and convenience, but she wished now that she'd insisted on Fergie. At least Judith's nurse would have the good grace not to glow as if she were the bride instead.

". . . as your lawfully wedded spouse?"

With that, the droning ceased. Startled, Monica looked up, realizing they waited for her answer. "Uh, yes," she said quickly before recalling the usual response. "I mean, yes, I do."

With a solemn nod, Father Doring turned to Derek, who answered with a grin. Gazing at him, Monica's heart began to swell. Must he always look so darned adorable?

"Do you have the ring?" Father Doring asked.

As Derek fumbled in his pocket, her heart swelled to double its size. How could she have ever doubted him? In spite of the circumstances, even in the panicked rush, Derek had found time to buy her a wedding band.

"The toast," Judith mumbled behind her oxygen mask. "First drink the toast."

With a smile, Derek nodded. Abandoning his

search for the ring, he reached for the five silver goblets waiting on the bedside table and passed them around. Confused, uneasy, Monica hesitated before accepting hers. Derek all but shoved the thing into her hands.

"To the continuation of the Sumner line," Judith panted. "May we live and prosper."

Sipping the strong, sickeningly sweet liqueur, Monica felt her uneasiness grow. She set her goblet down, sensing that something was going on beneath the surface—something the others knew that she did not.

Judith continued her toast, the words garbled by her mask, yet though Monica could make no sense of their content, she heard their building rhythm. Troubled, she turned to Derek.

With a reassuring smile, he put down his goblet to reach again into his pocket. As he took Monica's hand, Judith raised her right arm.

A pulse began to beat inside Monica's skull, pounding like primal drums, growing louder and more intense with each muffled word her aunt uttered. Judith's hand moved closer, inches away, until it came to rest on Derek's wrist.

With dismay, Monica noticed her aunt's finger was bare. Her gaze flew to Derek's opened palm, half-knowing what she would find there. Seeing the twin silver serpents, she instinctively yanked back her hand.

His grasp tightened. He seemed bewildered by her reaction, and perhaps a bit hurt, but no less determined to set the ring on her finger. It was as if Judith's incessant litany urged him on.

"No!" Monica cried as the ring glanced her skin, sending an icy chill into her bones. She flung out her hand, sending the ring flying, and it bounced off the bedframe with a resounding clank. Spinning like a dervish, it danced across the floor and disappeared.

There was an unnerving silence as everyone paused to gape at her bare finger. Monica tried to explain her panic, but no words came. In truth, she didn't understand it herself. It had been a gut reaction; she knew only that she must never let those reptiles close around her finger.

"Get . . . the . . . ring!" Judith shrieked, ripping off the oxygen mask and moving their frozen tableau to action. Amy, Derek, and Hartley began rooting around on the floor, while the priest, the doctor, and both nurses rushed to her side.

Monica alone stood where she was, paralyzed, numbly watching as her aunt alternately screamed vile obscenities and lapsed into spasms of coughs.

"You bitch . . ." Judith spat out, her eyes as dark as a fathomless hole. ". . . you promised!"

Monica edged back, stunned by the rage in Judith's unblinking gaze. There was nothing of her aunt in it; a stranger could be staring back at her, cold eyes blazing with malice.

Swatting the medical team away, Judith seemed to draw on that hatred as she forced herself up to grab for her niece. Paralyzed, Monica watched the skeletal hand approach, then falter, then drop with a lifeless thud to the bed.

Judith's eyes went wide with fear and disbelief. "You promised," she croaked. "Damn you, you promised!"

And then, Monica saw absolutely nothing in her eyes.

Badly shaken, she turned to the doctor, the priest, even Fergie, but their attention was focused on Judith. As Monica watched them work to revive her, she thought she saw a flash of glowing white under the sheet where Judith's left hand lay.

But she was dizzy suddenly; she feared she might faint. Confused and scared, she turned to Derek, still on his knees across the room. He glanced up, saw her, and quickly looked away—first to Amy and then Hartley. All three slowly rose to their feet, as if in silent mutual agreement there was no further need to search for the ring.

Derek came to her, all solicitation as he nudged her from the room. "Here, drink this." He urged the silver goblet to her lips. "It will calm you down."

Although Monica wondered briefly when and why he had picked up the goblet, she was still wobbly and too upset to dwell on anything more than her aunt's death. "She damned me," she whispered when she'd drained it. "The last words Judith ever uttered, and she damned me."

As Derek held out his arms, she fell into them, wanting nothing more than to stay there forever. She was vaguely aware of Amy and Hartley standing beside them, but her mind was too filled with the horror of Judith's last moments.

Derek stroked her back. "Hush, none of that now. She was out of it, there at the end. The ring, her toast—she was crazy, I tell you. Maybe the cancer went to her brain."

Monica began shivering. Crazy or not, her aunt had cursed her from her deathbed. It seemed a terrible legacy to drag around for the rest of her life.

Father Doring joined them with a mournful smile. "I'm afraid Judith has passed on," he said in his monotone. "She is in God's keeping now."

Passed on? Monica repeated dully in her mind.

Judith had used that quaint term in her typically arrogant fashion. Something as final as death could never touch Judith Sumner; oh no, she would merely be passing on.

". . . are we married?" she heard Derek ask the priest.

"I now declare you man and wife," the priest answered with a rare smile. "That should make it official for the church; but, legally, you were wed the moment you signed the marriage license."

"Good." Derek inhaled deeply, blatantly relieved. "Then in that case, I want to put my new wife to bed."

Hartley made some lewd remark Monica didn't catch; Amy hissed at him to shut his mouth. "I'm worried by how pale Monica is," Derek added. "I want her to rest. This has all been a strain—the wedding, the rush, and now Judith . . ."

As his voice faltered, Monica realized this must be equally awful for him. She tried to stir herself. "I'm fine, really. I'll call the undertaker. Judith wouldn't want to stay in that hospital bed any longer than necessary."

"You're not to worry your pretty little head about it," Derek insisted. "Amy and I can take care of things."

"But I should help." Anyone could tell her heart was not in the protest.

"Get to bed," her new husband ordered, "or I'll get the doctor to inject you with something. We'll need you more tomorrow, anyway. To smile and greet all the well-wishers who come to pay their respects."

An ordeal Monica dreaded. She knew Derek was right; rest was what she needed most. "Wake me in an hour or two, though," she told him as she let herself be shooed away. "I really do want to help. She was my aunt, after all."

Was my aunt? she thought as she entered her room. Just what was the difference between the Judith of yesterday and the one lying so still and lifeless on that bed? If there actually was a soul, as the priest would have them believe, had it left the moment the body ceased to function? If so, she wondered as she stripped down to her slip, just where had Judith's soul gone?

Dizzy, overwhelmed by drowsiness, she flopped on the bed. She tried to accept that her aunt was dead, to understand the finality of it all; yet she couldn't quite shake the sense of something not yet done.

The more she tried to think, the hazier her thoughts became. She kept seeing that faint white glow beneath the sheet, and as she fell off into a deep, dark slumber, the words, "you promised" drifted into her brain.

The same words were there, waiting to taunt her when she woke, though she couldn't decipher them. Holding a head that felt too heavy to lift, she tried to sit up. It was dark, she realized; the clock at her bedside read ten. She must have been out for two hours.

Only gradually did she remember that Judith was dead, that she was married now. Groggy and disoriented, she rose from the bed. Derek, she thought frantically; I need him.

He was her husband; he would know the words to make her feel better. From now on, she thought with a dreamy smile, Derek would be there whenever she needed comfort.

Still in a stupor, she moved toward his room. Hearing a low murmuring, thinking Hartley Buford must be with him, she belatedly realized she wore only her slip. About to turn back for a robe, she heard the soft female drawl.

"That was wonderful, darling," Amy Piersoll purred. "But shouldn't you be getting back to your wife?"

Remembering how Hartley had leered at Amy's chest, Monica felt a rush of pity for poor Nancy Buford.

But it wasn't Hartley; it was Derek. "Wife?" he snorted. "Spare me. God knows I'll have to be putting in the time soon enough. Jeez, did you see that sack she wore?"

Monica felt the ice-cold splash of shock. She didn't want to hear more, but her feet felt encased in cement.

"You won't get my sympathy, Derek. You had to go tie yourself to that cow when you could have married me."

"No one offered five hundred grand for you, sugar."

"You bastard. You lucky bastard. Do you realize how close you cut it?"

"Trust me, I knew what I was doing. She had said we had to be married before she died, remember? And I made sure we signed the license first thing—I wasn't about to let those loan sharks mess up this pretty face."

Monica's shock dwindled into humiliation. Judith *had* paid him to marry her.

"You weren't into them for more than fifty grand, Derek. I'd say you made yourself a tidy little profit."

Monica could almost hear Derek's grin. "Play

money, darlin'. Don't forget, I've got me a rich wife now; and, as Judith would say, I'm her family—the only family she has left."

Monica began to tremble. She didn't know which hurt more—his betrayal, Judith's manipulation, or her own stupidity.

"That sure was weird with Judith," Amy said in a puzzled tone. "What was all that stuff about the ring, anyway?"

"Who knows? She got real loony there at the end."

"Aren't you a little scared? I mean, you never did do what she asked."

"Scared of what? The wicked witch is dead, darlin'. Ain't nothing Judith can do about things now."

Monica ran, his callous words ringing in her ears. His conceit was incredible. With the door open, anyone could have caught him and Amy together.

There are some real stinkers out there, Geralyn had warned. What would she say when she learned Monica had married the biggest skunk of them all?

She stood in the hallway, fighting the grogginess that had yet to leave her, not knowing which way to turn. Like a sleepwalker, she drifted into her aunt's rooms. On some vague level, she knew she had to find Judith, had to finish whatever she'd left undone.

"You promised." A memory stirred, but it flitted away as she caught a heavy whiff of disinfectant. She reached for the switch, the sudden glaring light emphasizing the truth. There would be no finding Judith. Her bed was stripped, its plastic surface as cold and impersonal as the morgue in which her aunt most likely now lay.

Monica touched it anyway, looking for solace, even while knowing none would be found. Even Judith had betrayed her in those last few moments. No gesture of affection, no words on how to go on—just her awful screeching, "You promised!"

Monica took her hand off the plastic, the memory of another bedside confrontation flashing across her mind. She could see Judith as if she lay there still, the day she'd tried to press the ring in her niece's hand. "When the time comes," Judith had pleaded, "promise you'll wear it."

Monica went to her knees, groping beneath the bed, the nightstand, the dresser in the corner where she'd found the cigarettes and the awful black book. As she searched, she silently begged her aunt's forgiveness. No wonder Judith had been furious. The time had come and Monica had let her down.

It must have been the liqueur, clouding her mind. It still made her woozy, so much so it seemed all she could do not to lay her head down on the floor and go to sleep.

With a jolt, her fingers met the shock of the silver band. Swallowing her distaste, Monica pulled the ring out from under the dresser. Dizzy or not, like it or not, she had to keep her promise.

Yet she found it hard to place the ring on her finger. Going to the bed, having to sit, she told herself she need only wear it for a second, just to keep her word. This was for Judith, her family, the only . . .

Remembering Derek's ugly laughter as he'd mimicked the words, she felt a fresh wave of mortification. She was the ultimate cliché, taken in by a smile.

Trust me, he'd said, and she'd believed him. Oh,

how it had hurt to hear him say the same thing to Amy.

She sat on the plastic bedcover, its chill penetrating her slip. Eventually, she'd have to confront him. He could turn nasty, she realized, once he learned she had no intention of giving him control of her estate.

She knew an overwhelming urge to run away—to go anywhere—so she'd need never face him again.

Taking a deep breath, she looked at the ring. If only it were a talisman, the ruby slippers to aid her escape. "There's no place like home," she whispered, thinking of her dream family as she slid the silver band down her finger.

With an almost electric chill, her mind began to reel. Am I drunk? she thought, remembering how Derek had urged her to drink the liqueur.

Somewhere in her brain, she heard a low, rhythmic chanting, as if Judith had resumed her litany. It made her want to weave and dance, to answer its seductive call. The medicinal smell dissolved into a deep, earthy scent, the cold plastic enveloped her in a warm, bathing glow. A silvery white glow, as her head grew lighter, airier.

Part of her sensed that she should remove the ring, but her hand now seemed a million miles away. Her body grew weightless, insignificant, as she slowly stretched away from the ring. Taking flight, floating, up, up . . .

She looked down at the room below and there on the bed, remote and detached, lay her body. Confused, she tried to reach for it, yet the chanting kept urging her farther away.

My God, she thought, recognizing this scene from too many movies; I must be dying.

Monique

April 5, 1855:

Here I am—me, who finds it hard to sit still in one place—writing again in my diary. But I am so delighted with life, I cannot keep my thoughts to myself.

One day soon, I feel certain Robert Sumner will ask me to be his wife. Oh, he does not say this to me—he is far too reserved and formal—yet he is ever there when I wish to dance and his eyes follow my every move. In my more fanciful moments, I find myself wishing he were a warmer man, that his gentlemanly kisses could make me swoon rather than yawn, but my Gallic practicality accepts that a girl marries for position, not passion. Later, I can find lovers to satisfy that need.

It is a good sign, I think, that my parents and I shall accompany Robert tomorrow to his plantation. I cannot wait; I'm told River's Edge is one of the most beautiful homes on the Mississippi River, if not the most lavish, and I know I shall feel like a princess strolling through its halls.

I understand that exchanging long and frequent visits is a social entertainment for these southern planters, but I also know Robert is anxious for our families to meet. Why bother introducing them if he does not wish them to join?

Sarah Jane's reaction tells a tale in itself. I am glad she must stay here in town, for her own plantation, Bel Monde, lies but a short ride away from River's Edge. Since she claims I have betrayed her, stealing Robert away, I do not want her around, spoiling things with her snide comments and bitter frowns.

It will be difficult enough meeting Robert's family. Both parents are dead, but he has a younger brother and sister, and they are too-long accustomed to having the house to themselves. I shall have to charm this Drew and Abigail; I cannot risk having them stand in my way.

Rachel shall stay in America with me. I insist, despite my parents' protests, for I cannot leave her behind on that claustrophobic island. In part, I want to reward Rachel for her potions, knowing they have helped arrange all this good fortune for me; but more importantly, I see the wisdom in keeping her near. I just might need those potions again.

After all, one never knows what the future can bring.

Three

Pulled away with a slow, building rhythm as if she were being sucked out by the tide, Monica gave herself over to the hundred pleasant sensations bombarding her mind. The chants surrounded her, building in volume and speed, the low, guttural tones growing more insistent, more seductive. The delicate scent of ginger blossoms gave way to a blend of exotic spices, then a deep, enticing musk. Opening her mouth, she tasted each aroma with her tongue, savoring, being aroused by them. Velvet brushed her skin, became a soft fur, and then hot, rasping hands. Moving up and down in time to the rhythmic chants, Monica felt as if she rode some long-forgotten, primal creature. Part of her revelled in the wild, erotic sensations, but another part recoiled.

"No more," her mind cried out. "I want to stop. Now!"

With a twang, the movement ceased, and she was jolted back into her body. She grew slowly aware that the surface on which she rested was cold and damp, that the chanting was now merely the drone of insects buzzing above her head.

Drawing in a deep, fortifying breath, she realized there was a different feel to the air; it was fresher, cleaner, though still tinged with that deep, earthy scent.

She opened her eyes, blinking at the sudden daylight. Trees? she thought disoriented. How like crones the cypress seemed, hunched over their gnarled roots, their shawls of Spanish moss dripping like lacy tentacles from their limbs.

Slowly, she realized she lay on high ground in some swamp. The earth had been dug out around and beneath her, then lined with leaves, with a blanket of the same leaves covering her like a shroud. Was this her grave? she thought with a shudder.

It all came rushing back, her dizziness, the liqueur Derek gave her, his betrayal. She sat up, yanking the wedding ring off her finger.

A hand grasped her wrist. Startled, she turned to find a black woman kneeling beside her. She seemed concerned, and perhaps as confused as Monica herself.

"What is this?" the woman asked with a strange accent. "Must we try again?"

Monica shook her head, but she felt so dizzy and lightheaded, she could not seem to clear it. The woman seemed to know her, yet the odd accent and ragged, outdated clothes sparked no recognition on her part. Monica rose, meaning to question her, but the lightness seemed to extend to her body. Was this some blood sugar disorder? What *had* been in the liqueur Derek gave her?

"Monique?" The shout came from the right, beyond the trees. Male, and awesomely angry, the voice repeated the name, until mere seconds later

Derek broke into the clearing. For once, he was not smiling. He looked mad enough to kill.

Swallowing painfully, Monica slid the ring in her pocket.

As she took an unconscious step back, the black woman reached for her wrist. *Must we try again?* she'd said, but what if Monica was not included in that *we*. If the woman had instead meant Derek, one must wonder just what they'd tried before.

Monica looked down at the grave-like bed. Had they meant to poison her with the liqueur? Or had Derek merely drugged her, hoping the damp night air of the swamp would do the job? "My wife was distraught over her aunt's death," he'd tell the authorities with an angelic face, all the while plotting how to fritter away her inheritance.

Too bad she hadn't been obliging enough to die.

"Two days wasted, searching for you," Derek ranted as he approached. "I could have been working, getting things done."

As if he'd ever worked a day in his life. "Don't you dare come near me!" she shouted back, breaking free of the woman. "I swear, I'll call the police if I have to."

He halted, gaping as if she'd sprouted another head.

"I might once have been naive enough to think you loved me, but my eyes are wide open now. I want a divorce, Derek. You can keep your lousy five hundred thousand, but if you don't leave now, I'll tell everyone you tried to murder your wife." She inhaled deeply, trembling inside. Saying those defiant words was the bravest thing she'd ever done in her life. It wouldn't surprise her if he now tried to choke her.

But to her utter amazement, Derek turned to the black woman. "What is she talking about, Rachel? Who is this Derek? And what is this about murder?"

"She's been ill, Master Drew," the woman answered in a measured tone, studying Monica carefully. "Miss Monique's hit her head and cannot recall the past. She's come to me for a healing potion."

Monica felt strangely unsteady, as if the ground had been yanked out from under her feet. Master Drew? With an odd flutter in her stomach, she wondered what had happened to the shorts and tee shirt Derek habitually wore. He'd never be caught dead in those faded blue wool pants or the white cotton shirt with its fraying cuffs and collar.

Nor was she a prize, she realized, noticing how the leaves and mud decorated her skirt. Her long, *full* skirt. It lacked the hoop, and perhaps a petticoat or two, but she recognized the style. Vintage Scarlett O'Hara.

Was it Mardi Gras and they'd been to a Civil War masquerade? She shook her head, trying to shake off the grogginess. Why couldn't she remember?

"We know you don't want her visiting me in the swamp," Rachel was saying behind her, "but with you off to the city, she had nowhere else to turn."

"I'm not a fool, Rachel. Stop treating me like one."

"No, no, Master Drew. I tell you, Miss Monique is ill, not . . . not herself. Please, let her stay here with me to recover."

"Any recovery can be done at the house, in her own bed."

Staring at this *Drew,* truly seeing him for the first time, Monica saw he couldn't possibly be Derek. His features were stronger, sharper, as if chiselled from rock. From the proud chin to the determined glint in his eyes, he was a man who commanded respect. Besides, the Derek she knew wore his grin like a name badge; this version merely scowled.

It was zany, like a dream—yes, that had to be it—she was safe in bed dreaming.

"Come, Monique," he barked, turning back and clearly expecting her to follow. "I've wasted enough time as it is."

Monica had no wish to go anywhere with such an angry man, not when he looked enough like her treacherous husband to be his twin; but gazing at the shallow hole, she couldn't see how spending the night here was a good idea either. Looking into Rachel's cold, black eyes, she remembered the stranger who'd glared at her from Judith's dying face. She found the same loathing there, an utter lack of concern for her own humanity. Better to face whatever might happen "up at the house," than stay behind with Rachel.

Gritting her teeth, she followed after Drew. Oblivious to her struggles to keep up, his long, angry strides made no concessions to either exhaustion or femininity. Monica didn't know which she resented more, his cavalier treatment or the heavy skirts of her gown. If she had to dream about the past, she thought irritably, why couldn't it include the mini-skirts of the sixties?

As she stumbled through the undergrowth, the questions multiplied in her brain. She wanted to ask her escort who he was, who she was, and where she was supposed to be; but the perpetual scowl indicated that he just might bite off her head. Let him enjoy his stony silence for now, she decided; she would wait until they stopped.

But when they broke out of the wetlands to face what must be his home, Monica herself was speechless. She knew that house. Wasn't it River's Edge?

Confused, she turned to Drew. He was looking ahead, his gaze filled with utter longing.

It touched her, that proud and wistful turn of his lips, and she saw how wrong she'd been to think he couldn't smile. He, too, sensed the place was special, she realized; like her, he saw it as home.

And in that moment, their gazes locked. Empathy became something more, pulsing to life between them. She could see it mirrored in his eyes, deep beneath the anger he strove so hard to maintain. He wanted to kiss her, wanted to take her there on the spot; she knew it just as surely as if he had thrown her to the ground.

And deep inside her own body, she knew an answering heat, a steady throbbing that insisted she knew this man intimately, had once felt his hard, naked body pressed against her own.

He wanted her, yes, but she wanted him more.

Hearing a shout, he looked away. He muttered an oath and stomped off, toward the young woman gesturing from the side of the house.

Shaken, Monica stared after him, denying that she'd been physically drawn to a stranger, yet still trembling with a need to touch him. How could she be so certain of how hot his hands would be on her breasts, how cool his lips would feel on her face? What was going on here?

Knowing the question would never be answered by talking to herself, Monica hurried after him. As she did, she began to notice differences she should have seen already. The paint on the house was peeling; several shutters had come loose from their hinges. Blades of grass reached past her ankles, and the shrubbery likewise needed a trimming. Yet, while all else grew in wild abandon, the live oaks in the drive seemed shorter, less massive. And wasn't the levee a good ten feet lower than yesterday?

Could it be that she had wandered off in her daze and stumbled upon a similar house upriver?

"Thank heavens you've found her," she could hear the young woman say as she neared. "Reverend Byers will be here soon. He's bringing someone from the Children's Home with him."

"Dammit, Abbie, doesn't that man ever give up?"

"At least you've found Monique. That should help. Where was she this time?"

"In the swamp—with Rachel. They say she's injured."

"For two full days and neither thought to let us know?"

As they walked off without her, Monica felt unreasonably hurt. They spoke to each other, excluding her, as if what she thought or felt didn't concern them in the least. The inconvenience of her being gone seemed to upset them more than her actual disappearance.

She shook herself. She wasn't *Monique* anyway; why should she care how they felt? Somehow, she must make them understand that she was Monica

Ryan and she needed to get back to where she belonged.

And the moment she did, they'd be calling the looney doctors to cart her away.

She'd have to stay calm, choose her words carefully. Wondering how to begin, she studied the girl, Abbie. She was young, maybe eighteen, and she, too, wore a full skirt without the hoop. Her hem had frayed where it dragged on the ground and the faded blue cotton showed the toll of many mendings. Her honey-colored hair had been parted at the center and pulled back into a profusion of curls, but the pins had slipped, letting the curls cover parts of her pretty face. Still, the family resemblance was obvious; Drew must be a brother or cousin.

Who are these people? Monica wondered as they rounded the corner to the front of the house. And what in heaven's name am I doing here?

As if in answer, childish laughter erupted on the porch, drawing her gaze to the three urchins scrambling like little monkeys through the rail posts. She felt a pang in her heart, a recognition, as she watched the blond heads so absorbed in their play. It was so like her fantasy—how many times had she watched her dream children play this very game?

Perched on the railing, the oldest boy frowned at the others as if such childish antics were beneath him, though he couldn't have been more than ten. Another boy, a year or so younger, wiggled in and out of the posts like an agile lizard, laughing and taunting as the girl struggled to follow behind him. Her thin body was tiny enough to slip through the gaps, but her once-yellow skirt kept getting snagged on the splintered wood. She didn't cry or whine at him to stop; she just sucked in a breath, ripped the material loose, and tried again.

"Uncle Drew!" the kids shouted in unison, running to his side the instant they spotted him. "You're back."

"I've brought your mother," he said flatly.

Monica's smile dropped as the three eager faces turned to her with their uncle's scowl. Bad enough they could mistake her for their mother, but why such hostility? "I can't imagine what's happened," she tried to explain, "but actually, I'm Monica Ryan. I live in New York."

The bewildered children looked to Drew. Abbie continued to watch her, her gaze wary, yet curious. "I woke in the swamp." Monica smiled at her, hoping Abbie might listen. "I have no idea how I got there."

Drew shrugged. "Rachel claims she hit her head. That she's lost her memory."

"My memory is fine," Monica snapped. "And I'll thank you to stop talking as if I'm not here. I don't know who this Monique is, but if you'll just show me your telephone, I'll try to straighten this out."

All five faces started at her with the same blank expression. "Teleform?" Abbie asked.

"Telephone. You know, you dial and then talk . . ." Monica broke off, looking to the roof and finding no wires going to the house. No phone, no electricity, no cable TV.

Shaking his head, Drew took her arm. "I'd better get her to bed. Abbie, try to get the children tidied up before Reverend Byers arrives. God knows what he'll suggest if he finds Monique like this."

"Wait . . ." Monica tried to protest, but he was already dragging her into the house.

"Who is that lady?" she heard the little girl ask Abbie.

Monica wished she could talk with the child, but Drew was pulling her across the entrance foyer. A hazy part of her rejoiced that the marble tiles were gone, that a scuffed, hardwood flooring stood in their place. Stripped and waxed, the rich, vibrant oak would be beautiful.

Drew gave her no time to inspect the similarly neglected furnishings; but as he dragged her up the stairs, she saw that while the bannister would profit from a polishing, it was free of the awful white paint. Gone too was the chandelier, as were all Judith's touches—had someone turned back the hands of the clock?

But if this were the past, how on earth could she have gotten here? She thought of the ring, deep in her pocket, and remembered wishing it could be a talisman. One click of the ruby slippers and here she was in her own version of Oz. Lord knew, the ingredients for a dream-come-true were all here. The kids, a family, a house she could make her own.

As if to remind her that one vital piece was missing—a husband who would love her—Drew all but shoved her into her aunt's rooms.

It was much as it had been before Judith's illness, pale pastels and French Provincial. Monica hadn't liked it then; she felt doubly uncomfortable now. "I'd rather not stay here if you don't mind," she told him.

"Don't start," he said wearily from the doorway, though there was no mistaking the steel behind that tone. "You've stretched my patience thin enough. If I were you, I'd get out of those filthy clothes and into bed."

"Well, you aren't me. I'm not even me." She knew she was babbling, but she couldn't stop. "I mean, I'm not your Monique. I'm Monica. Monica Ryan. And I want to go home."

His lips formed a hard, tight line. "I don't know what game you're playing now, but I haven't the time for it. Not with Reverend Byers on his way."

"Stop yelling at me. It's not my fault if you're having trouble with the man."

"No? Then who called him a hairless toad? Granted, I wouldn't want to marry him, either, but did you have to laugh at his proposal?" He ran his hand through his hair, a gesture she'd seen Derek try a hundred times, yet Drew's distress seemed genuine. "Can't you see it's no laughing matter?" he asked, exasperated. "The man is bound and determined to brand you an unfit mother."

"Unfit?" Monica thought aloud, wondering how any woman could neglect those delightful children on the porch. "You can't think I—"

"I try not to think about you at all, Monique. Get it through your head our recent sham of a wedding was merely to stop Byers from taking the children. I'd just as soon see you in your grave than let them be taken from this house!"

The words seemed to reverberate in the ensuing silence. They were recently married and he talked to his new wife this way? She sure could pick them—that made two husbands who thoroughly despised her.

No, she repeated firmly to herself. It was Monique he hated, not her.

He grimaced, as if daunted by his outburst. "Get some rest," he said quietly. "And clean yourself up."

She nodded, tried to smile. "Can I use the shower?"

At his uncomprehending stare, she remembered the lack of modern conveniences. Eyeing the pitcher and bowl on the nearby table, she feared a sponge bath would have to suffice. "Never mind," she told him wearily. "I can make do."

"Do what you must, but don't leave this room."

He turned; but, irrationally, Monica wanted him to stay. "I'm not her, you know," she spoke out, wanting to get past the animosity to the man underneath.

He turned briefly, tilting his head as if something in her tone gave him pause. "Whoever you are," he said with a brief shrug as he left the room, "just do as you are told."

Monica stared at the empty doorway. It was impossible; she couldn't stay here. How could she manage with no shower and no phone? And how could she live with a man who'd just admitted he'd happily see her dead?

She thought again of the ring. If it truly were a talisman, why not try it? Just set it on her finger and she could go back to where she had been.

But why? Too vividly, she could hear Derek and Amy in bed, talking about her. Did she want to return to that?

She stood in the middle of the room, fighting the tears she'd been too distracted to shed. Damn you, Derek, she thought bitterly; I thought you were going to make sure I need never cry again.

"I don't mean to bother you," a small voice

called from the doorway, "but could we talk for just a li'l bit?"

Dabbing at her eyes, Monica turned to face the child. A ragged Alice in Wonderland in her torn yellow dress and dirty white apron, the little girl stepped in and eased the door closed behind her. "I'm s'ppost to be getting pretty for that awful Reverend Byers. Uncle Drew would paddle my backside good and proper if he knew I came in here."

She was adorable, all blond curls and pink cheeks, and Monica couldn't help but smile.

With a grin of her own, the girl moved closer. "Stephen says I'm too li'l to know anything, but I just had to see for myself."

"Stephen?"

"My biggest brother. Boys are silly, huh? Any girl can see you're too different to be our mama."

Guessing the child to be six or seven, Monica crouched down to be on eye level with her. "Different? How so?"

She shrugged. "Your smile. Your whole face does it, like you can't keep the good feelings all in one place." The girl frowned, suddenly solemn. "Mama just smiles with her lips. Never her eyes."

Disturbed by the child's observation, Monica spoke quickly. "You're right—I'm not your mama. My name is Monica. I'm a teacher from New York."

"You teach school?" The tiny face lit up, making Monica long to hug her. "Can you teach me to read?"

"Well, yes, I suppose; but you must surely be old enough to start school."

She shook her head. "That's what Mama said,

but Uncle Drew doesn't want me going all the way down to New Orleans. And Mama doesn't want us taking lessons from Reverend Byers."

Nor would I, Monica thought, if the man called me an unfit mother. Curious, she asked, "Reverend Byers is a teacher?"

"Back when I was real li'l, before the war got bad, he came here most afternoons. But then Papa died and Reverend Byers had that fight with Mama."

Ah, yes, the marriage proposal. "Can't your Uncle Drew teach you?"

"He's in the fields all day, 'cept when he does his 'counts." The girl sighed, the sound too adult. "He frowns somethin' fierce, doing those 'counts. But then, he hardly ever smiles any more. Abbie says somethin' bad happened to him in that rebel prison."

What had Drew been doing in a rebel prison? Living in Louisiana, wouldn't he have embraced the Confederate cause?

"I want to learn 'rithmetic too. So I can help Uncle Drew do his 'counts. But mostly, I need to read." A determined glint shone in her angelic features.

Monica knew she mustn't encourage her. "I'd love to help, but I don't really belong here. I have a home of my own—a life of my own."

"Please stay," the child pleaded. "Just till I learn to read that book."

"What book?"

Suddenly tense, the girl took a step back, glancing over her shoulder at the door. "It's nothin', just a silly old thing." She looked to Monica, her soft brown eyes wide and pleading.

"Just stay for a li'l bit. Please? I'll be the best reader you ever taught."

"I bet you would." Monica rose, feeling genuine regret. The ring seemed to burn a hole in her pocket. "The trouble is, even if I want to stay, maybe I can't. I don't know how I got here, so how can I be sure I won't be taken away again?"

The blond curls danced as the girl shook her head. "I know how you got here. I wished you."

"Wished me?"

"Uh huh. And I'm not ever gonna wish you away."

Monica started to deny this; but, in truth, did she have a better explanation? "I don't understand. Why wish for me?"

"We need a real mother, someone to love us and make us a family. Someone to make Uncle Drew smile again."

He needs me, Monica thought, remembering his fleeting smile as he gazed at the house.

And two seconds later, she'd practically pulled him to the ground. "You're forgetting one thing," she told the girl, but she could have been speaking to herself. "Your uncle doesn't much like me."

"He will. I'll just wish him to."

Monica found herself grinning. Smiling back, the girl flung herself into Monica's arms, nearly knocking her over.

With a giggle, she disentangled herself. "Stephen says I'm too 'petuous to be alive, but I had to hug you." She glanced back at the door. "I reckon I'd best get to changing clothes. Uncle Drew doesn't want Reverend Byers calling me a ragmuffin again."

Watching the child skip off, Monica understood

Drew's anger. She too would kill rather than let anyone take this precious child away.

"Wait," she called out. "I don't know your name."

"It's 'Lizabeth."

"How pretty. Don't you have a nickname?" At the child's obvious confusion, she added, "You know, a pet name that's yours and yours alone."

Elizabeth frowned, then her tiny face brightened. "I know, you can think up one for me."

With that, she was out the door, leaving Monica alone in the room, her smile slowly fading. The child made it sound so natural, so believable. I wished you here, she'd said.

And all at once, Monica wanted to believe her. This house, the children, the family, and yes, even Drew—it was all she had ever wished for herself.

Uneasily, she remembered saying those same words to Geralyn. If her friend thought Derek was too good to be true, imagine what she'd say to the irresistible 'Lizabeth and her good-looking uncle.

She knew what Geralyn would say—Monica was dreaming or going insane. This was some crazy psychological outpouring, her mind trying to compensate for Derek's betrayal.

She wandered into the bedroom, retracing her earlier steps to try to understand what had happened. She'd gone to the bed—no, she'd found the ring first. Digging in her pocket for the ring, she sat on the soft, feather-filled mattress. As she did, she remembered how she had seemed to float out of her body. Had she actually died?

Or had she just been transported to a different reality?

Looking at the ugly silver band with its evil serpents, she knew that everything had changed the moment she set it on her finger. Maybe it *was* a talisman. She had been wishing for a better life at the time.

Come home. As if her aunt stood beside her, Monica could hear Judith whispering the inevitable plea.

Monica knew she should go back. Holding the ring above her finger, she tried to gather the courage to put it on. Only by returning, by confronting Derek with his betrayal, could she begin to make sense of her life again.

But home is where the heart is.

She bit her lip. This was crazy. Could she actually consider choosing this dreamworld over reality? Breathing deeply, meaning to force the ring on her finger, she happened to glance at the full-length mirror before her.

A total stranger stared back.

Monica gaped at the alien face, its skin too soft and delicate to be her own. Touching the long, raven hair, she shook her head, but the stranger moved with her. She stood, and the image in the mirror rose to her feet.

"It's not me," she whispered to the reflection, exaggerating the movement of her mouth as she approached the mirror. The red, full lips mimicked every word.

Running a trembling finger down the elegant nose, Monica felt a rush of excitement. She twirled before the mirror, realizing why she felt so light. It wasn't blood sugar; she no longer carried the extra weight. She was not only beautiful, she was thin!

Touching the new body in a hundred places, she

pinched herself to make sure it was real. All her life, she'd ached to look like this. Time and again she'd watched it happen—with Judith and the girls at school—all the best went to the beautiful people. When you're lovely on the outside, she'd learned early on, there's no need to prove yourself; others see you and want to like the person underneath.

And by some miraculous twist of fate, she had become one of them. For the first time in her life, she could look in the mirror and believe someone could love her back.

Derek must have poisoned me, she decided. For surely I've died and gone to heaven.

No, not quite heaven. Considering Drew's hatred and the upcoming visit by Reverend Byers, perhaps this was more the *edge* of heaven, some sort of purgatory where she must first prove her worth.

She paused, her gaze going down to the ring in her hand. Just what had she done to prove worthy of such incredible luck? Set this ring on her finger? It wasn't even *her* ring.

Guilt flared. Had this face—this fate—been meant for Judith instead?

Judith was dead, she reminded herself angrily. Nor should she forget how the woman had paid Derek to marry her.

Here was her chance; she'd be a fool not to take it. Or did she mean to spend the rest of her life on the brink of happiness, always standing at the edge, seeing heaven's potential but never knowing its joy?

Thinking of Elizabeth's wish, and Drew's wistful smile as he gazed at the house, Monica knew that with a little luck and a lot of effort, she could one day make this place her own personal Eden.

It could mean the fight of her life, but what of it? River's Edge, the children, Drew . . . having a family like the Sumners would be well worth the struggle.

Shoulders squared, she marched to the dresser, dropped the ring on the floor, and kicked it firmly out of reach.

And there it could stay, she decided, out of sight, out of mind.

Four

Hurrying down the staircase, Drew cursed softly. If only he could wash away his anger as quickly as he'd scrubbed the grime from his body. He had no time for such nonsense—the plantation took forty-eight hours out of his day.

Damn that Monique. Was it her life's work to ruin him?

Reaching the bottom step, he scowled at the front door. Thanks to his new wife, Reverend Byers would be knocking any moment—the spurned suitor exacting revenge.

How much easier things would have been had Monique not refused the man. Drew had had to marry her, to prove the children had a proper family and home; but he now felt as trapped, and as helpless, as he had in prison. Life with Monique, he knew, would be the same living hell.

Hearing a carriage outside, he braced himself. The next hour or so wasn't likely to be any more pleasant. The good reverend's voice tended to rise in pitch when he was upset, and learning about their marriage was bound to upset him.

Ah, hell, best to get it over and done with.

Drew flung open the door as the man was readying to knock. For an awkward second, they both stared at the reverend's useless fist, until Byers meekly pulled it back to his side. "Captain Sumner, what a surprise. I thought . . . that is . . . I was told you'd gone to New Orleans."

"Sorry to disappoint you."

"Yes, well . . ."

"Good day, Captain Sumner," added a female voice, and Drew turned to the woman beside Byers. "I am Miriam Harweather," she said stiffly, extending a hand. "Matron Harweather, from the Children's Home."

Drew shook her hand. From the gray hair to the drab clothing, she was every inch the forbidding matron, yet something in her brief smile helped him relax. She might be strict, he sensed, but she'd be fair.

"Won't you come in?" Ushering them into the parlor, Drew watched Byers turn up his hawk of a nose, sniffing in disdain at the furnishings. Monique was right at that; the man was a hairless toad.

But the man's shortcomings weren't at issue today, Drew reminded himself. It was more important to convince Byers—and Matron Harweather—they had no reason to break up his family.

He gestured to the only decent chairs in the room. Their dark mahogany backs might be stiffly uncomfortable, but at least they weren't as shabby as the others, whose gold brocade was so worn tufts of stuffing poked through the armrests. "Please make yourselves comfortable," he told his guests, trying to divert Byers from studying the bare patches in the carpet. "I'll call the children."

"No need for that." Reminded of his purpose for being here, Byers puffed himself up in the chair. "After all, what must be said might not be fit for little ears."

He had no time to elaborate, for the children were already flying down the stairs. At the last step, Stephen slowed, demanding his younger siblings follow his lead. Watching the attempt at a dignified entrance from the parlor door, Drew barely suppressed a grin. If nothing else, at least they knew their manners.

"Ah, here they are," he said, herding the children forward. "My family. Stephen, Andrew, and Elizabeth."

To his relief, the boys executed their well-rehearsed bows without a hitch. Elizabeth—the little ham—performed her curtsy as if dipping before royalty and then stepped back to take Drew's hand.

He gave it a reassuring squeeze. "Children, you already know Reverend Byers. And this is Mrs. Harweather, from the Children's Home."

"Miss Harweather," Byers corrected, earning a frown from his companion. "If you will kindly leave us now, children, we have grave matters to discuss with your uncle."

Elizabeth shook her head. "He's not our uncle any more. He's our daddy."

Byers shook his bald head with feigned sympathy. "This is precisely what I feared. Poor children, forced to live without affection, transferring their emotions to the first available source. A source, I might add, who has proven unreliable by running off in the past."

Drew bristled. The only time he'd *run off* had been to join the army.

Elizabeth gave *his* hand a reassuring squeeze. "But Uncle Drew, didn't you become our daddy when you married Mama?"

"Married?" Byers grew so red, it looked as if he'd have apoplexy and explode on the spot.

It was time for Drew's performance. "Please forgive us, Reverend, Monique and I wanted you to be at the ceremony, but there we were in the city, with a dispensation from the bishop, and well, neither of us could bear to wait."

"You . . . why you . . ."

"What's wrong?" Miss Harweather eyed Byers with surprise. "This is wonderful news. You said yourself marriage was a means of providing security for the children."

Had he actually hoped to force Monique to the altar? Frustration could make a man dangerous, Drew thought. Byers might be doubly determined to get revenge now.

"You can't . . ." Eyes glittering, the reverend swallowed and tried again. ". . . you can't tell me the children are happy with this sudden turn of events."

The boys moved closer to Drew, presenting a united front. "We are too happy," Elizabeth said fiercely. "We love our new daddy."

"And what of Mon . . . er, Mrs. Sumner? Why isn't she here to share such 'happy' news."

"She wanted very much to tell you herself, but as luck would have it, she took ill this morning. She's been keeping to her bed all day."

"Oh?"

Drew itched to rearrange those smug features. "She especially wanted to tell you we've sold the house in New Orleans. She'll be making her home here at River's Edge from now on, with the children and me."

Though his speech was as carefully rehearsed as the boys' bows, Drew felt uneasy. Could he hope to make Monique play along? Not likely, the way she'd fought the sale of the house. And not two minutes after he'd left for the city, she'd gone running to Rachel in the swamp.

He couldn't watch her day and night, not with all the work to be done on the place, yet clearly someone had to. There was no predicting what the woman might do next.

As if to prove this, he heard the whisper of silk. Even before turning around, he knew he would find Monique at the door.

Gliding into the room, smiling in her deceptively angelic fashion, she made herself the focus of everyone's attention. Drew couldn't know what she was up to now; but, being Monique, it had to be trouble. She might have the face of an angel, he well knew, but deep down she had the heart of a witch.

As she swept her skirts past his leg, trailing the subtle scent of magnolias, it was all he could do not to reach out and throttle her.

She looked at Drew, blinking. "Where's your sister?"

"Yes," Byers said, jutting out his nose in his eagerness to trap them. "Just where is Abigail?"

"Busy in the kitchen." Drew didn't add that Abbie had wanted no part of this charade. She'd support Drew to the day he died, but she'd never approve of his marriage. In her mind, the children would be better off without their mother.

"We were told you were ill." Shifting focus, Byers turned to Monique with his irritating whine. "I must say you are looking remarkably well to me."

It was an understatement. Since Drew had left her, she'd put the time to good use. Parted at the center and pulled up at the sides by dark rose ribbons, her black curls fell charmingly behind her ears, emphasizing the glow on her delicate cheekbones. It was like looking at an older version of Elizabeth, innocence and female mystery combined, the personification of the pre-war idyll when women seemed fragile dolls to be pampered and protected.

Of the same shade as the ribbons, the gown was a paradox, managing to be both demure and provocative. It covered all the important parts of her, yet somehow made Drew all the more aware that they were there. Whispering secrets as she moved, the silk swirled about her limbs. Other women had abandoned the massive hoops for practicality; but, being Monique, she no doubt wanted everyone in the room wondering about those long, well-formed limbs.

She looked at him then with a gaze so direct his breath caught in his throat. Was she daring him to remember her legs wrapped about his own? Damn her—no matter how he tried, he could not stop the tightening in his groin.

What was wrong with him, letting her get under his skin? He had more than himself to consider; he had his brother's children to think of now. Robert would expect him to look after them; and, all things considered, it was the least Drew could do.

"I am feeling a bit faint," Monique said in a breathless voice as she sashayed to the only remaining chair. Dropping into it, she beamed up at their visitors.

The effect might be dazzling, but Drew focused on how her fingers nervously poked and pulled at the tufts of the chair. His irritation increased; must she call attention to how tattered the room—the whole house—had gotten to be?

Her smile found and centered on Elizabeth. As if it were an invitation, the child went running to jump onto her mother's lap.

Stunned, Drew wondered what was behind this rare display of affection. Only last week, Monique had shrieked at the tired Elizabeth for merely leaning against her skirts.

More surprising yet was how Elizabeth, who'd always avoided her mother in the past, seemed content to be sitting there. Either each was an incredible actress or they had forged some unexpected bond between them.

Drew waited nervously, wondering what in hell the she-witch was up to now.

Stroking the child's hair, Monique turned to their guests. "I hope we don't seem rude to you, but Elizabeth and I have been separated for a few days and we're still catching up on things, aren't we, sweetie?" Again, there was that silent exchange as the child enthusiastically nodded her head. "Why, we have such plans, the children and I. Have they told you? Starting tomorrow, we'll be doing lessons. It's time—don't you think?—they were reading and doing their sums."

"Well past time, if you ask me; but I must warn

you, Mrs. Sumner, I will no longer be available to school them."

She gave Byers a smile that would melt a stone. "I'd never dream of imposing so. I mean to teach them myself."

Elizabeth reached up to hug her, the motion fiercely spontaneous, but more surprising still was how Monique returned the gesture. Gazing at them, reminded of the Madonna with her Child, Drew felt that old familiar aching in his chest. He was the ultimate incurable romantic, always searching for a sign that love truly did exist.

This was Monique, he reminded himself. Couldn't he see by now when she was playing her endless round of games?

"We should be going." Miss Harweather rose to her feet. "I can see that we're not needed here."

Byers remained seated, his arms folded stubbornly across his chest. "You may trick the others, but you can't deceive me. I was here, remember, when you locked the children in their rooms to entertain the Yankee riff-raff."

Biting her lip, Monique set Elizabeth down and stood beside Drew. "The war was a painful time in my life—in all our lives," she said with a sad smile for Matron Harweather. "But it's now over, and I swear I will not fail the children again. Besides, I have such a fine new husband to help me." Placing her hands on Elizabeth's shoulders, she paused to smile shyly up at Drew.

Though his own response was a bit forced, Drew did his best to follow her cue. "I think what my wife is trying to say, Reverend, is that we ask only for a chance to begin again."

Monique's eyes searched his. As the aching

filled his chest, Drew almost gave in to the temptation to hold her close against his side.

He forced himself to look away. Oh, she was good, so good even he was almost suckered into believing her.

"A reasonable request," Miss Harweather said. "I think we can consider the matter resolved, don't you, Reverend?" She glared at him until he, too, reluctantly rose to his feet.

"My concern is for the welfare of the children. I will not rest until I'm certain they have a proper home."

"They shall have a loving home," Monique said fervently. "If I have to die giving it to them."

Drew knew he had to put a stop to this. She'd gone too far; not even Miss Harweather could swallow much more. Leading their visitors out of the room, he knew he had to get rid of them before Monique ruined it all.

The children took this chance to escape, scampering over each other in the race up the stairs. Byers shook his head disapprovingly.

"Leave the children be," Drew said softly as the man bustled past. "They're not the ones you're angry at."

Byers straightened his shoulders, but gave no other indication he'd heard. There would be trouble from that one, Drew thought as he closed the door behind him; this was far from over.

Strangely enough, Monique echoed his thoughts. "He's not finished, is he? He means to come back."

"It surprises you?" he snapped. What gall, playing the innocent, when she was the sole reason the man had come. "Did you honestly think your performance would convince him?"

She blinked, the perfect wounded doe, until Drew thought he would choke on his anger. "Don't bat your lashes at me. Your playacting might deceive a soft heart like Matron Harweather, but it hasn't worked on me for years."

She gazed at her hands. "Then you didn't mean what you said in there? About beginning again?"

"With you?" He laughed, bitterness rising like bile in his throat. "Even I can learn my lesson by now."

She looked up eagerly. "I might have changed, you know. I might be a . . . a new person."

"Yeah, well I've changed too. I'm no longer a gullible boy, Monique, eager to believe your lies. Maybe I don't know what it is yet, but I can see when you're up to something. From now on, I mean to be watching you. If you so much as frown at those children, I'll make you wish you'd never been born."

She stared at him, into him, with eyes so wide and hurt, he knew he'd either strangle her or kiss her.

"I've got to go," he said brusquely, turning on a heel to march away.

Watching him, Monica began to tremble. She could battle a hundred Reverend Byers, but it wouldn't make the slightest difference. Drew was determined to hate her.

She tried to insist it didn't matter, that the children were her sole concern, but her new body refused to listen. Even now, it shook with the need to be in Drew's arms.

Back in the parlor, it had taken all the willpower

she owned not to betray her yearning. Walking past him, standing at his side, she could think only of how it would feel to have his lean, strong hands brush up and down her naked skin.

She blushed. Where on earth did such thoughts come from? She wasn't precisely a virgin, but her few attempts at lovemaking were hardly the acts of grand passion. How would she know what it meant to have a man stroke her, to lose herself in such mindless pleasure?

Nor would she ever know, she thought sadly. Drew had made it clear that he'd rather see her dead.

"He'll like you someday," Elizabeth said, suddenly behind her. "Just give him a li'l bit."

Smiling ruefully, Monica squatted beside the child. "You're too wise for your years, you know that? Where did you come from? I thought you went upstairs with your brothers."

"I knew you didn't get to eat breakfast. I came to show you to the kitchen."

"Why thanks, sweetie, but I can find it. You go on and play. Go have fun with your brothers."

Elizabeth shook her head. "Andrew just plays with his frogs, and Stephen's angry. He says taking lessons from you is stupid and he isn't gonna do it."

"Did you fight with him?"

"Some. Did you fight with Uncle Drew? I heard him hollering. I came down in case you needed me."

Oh, yes, much too wise for her years, Monica thought, gently brushing the hair off the child's face. "Thanks for the concern, but I'm fine. You go along now and make up with Stephen and let me worry about getting him to take lessons."

Elizabeth looked up the stairs, then back at Monica. "If you're sure you don't need me . . ."

Monica stood. "Go on. Get out of here."

Watching the child race up the steps, she wondered if Elizabeth would try again to talk to her brother.

If so, she wished the girl better luck than she'd had with their uncle.

The man was impossible. Unfair and pigheaded. Maybe Monique had done terrible things to him; but Derek had betrayed her, too, and she didn't blame Drew for another's treachery.

Shaking herself, she decided she wouldn't waste another moment thinking about him or any other man. Lord knew, she had worries enough to occupy her, foremost being her rumbling stomach. With Byers gone, she found she was starving.

She went through the back hall to the kitchen, only to discover it was no longer there.

Instead of Judith's black, white, and chrome appliances, wooden shelves, cabinets and counters now lined the room. From the stack of trays in the far corner, she realized this must be a serving pantry, a "command central" for the slaves who would present the family meal.

The actual food preparation, she now remembered, had been conducted elsewhere. Back before air conditioning, planters designed their kitchens to keep the stoves away from the house, letting the slaves deal with the heat.

Catching the aroma of baking bread, she went weak with hunger. Mouth watering, she trailed the scent to a structure across the carriageway. An old-fashioned pump stood guard outside the door, its cast iron crank reminding about the lack of indoor plumbing.

The room inside held the same, quaint charm. Lit and ventilated by three windows, the large room welcomed her in. A mammoth hearth stood directly opposite; the cast iron stove set inside it no doubt produced those yummy scents. Above on the mantel, a colorful row of ceramic jars and utensils added to the impression of a busy, happy place. Pots and pans hung from hooks in a profusion of iron and copper, while various gadgets, whose use she couldn't guess at, lined the two long counters along either wall. Monica saw the sink, but no faucets, and she remembered the pump outside with a groan. Cleaning up after a meal would mean considerably more than stuffing things into a dishwasher.

Nor would there be an army of slaves to help, she saw as she watched the sole occupant of the room, Drew's sister, try to lift the huge iron cauldron off the wooden table.

"Let me help you with that," she offered impulsively, but the girl's stunned expression stopped her in her tracks.

"What are you doing here?" Abigail snapped, forgetting the pot for a moment.

"I was hungry. I-I smelled the bread." And up close, there were other scents, each better than the last, to fill her head with food fantasies. What she wouldn't give for a cheeseburger and fries. With a chocolate shake on the side.

"Oh. Well, it's not done yet. You'll have to wait." Abigail turned back to struggle with the pot.

Monica grabbed the handle and helped carry the

pot to the stove. "What are you making?"

"I'm fixing stew for supper."

"By yourself?"

Abigail turned, blue eyes flashing. "Who would help?"

"The slaves, er, the servants."

"Wake up and look around you. We can scarce afford the few workers we have, and every last one has to work in the fields with Drew. Someone's got to do the cooking, and it sure as spit isn't gonna be you."

Taken aback, Monica shook her head. "I'm perfectly willing to do my part. Just tell me how to help."

For a long moment, Abigail eyed her suspiciously. "The potatoes need paring," she said at last, nodding toward the table. "And that sack of carrots needs to be sliced."

Handing her a knife, Abigail turned back to the counter to chop meat. Monica looked at the pile of potatoes, trying not to groan. K.P. duty; wasn't it a punishment in the army?

Still, she didn't want Abigail doing it; the girl seemed overworked as it was. At her age, she should be out meeting young men, making the most of her looks, not spending her days in her brother's kitchen playing the drudge.

Grabbing the sack, Monica started slicing carrots. She'd put the potatoes off for as long as she could.

"If you're hungry," Abigail said without looking up, "why not nibble on carrots?"

"What I had in mind, actually, was more along the line of a cheeseburger and fries."

"A what?"

"Cheeseburger, with the works. Onions, pickles, mustard, ketchup . . ."

Seeing Abbie's bewilderment, she stopped. Fast food was a twentieth-century phenomenon. "Never mind," she finished lamely. "I was just rattling on."

No wonder Monique had the body of a model, she thought as she popped a carrot in her mouth. With all the good stuff out of reach, it would be easy to diet.

"You sure are acting strange," Abigail said, tilting her face as she turned toward her. "Did you really get knocked on the head?"

Monica decided she liked Drew's sister. In a lot of ways, the girl reminded her of her friend, Geralyn. And considering her precarious position in the household, Monica could sure use a friend now. "Listen, Abigail . . ."

"Abbie. No one ever calls me by my given name."

Except Byers, apparently, for that was where Monica had gotten the name. "Abbie, then. I guess amnesia must seem easier to accept than my being a stranger; but, truly, I'm not your Monique."

Abbie continued to study her.

To be fair, Monica supposed that if the situation were reversed, she'd find it hard to accept, too. "All right, say I am her and can't remember. You've got to see I need help figuring out what is going on."

"How so?"

"I assume the Reverend Byers' thing is jealousy rearing its proverbial head, but what about Rachel? It was pretty spooky, waking up to find her staring down at me. Who is she and why was I with her in the swamp?"

Abbie cocked her head, staring at her. "Sure is strange that you'd forget Rachel. She was your slave, brought with you from home. You two were inseparable."

"Were?"

"Rachel must have done something to make Drew angry, for next thing we knew, he'd banished her from the plantation."

Why banish her? Monica wondered, her mind racing. Theft, seducing a guest—or maybe the master himself? "What did she do?"

Abbie shrugged. "Drew won't talk about it. But I'll tell you this much. You and that Rachel were closer than any mere slave and mistress. Gave me the shivers, watching you together, plotting and whispering your secrets. And I wasn't the only one. There's not a worker in this parish that will walk within a mile of that woman's shack in the swamp."

The more Monica heard about Monique, the more she understood Abbie's distrust.

"There's been talk, about curses and enchantments. The fieldhands claim Rachel has her own brand of magic, more powerful than any of the voodoo that goes on in town."

It was Monica's turn to shiver. "Voodoo?"

"It's their way of explaining how you got away with what you did." Abbie went back to chopping with a flourish, her knife pounding on the board with quick, punishing strokes. "Myself, I think you made your luck by catering to the Union soldiers. They helped you live the good life in New Orleans while we all suffered here at home."

"Oh, Abbie, I had no idea . . ."

The girl didn't seem to hear her. "Can you

imagine how Drew felt, coming home after the hell he'd been through, to learn you'd frittered away the estate? Every day he goes out to the fields, slaving to make this plantation pay again, he's got to be cursing you for your deceitful, selfish ways."

Oh, yes, Monica could well imagine. No wonder he hated his wife.

"But I don't know," Abbie added quietly, resting the knife as she eyed the pile of carrots. "Maybe you have changed."

"More than you can guess."

"Elizabeth sure seems to think so. I declare, the way that child goes on, you'd think you were our salvation. I swear, if you get that little girl loving you and you let her down, there's no curse you and your Rachel can dream up that will stop me from making you pay for it."

Abbie turned with the knife, using it to accentuate her threat, and Monica suddenly felt too weary to fight. It seemed an uphill battle, convincing these people she meant them no harm. There was no sense protesting she wasn't Abbie's sister-in-law; she doubted she would ever be believed.

Abbie turned back to her work. The only sound in the room was the blade hitting the cutting block and Monica felt the accusation in each thud. Peeling potatoes in silence, she tried not to be discouraged. With all she'd been through in the past twenty-four hours, she was emotionally spent. It wasn't every day that your aunt cursed you from her deathbed or you found your new husband in bed with your maid of honor. How often did you find yourself in another body in a completely different time?

And, aside from the two hours she'd been drugged, she hadn't had much sleep lately. A good night's rest and, hopefully, everything would seem a lot less daunting.

She thought longingly of the bed in Monique's room. Forget it, she told herself; she had to peel the potatoes.

When she reached for the last one and sighed in relief, Abbie turned to look at her. "Good gracious, what did that Rachel have you doing in the swamp? You look tuckered out. Why don't you go on upstairs and take a nap?"

"I'm fine," Monica lied, fighting a yawn. "All I really need is a shower . . . er, bath."

"The tub is there," Abbie said, pointing at a copper contraption in the corner, "but I'm afraid I'm using the kettle for heating water."

Monica tried not to groan. She didn't much relish a cold bath; and, besides, she'd seen larger buckets at college parties, holding ice and beer.

Abbie must have seen her expression, for she smiled. "Why not rest now? You can bathe later."

Monica gave a weak smile. "I'd love to, but we've got to finish dinner. How else can I help?"

"You've got those vegetables done?" Abbie looked at the table, obviously amazed.

"Anyone can peel a potato."

"I must say I never expected to hear you say so. I'm enjoying this new you so much I'd love to dream up all sorts of chores; but, truth to tell, other than browning the meat and setting vegetables in the broth, there's nothing to do. Stew all but cooks itself."

"Maybe I can set the table."

Abbie shook her head. "No one sits down to a

formal meal in this house anymore. No, you go on up and try to rest. I'll call you when supper's ready."

"If you're sure . . ."

"Go on, you're cluttering up my kitchen."

Monica did feel exhausted. All at once the thought of sleep was more temptation than she could resist. "All right," she said as she went to the door, "as long as you promise to call if you need me for anything."

"I've got but one request," Abbie called out. "Just don't wake up being the old Monique."

Making her way into the house, Monica felt chilled by her words. After all, what control did she actually have over which body she inhabited?

One day, she realized uneasily, she might just wake up and find herself back in her old life.

Five

Monica woke slowly, Abbie's words returning to haunt her as they'd done when she first flopped on the bed. What would she do if she found herself back in her old life?

She hadn't bothered to undress, convinced worry would keep her awake for hours, yet she must have dozed off, for here she lay tangled up in her wrinkled gown.

Gown? Monica Ryan didn't own silk.

Taking heart, she opened her eyes to the dim light. She was here, in Monique's dress and room, safe and secure inside her incredible new body.

Safe and secure? Wide awake now, she sat up, wondering why she felt that way. Shouldn't she be running around, struggling to get back to her own life, like they did in the movies?

But this wasn't a movie. This was actually Monica Ryan, sitting here meekly accepting—no, actively wanting—her strange, new life.

Still, it would take some getting used to, this new existence. The gutted candle reminded her that there would be no electricity, no easy-listening radio station to wake her, no bracing shower to start the day.

Remembering the tub Abbie had pointed out, she added a soothing bath to her list of do-withouts. In the books she read, the hero was forever pulling the heroine down into the tub with him, but it was hard to imagine Drew, much less the two of them, fitting into that copper bucket.

She blushed furiously as she realized what she was thinking. Just when had she begun considering Drew as a hero?

Determinedly, she looked about the room until her gaze settled upon the ewer and basin on the dresser. That, she remembered from yesterday, was her sole hope of washing up.

Reaching back to unbutton the dress, she wondered what she should wear to dinner. From the sumptuous array in Monique's closet, she'd have assumed the Sumners dressed up, but Abbie claimed they never sat down to a formal meal. Swinging her feet to the floor, thinking more of what she would wear and less of where she was going, she knocked into the bedside table. It was then she noticed the tray.

Righting it, she found cold stew in a large bowl, with a generous chunk of bread beside it. An accompanying note had fallen to the floor.

She took the paper to the French doors, drawing the drapes aside for more light, but instead of the doors, she found a floor-length window. Oh yes, she remembered these, back when she'd first visited the house. Lift the window up and you had a doorway. It was yet another charming bit of the past Judith had swept away with her renovations.

Stepping onto the balcony—no, it was called a gallery—she was surprised to find the sun rising over the horizon. Had she truly slept through the night?

As if in answer, her stomach grumbled, reminding that she'd missed another meal. Had she skipped as many in her other life, she'd never have had to diet.

The note was from Abbie, its form and content as no-nonsense as the girl herself. Not wanting to disturb her sleep, Abbie had left both candle and meal in case Monique woke in the next hour or so.

Touched by her thoughtfulness, Monica vowed to do her best to help in the kitchen today. As she returned to the room to change, she left the window open, reasoning that the faint sunlight was better than no light at all. Cluttered with silly French furniture and myriad bric-a-brac, the room would be a minefield in the dark.

Unbuttoning her dress as she made her way to the basin, she found disrobing to be no easier than the dressing up had been. Underneath, she wore only a cotton slip—she couldn't guess what half the woman's underwear was for anyway—but the gown itself was a challenge. Who in her right mind would buy one with so many tiny fasteners? Wrenching and turning to get them undone was liable to twist her into a pretzel.

A few steps from the basin, the job almost done, she caught a glimpse of herself in the mirror. She stopped, her hand falling to her side. How bizarre it was, looking at the face of a stranger, knowing the delicately beautiful features now belonged to her.

The gown had fallen from her left shoulder, leaving an expanse of pure, white skin. Entranced by the vision, she inched the sleeve lower, watching the fabric slide down that slender arm.

As the silk dropped to her hips, and then the floor, only the thin, sheer cotton of her slip concealed the secrets of the perfectly formed body.

Shaking her hair free, feeling deliciously wicked, she let the tangled black curls cascade in a wanton riot about her shoulders. Miracle of miracles, she was not only thin, she was sexy, too!

She began to pose like a magazine model, pouting her lips, throwing back her head in a defiant pose. One graceful arm trailed up her side, reaching to lift the hair off her neck. Savoring the soft, morning breeze for a moment, she released the hair in a long, black cloud. It brushed her back like a lover's caress.

A lover.

He stole into her mind, a hazy, shimmering focus of all her desires. She began to imagine callused fingers sliding up her back, over her shoulders, trailing lazy circles around her breasts. She could almost picture his dark blond head bent over her neck, kissing the tender flesh at her nape.

Of its own volition, her hand moved to the strap of her slip, pushing it slowly down her arm. Deep within her, she felt an excitement growing; she felt daring, so alive. Soft cotton tugged across her breast until the nipple burst free into the cool, morning air.

Drew, her mind cried out in a jolt of desire.

Her hand tightened on the strap. Gazing at the mirror with embarrassed fright, she yanked the strap back into place. What had gotten into her?

It was outrageous, strutting like this before a mirror. Worse, it was completely alien to her nature. This new body seemed to have urges her other one had never known.

Trembling, she forced herself to look away.

Hurriedly searching for clothes, any clothes, she wondered again what was happening to her. It wasn't a long, soaking bath she needed; she had to find a numbing cold shower.

Or a swim.

Whirling, she looked to the window. The pool was no longer here, but what about the river? The Mississippi was renowned for its mud, but across the road should be a small cove, a bit of an oxbow where the water had settled enough for swimming. In her other life, Monica had gone there as a teenager, hoping to qualify for a lifeguard job at the town pool. Judith had squashed that opportunity, claiming it was beneath their social position, but Monica had spent many a happy hour paddling across that cove.

She reached for a dress, but rejected it in favor of a two piece outfit. The skirt might be ridiculously full and the blouse might reach to her knees, but at least she'd have a lot less buttons to cope with.

Once dressed, she could find nothing to pass for a bathing suit, so she decided to swim in her slip. She'd take a clean one to change into later, as well as one of the small tents that passed for a pair of panties.

Tying back her hair with a ribbon, she grabbed the underthings, along with the soap and towel by the basin. As she passed through the sitting room and into the hall, she felt the first real sense of purpose in days. She wanted a bath; and, by hook or by crook, she was going to get one.

At the top of the stairs, the sound of voices stopped her cold. With a sense of *déjà vu,* she remembered hearing Derek and Amy Piersoll whispering there—was it only the day before yesterday?—as she trudged to her aunt's room.

With an icy wave of humiliation, she realized she hadn't been paranoid after all; they had indeed been talking about her.

"Wait and I'll cook some breakfast."

"I haven't the time."

Monica snapped back to the here and now. This wasn't Derek and Amy; it was Drew and Abbie. And Monica Ryan seemed to be the last thing on their minds.

"You've got to eat, Drew. You'll get sick if you keep on this way."

"I'll eat later. I can't stop now—I should have been out in the fields hours ago. I can't believe I overslept."

"Ever think maybe you need the sleep? Not to mention the food. What are you trying to do, work yourself into an early grave?"

"If I don't get the crops in by summer, nobody in this house is going to eat. Thanks to Monique, I've already lost three days work."

"Maybe you could ask her to work with you."

Drew's laughter held a bitter ring. "Monique, lifting a pretty little finger to help? You must still be asleep, little sister, because I think you're dreaming."

"She helped me in the kitchen yesterday. And she plans to give the children lessons."

"And you believe her? That's the trouble with you, Abbie—you're too damned soft-hearted. If Monique is being nice, you can bet she's got a reason. A selfish one. Don't trust her for a minute."

"Maybe I am soft, Drew Sumner; but you've grown so hard, I scarcely recognize you at all. I declare, that rebel prison must have—"

"I've got too much to do to stand here listening

to your harping. I'll see you for dinner."

"And just when is that likely to be? Ten? Eleven?"

Drew didn't answer. He turned away, his shadowed form striding into Monica's range of vision. As he flung open the door and the pale sunlight outlined his features, a slow throb began in the pit of her stomach, radiating downward.

Long after he slammed the door behind him, the picture remained etched in Monica's mind. She half-heard Abbie muttering under her breath and stomping off to the kitchen, but every inch of her body stretched toward Drew. One look at those strong, lean features, and it was all she could do not to chase after him. Heaven help her but she wanted to grab hold of his arms, wrap her legs around him, and make him take her forcefully, right there against the wall.

She sat on the top step, trying to regain her composure. What was happening? This was how she'd been by the mirror; such thoughts didn't belong to Monica Ryan. In all her yearning for Derek, her fantasies had never gone past cuddling before the fire. She'd wanted to get married, yes, but she hadn't thought much past the "you may kiss the bride." How embarrassing—no, alarming—that she should now become so, well, so lurid.

Even now, her body burned for Drew. *I've got to get that cold swim,* she thought desperately. *Pronto.*

Hurrying out of the house and across the lawn, she prayed that she wouldn't run into either Sumner. They'd guess in an instant that she'd been eavesdropping; the way she was blushing, she must be the picture of guilt.

As she crossed the road, she saw Drew far ahead, making his way to the fields. Framed by the strengthening sunshine, he was even more beautiful than he'd been in the doorway. From the purposeful stride, to the proud tilt of his head, he was every bit the strong, virile male. What girl in her right mind wouldn't have the hots for him?

Running to the cove as if it were an oasis that would save her, she told herself firmly that she hated that macho stuff. A man had to have a lot more than overdeveloped biceps to impress her. He should have intelligence, sensitivity, a sense of humor . . .

Give it up, she told herself angrily. Such a man didn't exist.

But thankfully, the cove did.

Though, granted, it was more defined than she remembered, with a narrow inlet opening onto the river. It must have been dug out by man, not nature, though Mother Earth had certainly not spared her bounty on the place.

Definitely not New York, she thought fondly as she listened to the natural quiet. How peaceful it seemed, guarded by tall, sweeping oaks, the stately cypress. An early morning haze still lingered above the water, lending an almost magical air, as if nymphs and fairies actually frolicked in the lily pads on the far banks.

As if to guard the inlet, a small dock stretched over the far points, a wooden structure that storms and floods must have destroyed in the future. Gazing at it, she could think of nothing more divine than diving off its boards into the cool, bracing water.

She unbuttoned as she went, hurrying along the bank to the dock, dropping her things on the wooden planks. Clad in her slip, she dove into the water with a quick, fluid motion.

Surfacing, taking in air like a prisoner freed from solitary confinement, she made her way across the cove. As she swam lap after lap, she gave herself over to the sheer, sensual pleasure of water sliding over her skin, as if the motion could rinse away all the dirt and grime she'd collected. And perhaps a bit of her cares, as well.

A bit, but not all of them, for slowly, insidiously, images of Drew Sumner again invaded her mind.

She began to picture him, hot and sweaty from a day in the fields. It would be only natural to strip down, just as she had done, and dive into the river to cool off.

But there would be no cooling—not on her part—for the mere thought of his naked body made her own start to burn. Cold water and hot flesh, her own pale skin pressed up against that deep, dark tan.

"I wish I could do that."

Startled to hear a voice, she looked up at the dock to find Elizabeth. Monica faltered, almost taking in water, as she realized what she'd been thinking. Not quite a fitting subject for so young an audience.

Swimming slowly, she made her way back, taking time to compose herself. It seemed silly, since the child could hardly guess her thoughts, but Monica climbed up with extra care, and made a great deal of drying herself off with the towel.

Legs dangling over the side, Elizabeth watched her with a grin. "You move like a fish. Can you teach me to do that, too?"

"If you can't swim," Monica said sharply, still worried about the lurid direction of her thoughts, "then you shouldn't sit so near the edge. The water is deep here."

"Teach me now. It'll only take a li'l bit."

Monica dried herself vigorously. "Some other time. We're supposed to start school today."

"Today?" In her eagerness, Elizabeth stood up too close to the edge.

Automatically, Monica reached out and grabbed her. "Let's get off the dock." Leaning down for her clothing, she tugged the little girl to the bank. "Who let you come out here alone?"

"I can take care of myself."

"Did you ever stop to think you could drown? That no one would be here to save you?"

The girl looked up at her, her eyes puzzled and hurt. "I didn't mean to be bad. Why are you so angry?"

Why indeed? Sighing, releasing her hand now that they were on solid ground, Monica shook her head. "I'm not mad at you, sweetie. It scared me, seeing you in danger, and I guess I got a little crazy. It's criminal negligence, having that dock so close to the house and not teaching you to at least stay afloat. What about your brothers? Do they swim?"

Elizabeth merely shrugged.

"Hmmm. I'll have to teach you all, then."

"Today?"

"Definitely *not* today." Unwilling to remove her slip here, especially in light of her recent behavior, Monica decided she might better change at the house. She wiggled into her clothes, trying to ignore the uncomfortably damp cotton slip against her skin.

Once dressed, she took Elizabeth by the hand. "Besides, after I help your Aunt Abbie in the kitchen, you and I are going to start our lessons."

Falling into step beside her, Elizabeth all but skipped. "How long 'til I can read like you?"

Monica grinned. "Oh, I don't know; but, considering the student, I'd imagine it'll be just a li'l bit."

"I can't wait to show Robert and Andrew they should come to our lessons."

Elizabeth tried to sound defiant, but Monica could hear her disappointment, her loneliness. Remembering a childhood filled with much the same emotions, she resolved then and there to make today's lesson so much fun it wouldn't matter if either brother ever came to the classroom.

"If they don't want to learn, then we don't need them," she told Elizabeth. "In fact, it might be fun if it's just the two of us today."

As she began to catalog the various activities they would pursue, Monica felt an ugly sensation along her spine. At first, she thought it was her damp slip, chilling her skin, but the discomfort grew in intensity until she began to shiver.

Elizabeth stopped suddenly beside her, her tiny body as stiff as stone.

"What is it, sweetie? What's wrong?"

The child pointed forward. "You won't go with her, will you?"

Monica's gaze followed the gesture, only to be pinned by the cold, dark eyes of Monique's slave, Rachel. "No," she said quickly, half to reassure the child and half to convince herself. For there was something in the gaze, something that pulled at her and made her feet want to move forward.

Though the black woman stood a good way off at the edge of the swamp, it felt to Monica as if her angry eyes were an inch away. Monica could feel the animosity radiating out from them as if it physically brushed her skin. Once more an icy, ugly chill wriggled up her spine.

Instinctively, she moved closer to Elizabeth. She didn't know whether the hostility was aimed at herself or the child, but she wasn't about to hang around to find out.

Willing her gaze away, she tightened her grasp on Elizabeth's hand and fled back to the house.

Monique

May 27, 1857:

Mon Dieu, I have met him! The one man who can set my heart pounding and make me forget all that I have so carefully planned.

How can I explain how I felt, the moment I watched Drew rise from his seat on the porch to greet us? How do I describe his devastating smile, the easy, lazy charm that oozes from each pore of his perfect body?

How unjust, that the uninspired Robert should own River's Edge. For in my mind, they shall always be linked—beautiful Drew and that wonderful house.

Seeing them together, I knew I must have them both.

But I must start at the beginning, to make sense of this in my head.

Some might say that Drew is my forbidden fruit, and perhaps they would be right. It drove me mad, the way he ignored me at the start, for no other man has ever overlooked me before. But then, such is my point—Drew Sumner is no ordinary man.

Ah, what a challenge he is, my maddening Adonis. I am told no girl from here to New Orleans can resist his quick grin, his flattering words, and skillful flirting. Yet none of this attention means anything to him. All he cares about is running his family plantation, and proving himself worthy of the Sumner name.

He is a little boy lost, craving his brother's approval; but Robert does not understand this and belittles all Drew's attempts. I myself find no need to improve the slaves' quarters or to allow them to earn their freedom; but, unlike Robert, I see how such heedless laughter shatters his brother's dreams.

I would tell him there is no need to prove himself, that his good looks and charm are all any girl could ever want; but this is not what he wishes to hear. So I say Robert is a fool, he has no vision, and someday he will wish he had listened instead. All nonsense, of course, but how eagerly Drew responds to my words.

But it makes me insane, how he gazes at me with such undisguised longing, yet never, ever touches me. How silly these American men are with their outdated code of honor. What can it matter that I am an invited guest in his brother's home? We want each other, it is obvious, so why put us both through such torture?

Each day, I listen long and hard to his outpourings, telling him what he yearns to hear. I have trained myself to speak in the honeyed way these women have, striving to be one of the southern belles Drew favors. Even so, he continues to act the perfect gentleman—no, the perfect anachronism—while each night I crawl into my bed with a desire so fierce it is all I can do not to scream.

And then tonight, while we walked alone in the garden—blind, foolish Robert sees nothing wrong in this—Drew spoke of going away. A university friend has enlisted in the army, he told me, and he is thinking of joining him.

Unable to bear the thought, I became quite impatient. Why worry so about the future? It is time he relaxed and learned to enjoy life. Here, with me.

His features went solemn. It was vital to make his way in the world, he swore, for only then could he offer marriage to the woman he loves.

My first reaction was to find this woman and scratch out her eyes, but the intensity with which he then gazed at me warned that he was on the brink of making a declaration.

I panicked—I could not let him ruin everything—so I reached over and pulled him close.

It was heaven, that kiss, all I had ever hoped for and more. Even now, I can feel the tingling that radiated throughout my body. I think, *mon Dieu,* if he can do that to me with a simple kiss, only imagine what will happen when he takes me to bed.

But will he?

I cannot argue that it is part of his attraction, this inaccessibility. A challenge I cannot resist. He is strong, my Drew, an adamantly honorable man, and he thinks himself quite incorruptible.

But then, I have Rachel to help me.

Six

Trying not to wake him, Drew lifted his nephew off the floor and set him in the bed. From the tangle of bedcovers, it appeared Andrew had suffered another bad dream.

Drew knew about nightmares. Ever since the war and the ugliness of the prison camp, sleep had become a restless struggle for him, too.

In the pre-dawn dark, he could make out Stephen's rigid form in the other bed. How contained he seemed, even in his sleep. It wasn't right that a boy should sleep with the posture of a worried old man. He was a child, for God's sake; his most troublesome thoughts should be about eluding the punishment for the mischief he'd gotten into that day.

As he looked from one nephew to the other, Drew's throat tightened. Abbie was right. He should spend more time with them—show them the worst was over, that it was now safe to play and sleep.

But how would he teach them when he had his own nightmares to conquer? And where would he find the time?

As Andrew stirred, moaning quietly in his sleep, Drew felt another stab of guilt. He could dream up a thousand excuses but the fact would still remain: The children needed attention, a parent's attention. Tucking the covers under his nephew's chin, he vowed to find time. Somehow.

But not today, he amended silently as he moved down the hall. In the next few weeks, he had to get the crops in, repair the gas plant to supply fuel for the lamps in the house, and find some way to shore up the levee around the dock and artificial cove Monique had insisted upon building.

Besides, he wasn't the only parent in this house.

He paused before Monique's room, feeling old resentments engulf him. What mother didn't hear her son's nightmares or know how frequently he had them? But then, Monique would never squander precious beauty sleep on "childhood prattle." If Andrew were confused and frightened, she'd just as soon leave the task of comforting him to his older brother.

Enough was enough. As he'd told her when he married her, things had to change. There was no room for selfishness in this house. From now on, she'd have to take care of her children, just as a mother should.

The resentment built, needing an outlet. Shoving open the door, he entered the dark sitting room. Beyond, a candle beckoned from the bedroom as he strode forward.

Stopping in the doorway, he found Monique standing before her looking glass. She turned, clearly startled by his approach, and he noticed her pure white breasts were bare. Hot, forbidden lust slithered through him like a snake. He fought against it. The need to take her was a poison in him, one to which he must never again succumb.

Expecting her to laugh at his efforts, he was surprised when she reached frantically for her dressing gown, holding it up like a shield before her chest.

"Loving yourself?" he bit out as he gestured at the damned looking glass, using his anger for his own protection.

She further amazed him by blushing. "I-I was washing up." Her gaze went fleetingly to the table. "Truly."

Noticing the soap in the basin, the damp washcloth draped over the side, Drew felt suddenly foolish. "Why are you awake?" he asked sharply. "You never rise before noon."

"Abbie and I do the cooking early. So we can get most of it finished before the heat of the day. It leaves us free for other things."

"Other things?"

"Abbie does the housecleaning and I—"

"Spare me. I'd rather not know how you spend the day." He could imagine well enough. After two weeks of this loveless marriage, she was no doubt looking for some outlets of her own. "Just remember our agreement, Monique. You keep your end of it and I'll keep mine."

"Agreement?"

She looked so bewildered, he almost relented. "I asked only that you act like a mother. Don't you know Andrew has nightmares every night? Do you even care?"

She bit her lip and looked away. Anyone else and he'd think she felt remorse, but this was

Monique and "sorry" never entered her vocabulary. "And what about Stephen?" he went on, gathering steam. "That boy acts like the weight of the world rests on his shoulders. Ever notice how rarely they laugh, even Elizabeth? They're just children, for God's sake. How can you neglect your own flesh and blood?"

She looked up at him, her wide eyes alive with denial.

For a moment, looking into those eyes, Drew thought back to the moment they had stood watching the house, the day he'd brought Monique home from the swamp. Then, as now, it felt as if she had swallowed him whole, only to make him whole. His worries seemed to melt away; he felt eased, comforted . . .

He shook himself. Had he lost his mind? Monique didn't comfort, she lulled. She was setting him up, using him to get her way.

"Just keep our agreement," he said angrily, turning on a heel to leave the room.

She reached to grab his arm. "I would. I will. If I knew what it was."

Damn, but the feel of her fingers on his skin made the heat course through his body. He stepped back, out of her grasp, refusing to meet her gaze. "Ah yes, your amnesia. I wonder if it's contagious, since I keep forgetting you have it. Try this then. You play the model mother and I won't let them cart you off to jail."

"Jail?"

"Just behave yourself," he said over his shoulder as he quit the room. "As I've told you, I'd rather the children had no mother than a bad one."

As he left, he glanced back. She stood frozen

where he'd left her, her expression troubled, the dress still clasped protectively to her chest.

No, he told himself as he strode down the stairs. He would not be taken in by her wide-eyed stares and lost little girl charm.

He'd done that before and look where it had gotten him.

Later that day, Monica stood in the attic, wiping both perspiration and hair from her eyes. "Elizabeth?" she called, knowing the girl must be playing in another of this long series of rooms. "Can you come here and help me?"

Uneasily, she wondered if she should have let the little girl wander about in this clutter. With so few windows for light, what if she tripped and broke her neck?

"Elizabeth?" Monica called again, just as she saw the child wave from the end room. She grinned, understanding such curiosity. They'd found a veritable treasure trove here. A dusty trove, she added after another sneeze. "God bless you."

"Stephen!" she gasped, whirling to face him.

He held himself stiffly, ready for her to strike him, yet determined not to flinch. "I'm sorry." It sounded as if he said the words so often, they no longer had meaning.

"There's nothing to be sorry about. You just startled me. It's so quiet I thought I was alone up here."

He stepped back to the door. "Elizabeth is . . . has gone downstairs. I-I'll get her for you."

"The stairs are that way." Monica tried not to

smile; she knew he was trying to protect his sister. "But my bet is that Elizabeth is in the end room. She's fascinated by those old dresses."

"I'll get her."

"No, let her play," she said when he turned to go. "Grab that handle and help me move this trunk out so we can get at that little table. There sure is a lot of nice stuff up here. I don't know why your uncle doesn't use it, instead of the worn things you have downstairs."

He looked at her funny. "You're the one who put it up here. You said it was local garbage, that you'd never sit on a chair made of wood from a swamp."

Monique was a snob, for Monica could see nothing wrong with these furnishings that a good polishing wouldn't fix. And why belittle cypress when most of the house was built of that same sturdy wood?

As they dragged the trunk out of the way, Stephen bumped into the mirror behind him. It fell to the floor, crashing into what sounded like a million pieces.

He went white. "Y-your looking glass. I swear, I didn't mean to. . . . It was an accident."

"Stephen, it's all right," she soothed, hating to see his panic. "I'm happy it's broken. I brought it up here because I didn't want it in my room anymore."

What an understatement. It had done strange things to her, just looking into that mirror. She blushed as she thought of this morning. How humiliating, to be dreaming of Drew's hot, callused hands on her body, only to look up and find him staring from the doorway.

No, not staring. Glaring.

"Honestly," she added for emphasis, "I'm happy to see the last of it."

He looked at her as if she'd just announced she'd robbed the local bank.

"Help me carry this stuff downstairs to set up our schoolroom," she told him to change the subject. "Actually, I'm glad you came along. I was wondering how Elizabeth and I would manage on our own."

It was a cheap trick, playing the helpless female. None of this stuff was heavier than the furniture she'd dragged up the four flights to her New York apartment, but appealing to his gentlemanly instincts seemed a good way to reach him.

As they worked, she decided Drew was right about his nephew. Stephen was far too serious, a classic case of being *too* quiet, *too* polite. A great deal bubbled beneath the surface, and if it weren't soon given an outlet, the boy was liable to explode.

What had Monique done that her own children would be so distrustful—no, afraid—of her?

Jail, Drew had threatened. Was it a bluff or had the woman done something truly awful?

"We did a pretty terrific job," she said as they set the last table in place. "This is one super classroom."

It looked like what it was, an odd mix of tables and chairs. "It's nice, I guess," Stephen said, ever polite. "But why four desks?"

She wouldn't get much past this kid. "For you and Andrew. I know you're too busy for lessons, but I thought you might want to drop by and check on Elizabeth's progress. She seems a bit slow." A blatant attempt to exploit his protective instincts, but she had to involve him somehow. "With you here, she might not be so nervous. Maybe you can help me figure out what I'm doing wrong."

Before he could answer, Elizabeth bounded into the room, eager to begin. Monica suggested that Stephen shelve the box of books while she and his sister read. The boy frowned, but he went to work on the shelves.

As Elizabeth stumbled through the pages of her primer, he pretended to ignore them. When the lesson was done and his sister scampered off, though, he spoke up. "She won't learn if you jump in and correct her every time," he said defiantly. "Let her figure some things out for herself."

Monica knew this, but his observation impressed her. "You're right. I should have thought of that."

His brief, stifled grin left her wondering if anyone ever bothered to praise him. "Are you busy?" she asked, not quite finished with him yet. "I need help hanging this map on the wall."

He looked at the door as if wishing he could escape through it.

"I thought geography might be a good way to help her read," she went on as she held up the map. "Learning about other places could hold her interest better than that primer. Like maybe Hawaii. Or Alaska."

Seeing his blank expression, she realized that as exotic as those two states might be—and the most likely to pique his own interest—they wouldn't be part of the Union for a good many years. "Here," she told him, "hold the other end of this map while I tack it up. Actually, I should start in the northeast, where our country began. You know, the Boston Tea Party, the Declaration of Independence, the shot heard round the world."

Stephen snorted. "Yankee stuff."

Monica took her time tacking in her side of the map, wondering how best to answer him. She had to be careful; even in her own time, feelings were tender when it came to the Civil War. "It's not just Yankee stuff, Stephen. They were our forefathers. They fought for our liberty and freedom."

"So did President Davis and the Confederate army."

"You can't compare being taxed without representation to wanting to profit from another man's misery. Slavery was wrong and had to be stopped."

"The war wasn't over slavery. Uncle Drew says it was about money. He says war always is."

Drew Sumner, the ultimate cynic. She should have known such thoughts couldn't evolve in the mind of a boy. "He sounds like a rebel," she said, irritated. "I thought he fought on the Union side."

"You know he did." He seemed like a smaller Drew, blue eyes crackling with the same frustrated anger and hostility. "He couldn't stop being a Yankee soldier just because war broke out. Maybe you can change sides whenever it takes your fancy, but Uncle Drew keeps his word. But then, keeping your word has never meant anything to you."

He released his hold on the map, letting it swing downward as he turned to leave. Monica reached out to stop him, wishing she could get him to talk about what was so clearly bothering him, but she feared he would never confide in her as long as he thought her Monique. "Stephen, try to understand. I'm not—"

"Don't tell me you're not my mother. Only a baby like Elizabeth can believe she wished you here." The chill in his eyes could have frozen her. "I happen to know wishes don't come true."

Oh yes, far too like his uncle. Saddened by his cynicism, Monica loosened her hold. "I *can* keep my word," she told him softly. "I promised your sister I'd teach her to read, and I'm going to do it."

"What if you can't?"

"We can do anything, once we set our minds to it."

"Yeah? Can you stop Andrew's nightmares? Or keep the tax man from worrying Uncle Drew?" Shrugging free of her grasp, he ran off.

This time, Monica let him go. Feeling exhausted, she wondered what Monique had done to the boy to make him so bitter. Was there anyone the woman hadn't hurt?

Righting the map and securing it to the wall, she knew that however hard it might prove, she had to reach Stephen, He was a sharp one, that boy, both intelligent and innately curious; but unless someone could interest him in learning, his fine mind would go to waste.

There was so much she could teach him with the proper tools. All the computer and video equipment she'd taken for granted in New York—oh, how Stephen would have thrived on that. Here, she barely had paper. The Sumners were so low on supplies Abbie made lists on the backs of her aprons.

What she needed was books. Looking at the shelves he'd set up, she found grade-school primers, nothing to stimulate the imagination. If only she had access to a good library.

She thought of Judith's, stocked with hundreds of titles. Considering the relocation of the kitchen, the library might not exist now, but what would it hurt to look? With budding excitement, she hurried down the stairs to the first room on the left. To her disappointment, the door wouldn't budge.

Locked? But why?

She remembered a ring of keys hanging from the wall in the kitchen. One of them might open this door, but she didn't much relish the prospect of Drew catching her fiddling with his keys.

Across the hallway, she heard Abbie's voice. His sister should know which key. Better yet, she'd get the girl to let her in the room; Drew couldn't complain about that.

Stopping outside what had been Judith's living room, she heard a second voice. "Truly, Abbie, you look exhausted." From the voice, Monica pictured a prune of a woman. "The way you carry on, people will think you're one of Drew's slaves."

"He doesn't have slaves, Sarah Jane. No one does any more. Besides, I'm only doing what needs to be done. There's nothing wrong with good, clean work."

"How can you bear it? Why, your daddy entertained the governor here and your mama had darkies waiting on her hand and foot. You were born to a more gracious life."

"Robert died and left us to fend for ourselves long before I could play the belle," Abbie said in her no-nonsense tone. "And you know I'm more comfortable in the kitchen than in any ballroom."

"'Cept if that handsome Yankee friend of Drew's came calling. I'll wager you'd dig up all your old finery then."

"He hasn't been here since the war; and even if he did come, I have no finery. You know that."

"I suppose not." The woman sighed. "Everything nice in this house has always gone to Monique."

Monica cringed. Why hadn't she noticed that everyone else went around in virtual rags, while she had an endless supply of beautiful things? No wonder Drew thought she'd been loving herself in the mirror. She'd been so wrapped up in her fairy tale, she hadn't realized she'd been acting just as badly as Monique.

Well, she meant to change that. Gazing down at her gown, knowing she looked more like a maid than a prima donna, she wondered if she should join Abbie and her guest. If she could prove she wasn't afraid of hard work, that she was happy to do her part, maybe they'd come to accept her.

As she entered the room, all conversation stopped. The sudden chill warned that Sarah Jane could be added to the ever-growing list of people who hated Monique.

"My heavens, what happened to you?" Abbie gasped.

Monica's hand went to her hair, trying to straighten the tangles there. "The children and I were moving furniture. I came to ask a favor, but it can wait until your company has gone."

"Company? Don't be silly. Why, the Hawkins have been neighbors since time began. There's nothing you can say to me that Sarah Jane can't hear."

As Abbie spoke, Monica studied her guest. Surprisingly, Sarah Jane was close to her own age, not a prune at all, though she pretended to be one.

Poised at the edge of her chair, spine rigid, she wore a gray wool dress so prim it covered all but her face and hands. Her soft brown hair was pulled back from her face so tightly not one wisp escaped her severe little bun. Curled around the strap in her lap, her well-manicured fingers seemed to fear that the purse might otherwise sneak free of their grasp.

Yet despite the tightly-controlled exterior, Sarah Jane was a surprisingly attractive woman with creamy skin and the prettiest lashes a woman could ask for.

"Sarah Jane's inquired after our visit from Reverend Byers," Abbie hurried on as if afraid of a further lapse in the conversation. "She's here to offer help if we need it."

Not likely, Monica thought. The way the woman glared, she'd probably come hoping to find Monique dragged off in chains.

"Actually, I did have another reason for coming over." Sarah Jane turned to Abbie, her back facing Monica. "Do come with me next week to the city. I've discovered the most charming pawnshop over on Royal Street. Oh, I know how you feel about taking advantage of others' misfortunates; but, truly, those Yankee carpetbaggers have taken over every decent store in New Orleans. I can scarcely afford a ribbon, their prices are so dear. In this particular shop, though, the proprietor is a southern gentleman through and through. I declare, he's so adorable, I just about giggle each time I see him."

Monica stifled a grin as Sarah Jane's purse slipped unheeded to the floor. It did wonders for her, thinking about her pawnshop owner. Why, the woman actually smiled.

"I'm terribly busy," Abbie was saying. "I don't have time for going into the city."

"Oh, tsk, you can tell that Drew Sumner to fix his own supper for a change. I've a mind to tell him myself. How in creation does he expect his little sister to find herself a husband buried away in this old house?"

"Things are fine just the way they are, Sarah Jane."

"I declare, Abbie, you must still be carrying a torch for that Yankee . . ."

Sarah Jane halted as a blushing Abbie looked at Monica. Apparently, the girl didn't want her love life discussed in front of her sister-in-law. From what she'd learned of Monique, Monica couldn't really blame her.

The clock in the hallway chimed five and Sarah Jane jumped up as if from a spring. "Will you look where the time has gone?" she said in a fluster as she retrieved her purse. "I declare, ever since Mama died, Papa has no sense at all. If I'm not there to stop him, he'll be knee-deep into the bourbon by sundown."

She hurried out of the room, followed closely by Abbie. Trailing after them, watching them part at the door, Monica was again struck by how attractive the woman could be.

"She's so pretty when she smiles," she said when Abbie closed the door. "She should do it more often."

"I don't imagine she has much to smile about," the girl said brusquely. "Marrying was her one hope of escaping that hard-drinking father of hers. You can't expect her to smile at you when you stole

Robert away."

So that was why the woman acted like an old maid; Monique had made her into one.

Abbie rubbed her hands on her skirts. "I've got things to do in the kitchen. I can't be chatting the day away."

"Let me help."

Looking her over, Abbie gave a reluctant grin. "Maybe you'd best just get cleaned up. I'm planning a special supper tonight. We're going to have us a real family meal."

Monica felt the stirrings of excitement. To date, she had sat alone with Abbie each night in the kitchen. There was no need to set the dining room table when Drew never made an appearance. Night after night, his meal was left waiting on the stove.

"Drew's promised to be home early tonight," Abbie went on, beaming. "I'm digging up the china and polishing what's left of the silver. We'll get dressed up and look our finest, make it a grand occasion, just like before the war. I want Drew to realize he hasn't lost everything. That if nothing else, he still has us."

Us. Monica felt warmed, happy to be included. "In that case, let me help, so you'll have time to get prettied up, too."

Abbie shrugged, turning for the kitchen. "It won't take but a minute to change into my flowered cotton."

Monica remembered that dress—once too often mended and far too small. "Surely you'll want to wear something else. After we're done here, let's go up and rummage through your closet."

With a hmmf, Abbie pushed through the door.

"As if I'd have a closet. The way the government taxes each room, we can't be keeping up ones that don't serve a purpose. Not when we have more than enough armoires."

"But *I* have a closet."

Abbie merely smiled, as if she'd made her point; and, picturing the rows of gowns hanging upstairs, Monica supposed she had. Sarah Jane was right; all the best went to Monique.

"Then we'll rummage through my things," she told the girl, remembering a pretty blue silk that would match Abbie's eyes. "I have the perfect gown for you."

Abbie stopped at the kitchen door to face her, her gaze bewildered. "You're offering me a dress?"

"I think it should fit. We're about the same size, and my blue silk will look much better on you."

Abbie shook her head. "That knock on your head sure changed you." All at once, she began to grin. "Truth to tell, I'd just about sell my soul to wear your blue dress."

Monica returned the grin. "There's shoes to match. Now what needs to be done?"

They spent the next two hours in a flurry of activity that left little time for talking. Through it all, though, Abbie kept giving her surreptitious glances, as if waiting for her sister-in-law to revert to form.

When the table was set and the food left to simmer, Monica raced upstairs for the gown, determined to prove the old Monique was gone for good.

But as she searched through the closet, she discovered the blue slippers were not on the shelf where she'd left them. They, like the straw bonnet and beaded purse, were scattered on the floor.

Surveying her bedroom, she found the basin on the wrong side of the dresser. Several other items had been moved as well, though so subtly she might not otherwise have noticed.

She stopped, listening to the sound of her rapid breathing, her thoughts tripped along at the same pace. She saw the fluttering drapes by the balcony, the unlocked door to the hall, and realized anyone could have come in here in her absence.

Don't be ridiculous, she told herself. It must have been Abbie, cleaning. Or one of the kids, playing a game. She was silly to feel such uneasiness.

Logic might tell her this, but with a tiny shiver, she grabbed the blue dress and dashed out of the room.

Seven

Drew looked at the rusted machinery, then back through the open door behind him where the sun was dropping below the distant trees. "Get some light," he told Jasper, the seven-foot former slave who had become his right-hand man. "We'll never get the gas plant operating again if we can't see what we're doing."

Drew saw the frown. Jasper knew about his promise to join the family tonight, and he also knew Drew hadn't a prayer of keeping it.

Damn Robert for letting things go, Drew thought. "While you're up at the house," he told Jasper tightly, "you might as well tell my sister I won't be making it home for dinner."

Jasper nodded. "Want me to say why?"

Drew shook his head. No sense having Abbie take out her anger on Jasper. "Just tell her not to wait for me. I'll take care of the apologies later."

Going to the door, watching the black giant make his way back to the house, Drew could see Jasper was upset. He might understand the pressure Drew was under, but Jasper would rather see the whole place fall down than watch a single tear form in his mistress' pretty eyes.

Hell, did he think Drew enjoyed disappointing his sister? Jasper had to see that the house needed a cheaper source of light; they couldn't afford to keep buying candles.

At times like this, Drew wondered why he bothered to fight this constant uphill battle. Between Monique's extravagances and his brother's refusal to face the facts, he'd inherited one giant sinkhole of disaster.

River's Edge, he thought with a sigh, gazing at the fields with a reluctant sense of pride. However relentless the struggle, he knew he would fight with his last breath to keep the plantation going. It was more than his heritage. It was his home.

As if she now stood beside him, he pictured Monique's face when he'd brought her home from the swamp. He knew it was impossible, but for a moment, he could have sworn she had felt it, too, that she shared his need to build a future here.

Wallowing in his yearnings, he let himself envision walking back to the house, tired and yet proud of a good day's work, lured by the scent of a hot, cooked dinner. Every window would glow with soft, welcoming lamplight, while his family waited to greet him at the door. His wife, her arms open wide . . .

He looked at the house, so dark and distant, and told himself to stop such nonsense. How many times must she spin her black magic around him before he accepted the truth? Monique would never be the wife he wanted. Whatever he'd seen in her eyes that day was sheer illusion.

Running a hand through his hair, he forced himself back to work. He had to think of the children. They would have a better life—if he had to kill himself to provide it. Hard work and sacrifice, that was his lot.

And considering what he'd done to Robert, maybe it was his atonement.

Leaving Abbie preparing a plate for her brother, Monica reluctantly walked out of the kitchen. She personally felt that Drew could get his own meal if he hadn't the decency to show up for dinner, but it had been a mistake to tell his sister so. Abbie's sudden cold shoulder gave Monica no choice but to quit the room.

It was all Drew's fault, she thought angrily as she went into the house. He was just like her father—and Judith—always letting work come before family. Stephen claimed Drew always kept his word, yet how could the man neglect his promise to Abbie?

Hours ago, excitedly twirling before them in the blue gown, Abbie could have been the belle of anyone's ball; but after Drew's message, she'd seemed as deflated as their untouched chocolate souffle.

And the children had been just as disappointed. The way they'd trudged up to bed, you'd think someone had cancelled Christmas.

And what about you? a tiny voice taunted as she climbed the stairs. *Does all this righteous indignation have anything to do with your own disappointment?*

She shook off such thoughts. Being part of a family celebration might be wonderful, but she knew she'd be better off if Drew stayed in the fields. It was hard enough to keep her composure on their rare, brief encounters; how would she still her strange yearnings when he sat mere inches away at the table?

Besides, her own feelings were unimportant. Someone had to make up for Drew's neglect, she told herself as she marched upstairs. The children needed to know that she, at least, would always be there for them.

She went to Elizabeth first, her best hope for a favorable reception; but, as Monica stepped into the room, Elizabeth started and jammed whatever she'd been holding out of sight under her pillow. The action was hurried, furtive, as if the child meant to hide the object from view.

From me, Monica amended, trying not to feel hurt. "Are you all right, sweetie?"

Elizabeth nodded, lying down on the pillow as if she were settling into bed, though Monica suspected she was more likely trying to guard whatever she'd hidden.

"I hope you're not too disappointed your Uncle Drew didn't come to dinner tonight."

The girl shook her head. "Nuh-uh. I know he would be here if he could. 'Sides, I have his mormento."

"His what?"

"His favorite handkerchief. It's for me when he can't be here. If I have his mormento, I still have part of him with me."

A *mem*ento. At Elizabeth's age, left alone while her mom accompanied her father on his frequent business trips, Monica remembered creeping into their empty room. She'd paraded about in shoes, preened before the mirror in hats and gloves, finding comfort in being surrounded by her mother's things.

Once, she'd taken a scarf, redolent with the scent

of lilacs, to hide beneath her pillow. Whenever she was scared, or so lonely she could cry, she'd take out that scarf and inhale her mother's essence. For years after her parents died, she'd clung to the silk square like other kids did their security blankets.

Maybe it was Drew's handkerchief the child had hidden under her pillow. Or, considering how her own room had been disturbed, maybe it was a *mormento* from her mother that Elizabeth guarded there.

As she pulled the covers to the girl's chin, Elizabeth smiled up at her and Monica felt herself melt. Another woman might confront the child with her theft, but she was content to wait. Elizabeth would confess eventually; and, even if she never did, what did a missing trinket matter? To keep this child feeling safe and secure, Monica would sacrifice a hundred scarves—she'd give up everything she had.

"You know," Elizabeth said as Monica placed a kiss on her forehead, "I've been thinking 'bout what you said."

"Really? About what?"

"'Bout a nickname. You should have one too. Monica is too long to say."

"Some people use Mona," Monica offered.

"Nuh-uh. I want something pretty and nice, like you. I'm gonna call you Nicki."

Monica had never had a real nickname; no one had ever bothered to think of one for her. She'd spent her life as solid, stodgy Monica; and now, with a wave of Elizabeth's magic wand, she became a capricious *Nicki*.

Monica smiled down at her. "Nicki it is then, but we really should have a name for you, too, so we can save Elizabeth for when you're grown up.

I'm going to call you . . . well, how about Li'l Bit?"

"Li'l Bit?"

"Not li'l, as in too-small. Li'l as in so-cute-I-want-to-keep-you-in-my-pocket." As Monica tickled her through the covers, Elizabeth giggled. It was such a normal, happy sound, she wanted to keep the child laughing forever.

"I'm glad we have our special names," Elizabeth said, sobering, "'cause this way, if Mama ever should come back, I'll know right out she isn't you."

"Ah, sweetie, I'm not going anywhere."

"But you said maybe you can't help it. Stephen says one day I'm gonna wake up and find you're the same mean, old mama you always were."

Monica started to refute this, only to realize Stephen could be right. If Monique wanted her life back and knew the way to claim it, what could Monica do to stop her? "You know what I think?" she asked in a light tone, trying not to betray her fears to the child. "I think Stephen's terribly angry right now. We need to be patient."

Elizabeth nodded, that too-old knowledge in her eyes.

Leaning down to kiss her cheek, Monica tried to reassure her. "Just wait, he'll come around."

"I love you, Nicki," the girl said quietly as Monica turned to go. "I hope you never have to go away."

"If I do, Li'l Bit, they'll have to drag me off kicking and screaming."

"If it happens, don't worry. I'll just wish you back."

Stephen might also be right about wishes not coming true, but the world could certainly use more optimists like Elizabeth.

Monica went to the boys' room next, not with any real hope of being welcomed but knowing she should at least try to cheer them up about their uncle's absence.

To her surprise, she heard laughter as she paused outside the door. Not the rowdy, boyish chuckles one might expect—but a low, secretive giggle. And when she knocked, the sound was cut off abruptly.

Opening the door, she found an orderly room, far too neat for boys that age. Stephen sat at a desk in the corner; and the speed with which he closed his notebook made her think it might be a diary, filled with private thoughts he'd rather die than have her see. Did everyone in this house feel the need to hide things from her?

In the corner, crouched over a makeshift cage, Andrew, too, shielded something from her gaze. The occasional croak indicated he might keep his frog collection there.

Neither seemed particularly happy to see her.

"I-I thought I'd look in before going to bed," she said awkwardly. "I hope you're not too disappointed about tonight. I'm sure there will be many other times when Uncle Drew can sit down to dinner with us."

Stephen looked at her with disdain. Andrew ignored her entirely.

"Are those your frogs?" she asked.

"It was cold, so I brought them in." He huddled over the cage, his brown hair hiding his face. "I won't take them outside again. You can't make me."

"I didn't mean to."

"We'd like to sleep now," Stephen said from his

desk. The words were polite enough, but there was frost in his tone. "If you will excuse us?"

"Oh, yes, of course. Do you want me to tuck you in?"

The disdain became contempt. "We've been taking care of ourselves for a long time now. Haven't we, Andrew?"

Though he nodded, the younger boy continued to look down at his frogs. Knowing she'd been rebuffed, Monica wished them good night and closed the door behind her.

Entering her room, she tried not to be discouraged. As she'd warned Elizabeth, she had to be patient. Sooner or later, she'd find a way to win the boys over.

First, she had to lure them into the schoolroom. Maybe if she caught a frog for Elizabeth's lessons and then told Andrew it was ill, he might be tempted to help. After all, it was too cold for a frog . . .

She stopped, realizing that it was a good seventy degrees tonight. Why on earth would Andrew say it was too cold?

Suddenly suspicious of their secretive laughter, she tore down the covers. It would be just like boys to think finding a frog in bed with her would make her scream.

She was almost disappointed to find the bed empty. At least a prank would mean they didn't intend to ignore her entirely.

Reaching for a demure cotton nightgown, she prepared for bed. She told herself not to be silly, that Andrew had probably brought his pets in the house because he was lonely. Drew mentioned bad dreams; maybe the night music of the frogs helped lull the poor boy to sleep.

But as she blew out her candle and heard the teeltale croak, she abandoned that theory. Who was she kidding? The racket would keep Rip van Winkle awake.

She jumped out of bed and relit the candle. Listening for the frog's location, she got down on her hands and knees to feel about on the floor.

She was groping under the dresser, remembering how Derek and Amy had crawled about like this at her wedding ceremony, when her fingers closed around cold, hard metal.

Judith's ring!

Shuddering, she yanked her hand away. She hoped the boys never learned that she was more afraid of that ring than any swamp-dwelling creature.

She sat back on her heels, immobilized, filled with the same dread the ring always induced in her. Part of her knew she should just get rid of it, toss it somewhere deep in the swamp, but she could not bring herself to touch the icy silver. Maybe it was better off left where it was—out of sight, out of mind.

As if to affirm this, the frog jumped out from beneath the dresser, distracting her from all thoughts of the ring as she chased Andrew's pet about the room. Imagining how ridiculous she must look, bouncing from one corner to the other, she prayed she would catch the silly frog before someone came in to ask what she was doing.

It took half-an-hour and several odd contortions of her body, but at last she had it corralled. "You are going back to Andrew," she said, looking into its beady eyes. "We'll show him I'm not scared of any old bullfrog."

But as luck would have it, both boys were fast

asleep, looking like angels. Using the moonlight streaming in the window to see by, she set the frog in the cage, taking care to secure the cover. She smiled, imagining both boys' faces when they discovered it here in the morning.

Looking down on Andrew, she saw him start to twitch, as if at the start of a nightmare. Instinctively, she went to her knees beside him, placing a firm hand on his forehead. "Hush, it's all right," she whispered softly, not wanting to wake him or his brother. "I'm here now and I won't let anything hurt you."

He stilled then, and she smiled, feeling a mother's relief. For once, Andrew hadn't wrenched free of her touch; she'd comforted him, if just for a moment.

Standing slowly, she glanced down at Stephen, his young body so rigid she feared he'd snap. She wished she had the magic to help him relax too. If only she could make him giggle the way Elizabeth had.

The poor kids, she thought with a strong, protective surge. A possessive surge. God, she loved these children as if they were her own.

She looked down to find her hands resting on her belly. Within this body, she realized, she'd carried all three kids to full term; she could almost feel their tiny limbs stretching inside her now. When she thought about it, in some ways, they *were* her own children.

Bonds had been forged, ones that could never be broken. Monique might have let motherhood dwindle into little more than a physical link, but Monica meant to become an integral part of the children's lives. She'd find a way to teach them to trust her.

Tomorrow, she would show Andrew she was interested in his collection of frogs. If necessary, she'd even help catch the flies to feed them. As for Stephen . . .

The books! In the excitement of Abbie's family dinner, she'd forgotten about getting the key for the library door.

She could wait until morning to ask Abbie to let her in or she could get the key now, when no one would know.

Drifting downstairs to the kitchen, curiosity getting the best of her, she knew she had to see what was in that room. With a grin, she wondered if Drew locked it because he had some deep dark secret to protect. Like Dr. Frankenstein, did he hide a hideous monster? Or a mad wife, perhaps, à la Jane Eyre?

As she went out the back door, she found the moon cast an eerie glow across the carriageway, making a perfect setting for a gothic tale. Venturing out in her trailing white nightgown, she must seem the ideal foolish heroine.

A feeling that intensified as she stopped at the kitchen door and faced the sole candle flickering upon the mantel. It seemed straight out of the movies, shadows leaping on the wall, a silence filled with expectation, the lonely figure seated at the far end of the table.

Drew.

He slumped in the stiff-backed chair, arms dangling, a half-eaten chicken leg clasped in one hand. Staring into space, he looked so tired, so lost, she forgot how he'd let them down. She stepped forward, wanting to offer comfort.

As she did, he seemed to collect himself, sitting up to set the chicken leg on the plate. As he pushed the dish away, Monica's gaze went to the table, taking in the long empty expanse of its wooden surface.

Desire, intense and primal, rocked through her frame.

Grab me and push me down on the table, her mind seemed to whisper. She could almost feel the rough boards beneath her, the cool night air, and his fevered hands against her bare skin. Her breasts swelled as if he'd already engulfed them with his hot, demanding mouth; she throbbed at the thought of insistent fingers probing between her thighs. She knew a desperate need to have him in her, swelling with every thrust, touching her deepest, hungriest parts. *Take me,* she thought with a triumphant laugh. *Take me now!*

"What the hell do you want?"

The vision evaporated; all that remained was an angry Drew, glaring up from his chair. Suddenly weak, Monica saw that she stood mere inches away. "I wanted a book," she said lamely, grasping the solid pine of the table for support.

"In the kitchen?"

"No. No, of course not. The door was locked, so I came in here for the key."

"What door?"

"In the hall, the first one on the left. I-I thought it was the library."

He reached for a towel to wipe his hands. "I've never seen you pick up a book; yet suddenly, at this hour of night, I'm expected to believe you've developed an intense desire to read?"

"It's not for—"

"Enough, Monique. I'm sick of your prowling around. All this intrigue."

He talked to her as if she were a naughty child

caught in some prank. If she were Monique, then this was her house, too, and she had every right to enter whatever room she chose. "I wasn't prowling." If only she could remember more of her anger and less of what she wanted to do on the table. "I'd have gotten the book this afternoon if you hadn't locked the stupid door. If you ask me, you're the one who acts like he has something to hide."

"What?"

"Nobody locks a door for the fun of it. Just what have you got in that room, anyway?"

Tossing the towel down, he pushed back his chair and stood. "I lock the door because my ledgers are spread across the desk. You know full well I can't have those frogs setting up camp on them again."

So much for a deep, dark secret. Though the way Drew scowled at her, he could still pass for Mr. Rochester.

"Oh, but that's right," he continued as he came nearer, his blue eyes glinting like forged steel. "You probably can't remember. You and your convenient amnesia."

He stopped, his gaze holding her in place. Daunted by his nearness, Monica felt her throat go tight, her heart begin to race. "It's not convenient," was all she could think of to say.

He loomed before her, tall and so overpoweringly male. "No? Then how is it you can forget your son has nightmares, yet have no trouble remembering one hell of a lot about you and me?"

Monica shook her head vehemently, half-wanting to back away, half-hoping he'd kiss her.

"How could you know what we did in this room?" He moved closer yet, angrily grabbing her arms. "I heard your laugh just now—I saw your face."

Monica could barely breathe. All she knew was that her treacherous new body wanted to be driven back to the table. *Take me,* her mind was repeating. *Now.*

"You and your damned deceits," he hissed, his grip tightening on her arms. "Did you come here to seduce me? Or were you hoping to find someone else?"

"No." The denial was the merest whisper. "I swear to you. I wanted a book. For Stephen."

Doubt softened the glint in his eyes.

"For his lessons," she added, her voice gaining substance with her need to be believed. "Simple primers are no challenge to a smart boy like him."

Looking at him, seeing his confusion, she remembered how tired and lost he'd first seemed. He wanted to believe her, she sensed, but common sense warned him against it.

Every inch of her wanted him still, but her need had softened, gone gentle. *Come to me,* she tried to tell him with her eyes. *Come let me love you.*

And for a miraculous moment, their gazes linked. She could feel his own need as if he'd physically touched her with it. His need for her, Monica—not Monique.

His eyes searched hers, strenghtening that link, even as his lips sought her mouth. He was so close she could feel his heat, could hear his heartbeat pounding the same accelerated rhythm as her own.

His kiss was electric, a jolt of pleasure that went shooting through her veins. It set off a hunger so strong she forgot everything and dug her fingers into his hair to pull him closer.

He yanked free, drawing back as if she'd slapped

his face. "You made your point—my flesh is weak," he said, wiping his mouth with the back of his hand. "Are you satisfied?"

"But I—"

"No, you won't be happy until you destroy us all."

"Drew, please listen—"

"Get it through your head. I know better than to go through your parody of love again. It makes me sick, just to think of touching you. Stay away from me, Monique, or we'll both live to regret it."

Where was the link now? Monica thought desperately. The glint was back in his eyes; they were as shuttered as if he'd slammed a door. All that remained was his loathing and her own sense of loss.

"Go." He spun her around and headed her toward the door. "Go on. Get out of my sight."

Monique

June 1, 1855:

That potion of Rachel's, I will not rest until I know how it's concocted.

But I get ahead of myself. I feel so wonderful, it is as if I walk on air. I had not known a man could be so . . . so inspired.

But Rachel knew. Oh, how she smiled when I went to her, complaining that Drew was caught in his frustrating gentleman's code. With a slow, spreading grin, Rachel insisted any man can be brought around. A few drops sprinkled in his food and even the most reluctant suitor can be lost to his passions.

When I protested that it didn't work with Robert, her smile merely deepened. She would not waste her best magic on that cold fish. The brew we'd given to Robert was meant to inspire admiration and devotion; the one she would make for Drew would evoke passion.

And at that, my smile mirrored hers.

And yet, it was nothing to my satisfaction now. Oh, the things he made me feel, the things he had me do. I must talk about them or I shall surely explode.

It was a perfect night for my plan, the moon so full and large it seemed you could reach up and touch it. Robert paid little heed to me; he was laughing and drinking with his bachelor friends from the city.

How easy it was to sprinkle Rachel's concoction into Drew's soup; it was far more difficult to wait for the interminable meal to be over. You would think I had taken the drops, so fevered was my anticipation.

I used my flushed condition as an excuse to get outside, knowing full well Robert would ask his brother to accompany me. He is so blind, my husband-to-be, and for that alone, I can love him. However unwittingly, he will provide me with everything I desire most.

The night was warm, the air as sultry as a lover's breath. Dropping my shawl slowly, letting the silk caress my shoulders, I smiled back at Drew as I strolled a few inches before him. In a patch of silver moonlight, I stopped to pull my hair up off my neck, as if inviting the breeze to kiss the flesh I'd bared there.

Poor Drew, he eyed me like a man lost in the desert watching water drip mere inches away from his parched tongue.

Myself, I savored the moment of deprivation, coming alive as a fire ignited inside me. As I twirled before him, smiling over my shoulder, I tempted him to nip at my neck, His eyes glowed from the flame that clearly now blazed within us both.

With a curse, he clenched his fists and turned to walk away; but this night, I would have none of that. "Oh Drew," I said, my voice as breathless as any of his southern belles, "I do believe I'm about to faint."

I swooned then, timing my fall so he'd have opportunity enough to catch me. And once in his arms, I let Nature take its course.

With a groan, he buried his lips in my neck, holding me as if his life might end if he let me go. I threw back my head, revelling in the feel of his sweet, cool lips trailing along my sensitized skin. "You're so damned beautiful," he chanted, dazed. "I've got to make you mine."

"I *am* yours," I whispered into his ear.

He was lost then, and we both knew it. Lowering me to the ground, he took my lips with the pride and skill of a conqueror. Oh, how I relished it, his tongue mastering mine, his work-worn hands rasping against my skin.

Lifting up my skirts, barely bothering to unbutton his trousers, he took me like the master using his slave in the fields. We were animals, groping for each other, pounding our bodies in a primitive dance of love. It was glorious, and when we reached a dizzying climax in perfect harmony, it was all I could do not to scream out in triumph.

But when it was over, Drew said, "Dear God, what have I done?"

I suffered through his pleas for forgiveness, content to let him think he had raped me. From Rachel, I knew how to make a man think me a virgin, and I'd put such knowledge to good use. "But I love you," I sniffed on his shoulder. "It doesn't matter if it wasn't as . . . as nice for me."

I am no fool. I know what that does to a man's pride, and Drew did not disappoint me. If I could but describe what pains he took to prove it could indeed be as nice for me. There was not one part of my body he did not kiss, not one inch of me he failed to brand with his tongue.

By the time he was done, several wonderful hours later, our clothes were so scattered over the garden it took an eternity to locate my slippers.

The potion must have begun to wear off as he slid them on my feet, for, once again, I could hear the regret in his tone. He was wrong to do this, he kept repeating, but somehow, he would make amends.

It was all I could do to keep the panic from my eyes. He must not confess to his brother, I tried to convince him. Robert and his cronies were well into their fifth bottle of brandy by now; did he wish to face their scorn?

I might know he loved me, I told Drew, but his brother would denounce him for bedding a woman he could never support.

He swore he would find some way to take care of us as he took my hand to help me to my feet. But until he did, there would be no more of this.

I smile now as I think of his noble intentions, for, of course, I know better. I have Rachel's potion. Oh, yes, we shall have many more nights like this.

And every one will be without the benefit of matrimony.

For as I said at the start, I mean to have him *and* River's Edge.

I mean to have it all.

Eight

Monica stood in the empty kitchen the next morning, staring at the wooden table. Blushing, she heard Drew's question echo in her mind as if he still stood before her.

How *could* she know, so vividly, the intimacy he and Monique had shared?

She didn't like to think that so intense a reaction could be sparked by something he and another woman had shared in the past. That her body could behave so luridly on its own was daunting, but she was beginning to fear that her mind had its own contributions to her lust.

"You're up early this morning." Abbie bustled into the room, donning an apron as she sailed past.

"I couldn't sleep." Monica had no wish to elaborate. Seeing the table had her flustered enough.

Abbie hurried about the room, gathering flour and pans to make bread. "That's the trouble with living by a river on a warm, spring night. Can hardly hear yourself think with the noise the frogs make."

"Especially when Andrew keeps them in his room," Monica added, happy to be distracted. Looking up, she saw Abbie's struggle to hide her grin. "Abbie Sumner, did you help those boys put a frog in my bed?"

Setting a bowl on the counter, Abbie was not smiling now. "It was a prank, Monique, something all boys do. I didn't help; but, truth to tell, I'm glad to see them kicking up mischief. It's not natural to be so well behaved."

Monica held up her hands. "I'm not yelling at anyone. I'm a school teacher, well-accustomed to pranks. Besides, frogs don't frighten me."

"They used to." Abbie eyed her curiously. "I recall once watching you let that awful black snake of Rachel's crawl on your arms; but let one teeny little tree frog jump within a hundred feet, and you'd be running and shrieking like a gangful of pirates was chasing you."

Monica almost protested, but what was the use? Abbie needed time to accept that she wasn't Monique, more than the week they'd been working together in the kitchen.

Monica moved about the room, doing her morning chores in the awkward silence. Reaching for the coffeepot, she caught Abbie watching her, though the girl quickly averted her eyes.

"You know," Abbie said suddenly, "if you're not afraid of frogs, you might try showing Andrew so."

"I beg your pardon?"

"He goes down by the river most mornings. If you were to happen by and catch one yourself, might be he'd look at you in a new light."

"I declare," Monica teased, wondering if this were a test, if Abbie, too, would look at her differently. "You sure have a devious mind, Miss Abigail Sumner."

Her back stiffened. "Maybe I've had a good teacher."

Monica sighed. Dealing with this family was like running an obstacle course.

Abbie spoke slowly, choosing her words with care. "I'm sorry, I don't mean it the way it sounds. It's hard, is all. Working together like this, I can almost believe you're not Monique, but then you get that look in your eye and I can't help but recall all the awful things you've done."

Did Drew see that same *look?* Was that how he could act as if he wanted to devour her one moment and, in the next, act as if he'd just tasted something vile?

Abbie wiped her hands on her apron. "I don't suppose you recall Christmas two years back?"

"No, you know I can't."

Abbie gestured to the table and they both took a seat. "I'm thinking back to that Christmas for a reason. It was a bleak one. We'd buried Robert and heard Drew was missing. When the boys came asking if there would be a Christmas this year, I took one look at their grieving faces and vowed to find some way to make the holiday special."

"Oh Abbie, you had to have been a child yourself."

She held up her chin. "Seventeen is plenty old enough. And you offered to help me. Looked me straight in the eye and said you'd do your best to put together a holiday meal."

Abbie looked ahead, as if she could see the past on the wall, her pose defiant and determined. "A lady downriver made these dolls and I had my eye on one for Elizabeth. She agreed to give me a doll if

I took in her laundry. I knew you'd toss a fit if you learned I was doing slave work, so I had to creep home each night with my dirty wash and sneak out with it before dawn."

"Oh, Abbie."

"I'm not looking for pity," she said, stiffening again. "I found there were lots of chores no one else cared to do. In the end, I saved enough not only for that doll, but for slingshots and maybe some to add to the dinner you promised. It was far from a fortune, mind you, but it would have meant a holiday for children who had already lost too much."

She paused, as if gathering steam. "So you can just imagine how I felt when I came home to find the house full of Yankees, eating the candy I'd saved for the stockings. When I went to you, you laughed. I can still see you, shaking your head, telling me I was going to end up a bitter old maid like Sarah Jane. I should have used my silly little cache to buy myself a new dress, you said, for that was what you'd done with it. As you twirled in front of me in yards of crimson satin, all paid for with my money, I saw only red. I wanted to scratch your eyes out."

Monica winced at every *you.*

"But you kept on laughing," Abbie went on, "letting me know how truly powerless I was. That night, I shut myself in with the children and had a good cry. I hate to think how much I cried; but come morning, I was as dry and cold as a winter wind. I went to your room to tell you—and the Yankee soldier in bed beside you—to get out of my brother's house."

Abbie stuck up her chin. "You just laughed. You meant to leave this old relic anyway; the city was more fun. When I insisted the children stay, you said I was welcome to the brats. Then you gestured at the door. There were Stephen and Andrew, with eyes so wide and wet, it hurt to look at them." Her sigh seemed to echo across the room. "So you see, now, why I find it hard to forget and forgive?"

Horrified by the tale, Monica wanted more than ever to protest she wasn't Monique, but she did understand Abbie's position. In her place, she'd find it hard to trust anyone who even remotely resembled the woman.

"Don't you see?" Abbie went on. "It's too weird, looking at you, thinking you might not be you."

"Oh, I most definitely see. It's weird for me too. I mean, here I am in a kitchen that doesn't even exist in my time, trying to make a decent pot of coffee out of chicory when I don't have a microwave or even a gas stove. I keep thinking that if we had a refrigerator—or better yet, air conditioning—we wouldn't need to get up at the crack of dawn. Heck, we could just call up Pizza Deluxe and, within twenty minutes, the delivery van would drive up to the door."

Abbie shook her head, plainly bewildered. Knowing she must sound hysterical, Monica inhaled and tried again. "Try to imagine how it would feel if you woke up in a whole new world and everyone treated you as if you had the plague, if they hated you just for looking like someone else."

With a frown, as if she didn't want to empathize, Abbie stood. "What do you expect with the way you've been acting?"

"Acting?"

"The way you look at Drew . . ." Abbie blushed.

"Well, I can't help but think you're up to your old tricks."

Remembering the scene last night, Monica could hardly blame Abbie for thinking she was coming on to Drew. Each time she lost control to those sudden, alien urges, she wondered herself. Did part of Monique remain in her body? Was she doomed to repeat the woman's mistakes?

But then she remembered the strong, maternal urge she'd felt for the children last night, how the greed for Drew's touch had gentled into a more loving, caring desire. Maybe she had more control over this body than she thought. With a little effort, could she teach it to behave as it should?

"Forget how I look at Drew," she told Abbie. "That's between him and me and has nothing to do with my being a good mother and friend. Try to judge me by what I do now and not by what your sister-in-law did in the past."

Abbie studied her a long moment. "Time will tell, I suppose," she said brusquely, turning back to making bread. "For now, you'd best start fretting over breakfast. Those children are like hungry bears in the morning. You won't want them growling for their oatmeal."

Oatmeal, Monica thought with a grimace as she reached for the pot. The ultimate test. The few times she'd tried to cook the stuff, it had come out looking—and probably tasting—like wallpaper paste.

"Knowing how I cook," she joked, "try to keep in mind that it's the effort that counts. If I at least try to be a good mother, will you accept me?"

Abbie just shrugged. "We have a saying: The proof is in the pudding."

"As long as it isn't in the oatmeal."

Abbie laughed. She'd seen Monica work in the kitchen.

Watching the finished product plop off the ladle and into the children's bowls, Monica braced herself for more teasing from Abbie. She wondered how any of them were going to swallow this latest disaster.

Stephen ate quietly, albeit determinedly, while Andrew gobbled his down. Elizabeth alone, like the child in *The Emperor's New Clothes,* spoke what was on her mind. "Yuck. This isn't oatmeal."

Sitting down with her own bowl, Monica shared the girl's aversion. "I know it's awful, but please try to eat it, sweetie. We're so short of supplies in this house, I don't dare throw it out and try again."

"Can't afford to waste food," Abbie reminded as she set the bread to rise on the counter.

Elizabeth looked at her bowl as if she feared spiders might crawl out of it, but she took up her spoon and began to eat with the same perseverance as her brothers.

"I'm going outside to weed the garden," Abbie announced as she removed her apron. "Why don't you go on with your lessons this morning? You can help me later."

"If you're sure . . ."

Abbie glanced at each of the children. "I'm sure. Time to be making some pudding, I'd say."

Monica smiled as the girl left them. Her pleasure was short-lived as, moments later, Andrew shoved back his chair and bolted out of the room.

She called after him, but Stephen shook his head. "He's gone now. You'll never get him back."

Laying down her spoon, she looked him in the

eye. "If he has no wish to be included in our adventure, then I have no intention of forcing him."

"Adventure?" The boy didn't want to be curious; he just couldn't help himself.

"On Tuesdays, Li'l Bit and I take a nature walk. You, of course, are invited to join us."

Elizabeth's brow raised a fraction, but she gave no other sign that this was the first she'd heard of such walks.

"She talks strange," Stephen said to his sister. "Mama never used words like *kid* or *cooped up.*"

"O' course not. She's not Mama; she's Nicki."

Odd, how children noticed what adults did not. She'd never stopped to think how different she must sound.

"Why do you call her Nicki?" Stephen seemed suddenly suspicious. "And why does she call you Li'l Bit?"

"We gave each other nicknames," Monica interrupted. "If you'd like, we can think one up for you."

He sat straighter in his chair. "I don't need one."

Oh, yes you do, Monica thought to herself, but now was not the time to press. "Let's do the dishes," she said, standing abruptly. "That is, if you've eaten enough?"

Elizabeth popped up instantly. Stephen dallied, pride battling with curiosity; but, with one last look at his bowl, he too set down his spoon.

After tidying the kitchen, she led them outside, waving as they passed by Abbie. How much nicer the place looked as a garden than as Judith's expensive swimming pool. Nestled in the oaks beyond it, the long white building would one day be turned into gaudy cabanas; but today it was still the *garçonnière,* a place to house visiting males or the young men of the household when they began to show interest in the ladies. One day soon, Monica thought with a pang, Stephen and Andrew would be conducting their own escapades there.

She sighed. As much as she might want to prevent their growing up, she'd let the tradition stand. Unlike Judith, she didn't want to change things. Despite its lack of paint, its untrimmed shrubs, River's Edge had never looked better to her. Gone was the haunting sense of loneliness. People loved and worried about each other here; they were a family.

She had the urge to hug both children, but she knew Stephen would shove her away. Taking Li'l Bit's hand instead, she led them across the road, over the levee, and down through the bushes to the cove.

The mosquitoes were out and buzzing, making her glad she and Abbie had brought down the netting to cover the beds at night. Time to be "dressing the house for summer" Abbie had called it.

Summer, a time for family picnics, for boating and fishing.

Eyeing the distant dock, Monica vowed that one day soon, she would teach the kids how to swim.

But not today. Intent upon finding Andrew, she glimpsed a flash of white in the trees. Just in case he watched from a hiding place, she led her charges to the reeds on the near bank. "This is a good place," she said loudly, hoping to lure their brother closer. "Roll up your sleeves. We're going to catch us a frog."

Stephen's startled expression went to astonishment as she stepped free of her skirt. She supposed it was shocking for a lady to expose so much leg, but her blouse did reach past her thigh and she needed her limbs free to go splashing about in the water.

Soon, all three were too busy chasing frogs to notice her legs. Li'l Bit squealed each time her quarry slipped through her fingers, while her brother pretended he wasn't startled at all. "Watch," Monica told them after a time. "When you find a frog, approach him quietly. They have ears too. Not like ours, maybe, but they can hear you. The trick is putting a hand in front to distract them while grabbing them from the back. Like this. Ha, I got one!"

Andrew materialized behind them, blatantly curious. "Meet King Arthur," Monica told all three, holding up the frog, "who's agreed to hold court in our schoolroom."

"You're gonna keep him?" He might be curious, but Andrew eyed her warily.

"For a time, while we learn about him. Then we'll put him back in the river with his family."

"You don't know anything about frogs," he snorted. "You don't even like them."

"I happen to have studied a good deal about amphibians," she told him. "Do you have a bucket we can keep King Arthur in until we get him back to the house?"

"Yeah, but—"

"Get it please?" She spoke quickly, with no chance for refusal. That was the trick with these kids, she decided; you had to steamroll them into having a good time. As Andrew went off grumbling, she turned to Stephen. "We need to gather moss for the bottom of his cage and, of course, lots of water. Frogs take in fluids through their skin."

"Want me to get some lily pads for him to eat?" Li'l Bit asked eagerly.

"It will make him feel at home; but, actually, he eats insects. We'll put a piece of meat in a jar to trap flies."

Andrew, who'd returned with the pail, shook his head. "They just fly away when you put them in the cage."

"Not if you take off a wing first." Derek had taught her that, she thought with a shudder. In truth, she'd hoped to persuade Andrew to supply the flies.

Elizabeth made the appropriate girl-sounds of revulsion, but Andrew looked at her as if she'd just invented the wheel. "I never thought of doing that," he said to himself.

"I don't want to do frogs anymore," Elizabeth broke in, tugging at Monica's blouse. "Remember? You said you'd teach me to swim."

"I will, but not now. Let's put King Arthur in the pail. Oh, good, you have a top. I'm told bullfrogs can leap a good five feet."

"I once had one that jumped six feet." Andrew was so excited he'd forgotten he hated her.

"Nicki, it's hot. I want to swim."

"I know, sweetie. Maybe later. Actually, I thought we should find a friend for King Arthur. A Lancelot, maybe."

The boys needed no further encouragement. They raced to the riverbank, determined to find the biggest frog ever. As she helped them, Monica felt uneasy. Some sixth sense made her look up to see Li'l Bit running along the dock.

"Sweetie, no!" she called out, her feet already moving as the child stumbled, hit her head, and went tumbling into the water.

Monica dove, taking no time to see if the water was deep enough. All that mattered was that she could see no head, not even hands, clawing for the surface.

Were her heavy skirts weighing the child down? Or worse, had she hit her head so hard she was now unconscious? Monica refused to consider a third possibility. Elizabeth couldn't be dead. Not her Li'l Bit. She wouldn't allow it.

Please let me find her in time, she kept chanting as she dived deeper and deeper. As her eyes searched underwater, she saw the pilings for the dock, then a scrap of blue. Knowing it was the color of Li'l Bit's dress, she kicked with all her might. Closer up, she could see the child wasn't moving.

Grabbing her beneath the arms, Monica kicked them both to the surface. The lifeguard training came rushing back, and, as she swam, she planned out how to administer CPR. In her preoccupation, she didn't hear the boys shouting.

Drew heard the first cry for help as he rode down the River Road from the upper fields. Recognizing Stephen's voice, knowing the boy was not one to panic, Drew urged his horse toward the sound. He saw his nephews cross the road ahead and called to them even as he dismounted.

"It's Elizabeth," Andrew shouted breathlessly. "She fell in the water."

Touching ground, Drew felt his temperature drop thirty degrees. "Take my horse and hitch up the wagon," he told the boys. "Then come wait for me here at the road."

Tearing through bushes, he arrived at the riverbank to catch Monique squeezing her fingers over Elizabeth's nose. "Damn you!" he shouted, running up to pull his wife away. "Are you such a monster you'd harm your own child?"

Below them, Elizabeth began simultaneously to cough and cry. He shook with anger and he leaned down to lift her in his arms. Cradling Elizabeth, he looked at his wife.

A white cotton blouse clung to her body, outlining her well-remembered breasts. She looked half-drowned herself and just as short of breath; but, unlike Elizabeth, she'd taken time to remove her skirt. Had this been premeditated? Dear God, had she deliberately tried to drown Elizabeth?

"Enough is enough," he spat out as he turned away. "I warned you not to hurt the children. This time, you've got to be stopped."

He kept walking, for he knew if he stayed there a moment more, he'd kill her.

Monica watched him go. I'm not the enemy! she wanted to shout, but what was the sense? Drew would believe the worst; nothing she could say would ever change his mind.

Wearily, she reached for her skirt and donned it. "Come on, King Arthur." She leaned down to grab the forgotten pail, hearing again the anger in Drew's words. Had he truly thought she meant to harm Elizabeth? How could he think she could ever hurt a hair on that adorable child?

"You've got to be stopped," he'd said; and, slowly, she remembered his earlier threat about jail. It was one thing to be ignored or even hated for what Monique had done, but she certainly had no wish to face a prison term. Considering the culprit, it could mean a life sentence. Or worse.

Her hand went to her throat as if she could already feel a noose there. She didn't want to pay for another woman's crimes. *I have to go back,* she thought in a panic, *back where I belong.*

As if materializing out of the air, a hand appeared, to encircle her wrist. "You don't belong here," a deep, rich voice echoed. "Come with me—I can help you."

Monica's pulse raced. She hated to think anyone could sneak up on her like that, especially mysterious Rachel. "How did you . . . where did you come from?"

Rachel merely smiled. "I have come to help you. You cannot want to live with that—that man."

"You mean Drew?"

"Oui. Soon, he will hurt you, and then it will be too late. Come, I will help you escape."

Her voice was soft, honeyed, hypnotizing. Gazing into her dark black eyes, Monica found herself nodding. She was hazily aware of her hand being turned over.

The black eyes went sharp, hateful, as Rachel flung down her hand. "Where is it?"

At the question, so quick and unexpected, Monica felt her vision clear. For a moment, she had been tempted to go back to her old life, had so very nearly fallen into the old pattern of running away.

But what about Li'l Bit? she thought now. The girl had revived on her own and would probably be okay, but she would need someone to sit by her, to spoil her with stories and hugs until all the scariness was gone.

And it wasn't just Li'l Bit. It was the boys, stiff

and wary—Abbie, so overworked—and Drew, his handsome face ever bereft of its smile.

She could help these people, she knew she could, if she could only get past their suspicions. She had to gain their trust, which she'd never accomplish by running away.

"No!" she said, edging back. "I'm not going anywhere with you."

With a low, unintelligible oath, Rachel whirled and vanished into the trees.

Stunned, Monica stared at where she'd been. Odd, the way the woman ran off. She glanced at her hand, wondering what Rachel could have seen there to make her give up.

No, she hadn't given up; the woman would never back down from a fight. Uneasily, Monica sensed that her business with Rachel was far from over.

Monique

July 15, 1857:

The worst has happened.

I cry when I think of all those nights, our wonderful idyll, coming to so abrupt an end. There will be no making love on the kitchen table, no more tempting Drew before my mirror, no pulling him down into my hungry body in the sheltered paths of the garden.

I want to scream and rage and pull out my hair; but, no, I am trapped in the prison I've made for myself. Each day I must smile and act as if I haven't a care in the world.

Damn that Robert. I sometimes wonder if he guessed why Drew and I went off together. Could he see, in our glances across the table, the passion that sparks between us?

Most times, I doubt this. More likely, it is that little bitch, Abbie, who put the worm in his ear.

It hardly matters; the outcome is devastating in any case. What ill-timing! A few weeks more and winter would have made travelling north impractical. But, no, Robert must make his announcement last night.

I thought my heart would stop when he held up his glass to salute me; for I knew, even before he spoke, that the moment had come. A pin? *Non,* I could have heard a feather drop in that room when he finished pronouncing we meant to be married. He was oblivious to the lack of enthusiasm, and I alone seemed to notice his brother had gone white as the linen gracing the table.

Oh, how I longed to go to Drew, to make him understand that nothing need change; but Robert had clasped my hands, the proudest of suitors, and I'd no choice but to return his salute. He is, after all, the one who shall pay my bills.

It was not until late that night, when I crept into Drew's room, that I could even begin to explain. He was going away, he told me coldly as he rose with deliberate haste from his bed. Up north, to New York, where he would join his university friend in the army.

I went to him, trying to embrace him, but he pushed my hands away. What about us? I asked, startled by his rejection.

His laughter was such a bitter, ugly sound. "There is no us," he spat at me. "You belong to Robert now."

I told him we could go on as before. Nothing need change.

"You knew?" he shouted at me. "All this time, with all that we did, you meant to marry my brother anyway?"

I shudder to think how he looked at me then. So cold and distant, as if he did not care to know me at all. "I love my brother," he added, each word like a shard of ice. "I'd rather die than betray him. I would hope his wife-to-be might feel the same."

I called him a fool, becoming angry myself. I would be his brother's wife, yes; but he and I would always be lovers.

I heard him mutter, "God forbid," as he ushered me out of his room.

In my pique I stomped away. After all, I still had one last card to play, one last means of keeping him beside me.

But I should have remembered Drew's absurd code of honor and where it would lead him. This morning, when I went looking, he was already on his way to New York.

I never did have the chance to tell him how late I am for my monthly courses.

Nine

Drew looked out the window. In his mind, he could imagine a clock ticking, the minutes rapidly passing him by. Nothing moved out in the fields; without him there to drive them, his two field-hands would stop working the land. He had to get out there, now.

Yet when he turned and saw Abbie tucking the covers in around Elizabeth, his heart flipped over. All at once, the fields, his anger, *everything* paled in comparison to the fact that they'd almost lost this child.

"Go on, get back to work." Sometimes it seemed his sister could read his mind. "Elizabeth and I will be fine."

"You have your own work." He sat on the bed, trying not to scowl. He didn't want to take his anger out on these two. "Besides, it's time this little imp and I had a good talk."

"He's gonna scold me," Elizabeth said, her blue eyes sparkling as if she were proud of the fact.

"I doubt that." Abbie eyed him speculatively. "I imagine he's more interested in what your mother did to you down by the river."

"Mama? Oh, you mean Nicki. Nuh-uh, she didn't do anything."

Abbie leaned down to press her palm to the child's brow. "Don't be shaking your head until we see what your bump's going to do. How did you get it, anyway?"

"She fell off the dock," Stephen said somberly from the doorway.

Andrew nodded next to him. "She wanted to learn how to swim and didn't listen when Nicki told her to wait."

"And Nicki had to jump in after her."

Looking at Stephen, so controlled and solemn, was like seeing a younger version of Robert. Many was the time Drew had watched his older brother step forward, taking the blame for their mischief.

Stephen *had* to be Robert's son; it wasn't the sort of secret Monique would keep to herself. He was imagining things, refining too much upon Robert's unexpectedly hasty marriage. Yet though he should be relieved to share no more than a family resemblance with the boy, the realization filled him with regret.

Shaking himself, Drew gestured the boys into the room. "Let's sort this out. When you say Nicki, you mean your mother? Are you saying she was trying to *save* your sister?"

"She's not Mama," Elizabeth insisted.

Stephen frowned as he approached the bed. "Actually, we've been talking about it, Andrew and I; and we decided we're not really sure she *is* our mother."

Drew looked to Abbie for clarification, but she carefully avoided his eyes.

"Nicki likes frogs, Uncle Drew," Andrew said eagerly. "She knows all about them, even how to keep the flies in the cage."

"And she's good with Elizabeth," Stephen added. "During lessons, Nicki even lets her sit on her lap."

None of this sounded like Monique, who had often slapped the child for wrinkling her skirts.

"Do you think she really *is* a different person?" Abbie seemed like a child, wanting proof that magic did exist.

All four faces turned to him, so young and trusting, the perfect victims for Monique's deceit. "Don't be ridiculous," he snapped. He had to be brusque to put a stop to this. "People don't change overnight."

"Mama's the bad one, not Nicki." Crossing her arms stubbornly over her chest, Elizabeth frowned at him. "You shouldn't have said those mean things to her. You hurt her feelings."

Had he? Or was her wounded expression merely to mask her frustration? Why would she stand there flaunting her wet, luscious body if she hadn't meant to seduce him? If the pose were not planned, where were all the undergarments with which women normally armored themselves?

After all, it wasn't the first time Monique had played the helpless kitten when her true goal was seduction.

"It might have been an accident this time," he told the children while looking Abbie in the eyes, "but we must be careful. Your mama's terribly clever about getting what she wants."

"It's not Mama," Elizabeth insisted. "It's Nicki. I know, because I wished her here."

"Is that what she said? Can't you see she's using you?"

"Drew, enough." Abbie bit out the words, her

eyes signalling toward the door. She turned and walked through it, clearly expecting him to follow.

Gritting his teeth, Drew joined his sister in the hall. "You shouldn't be saying such things to them," Abbie said fiercely. "They're only children."

"God, Abbie, don't you think I wish it weren't necessary? How many times do they have to be hurt before they learn to protect themselves? How often before you do, too? I'd have hoped by now you'd know better than to trust a word that woman says."

"Monique, yes, but—"

"What? Nicki? Don't tell me you believe Elizabeth wished her here too?"

"No, not exactly, but Monique *has* changed since you brought her back from the swamp. Maybe her head injury has her seeing things differently. She asks to be judged by what she does now, not by what Monique did in the past."

"How many times has she asked for another chance? And how often must we grant it, only to have her make our lives miserable?"

"But there's something about her, Drew. Something different. I find myself wanting to believe."

"You can't. Dammit, we have the children to consider now. Whatever we might want, we can't risk letting her hurt them again."

"We?" Abbie searched his eyes. "Then you feel it too? This need to believe her?"

"No!" Yet even as he denied it, Drew knew that he did. It was a weakness in him, and one he was determined to expel. "Even if I did, Abbie, I've learned my lesson. Mark my words, she's up to no good. Monique is always her most disarming when she's planning to stab you in the back."

He turned, meaning to join the children, but Abbie reached out to detain him. "Let me go to them. The mood you're in, you're liable to make things worse."

"I don't want you encouraging—"

"Don't worry, I'll make sure they know their mother is the big, bad wolf."

He shook his head. "This isn't a joke, Abbie, I'm serious."

"I know," she told him sadly. "You've grown cynical, Drew Sumner. But maybe we need to believe that wishes come true. We need someone like Nicki to show us how to laugh and dream again. You most of all."

The words stung. "Wake up, Abbie. Can't you see how she's already got us taking sides? How she's driving a wedge clean through this family?"

"Is she? From where I stand, it looks as if it's just you, stubbornly standing apart."

She turned to join the children then, leaving Drew alone in the hall, her words echoing in his mind.

Monica gazed up the stairs. If she thought she had a prayer of being let in the room, she'd be up at Elizabeth's bedside with everyone else.

But Abbie had cautioned her to go change and then wait downstairs until either Drew cooled off, left the room, or she herself could come down to talk.

Knowing there was no sense standing around wringing her hands, Monica decided to keep busy. It was a long time since she found a book for Stephen to read.

She got the key from the kitchen and let herself into the room. She left the door open behind her so she could hear Abbie the instant she descended the stairs.

To Monica, the room seemed a gloomy place, its three windows concealed by miles of heavy velvet. It was a sign of wealth, she knew, to let the draperies pool at the bottom, but all that dark green overpowered the senses.

It was not a library, after all. A lonely desk, a huge expanse of almost-black wood, covered most of the faded Oriental carpet in the center. There was a single bookcase, sporting the same dark wood, built into the wall behind it. Two rows contained books—the remaining shelves held only dust.

The room needs light, she thought, crossing to a window. Flowers would help, a vase or two set on either side of the books. Pulling back the drapes, she allowed sunlight to stream into the room, a definite improvement though dust motes danced along the narrow beam. The place could also use a good cleaning.

She went to the shelf to scan the titles. Passing by the agricultural volumes, she looked for something more suitable for a boy. She wished she could find *Tom Sawyer,* but then, Samuel Clemens must just be starting his career.

She did find a collection of Dickens. Reaching for *Oliver Twist,* she spied the more romantic *A Tale of Two Cities*. Smiling, she reached for it, deciding it was perfect for a boy like Stephen.

Turning to leave, she noticed more books sprawled across the desk. Drew's accounts? Curious, she moved closer for a peek. Having been a bookkeeper while working to win financial independence from Judith, she found herself smiling at Drew's entries. Neat, he was not.

Nor was he joking when he ranted about not having time or money to waste. The more she saw, the more concerned she became.

"What are you doing in my study?"

Drew stood in the doorway, his harsh tone startling her so she nearly dropped her book. "Do you know you pretty near scared the Dickens out of me?" she quipped nervously, holding up the volume.

She could not see his expression, for his face was obscured by shadows, but the tautness with which he held himself suggested he was not amused. He seemed to radiate a coiled energy, like a predator readying himself to spring.

"I came for a book," she added lamely. "For Stephen."

"Again?"

"I never got it last night. After we . . ." Monica broke off, blushing. Was he, like herself, remembering where a similar conversation had led them? "I just thought that now, more than ever, Stephen might need a diversion."

"How considerate of you." His voice reeked of sarcasm. "And how selectively so, considering your daughter lies half-conscious in her bed."

"Half-conscious?" Monica felt cold with dread. "But Abbie said she'd be fine."

He shrugged, but his posture lost none of its tension, much like the wariness with which Stephen always regarded her. "She is, but a real mother would want to see for herself."

"I did. I do." Monica bit her lip, wishing she wasn't so flustered. "Abbie asked me to wait until you left the room. She feared there might be a scene, and we both felt Elizabeth didn't need that right now."

"You're good," he said softly, as if to himself. "You manage to have an answer for everything."

"And you always manage to have an accusation."

He tilted his head, as if her bitter tone surprised him. Lord knew, she was surprised as well. Standing up for herself was a new experience.

"Why not tell me what happened?" He moved closer, stopping on the other side of the desk. "The boys say Elizabeth fell off the dock and you jumped in to save her."

"She struck her head, wasn't coming up on her own." Monica shivered, the shock just now hitting her. "Thank God for all my lifeguard training. I never thought I'd be so grateful to know CPR."

"Who?"

"Not who—what. It's the initials for a lifesaving procedure. Actually, all I used was artificial res . . ." She broke off, realizing he probably wouldn't know that term either. "When a person has been underwater, you often have to help them start breathing again."

He raised a brow, clearly skeptical.

"Through the mouth," she added. "You hold their nostrils to make sure the air you blow goes into their lungs and not out their nose."

Something changed in his expression; his posture seemed to loosen. "Is that what you were doing when I found you?"

"I had to get the water out of her lungs first, so I'd just started. As much as I'd like to take credit, I think she actually began breathing on her own."

"How can you know this?"

"Because Li'l Bit is a fighter."

"No, I mean, how did you know about this . . . this CPR?"

"I told you, in lifeguard training." He looked at her blankly and she realized there would be no lifeguards—especially female—in the mid-nineteenth century.

"It doesn't matter. Just as long as you understand that I wasn't hurting Elizabeth. I was trying to save her life."

"So everyone tells me."

"Everyone?" Odd, how that one word could warm her heart. "Even the boys?"

"Andrew is quite impressed with your knowledge of frogs."

She couldn't help but smile. "Then you believe me?"

He looked at her, studying her, and Monica held her breath. If only she could go to him, smooth the worry lines off his brow, hold him—but she knew that more than this desk still separated them.

"I won't be going to the authorities, if that's what worries you," he said at last, crossing both arms over his chest and returning to the same, stiff pose. "But don't think I'll let down my guard. I'll be watching you, Monique. One wrong step and I'll—"

"You keep threatening me. Just what happened to make you distrust me so?"

"You know damned well what you did."

"All I damned well know is that you're being difficult. Okay, maybe it's hard to accept that I'm not your wife, but you've got to see some difference. What must I do to prove I'm not your enemy? That I want to help?"

He laughed bitterly. "I don't need your kind of help."

"No?" She pointed down to the ledgers. "You plan to climb out of that financial hole all alone?"

"You read my ledgers?" From his tone, it was hard to tell if he was stunned, skeptical, angry—or all three.

"It's one of many things I do that your Monique didn't, but I suppose you'll find some rationalization for that, too. My point is, your books tell a grim story. What your brother's mismanagement didn't destroy, the war did. From what I can see, you're high on expenses and low on capital. Is that why you're growing vegetables?"

He stiffened, instantly defensive. "People need to eat. Until someone makes a better suggestion, I'll grow whatever will bring me cold hard cash."

"But this is a sugar plantation. Isn't changing crops a gamble?"

"You sound like Ben Hawkins. Next you'll be telling me that raising food is not a gentleman's occupation."

"I didn't mean—"

"Is it better to let the land lie idle? No one wishes more than I that life could go back to the way it was, but I'm not about to sit on my porch swilling bourbon and blindly denying that times have changed. If we want to survive, we have to change with them. Why can't anyone grasp that?"

"I do understand. More than you can know."

He looked at her for a moment, really looked at her, and Monica again felt that instinctive linking. Why were they fighting? Deep down, they wanted the same thing.

"I can't grow sugar," he said, pounding a fist on the ledger. "Not in any great quantity. If you can read these, you can see there's no money to hire the fieldhands to harvest it or even buy more cane.

That's why I plant vegetables. It might be beneath a Sumner to take his crops to market, but I'd rather have my aristocratic forbearers turn in their graves than see my family go hungry."

Monica shook her head. "I wasn't accusing you of anything. I only wanted to help."

"Help?" He gave another bark of laughter. "Like you helped Robert? Spare me, please."

He was determined to be nasty, she decided, but she was not going to let him provoke her. "Let me keep the books. I've had training. I can make them legible."

"I don't need someone to jot down profits I don't have," he snapped. "I need money. So unless you're willing to part with the jewels you've been hoarding, I don't need your kind of help, Monique. I can ruin River's Edge all on my own."

As he marched off, Monica stared after him, his words echoing in her mind. Jewels? What jewels?

Drew paused outside the house, wondering why he had let her get him so angry. This wasn't the way to handle Monique, he well knew. If he didn't keep a cool head around her, she would soon be mincing him to bits.

He winced as he thought of her face as he explained his situation and then when she'd offered to help. For a moment there . . .

He muttered an oath, thinking of Abbie's words. Damn, he did want to believe.

But that path, he knew from experience, could only lead to ruin.

Monique

June 11, 1858:

It is done.

For a year now, I have been Mrs. Robert Sumner, mistress of River's Edge, just as I had planned. Is it not strange, though, how our dreams do not always turn out as we imagine? I am no longer certain I want this gilded cage Robert offers, but then, what is my choice? Drew has abandoned me.

It was Rachel who pointed this out. Drying my tears the morning he left me, she said, quite rightly, that no man was worth such suffering. Drew was gone; I had my future to consider. If Robert were to learn I was with child—which he would soon enough—I would be left with nothing.

Give Robert the same potion his brother had taken, she ordered, and let his sense of honor do the rest.

Yet even with those drops, he could not make love like Drew. I told myself it didn't matter, that it was only important that Robert feel guilty for deflowering me and thus be moved to offer instant marriage.

On one thing, the brothers are quite alike. Since Robert has the same rigid sense of honor, our marriage took place at once.

But, alas, our hastily planned wedding trip was utter disaster. With the potion, Robert was an uninspired lover at best; without it, he viewed the act as merely a duty to perpetuate the family line.

For myself, I cannot help but compare what I have and what I have lost. Each night as I lie in my bed—thank God Robert does not insist upon sharing one—my body twists and writhes, longing for the magic of his brother's agile fingers.

But Drew is lost to me, vanished as surely as if he were dead, leaving me nothing but the brat squawking in the next room.

I had but two choices, Rachel explained nearly a year ago. She could brew me a concoction to do away with the child, or I could wait a month or two, tell Robert the happy news, and insist upon going back to my parents' island plantation to have my baby.

Oh, to have it to do over. To a girl of seventeen, the thought of carrying my lover's child was a romantic idyll—I had no idea I would face weeks of retching, months of waddling about, hideously swollen.

And for what? As I lay in a pool of my own blood and that ugly, slimy creature was set upon my chest, I screamed at them to take it away. I swore then that I would never again let such horror happen to me.

My parents shook their heads in dismay as I told them to hire a wet nurse; but, after giving up my body for nine long months, I was not about to let that thing suck at my tender breasts. I had no intention of waking at ungodly hours to offer up myself like some mindless cow.

The six-months stay my parents advised for the baby's welfare seemed a prison sentence. Able enough to sail to River's Edge, I'd have left Stephen behind—I had no doubt my parents would provide an avalanche of loving care—but I knew Robert would be furious if I did not bring his precious heir home with me.

For three months I paced my parents' floors like a tiger trapped in his cage. The moment I presented Robert his son, I would go to New Orleans to dance and drink and be loved by every man who took my fancy.

On the ninety-first day, I demanded that Papa book my passage. He tried to dissuade me, warning that I'd be sailing alone as Rachel must stay with her dying mother, but I was determined to leave. I'd married to escape my parents' smothering affection, after all, and I did not mean to end up where I'd begun.

At first, returning to River's Edge was wonderful. I felt like the hero, marching home from war, until I realized it was actually my son's arrival that everyone celebrated.

Robert was like a child with a new toy, the way he fussed and preened over Stephen. I wanted to tell him the truth, that the boy was Drew's, but I had sense enough to keep such knowledge to myself. I contented myself with announcing my intention to winter in the city instead.

To my utter amazement, my husband said no. One son might strengthen the line, he pronounced; two would secure it.

We were in my bedroom, Robert staring at my reflection in the looking glass. His eyes went cold, hard, as I protested. He insisted I must stay at

River's Edge and provide Stephen with a brother.

I laughed at his image, confident I could persuade him differently, for I had easily controlled Robert in the past. I told him I would go to New Orleans and there was nothing he could do to stop me.

It was rather like waving the cloth before a bull, showing my contempt for his masculinity. Let me tell you, I mean never again to make that mistake with a man. Such scorn is a challenge to them, a gauntlet being thrown down.

And Robert had been drinking that night, heavily. I watched his expression change in the looking glass, saw the fire in his eyes; and, before I could so much as whimper, he grabbed my arm and dragged me to the bed. Flinging me down as though I were no more than a sack of garbage, he climbed upon me, tearing open my bodice so he could slobber over my breasts.

These southern gentlemen might call it exercising their husbandly rights, but what Robert did to me that night was pure and simple rape.

And in some ways, I almost enjoyed it, for it was the closest to passion I've ever seen him. But he'd done it without my consent, without my *control,* and for that I can never forgive him.

Though I must admit, I did learn a valuable lesson. Never push a man beyond his limits; yet, if you do, be certain he suffers the ultimate guilt. Always make him pay.

When he was done, Robert seemed remorseful enough, but I made certain he wallowed in guilt. As his apologies grew into pleas for forgiveness, I let him understand that only jewels could comfort me, that pearls alone could help me forget this monstrous thing he'd done. And nothing less than a ruby would get me into bed with him again.

Thanks to his conscience, I now have my pearls, a string so finely matched, who could not find them a source of comfort? And since I find myself with child once more, I know I shall soon have my ruby.

In return, I have taught Robert his first real lesson about women: We do not come cheap.

And after he holds his second son in his arms, I mean to teach him just how expensive we can be. He can complain all he wants about rising costs and the vagaries of weather, but the fact remains: If he expects any more children, he must next seduce me with diamonds.

Ten

"Nicki!"

Following Elizabeth's gaze, Abbie looked to the door. Monique stood there clasping a book to her chest, waiting, as if shy and unsure of her welcome. "How's she doing?" she asked Abbie, nodding in the girl's direction.

She looked so worried, Abbie wanted to smile. If Drew could see her, he'd have to admit Monique had changed. Two weeks ago, no one would have dared call her "Nicki," yet it was now hard to think of her otherwise. I'm going to call her Nicki, too, she decided; the name somehow suits her.

"Elizabeth is doing very well," Abbie said, placing a hand on each of the boys' shoulders, "but as I was just explaining to Stephen and Andrew, we should let her sleep." She paused, glancing meaningfully down at the boys. "Which she won't do if we keep fussing over her."

With a nod, Nicki seemed to understand that the boys were *too* concerned, *too* protective. "Actually, I'm here to borrow Stephen and Andrew," she said quickly. "I need a home for King Arthur and I'd hoped they'd help me build it."

"King Arthur?" Confused, Abbie looked from her to the boys.

"He's the frog we caught." Andrew seemed ready to burst with pride. "He's the biggest one on the river."

Nicki nodded. "That's why he'll need a cage at least as big and strong as the one you built for your frogs."

"Uncle Drew made most of it." Stephen's words were curt, but his watchful gaze was much like Abbie's own. He seemed to be waiting, as if he too hoped Nicki would prove she wasn't Monique.

"Maybe." Nicki grinned at both boys with obvious affection. "But we can accomplish anything, once we've set our minds to it. Why, I bet you build a regular palace. Let's see, we'll need wood and wire—do you think you can find those things?"

With an eager nod, Andrew hurried out of the room. Stephen hovered by his sister, who was whining, "I wanna help."

Nicki stepped over to the bed. "You will, sweetie, but let's wait for the boys to finish the frame. Later, you and I can decorate the inside. We'll get those lily pads and some moss and we'll fix him a house fit for a king."

Elizabeth giggled. "Will we make him a throne?"

"I don't know. We'll have to ask the master builder. Can you make a throne, Stephen?"

It took a few seconds, but a slow grin spread across his face. "Like you said, I suppose we can accomplish anything—if we set our minds to it."

He looked up at Nicki then and as she gazed back at him, Abbie could almost hear something click into place. Drew just had to be wrong about her.

The moment didn't last long. Suddenly embarrassed, Stephen turned to hurry after his brother.

"Stephen?" Nicki called out and Abbie held her breath. *Don't push,* she wanted to caution. *The boy's so skittish, you're liable to lose him.*

Nicki held out the book she'd been holding. "I found this in your uncle's study," she went on in a rush, "and thought instantly of you. I loved this story when I was your age."

Stephen took the book, eyeing it suspiciously. With a nod, he tucked it under his arm, thanked her politely, and quickly left the room.

"What about me?" Elizabeth fidgeted on the bed, her tone testy. "What about our lesson, Nicki? I'm never gonna learn to read."

Though she spoke to the child, Nicki looked to Abbie. "As long as you stay quiet, I think we can read a story together. Wait here while Abbie and I get the storybook."

"I want Cinderella," Elizabeth requested. "It's my favorite."

Nodding, Nicki bustled Abbie from the room. "She really is okay?" she whispered as they walked down the hall.

"Oh, Kay?"

"It's an expression. I meant to ask if she was all right. You weren't just saying that for the boys?"

Abbie smiled, touched by her concern. "No, she's . . . o.k. She just needs to be quiet. She's got quite a bump."

"Head injuries can be tricky. Maybe she should be watched."

Abbie gave her niece's room a harried glance. "But I have dinner to make and the garden to weed." Suddenly, she could feel the humidity close in on her. "And there's the mosquito netting I've yet to attach to your bed and mine."

"We, Abbie. There's two of us to do the work. If I thought anyone would want to eat it, I'd gladly do the cooking." She matched Abbie's grin. "Maybe I'd better be the one to sit with Li'l Bit for the day."

In truth, Abbie would feel better knowing someone watched over her niece. And she could hardly object to fixing dinner alone; she'd been doing so for years. The trouble was, Drew's warning kept creeping into her head. *Don't trust her,* he'd insisted. *She's using you.*

Nicki stopped at the schoolroom door, her expression both concerned and expectant.

"I don't know," Abbie found herself answering. "I'm not sure Drew will like it."

Nicki leaned back against the doorframe with a sigh. "I'd never hurt Li'l Bit, Abbie. Don't you know that by now?"

Abbie felt torn. Drew asked her to be cautious; Nicki asked to be judged by her actions. Logic and past experience warned her to be wary, yet instinct urged her to trust the woman who had just saved her niece's life. "Drew will be out in the fields all day," she said slowly, giving in to her instincts. "I suppose what he doesn't know can't hurt him."

As Nicki smiled, Abbie thought, *Don't make me regret this;* but aloud, she merely said, "I'd best be talking to the boys. They expect your help making a cage this afternoon."

"I forgot." Nicki stood straight, biting her lip as she looked at the stairs. "I can't disappoint them."

She looked so stricken, Abbie hastened to reassure her. "They'll understand. You just worry about Elizabeth. I'll stop by now and again to see how she's getting on."

Nicki's smile held a note of resignation, as if she understood that Abbie would be checking on her as much as her niece.

Moving to the stairs, Abbie felt bad about being so cautious. Maybe she needn't come up all that often. Just enough to show Drew he was wrong.

"One other thing," Nicki called out behind her. "About Drew."

Stopping at the head of the stairs, she saw Nicki was still in the doorway, chewing her lower lip. "Can you tell me why Drew keeps threatening to send me . . . Monique . . . to jail?"

Abbie shrugged uneasily. "He's become a private man. Since the war, he keeps his thoughts to himself."

"He mentioned that Monique had a hoard of jewels."

Her apprehension intensified. Monique had often boasted that those precious stones were her security and financial independence. What was Nicki's interest in them now?

"I just wondered," Nicki went on, "if his threats meant that she stole them?"

Abbie shook her head, unable to hide her bitterness. "Not so she'd go to jail. But she sure robbed Robert blind with her demands. He all but ruined River's Edge buying that jewelry for her."

A strange look came into Nicki's eyes and she stopped worrying her lip. "I don't suppose you know where the jewels are now?"

The heat in the hallway seemed suddenly oppressive. Wiping her forehead with a hand, Abbie said no, she didn't, more and more disturbed by her sudden interest in the jewels.

"Do you have any idea?" the woman pressed. "I

mean, is there a vault or some other place she kept her valuables?"

"Not that I know," Abbie said sharply. "But then, I'd hardly be the one she'd confide in."

"They must be worth a great deal." Clearly preoccupied, Nicki stared into space.

Abbie might want to ask why Nicki wanted to know about the jewels, but she kept hearing her brother. *A person does not change overnight,* Drew insisted. Even if Monique did have amnesia, he'd say, this proved she was still as greedy—and devious—as ever.

"I guess I should get that book," Nicki said abruptly, flashing a brilliant smile. "Li'l Bit will be wondering where I've gone."

Watching her hurry off, Abbie fought the urge to call her back, for what good would it do to question her if Nicki *were* Monique? Her sister-in-law had always been able to lie with an innocent face.

Slowly descending the stairs, growing increasingly nervous about leaving Nicki alone with Elizabeth, Abbie decided she might have to visit them more than she'd planned. She tried to tell herself it was crazy, that Nicki cared about the children, that she was wonderful with them, but Drew's words would not let her be.

Monique is always her most disarming, he'd warned, *when she's planning on stabbing you in the back.*

That night, snatching up her pillows and blankets, Monica stepped quietly across the hall to Elizabeth's room. Abbie would frown if she saw her; she'd insist the child was fine and had no need of a night nurse. Still, it was a traumatic thing to nearly drown, and Monica wanted to be there if Li'l Bit should wake and need soothing. Her own comfort didn't matter; she'd slept in worse places than the floor.

As she set up her makeshift bed, the child's even breathing reassured her. It was hard to explain, even to Abbie, how much the accident upset her. If anything happened to Li'l Bit, Monica would never be able to forgive herself. If she'd been listening to the child's pleas, if she'd been watching more carefully . . .

She glanced again at the child, snugly tucked inside the mosquito netting. Li'l Bit slept on, seeming less disturbed by her near-drowning than Monica herself. God, she loved that little girl so fiercely it made her throat hurt just to look at her. She wanted to spoil her rotten, buy her every silly toy her heart desired, dress her in satins and silks.

Good luck, she thought. She'd seen Drew's books; she knew they hadn't a dime to spare.

Unless, of course, she could find Monique's hoard.

She smiled. It was a relief to know the woman hadn't stolen the jewels—although it might have been a mistake to ask Abbie for information. The way the girl had studied Monica on her too-frequent visits all day, it would seem things were back to where they'd started.

Maybe she should have explained that she didn't want the jewels for herself, but she'd assumed Abbie would understand she meant to give the jewels to Drew. It hurt that Abbie could doubt her, and protesting was a waste of time. Monica would just have to find the hoard herself and let her actions speak louder than her words.

Hearing a faint whimper, she dropped the pillow. She looked to Li'l Bit, but the child slept as serenely as ever. Puzzled, Monica tilted her head and heard a second whimper.

Taking her candle into the hall, she realized the noise originated in the boys' room. Poor Andrew must be having a nightmare.

She hurried to their room and found the boy flailing his arms, twisting himself up in his bedcovers, a far more violent expression of inner demons than the last time she'd soothed him. She hesitated, having little experience with nightmares. It was bad to wake sleepwalkers, she remembered once hearing; did the same hold true with dreamers?

Unable to bear his obvious fright, she decided that whatever the consequences, this had to be stopped. She set the candle on a stand by the door and went to sit on the bed. Lifting the boy in her arms, she held him tight to her chest. "Shh, Andrew, it's all right," she whispered, stroking his hair. "I'm here now, I won't let anything hurt you."

"Nicki?" he asked groggily. He stopped thrashing, but he went stiff. "Did you find my frog?"

She looked at the cage, half-expecting to find the top removed, but everything seemed secure. "They're all here," she told him. "I won't let anyone hurt your frogs, either."

"I couldn't hear them." His voice began to tremble. "It was so dark in the closet. I couldn't see anything."

Monica rocked with him, speaking softly to banish the awful dream. "It's all right, Andrew. Listen, can't you hear the tree frogs? You're not in any closet now. You're here, safe, in your room."

"I'm here too," Stephen said to her right, materializing out of the dark. "Me and Nicki. Mama's gone."

And with those magic words, Andrew relaxed in her arms, his body as loose as if his bones had melted in the heat. "He'll sleep now," Stephen whispered. "You can lay him down."

"Amazing," Monica said as she settled Andrew in bed, arranging the covers around him. "How did you know what to say?"

"He has the same dream most every night. After a while, I figured out what's bothering him."

"Which is?"

"Mama used to lock us in the closet when we were bad or in the way. I didn't mind being alone so much, but Andrew can't bear being in dark, tight places."

In the way? Monica thought, her stomach turning over. Was he saying the woman had locked her children in a closet because she found them inconvenient?

"That's why he likes to be outside so much. It was good for him today, having lessons down by the river. At least until Elizabeth got . . . hurt."

His voice caught on that last, and Monica ached to hold him in her arms to reassure him. "Don't worry," she said gently instead. "I just left her and she's fast asleep." He'd never let her hug him, but maybe he wouldn't mind being fussed over. "Come to think of it," she said in her best mother-to-son tone, "you should be in bed, too. Do you want me to tuck you in?"

"No, thank you." He moved quickly, jumping under his sheet. "I can get myself into bed."

Monica tried not to be hurt. She must remember that he was older and had a certain male dignity to uphold. "Sleep well, then. And if Andrew has another nightmare, come get me. Maybe we can help him so he need never again have such awful dreams."

"I don't know. He spent a lot of time in the closet."

And how much time did you spend there? she wanted to ask, but she knew better. It would take time before he felt safe enough to confide in her. "We'll have to be patient," she told him—and maybe herself as well. "Good night, Stephen. Sweet dreams."

"Nicki?" he called out as she turned to leave. "I've been reading the book you gave me. *A Tale of Two Cities.*"

"Have you? Do you like it?"

"It's very good. You know, it's a lot like what's happened to us."

"I thought so, too." She was pleased; she'd hoped he'd see the connection. "I guess lives are always being torn apart by war; but isn't it nice to know that with a lot of love, we can always build again?"

"I guess, but I was thinking more about the two people trading places. I got to thinking being here must feel that way for you. Like you're in prison and can't get out. It made me feel bad for the things I said to you."

Monica again felt that throat-tightening emotion. "You want to know the truth?" she said hoarsely. "Coming here is the best thing that ever happened to me."

"Then you won't leave? You won't let Andrew and Elizabeth love you and then just go away?"

"Not on your life." Crossing her fingers, she prayed that nothing would ever force her to go back on that promise.

"Good." He rolled over on his side. Having learned what he wanted to hear, he was now ready to sleep.

For a moment more, Monica stood watching him. She wanted to hug him so badly her arms ached. If she wasn't mistaken, Stephen had just told her he, too, wanted her to stay.

The hugging could wait. One of these days, he might even let her tuck him in.

Feeling a surge of emotion, she turned to collect her candle; but when she went to the door, she found Drew blocking the way.

Drew had heard Andrew's whimpers, and he'd reached the room in time to find Monique with the boy in her arms. He'd started forward to stop her, but then Stephen had gone to her side. They made quite a picture, a mother with her two sons. Utter amazement had rooted him to the spot.

Her conversation with Stephen was equally surprising. Listening, Drew almost began to believe her claim, that she was indeed a different person inside that beautiful shell. Monique didn't have it in her to be gentle or sensitive to the boy's needs. Moving slowly and gracefully to retrieve her candle, this stranger seemed to radiate a mystical glow. Everything she did seemed to hold such an unreal quality he found himself wondering if he were the one in a dream.

But then she turned, all but colliding with him, and he grew conscious of her slim, alluring body beneath the thin nightdress. It was Monique, he must remember, and he had to resist her.

He moved into the hall, gesturing her to follow,

not wanting to bother Stephen. "It won't work," he whispered when she'd joined him. "I don't know what you want of me this time, but I won't let you use those children to get it."

She blinked in bewilderment.

Drew refused to be taken in. "Whatever it is you want, deal with me."

"All I did was comfort Andrew. He had a bad dream."

She *was* getting to him, dammit, with her gentle speeches and soulful eyes. Looking at her made him feel like a brute, a careless hunter slaughtering the helpless doe. "Forgive me if I find the comforting mother pose hard to believe, but Andrew wouldn't be having the nightmares if you hadn't caused them."

To his dismay, her eyes began to fill, pools of moisture that spilled onto her cheeks. "You can believe whatever else you want of me," she told him with surprising fierceness, "but I would never, *ever* lock a child in a closet."

The candle began to tremble, and she set it down. It's all an act, he tried to tell himself, but then she swiped at her eyes, turning away so he could not see. He stared, a bit puzzled himself, for it wasn't like Monique not to milk the moment for all it was worth.

"My Aunt Judith locked me in a closet when I was his age," she said, her voice brittle. "I know how it feels to lose everything—sight, sound, air, trust. Adults are supposed to protect you. Once you know they won't, that they can hurt you instead, you haven't got much of a childhood left."

She seemed suddenly no older than the boys and less able to protect herself from the outside world. It wasn't conscious thought that had him reaching

Heartfire Romance
GET 4 FREE BOOKS

out to draw her into his arms. He just saw her trembling, felt her suffering; and, in that moment, she was no longer Monique.

As he held her, she looked up with eyes so soft and luminous something grabbed in his gut. His emotions shifted gears, became desire.

He grew steadily aware of the closeness of their bodies, of how little her nightdress concealed her form, her warmth. He longed to run his hands up and down every curve of her; and, even as his mind tried to catalogue the reasons he must not, her hands reached around his neck to urge him closer.

And gazing into her eyes, he knew it was no longer he who offered the comfort. The sweet, melting warmth of her was beyond his power to resist.

Cradling her head with his hands, he kissed her. And as he touched her trembling lips, as they opened to welcome him in, passion burst like a rocket throughout him. He had to have her; he wanted this woman more than anything he'd ever wanted in his life.

He lost himself then, his hands moving over her eager body with a will of their own. They pulled and tugged, yanking up the nightdress to feel her hot, willing flesh. As his hands slid up to cup her breast, she moaned, deep in her throat, the sound barely stifled by his mouth covering hers.

He wanted to go on devouring her, kissing her until he died; but he wanted to taste her ripe, swelling breast as well. Kneading the soft mound with his hands, savoring the fullness of it, he drew his thumb across the hardening nipple.

Some sane part of him realized that the next groan had not come from her lips, but he could not bring himself to end their kiss—not until he heard the "Nicki?" coming from inside the boys' room.

He pulled free of her mouth, but so slowly, their lips seemed to cling until the last possible moment. He looked down at her, saw her confusion, and registered the fact in the far, rear portion of his brain.

"Andrew," she whispered, snapping the spell between them. Like marionettes whose strings had been pulled, they stepped apart, she busily rearranging her clothes, he standing there watching and feeling an utter fool.

Good God, what had come over him?

As she reached for the candle, he noticed she was trembling even more now. Bemused, he didn't realize until she was nearly inside the room that she meant to go to his nephew. "I'll go," he said sharply, stepping forward to block her way.

She looked up, hurt, and Drew felt as if he had slapped her face. To his surprise, she didn't argue: She merely turned and hurried down the hall.

Watching her go, he shoved a hand through his hair. He had the insane urge to call her back, to apologize, but in truth, what could he say? I'm sorry, I thought you were someone else for a moment? Someone I could trust and love?

Angry with himself, he went in to Andrew. It was darker than before, and he was haunted by the thought that the candle was not the only light missing from the room. He kept thinking of how at home Monique had seemed on Andrew's bed. Sitting where she'd sat, Drew could feel her warmth, could smell her scent, and he ached to touch her again.

No, he had to stop this.

Reaching out, he smoothed Andrew's hair, trying to remind himself what the woman had done to this boy. Instead, his mind kept asking why, if she were so dreadful, did Andrew call out for her? And why did Stephen—overly cautious Stephen—ask her to promise she'd never go away?

Stephen believed in her. So did Andrew, and Elizabeth, and even the pragmatic Abbie. Was Drew clinging to his hatred, just to be stubborn, as his sister accused?

Could one person change all that much? He thought back to Timothy Sanders, back in the godawful prison. Poor Tim had come in young and innocent and nice, but once the guards were done with him, he'd been as twisted as they.

Drew didn't know much about the medical field, but maybe a whack on the head could also alter a person's outlook. Deep down, maybe Monique had been as sick of her selfishness as he was and, in some unknown way, felt a need to atone.

Yeah, and maybe his horse could fly.

Strange, though, how his bitterness had lost its edge. Could it be he wanted to believe in this new Monique, too?

Tucking the sheet around Andrew, he knew his questions wouldn't be answered tonight. He had to stay calm, watch her, weigh her every word and action. And one thing was certain, there could be no more kisses in the hall.

Shutting off that memory, he stepped out of the boys' room, only to see the the light glowing down the hall. All his good intentions evaporated as he strode forward angrily. What the devil was Monique doing in Elizabeth's room?

Monica lay on her blankets on the floor,

knowing she should get up and snuff out the candle before Drew yelled at her for wasting candles, too, but it took all her energy to still her beating heart. What must he think of her, giving herself to him like that.

The worst of it was, even if she had it to do over again, she knew she would do the same.

Hearing angry footsteps, fearing it was Drew, she feigned sleep. The last thing she wanted was to talk about the kiss, to be told it was a mistake they must never repeat.

But curiosity got the best of her. She had to see his face, had to know what he was thinking.

She should have kept her eyes closed. It helped nothing, seeing how angry he actually was.

He looked at her a long moment, glanced at the sleeping Elizabeth, then strode into the room with a determined sigh. Monica tried not to cringe. In her mind, she imagined him yanking her up and dragging her away, but instead he went to Elizabeth's bed to yank out the trundle bed resting beneath it. "I think you'll find this more comfortable than the floor," he offered gruffly.

Feeling foolish, Monica gathered up the bedclothes. As he helped arrange her blankets and pillows onto the trundle bed, he made no mention of their encounter in the hall, though, irrationally, she wished he would. Better to feel ashamed of herself than to suffer his polite silence, which left her wondering if she had dreamed the entire thing.

Without another word, he turned and marched off, leaving the candle burning on the dresser. Flopping to the bed, Monica shook her head. How could a man kiss her like that and so easily put it out of his mind?

She must have dozed off, for when she woke, the candle was extinguished. A faint stream of moonlight filtered through the windows and in its glow, she could see the outline of a man, hunkered down next to the bed, his hands moving in the darkness.

Oddly enough, she felt no fear. Though still half-asleep, she knew it was Drew.

He stood, hesitating for a moment, before leaving the room as quietly as he had entered it.

Reaching up, Monica felt the mosquito netting, safely cocooning her. Had he returned, merely to blow out the candle? Why, then, had he tucked her in?

It changed nothing, she told herself. Come tomorrow, Drew would no doubt be as nasty as ever. Still and all, for tonight, she would nonetheless fall asleep with a smile.

Monique

February 12, 1860:

Rachel has returned at last. It took her mother forever to die, an eternity where I was left on my own without my slave—and more importantly, without her potions.

Not that I have not used the time well. It is amazing, what a husband will grant you, once you provide him with two sons. As I look about at the improvements to this house, I think it almost worth the torture of childbirth.

River's Edge, I tell Robert, must be more lavish, more modern, than any other home on the river, or people will cease to respect him. While he sees the sense in this, the idea of making plans appalls my husband. The details, he leaves to me.

It is like playing with my old dollhouse again, designing this place as I wish it. My first demand was gas lighting, having seen it in houses in the city, and a gas plant of our own to supply the fuel. I next insisted upon a dock, built into the levee, so the steamboats can come right up to our doorstep to take us to town.

Ah, what pleasure I derived from designing my rooms. I went to Paris myself, buying the very best furnishings France had to offer. And since I could not resist those delicious French fashions, I've had a closet built into my bedroom as well. Robert grumbles about the extra taxes for a useless room, to which I point out the Beadleys have three in their house and you never hear Edward whining about money.

Downstairs, our fireplaces now burn coal and I have convinced Robert to order one of those cast iron ranges from Europe. Not that I have the slightest interest in cooking, but so few houses have them and those that do, I'm told, have some method of using its heat to warm pipes of water to send throughout the house. Imagine, having hot water at your fingertips, any time you wish it. I do believe I'd spend half my days lounging in a tub.

For the time being, I've had the slaves dig an artificial lake behind our new dock, filling it with water from the river. In deep summer, the mosquitoes can be unbearable, but now, in late spring, I often go out there naked, late at night. As I move through the velvety water, I dream of Drew; and I wait.

Tonight, sensing he meant to hide something from me, I crept into Robert's study. There, on his desk, I found the letter he plans to post tomorrow.

Steaming it open, scanning the lines, I could scarce contain my excitement as I realized Drew had written to him, begging to be allowed to come home for one last visit before the inevitable war.

My mule of a husband refused him. No Union soldier will step foot on Sumner land, Robert swore in his letter. Sometimes, truly, the man can be such a pompous ass.

But this time, Robert's arrogance fits well with my plans. By not letting Drew come home, by likewise refusing to meet him in the city, he has delivered his brother to me on a silver platter.

For I have written my own letter, imitating my husband's hand, sealed with his official stamp. Robert's original missive shall disappear, and he will never know his brother is coming to meet him in New Orleans.

And when Drew does, I shall be waiting.

Eleven

Monica polished the scuffed oak floor, working to restore it to its original state, struggling to keep her mind from straying to thoughts of the night before. With Li'l Bit still abed and the boys hammering away on the cage, she had to find some way to keep busy. Especially after Abbie insisted she needed no help in the kitchen this morning.

She sat back on her heels, surveying the section she'd completed. It looked wonderful shined, so much warmer and more welcoming than Judith's marble tile.

Yet it was not pride in her accomplishment that had Monica smiling; it was the memory of Drew, tucking the mosquito netting around her. Would he have done so, she wondered, if he had known she was not asleep?

No, she was not going to think about that, or him, and she most certainly was not going to think about the way he had kissed her. If she did, then she'd let herself imagine him smiling at her the next time they met. A hope, she knew, that was as foolish as it was futile.

Unconsciously, her hand went to her lips, her

fingers tracing the soft flesh there. Strange, how Drew's words told her one thing and his body another. If the man did despise her, how could he kiss her so tenderly, so thoroughly? And how could he always leave her aching for more?

At the knock on the front door, her hand dropped to her side and she stood abruptly. So much for her resolution not to think about last night. If she wasn't careful, she'd soon be discussing that kiss with whoever walked into the room. Taking a deep breath, as if the extra air would bolster her better sense, she went to answer the door.

Grinning down at her stood a poster-perfect officer in Union blue. Tall, broad-shouldered and glowing with good health, he could pass for a modern-day model urging television viewers to "Be all that you can be." His handsome face was tanned and smooth-shaven, his auburn hair clipped close to his ears, but by far his most arresting features were his twinkling blue eyes and engaging grin. Monica couldn't help but like him on sight.

"Forgive the intrusion, ma'am, but I'm Darcy O'Brien, from New York." She must have shown confusion, for he hastily added, "A good friend of Drew's."

"Come in, Mr.—excuse me, I imagine you must have a rank of some sort?"

"It's colonel, but please, I'd be more comfortable if you'd just call me Darcy."

Gesturing him inside, Monica held out a hand in greeting before realizing it must reek of lemon oil. "I'm Monica Ryan," she said, pulling the hand back and wiping it on her apron. "Er, Sumner. By coincidence, I'm from New York too."

"I'd heard Drew had married, but I know he hasn't been up north of late. Wherever did he stumble upon someone as lovely as you?"

"I just blew in on the breeze," she said capriciously, responding to that twinkle in his eye. "Drew turned around and here I was."

He looked at the bucket and brush, then her apron. From his puzzled grin, he obviously hadn't expected to find the lady of the house scrubbing his floors. "I'd wager it wasn't the first surprise you had for him, either."

"No, not quite." She knew she should probably explain that Drew thought she was Monique, but the story was so complicated. And would this stranger believe her, when no one else had?

"Nicki, did I hear the door?" Bouncing down the stairs, reminding that someone *had* believed her, Li'l Bit rushed to her side. "We have a caller?"

She seemed so excited, and healthy, Monica impulsively reached down to draw her close. "Hi, Li'l Bit. I'm glad to see you up and about. Come meet Colonel Darcy O'Brien, a friend of Uncle Drew's." Turning her to face Darcy, Monica held Elizabeth against her skirt, draping her hands over the girl's shoulders.

"Darcy?" Li'l Bit asked, looked back up at her. "That's a funny name."

"Not if you're Irish." He hunkered down to be on eye level with the child. "And who might you be?"

"I'm 'Lizabeth."

"Robert's youngest. Robert," Monica explained, "was Drew's older brother."

"It just so happens, Elizabeth, I knew your daddy well, back before he met your mama. I summered here with your Uncle Drew in our university days." He looked at Monica, the humorous glint gone from his eyes. "Before the war forced us to choose sides."

Puzzled, Monica cocked her head to the side. "I thought you and Drew both served in the Union army."

"We did. Robert chose differently. Drew enlisted to escape . . ." he paused, with a quick glance at Elizabeth, ". . . certain difficulties here at home, long before war broke out. When it did, Robert expected him to desert and join the Confederacy, but Drew felt bound by his oath of loyalty. In Robert's eye, he became the enemy and was no longer welcome in this house. Nor, naturally, was I."

Poor Drew, Monica thought, knowing him well enough by now to understand what it would mean to be banished from his home. Television coverage had shown her how ugly war could be, but for Drew, with nothing to return to, it must have been sheer hell.

And his reason for joining the army, his "difficulty at home," must have had a great deal to do with Monique.

"Then, too," Darcy went on, reinforcing this, "I doubt his sister-in-law helped things. From what Drew tells me, Monique thrives on creating conflict. Have you met her yet?"

I should tell him, Monica thought. Sooner or later, someone would call her Monique. Once they did, she could say goodbye to his likeable grin. She'd be lucky if Darcy O'Brien even spoke to her again.

Smiling at him as she tried to form an explanation, she caught Li'l Bit's scowl. "Nicki's not going with you," the girl said unexpectedly.

"She and Uncle Drew are married."

Darcy tousled the girl's hair. "Your uncle's a lucky man."

Li'l Bit backed away from his touch. "She's staying. With us. She's our mama now."

Monica realized the girl must feel threatened. Any time their mother had smiled at a handsome man, the kids had been abandoned—or locked in a closet.

Giving the tiny shoulders a reassuring squeeze, she steered Li'l Bit toward the kitchen. "Go on out and tell Abbie we have company." Feeling resistance, she added, "Hurry back, though. We have our lessons to do, and don't forget we still have to decorate King Arthur's cage."

Though Elizabeth gave one last suspicious glance at Darcy, she raced to the back door.

"I'm sorry if she seemed rude," Monica told their guest, "but she's had a rough time of it. All the children have."

"They must be quite a challenge. Three of them and Abbie, too, of course." He smiled, his expression tender. "Last time I saw her, Abbie wasn't much older than Elizabeth, but I imagine she must be quite the young lady by now."

Before Monica could warn that Abbie was somewhat more than a young lady, Drew barged in the door, striding over to clasp his friend by his shoulders. "Darcy, you old devil, it *was* you! I saw someone charging down the River Road and I thought: Only one person in the world can sit a horse that poorly."

Darcy returned the clasp with equal enthusiasm. "As if you're one to judge! How many times did I unseat you at those jousting tournaments you hold down here?"

"Once, and it was only through trickery. You shouted that Mary Lou Jenson had followed me out onto the field, and I was fool enough to turn and look."

"And why not? Women were always chasing after you."

As Drew shook his head fondly, Monica watched in fascination. So the man could smile. With a wave of longing, she wished she could step up beside him, join in their conversation, be part of that easy camaraderie. If only she could have known Drew before the war. Before Monique had ruined his life.

Drawing back, Drew looked his friend over. "It's great to see you. What brings you down south? Military business?"

"Inspections in New Orleans. But I wasn't about to come all the way to Louisiana and not drop by. I figure you owe me some of that fine old southern hospitality."

"I've still got a bit of Daddy's old bourbon, but I won't be able to entertain like we once did. I wish you had let me know you were coming."

"I didn't know until last night if I could get away." Darcy paused, looking around the hall, no doubt comparing its shabby state to his last visit. "Relax, Drew. We served in battle together—you know my expectations aren't high. Just give me a bed and three squares a day, and I'll consider your daddy's bourbon a bonus."

"Abbie's coming!" Elizabeth cried as she raced into the hall. She skidded to a halt before Drew, clearly relieved to see him.

"Whoa." Drew reached out, swinging her up into his arms. "Slow down a minute, I want you to meet someone. Darcy, this little imp is my niece, Elizabeth."

"We've already met."

Darcy nodded in Monica's direction. As Drew followed the gesture, his smile dropped, became a scowl. "I see. Then you've already met my wife, Monique?"

"Monique?" Clearly puzzled, Darcy looked from one to the other of them. "Didn't you say Monica?"

She'd been looking at Drew, hoping against hope that he'd show some of the same tenderness as the night before, but she should have known better. "My name *is* Monica," she told Darcy, though she meant the words more for Drew.

Lips twitching, Darcy's gaze went from one to the other. "Then who, if you don't mind my asking, is Nicki?"

"She is," Elizabeth told him irritably, pointing at Monica. "Don't you listen?"

"Mind your manners," Drew said sharply, setting the child on her feet. "Is that how a Sumner talks to company?"

Biting her lip, Li'l Bit shook her head. As her uncle continued to look down on her, arms folded across his chest, she stammered out an apology.

Darcy waved it off. "First of all, I've been here often enough not to be called company; and, secondly, she's right. I couldn't have been listening very well, or I would know why everyone calls your wife a different name."

"It's a long story. I'll explain later."

Monica had little doubt that he would. "The story is indeed long," she added, "but Drew's version will be a good deal different than my own."

Once again, Darcy's lips twitched. "In that case,

I look forward to hearing both."

"Nicki can't talk to you." Elizabeth tugged on Monica's skirt. "C'mon, we have to start our lessons."

Looking down at her, Monica remembered what had happened yesterday when she'd ignored the little girl's pleas. "Li'l Bit is right," she told the men. We should have started hours ago. If you gentlemen will excuse us?"

She turned abruptly, only to bump against the bucket of soapy water. The pail remained upright but the scrubbing brush went skittering across the floor.

"What is this?"

Drew's irritated tone nearly undid her. "I was trying to polish the floorboards," she snapped as she gathered up the cleaning implements to set them against the wall. "I didn't mean to leave a mess, but I wasn't expecting company."

Darcy stepped up to take the pail from her hands and set it out of the way. "You go on with Elizabeth, Mrs. Sumner. As I said before, I don't consider myself company and I wish you wouldn't either. I'd rather you thought me a friend."

As he took her hand, there was understanding and compassion in his eyes. He wasn't flirting; it was more like he was trying to figure her out.

"Let's get you settled, Darce," Drew said suddenly beside them. "Are these your things?"

Darcy merely nodded, his gaze never leaving Monica's face. "I hope it won't be long before our next encounter, *Monica.*" He bowed low over her hand. "I find I can't wait to hear your version."

When Elizabeth pulled again, Monica let herself be dragged away. Drew scowled behind her and up ahead Li'l Bit seemed no happier, but she herself could not stop smiling.

Darcy had called her Monica, and Drew had not corrected him.

Darcy O'Brien! Abbie stood back against the doorframe, her heart thundering in her chest. After all this time, here he was, bigger than life and twice as handsome.

He mustn't ever see her like this.

She glanced down at her torn hem, at the flour dusting the faded yellow tiers of her skirt. So much for her hopes that Darcy would take one look at the grown-up Abbie and fall desperately in love. This man had wined and dined the most beautiful and sophisticated ladies in New York. How could she hope to become the woman of his dreams when, in truth, she looked more like a scullery maid?

Especially when her sister-in-law had gotten to him first.

Abbie tried to ignore the stab of jealousy. It was petty and small of her, and it wasn't fair to Darcy. Even if Nicki *were* Monique, he would see through her facade in a blink, for he was the most down-to-earth, the most honest, and the most considerate man Abbie had ever known.

Back when he'd come visiting, when she'd been too young and foolish to hide her adoration, he'd never once laughed at her. Even though she'd stuttered and acted like a clumsy colt, he'd never ordered her away. Women chased him as much as they did Drew, but Darcy always found time to answer her endless questions, to spare a smile. Monique or no Monique, that would never change.

Besides, Abbie was a woman grown now, and

she knew Darcy better than Monique ever could. She'd make his favorites for supper, gumbo and berry pie, all served on the china and polished silver. She could get dressed up real pretty . . .

Her excitement stilled as she recalled returning the blue silk. She didn't dare ask for it; it would be just like Monique to loan the gown, then tell Darcy how hard Abbie had worked at making herself pretty for him. By the time Monique was done, everyone would know what a hopelessly adoring child she still was until Abbie was stammering again and stumbling over her feet.

And then in would waltz Monique, gowned and jewelled and utterly beautiful, demanding that every male in the room look at her. No, there was no way Abbie could ever compete with that.

Squeezing her eyes, Abbie tried to shut out the image of Darcy bowing over her sister-in-law's hand. She's Nicki, Abbie told herself, crossing her fingers behind her back.

But what would she do if she truly were Monique?

Following Drew outside, Darcy O'Brien looked fondly at the long white building beneath the oaks. On his first visit here, as a youth of fifteen, he'd thought the *garçonnière* meant banishment; but, smothered by his parents' rules and expectations in New York, he'd soon discovered residing there was a much-relished freedom. Ah, the memories he and Drew had created in those long-ago days.

"I thought you might like your old quarters." With a smile, Drew opened a door and gestured inside the distinctly male room.

Tossing his bags inside, Darcy wanted to ask about Monique. Many a night throughout the war, he'd sat up listening as Drew cursed her, and he certainly hadn't shown any great love for the woman back in the house.

But as curious as Darcy was, he decided to wait until Drew was ready to talk about it. "Are you in the next room?" he asked instead. "Like old times?"

Drew shook his head, grinning ruefully. "These days, I stay up at the house."

"Ah, yes. Marriage."

"No, I like to be near the children." The grin vanished, replaced by a look so dark, Darcy's curiosity almost got the better of him after all.

"Can we walk around a bit?" he asked, hoping a stroll might induce him to talk.

With a quick glance at his pocket watch, Drew shrugged. "If you like. I can always use the exercise."

Darcy doubted it. He had never seen his friend look more fit—or more weary. "I hope I'm not taking advantage of your hospitality, but you can't know how much I've wanted to come back here again. It's been too long since I've been to River's Edge, Drew. I think I've missed this place almost as much as you."

"Yeah, well, things have changed, Darce."

Darcy let the words hang between them. "Things" had indeed changed, his friend most of all. The old Drew laughed and joked constantly; this stranger seemed to eke out every smile. Staring off into the distance, Drew radiated a restlessness, an urgency, as if he'd rather be elsewhere. As he followed the man's gaze to the half-planted fields, Darcy realized he must be worrying about the work to be done. "You don't need to entertain me," he said. "I know you have things to do."

Darcy would offer his help, but he knew it would be taken as an insult. Like all southern planters, Drew would rather break his own back than have a guest lift a finger.

"Don't be ridiculous." Drew spoke abruptly, swinging around to face him. "It's not every day an old friend breezes into town."

"I'm serious. I didn't come to disrupt your schedule. We'll have time to talk in the evenings. Besides, you're not the only one I came to visit. Where is Abbie, anyway?"

"Probably in the kitchen. But I'd better warn you, she doesn't take kindly to being interrupted while working."

"Working?"

"She's taken over care of the house. Does the cooking and cleaning and who knows what else."

"But not the floors." At Drew's puzzled expression, he added, "Your wife. She was scrubbing in the hall."

His face clouded. "I imagine she had a reason for that. She always does."

"I must say, she's nothing like what you led me to expect."

"Don't let the angelic face deceive you."

Darcy wished he could tell his friend that it was more than her beauty that influenced him, but he'd never told anyone, not even Drew, about his unique gift. Sometimes it frightened him, how he could take a person's hand and "see" things. Buried things, like fear, and anger—and sincerity.

He decided to change the subject. "So, are you going to tell me why she goes by three different names?"

Drew shrugged, seeming confused. "Maybe it's amnesia. She claims she fell and hit her head."

"My, we sound skeptical."

"I guess I could come to accept the amnesia, but now she expects me to believe she's someone else altogether. If she's a new person, the reasoning goes, her slate is wiped clean."

"Forgive and forget. Something, I take it, you're not prepared to do?"

"I can't. You don't know what Monique is capable of, Darce. You don't know what she's done."

No, he didn't. All Darcy knew was what her hand had told him. And he hadn't gotten as far as he had in both the military and business worlds by reading his gift wrong.

From the start, he'd felt a warmth in the woman; and, after touching her, he could no longer believe her capable of any real evil. She genuinely cared about Drew and the children. Darcy didn't need to touch her hand to see that; it was right there in her eyes.

But he knew better than to think he could convince his friend. Drew would have to discover it himself.

Letting the subject drop, Darcy walked beside him toward the distant fields. He wondered if Drew realized they were heading in that direction or whether the pull was too strong for him to ignore.

Probably both. Drew might wish to spend time with him, but he was clearly driven to get back to work. "I can't help but notice that River's Edge has fallen on hard times," Darcy said softly. "If you need a loan—"

"No. Thanks, but I want to do this myself."

The man was proud to a fault. "You know I've got money to spare. What are friends for if they can't bail you out of a tight spot now and then? It's only a loan, Drew. You can't want the place to fall around your ears."

Drew turned to him, a determined look in his eye. "It won't. Not as long as I've got strength in these two hands. I'm starting slow, Darce. I've planted a small rice crop, and some vegetables, and what little was left of the cane. If I'm careful, if taxes and the weather don't finish me off, I mean to build this place back up. Maybe never to where it was before the war, but it will make a profit again. And I'll have proved I can make it on my own."

It was quite a challenge Drew faced, the American dream of building something from nothing. "I must say I envy you. You are truly blessed, Drew Sumner. All this fertile land, a beautiful wife at your side . . ."

Drew looked at him oddly. "I've told you what Monique is like. How can you call her a blessing?"

It was almost as if his friend wanted reassurance, as if he too entertained doubts about the woman's capacity for evil. Darcy merely shrugged. "It's just a feeling. If she wants to help you, why not let her?"

Drew snorted. Clearly, Darcy hadn't told him what he wanted to hear. "I thought she meant to help me once, but I've since learned better. You be careful, Darce. Don't you fall under her spell."

"You're wrong about her." As Drew frowned, Darcy considered telling him about his gift. No, the man was not likely to accept anything so extraordinary in his present mood. He was liable to think Darcy had lost his mind.

"You're wasting time, standing here arguing

with me," he told Drew, laying a hand on his back. "Go on, get back to work. You and I can fight later."

It wasn't a laugh, it wasn't even a smile, but the slight crinkling at the corner of Drew's mouth showed a ghost of his old sense of humor.

Watching him hurry off, Darcy decided the man needed to smile more often. And in his opinion, the only way that would happen was if Drew learned to forgive his wife.

For in touching Drew's back, Darcy had felt through his friend's anger, down to the yearning underneath. Deep inside him, on some unconscious level, Drew recognized that Nicki could help him realize his dream, that she was the one woman who would make it complete.

Far be it for Darcy O'Brien to interfere, but someone had to get those two together.

Monique

March 19, 1860:

In books, they say revenge is sweet.

I admit, vengeance holds a certain satisfaction, but I would not say I am left with a pleasing taste in my mouth. Then, too, perhaps the planning and preparing provide more joy than the actual act.

And so I write this, to rekindle the excitement I felt as I spun my web around Drew.

Foolish Robert, home adoring his precious sons, had no idea what I was about when I set off to the city. He truly believed I meant to shop for the nursery. As if I'd waste a penny on his precious brats.

I brought Rachel with me. Never again do I wish to be separated from her potions and magic, especially when they are so crucial for what I mean to do.

From his letter, I knew Drew would arrive at his hotel that afternoon and would then wait in the taproom for his brother to make an appearance. Using Robert's stationery, imitating his hand and fabricating a delay, I asked a friend of my husband to keep Drew entertained until Robert could get away to meet him.

I timed my entrance to arrive just before dinner, when Drew would be well into a bottle of brandy, yet not too far gone for my purposes. And for good measure, I brought Rachel's potion along.

Well-armed in a gown of burgundy satin trimmed with a delicate beige lace, I knew I looked my best. Its neckline rode low on my shoulders, its deep, warm color showing my pale flesh to advantage. A teardrop diamond pendant sat above the cleft between my breasts, calling attention to their generous swell, while matching earrings dangled from the lobes Drew loved to kiss.

Once I smiled in my special, seductive fashion, I knew no man would ever resist me.

But once again, Drew proved himself no ordinary man. He stiffened as I entered the taproom and stood at once to lead me away. He asked if I were mad, going into that bastion of masculinity, to which I told him sadly that we had to talk.

Damn him, he meant to leave me in the lobby. I could see in his eyes that he wanted to turn and run and never speak to me again. I was forced to use his concern for his brother as bait before Drew would agree to take me to dinner. I had to eat, I told him, before I could explain.

How glad I was that I had brought along the potion.

We had wine, Drew consuming most of it, unaware the carafe had been liberally laced. In no time, he was fidgeting in his chair, his eyes straying constantly to where my hands toyed with the diamond. By dessert, I knew I'd have no trouble leading him back to my townhouse, to the room Rachel and I had painstakingly prepared.

He seemed lost as I led him into that candle-drenched den, his drugged eyes unable to take it all in. From Rachel, I knew the purpose of each doll and symbol, just as I knew the steps of the dance that would bring this man to his knees.

I went to the mirror, standing at an angle so Drew could best see my reflection. Smiling back over my shoulder, confident that he could not take his eyes off me, I undid the buttons of my gown, letting the sleeves inch slowly down my shoulders, until my breasts were exposed. Part of him had to be thinking it was scandalous to go out without a single foundation; yet from the glow in his eyes, I could see the thought tantalized him far more.

As the gown fell slowly to my waist, I began the chant Rachel had taught me, a soft, building rhythm timed to my actions. Thrusting out my breasts for a better view, I swayed before the mirror, letting the satin drop inch by inch with each swirl of my hips. Drew stood transfixed, barely breathing, as his eyes followed every movement.

He's mine, I thought with growing excitement; tonight, he will do whatever I wish him to do. As I relished my sense of power, my chants deepened in pitch. I imagined his work-roughened hands rasping my skin where satin now brushed it.

The gown slid down, down, and as it dropped to the floor, there was a sound that could have been the satin pooling or a gasp of surprise from Drew.

I cared little about the source; by now, my chants had grown fevered as I became caught up in the spell. Throwing back my head, I let my hair sway across my back as I reached up to stroke the breasts thrust enticingly upward. In the mirror, I saw Drew take a step nearer.

Heady with power, I laughed. Not even the kiss with which he then tried to smother me could still my victorious laughter. My chants became less Rachel's and more my own. "He's mine!"

I ripped at his shirt, his trousers, everything that stood between us; and then I jumped into his arms, straddling his waist until he was backing up, taking me right there against the wall.

I almost shock myself as I write this. No southern lady would ever admit to rutting like some barn animal throughout the night, but even now, I ache to feel that force again. I feasted on Drew like a woman starved, demanding he take me over and over before each of the altars set up across the room. In my frenzy, I felt certain of Rachel's promise that this night would bind him to me forever.

Imagine my dismay when I woke on the floor to find him dressed and ready to go. His look of disgust was like a splash of ice water across my bruised, yet sated body.

I leaped up and grabbed for him, but he pushed me away. When I told him not to be a fool, that we were destined to be together, it was his turn to laugh. He'd rather burn in hell, he swore as he stomped off.

I raged at him, cursed him, all to no avail. I kicked out at the altars; but this, too, changed nothing. In truth, I had no real power. The only way I could control Drew was by using Rachel's potion.

I made a vow then, and I intend to keep it. Before I see Drew again—and I shall—I will know everything Rachel can teach me. That god of hers projects a mighty force; and, having tasted it, I am hungry for more.

These Sumners will pay for thwarting me, and they will pay dearly.

Twelve

Descending the spiral stairway, Monica chewed at her lower lip. After putting Li'l Bit in for a nap, she'd gone to her room to freshen up, only to find her hairbrush on the wrong side of the dresser.

Since the hair had been removed from its bristles, Abbie might have cleaned it; but other, more personal, items were moved as well. Today was not laundry day; why would Abbie tamper with her lingerie shelf?

It seemed someone had been in her room again.

It was time to find out who and why. Pushing through the back door to go help in the kitchen, she decided she'd start by asking Abbie.

But when she reached the kitchen, she found the girl had company. Sarah Jane Hawkins sat at the table, snapping beans. "I declare, Abbie," she was saying. "How can you bear all this drudgery? You and Drew should just sell out and move into the city. That's what Papa and I plan to do."

"You're leaving Bel Monde?" Abbie gasped. "Oh," she said flatly as she looked up to meet Monica's gaze. She turned abruptly to stir the pot on the stove.

Seeing Sarah Jane's frosty glare, Monica stayed in the doorway, feeling like an intruder. "I came to help with supper."

"Thank you," Abbie said stiffly. "But with Sarah Jane here to help, there's no need for you to bother."

"You know it's no bother." Bewildered and hurt, Monica looked from one female to the other. Sarah Jane grinned smugly. Abbie kept her face to the stove. "You can rest up the next few days," she offered coldly, "since Sarah Jane will be staying for a nice, little visit."

It was a charming southern custom, these frequent extended visits, but something in the looks the two women exchanged indicated that they meant to close ranks against her. Abbie might not have said, "We don't want you here," but it was nonetheless there in her tone.

Sarah Jane was not so subtle. "Heaven knows, it's hot enough in here without adding an extra person. We're stumbling over each other enough as it is, aren't we Abbie?"

Extra person? Trying not to let the words bother her, Monica looked to Abbie, but the girl continued to look away. So much for becoming friends; it was as if their cozy chats had never been.

As Monica left—what else could she do?—she heard Sarah Jane. "Maybe we should have had her stay, to watch her. You know Monique can't be trusted with a new man around."

Cheeks burning, Monica walked blindly across the yard. Did they think she meant to seduce Darcy? The coldness was because Abbie thought Monica meant to betray her brother?

And why wouldn't she? Apparently, Monique had been capable of much worse.

Yet though Monica understood this, deep down, she was the one who felt betrayed. She genuinely liked Abbie and wanted to be her friend; but the girl made it clear that with other—better—friends, she had no time for anyone who looked so much like Monique.

Feeling sorry for herself wouldn't help anything, Monica knew. She might better work herself senseless scrubbing the stupid floor and at least have the satisfaction of a job well done.

But she kept walking away from the house, not toward it. She was wallowing in a swamp of self-pity when she heard the low moan.

Thinking back to Andrew's nightmares, she was startled to find herself not in the upstairs hall but rather between two rows of wooden cabins divided by a wide, dirt road.

Judith had torn these "worthless shacks" down to replace them with tennis courts, but Monica realized that this must be where the Sumners had originally housed their slaves. She hadn't known anyone still lived here. After the Emancipation Proclamation, she'd have assumed the slaves would be long since gone.

Like the Big House, the slave quarters had seen better days though a few cabins were kept up. Especially the large one facing her at the far end of the road, inside which the moan was repeated with a note of urgency—and perhaps pain. Responding to it, Monica raced up the steps of its porch.

Inside the open door, she found a small black woman writhing on the floor. Hurrying to her, Monica went to her knees. "What's happened?"

she asked gently.

The woman pulled away, eyes wild with fear. "Bottle, it no break," she rasped out. "I keep it safe."

She held up a small, stoppered vial for inspection. Wondering what caused her fright, Monica looked past the woman to a toppled stepladder, white cotton towels draped haphazardly over its rungs. Above it stood a large cabinet, its doors wide open, revealing shelves of linens and assorted bottles. A medicine chest, she realized. Looking about, seeing the cots along the walls, the shelves of bandages and the long operating table in the center, she knew this must be an infirmary, what the planters would call a slave hospital. She wondered if it were still in use, since it was clean and relatively dust-free.

The woman moaned again; and, concerned that she might have hurt herself in the fall, Monica began to examine her. "Oh God," she said, noticing the swollen belly. "You're going to have a baby!"

The woman grimaced, the lines of her face etched with pain. Monica had never felt so helpless. She'd read the books, seen enough doctor shows on television, but this was up close and personal. From the looks of things, an actual birth could be moments away.

Though she threw a panicked glance at the door, she feared there wouldn't be time enough to summon help. This woman needed someone now, and even an inept someone had to be better than going through childbirth alone.

Praying the woman hadn't damaged her insides in the fall, Monica reached for her hand; but once more, the woman shrank back. "I—I be quiet, missus. I send for Jasper—he come soon."

She must be Monique's former slave, Monica realized, with her own sad tales of abuse. "It's all right. I'm not your mistress. I just look like her. Please, let me help."

The woman looked confused; but then another spasm hit, making her insensible to anything else. Suffering with her, Monica wondered how on earth they were going to pull this off.

She knew one thing—showing fear and doubt wouldn't help anyone. "I'm not going to leave until that baby is born," she said with false bravado, reasoning that by talking a lot, she could take the woman's mind off her torment. "So you'd better get used to having me around. My name is Monica, by the way. Monica Ryan. It sure would make things easier if I knew your name, too."

The woman didn't answer. Holding Monica's hand, fingers squeezing painfully, she tensed for another contraction.

Monica kept talking. "I think our first step should be to make you comfortable. Let's see if you can move so we can get you up on this bed."

The woman's movements were stiff as she let Monica help her up and prop her in the bed with pillows, but at least she seemed to have no serious injuries. With the patient settled, though, Monica had no idea what to do next.

In the movies, they ran about, boiling water. She saw a pitcher and bowl on the table; but, unless someone strolled in with a microwave, there would be no time to heat it. The contractions were now barely a minute apart.

"Hold onto my hand," she coached as the

woman groaned again. "Go on, squeeze to your heart's content. We're going to bring that baby out into this world. Just a few minutes more, and you'll be holding him in your arms."

Lying back, spent with the effort, the poor woman looked at her through glazed eyes. Monica felt a cold dread as she thought about possible complications. On television, they were always having breech births, where they had to reach inside to turn the baby around. The woman was so tiny; what if her baby was too large for the birth canal?

This was no time to be squeamish. "Okay, let's do this thing," she told her patient, hoping she sounded more confident than she felt. "If you can just scoot down here to the end of the bed." Releasing her hand, she went to kneel at the bottom of the cot. "That's it, go on and groan. Scream your lungs out—I'm told it helps. Just keep pushing so I can catch this little. . . . Oh, I see him. Here's his head."

Monica was so happy to see the dark patch of hair she began to babble. "That's it. C'mon, push him on out to me. He's coming; oh, yes, push out that head."

She saw his shoulders, then torso; and then with a final thrust, a tiny, precious body dropped into her grasp. She cradled the baby gingerly, awed, sensing the pettiness of her own struggles compared to the genuine miracle she held in her hands.

A very messy miracle. She realized she would have to clean him up.

"Swat his rump," the woman whispered feebly. "He got to breathe."

Monica looked at her patient in horror. "Spank

him?" she asked, thinking that a cruel finish to what had been an already traumatic journey.

"Here, give him to me." Drew strode in the door to stand beside her. "Unless you mean to try that CPR of yours."

As he held out his hands, she unthinkingly handed over the child. Drew gave the bottom a light tap, just enough to get the baby screaming in outrage and thereby drawing oxygen into his lungs. That done, he asked for a knife, directing her to the medicine cabinet. "The cord," he said in answer to her blank expression.

Hurrying to the cabinet, she found a knife—which she washed the best she could in the bowl—and cotton towels for wrappings. It might be hot outside, but they couldn't risk that poor little thing catching a chill.

Taking the knife, Drew efficiently severed the cord and tied it. "How do you know what to do?" she asked, impressed.

"Drew once had to deliver a baby at a farm we were stationed at," Darcy said suddenly from the doorway. "As they say, war truly is hell."

Swaddling the child in the towels she gave him, Drew cradled the baby against his chest. Monica watched him, her respect deepening as he calmed the infant's fears. She'd had a taste of such gentleness, last night when he'd tucked her in; but, just once, she wished he'd smile at her like he did at that baby.

"You might want to look at the patient," Darcy said at the doorway. "I think she needs your attention."

With a low oath, Drew strode over to shove the baby in his arms. "Here, Darce, clean him up."

"Me? What do I know about babies?"

"Sorry, but the other one's on its way."

"Other one?" Monica asked, following his nod. Their patient did indeed require attention. Between the continued writhing and the still-swollen belly, it would appear she was about to deliver twins. "But she's so tiny," Monica protested, wondering where the poor woman would find the strength.

Drew's expression was grim. "Just hold on," he told the woman. "Jasper went for the midwife."

"Not Rachel?" Her eyes were wide and fearful.

"I hope not. He didn't say. He just asked me to come, just in case, since I'd done this before."

"We do baby now. No Rachel. With her," she said, nodding at Monica. "I be Sadie."

Monica smiled at her, touched. By giving her name, Sadie had offered her trust. "Just squeeze my hand, Sadie. We've done this once, we can do it again."

Knowing Drew was near gave her added confidence. She felt they could manage any complication; but, thankfully, there was no need. Taking less time than his older brother, Sadie's second son came into the world screaming. "I guess he wanted no part of the spanking," Drew said with a relieved laugh.

"Don't expect me to clean him," Darcy said stubbornly. "I'm having trouble enough with this one."

His movements were so awkward, Monica took pity and hurried over to take the baby from his grasp. "Go on outside," she told him with a laugh of her own. "I can take over from here."

Gratefully, Darcy went for the door. Drew

joined Monica with the second child, standing silently at her side as she sponged off the first. When he was clean and wrapped in fresh linens, they traded babies. In the exchange, Drew looked at her with a guarded expression, but she thought she saw a flicker of shared understanding in his gaze. She wanted to say, "See how much we can accomplish together," but her throat felt as raw as her emotions.

When both boys were snug in their coverings, they brought the twins to their mother, presenting them from either side of the bed. Sadie looked weary, yet so happy it was enough to make Monica cry.

Blinking rapidly, she looked up to find Drew watching. "I cry at weddings, too," she said, feeling foolish. "I can't help it. Beautiful things get to me."

He continued to stare at her, into her, as if trying to figure out what made her tick. "I-I have never seen a birth before," she stuttered. "It's pretty amazing, isn't it?"

Whatever he might have replied was lost as Rachel burst through the door to fill the room.

She held a covered basket, which she set gingerly on the floor. "You!" Rachel hissed as she neared. "Interfering, always interfering—"

"That's enough, Rachel." Drew stepped forward as if to shield Monica. "You're not needed here."

As Rachel looked to the bed, Sadie gathered her sons closer to her chest. Training her gaze on Monica next, Rachel's black eyes narrowed. "One day soon, you will come to me," she said, her voice braced with steel. "I alone have what you want."

Turning on a heel, she took her basket and quit the room.

"Never go," Sadie warned, her whisper eerily filling the void left by Rachel's dramatic exit. "She voodoo, that one. She give, yes, but she take more."

Shaken, Monica could only stare after Rachel, trying not to show how much the words disturbed her.

But Sadie wasn't finished. "She say her gris-gris make baby, so baby now hers. I say I not give my sons to make voodoo. But Rachel, she know when babies come and she come here to take them away. You save babies, see?"

Voodoo? Confused, Monica looked to Drew, but he hadn't heard. He was greeting the tall black man now looming in the doorway.

"I couldn't find the midwife," the man panted. "Then I saw Rachel, coming this way."

"It's all right, Jasper," Drew told him. "Rachel is gone and all is well. Better than well. You're now the proud father of two very noisy sons."

Jasper must be Sadie's husband, Monica thought, watching the man swell with pride.

"*Two* boys?" he asked his wife.

As Sadie smiled up at him, Monica knew the rest of the world had vanished, that for Jasper and Sadie, all that existed were them and their sons. It was a private moment, and time for an exit.

As if reaching the same conclusion, Drew gestured toward the door. "Take the day off," he told Jasper as he ushered Monica onto the porch. "I've a feeling Sadie will need you more than I."

"But the crop—"

"The crop can wait. Stay and be with your

family. This is where you belong."

"The same could apply to you," Darcy chided, waiting for them on the porch. "You can take a day off as well."

"Can't afford it. There's a full five hours of sunlight left and I aim to use them." Drew looked at Monica, hesitating as if he would say something more; but, with a deep, indrawn breath, he turned and walked away.

Darcy shook his head as he stared after him. "That's one stubborn man you've married, Mrs. Sumner. Looks like I'm going to have to help him now. Without Jasper, he'll need an extra pair of arms."

"You do realize he never quits at sundown. He's forever disappointing Abbie by not showing up for supper."

"He will today. I'll see to it myself."

"I wish you luck, colonel. As you said, he's a stubborn man."

"I can be mule-headed too." He grinned audaciously. "The trick with Drew is in making him think everything is his idea. And I've got lots of ideas for him."

"Is that so?"

The grin tightened. "It's all an act, you know. His gruffness, his indifference. Sometimes people put up walls to hide behind because they feel vulnerable. I think Drew isn't as angry as he pretends. Nor nearly as indifferent to you as he wishes to be."

Monica shook her head in denial. Darcy O'Brien, she told herself, was an incurable optimist.

"I suppose I'd best be getting to work," he said jovially. "Wish me luck, will you? I have a feeling the next five hours just might be the longest of my life."

"Talk about pretending. We both know you mean to enjoy yourself thoroughly. You thrive on hard work."

"How perceptive of you." His sheepish grin turned somber as he looked over his shoulder to the swamp. "But I have my own perceptions. Don't ask me why or how I know this, but that Rachel. . . . Well, just let's say I agree with Sadie. Please, stay away from her."

She shivered, once again feeling an awful chill. "I plan to," she told him and was rewarded by the patented Darcy O'Brien grin.

She shooed him off, insisting his place was with Drew; but as he walked away, she battled the urge to call him back.

Alone now, she could hear the breeze as it whispered through the surrounding trees. Overhead, clouds gathered to block out the sun, darkening the sky degree by degree. A storm was imminent, she thought; soon, it was going to pour. Looking back at the infirmary, Monica hoped its roof was intact. She'd hate to think of these beautiful new babies getting soaked by the rain.

"Where is it?" Rachel hissed behind her, reaching out to dig her claw-like fingers into her arm.

Monica didn't want to stammer or in any other way betray her alarm; but seeing Rachel's mysterious basket, now uncovered, she kept hearing Darcy's warning. "I-I d-don't know what you're talking about," she said, wanting nothing more than to stay away from this woman.

"You know." Black eyes gleaming, Rachel all but snarled. "The Gem of Zombi. What have you done with it?"

Gem of Zombi? Having no idea what Rachel was talking about, Monica could hardly reply. Uneasily, she wondered if the woman would hurt her. She certainly seemed deranged enough, with her taut features and intense stare.

"I don't have it; I gave it away," Monica lied, taking advantage of her captor's shock to break free. She wanted to run off, but she knew she might better risk a frontal attack than ever turn her back to this woman.

To her surprise, Rachel merely stood there, studying her, until with utter inconsistency, the woman threw back her head and laughed. There was little mirth in the sound; if anything, it rang with a bone-chilling triumph.

And as she did, a black snake slithered out of the basket to climb up the side of Rachel's dress. Monica watched in morbid fascination as it twined around the woman's neck.

"You will bring it to us," Rachel said, cutting off her laughter as abruptly as it had begun. Then, with an icy smile, she unwound the snake and set it back into the basket before melting back into the trees.

Monica stood there, as shaken as always by these encounters. What had she meant by "it"; what could Monica possibly bring to Rachel?

Hastening back to the house, to the relative safety of her room, she tried to think what it was the woman wanted of her. The *Gem* of Zombi, Rachel had said.

With a flash of inspiration, she realized it must

be part of Monique's hoard of jewels.

Looking about her room, she decided it was time to start her search in earnest. No more being distracted by injuries or visitors or unknown persons searching through her things.

Then again, maybe that was what her mysterious searcher had been after. Did someone else want to get her hands on those jewels?

"Nicki?" Li'l Bit stood in the doorway, rubbing her eyes. "Where were you? I looked but you weren't here."

Monica held out her arms and, as the child ran into them, she remembered thinking Li'l Bit had been the culprit. Why did the intrusion suddenly seem far more sinister than a child seeking a *mormento?*

That was a silly question. After seeing Rachel with that snake, anything, would seem sinister.

"I was just out back with Sadie," she told the child as she lifted her in her arms. "She just had two beautiful baby boys."

Li'l Bit stiffened. "You're not gonna be their mama now, are you?"

"Of course not," Monica reassured, sitting with her in the rocking chair. "They have their own mama."

"What about *him?*"

"Him?" Puzzled, she forced the child to look at her. "Li'l Bit, what's this all about?"

"The man with the funny name. I don't like the way he smiles at you. The way you smile back at him."

"Darcy?" Monica almost laughed, but she knew she mustn't make light of the child's fear. "Colonel O'Brien is a friend and I like him very much, but that doesn't mean I'll go away with him. King Arthur makes you smile, but do you mean to follow him into the pond when he goes home?"

"O' course not."

Encouraged, Monica pressed her point. "I don't belong in Darcy's world any more than you belong in the pond. I belong here. With you."

"You don't love him?"

"No."

"Do you love Uncle Drew?"

It was on the tip of her tongue to repeat that no, but she kept seeing Drew, cradling the little baby. "Yes, I suppose I do," she said, awed by how deeply she felt that emotion. "I love him very much."

Li'l Bit sighed, her body relaxing as she snuggled into Monica's arms. "He's gonna love you, too. I'm gonna make him. Soon as I learn to read."

All at once, her little body tensed up again. "I gotta go now." Li'l Bit pursed her lips and jumped off Monica's lap.

She'd have been out the door had Monica not grabbed her arm. "What is this? Are you feeling guilty about something?"

"I didn't steal it," she cried out, looking at the closet door. "I swear, I mean to give it back."

So Li'l Bit *was* the one? Monica weighed her words carefully. "I know you want a memento; but, sweetie, you really should ask before you take it."

"I couldn't. It wasn't yours, and I can't ask Mama."

A valid point, but Monica had one of her own

to make. "The thing is, this is my room and it was an ugly feeling to walk in here today, knowing someone had been going through my private stuff."

"But I wasn't. Not today." Li'l Bit looked up at her with absolute innocence.

"You didn't come in here to play with your mama's things?"

The girl shook her head vehemently. "Nuh-uh. I was just in here once, and I let those jewels be."

"Jewels?" Feeling a rush of excitement, Monica held the girl by both arms. "Do you know where they are?"

Li'l Bit nodded, pointing to the closet. "In the floor. Mama thought it was a secret; but one day, when I was hiding from Andrew 'neath her bed, I saw her hide something there."

"Can you show me?"

Nodding, Li'l Bit pulled her to the closet. Monica's heart drummed in her chest as the girl lifted up the rug, then tapped on the floorboard. A slat popped up to reveal a square box. Opening it, Monica found it filled to the brim. "There's a small fortune in here," she gasped, holding up a tear-shaped diamond pendant. It seemed familiar, but she was distracted by all the other glittering gems. "I can't wait to show this to your Uncle Drew."

"Don't." Shaking her head, her face solemnly adult, Li'l Bit placed a hand on Monica's arm. "He'll just think you're Mama."

Monica sobered. The child could be right. If Monica presented the jewels, he'd consider it proof that she was Monique. Even if she claimed Li'l Bit led her to them, he'd insist the child merely lied to protect her. He was always twisting things around, shoring up that wall Darcy claimed he hid behind.

She might better sell the jewels and hand him the cash.

"Okay, I won't tell if you don't," she said, closing up the chest. "For the time being, it can be our little secret. This is it, though?" she asked, seeing the child's continued discomfort. "You don't have other secrets to share?"

Shaking her head, the girl looked at her feet. "Can I go now?"

Monica sighed. If she'd taken her memento, Li'l Bit wasn't about to confess today. "I suppose. But no more sneaking in here, okay?"

With a quick nod, Li'l Bit was out the door before Monica could call her back.

She should have explained better, she thought as she left the closet. Should have made the child see she was entitled to some privacy, that there might be things a little girl shouldn't play with.

Oh God, she thought with a spike of fear—not the ring!

Praying she was wrong, she dropped to her knees before the dresser. She'd been crazy, leaving it where anyone could find it. In her mind, she could see Li'l Bit hiding the hideous band under her pillow, taking it out to play with. . . . At the thought of the silver snakes closing around her little fingers, Monica felt physically ill.

As her own fingers brushed against metal, she went giddy with relief. Thank God, the ring was still there.

Grabbing her hairbrush, she poked and shoved until the ring lay on the floor before her. A memory sparked. Judith, laughing with friends in

New York about the quaint Louisiana customs had once mentioned a voodoo deity, a snake-god the locals called *Le Gran Zombi.*

She was jumping to conclusions, she told herself. Maybe Rachel had seemed overly interested in Monica's ringless hand the day Li'l Bit had almost drowned, but there was no gem—of Zombi or otherwise—in that band.

Or was there? Poking with a hat pin, she conceded that a proper cleaning might reveal a jewel beneath the fangs, as if the serpents had been formed for the sole purpose of guarding it.

Shuddering, she wanted to kick the hateful thing back under the dresser, but she couldn't risk Li'l Bit—or anyone else—innocently slipping it onto their finger. Gingerly lifting the ring with the hat pin, she dumped it in her pocket.

And there it would stay, she swore, until she could find some way to get rid of it.

Darcy stood before his room in the *garçonnière* that night, listening to the unexpected rain and looking up at the house. The faint light emanating from Abbie's room had him wondering what she was doing. Reading, sharing secrets with Sarah Jane, readying herself for bed?

Arrested by that last image, he smiled, then shook his head fiercely. What was wrong with him, entertaining such thoughts about his best friend's sister. God help him, but who could have guessed the charming little Abbie would grow into such a beautiful woman?

Not that it mattered, he thought unhappily. Abbie couldn't be less interested. She'd barely looked at him tonight; and she'd spoken only to Sarah Jane throughout the long, formal dinner. If not for Nicki, he'd have had no one to talk to at all.

At that, Darcy found himself grinning. He'd seen how hard Drew tried to ignore his wife. The man might have a lot on his mind, as he claimed, but money worries didn't cause his taciturn silence. The way Drew watched her, it was obvious Drew was a good deal more interested in Nicki than he was willing to let on.

That's why Darcy had engineered the trip to New Orleans tomorrow. True, Captain Stargell did owe Drew a favor, but Darcy could have asked the man himself. He'd insisted Drew come along because he wanted to get the Sumners together, away from this place and its memories.

And considering how eagerly Nicki had jumped at his invitation, Darcy knew there must be one beaut of a story here.

He wouldn't rest until he heard both versions.

Monique

January 18, 1861:

I was right about that night with Drew—I do indeed have something now to bind him to me forever. In the other room, our baby daughter waits for her daddy to come home.

Through Elizabeth, I shall yet have my revenge.

But until that time, I am content with the diamond broach Robert gave me for producing his daughter. It cost a small fortune, but oh, how delightfully it glitters upon my breast. I am so fond of it, I think I might ask Drew to buy the matching bracelet.

If he could but see how absolutely Robert adores our daughter. Many nights, I go to sleep dreaming of the day Drew will finally come home. In my vision, I see us standing together, watching Robert play with the children, as I casually mention how it will kill my husband to learn his precious Stephen and Elizabeth are not truly his.

I will give Drew a choice. If his military salary does not stretch to diamonds, that is his problem, not mine. As far as I can see, he has two options:

He can pay my price or he can watch his brother's face when I tell him the truth. Either way, I win. I have my revenge or I add to my collection.

And right now, I cannot imagine getting another gem from my husband. Not only does Robert cry poor mouth incessantly, but, with three healthy children, he has lost all interest in taking me to bed.

I have taken to the city for both my jewels and my fun. There are men there, grateful men, happy to grace my beauty with gems of their own. Though I must say, even New Orleans is grim these days with all this talk of secession and war.

I find it unbearable, the thought of uncouth soldiers tramping through the house. Not that I fear for my life—I little doubt I can charm them into sparing it—but no officer with any sense at all will allow me to keep my jewels.

To safeguard them, I have fashioned a hiding place in my closet. No one knows of it, not even Rachel, for I will not risk idle tongues revealing its location. Those precious stones are my security, my insurance that, no matter what happens, I shall continue to live as I wish.

For good measure, I shall tuck this, my journal, in the same, safe place. I'm not certain why, just yet, but I have the feeling I must not let anyone know my private thoughts.

Thirteen

Abbie fidgeted at the foot of the stairs, her eyes searching for signs of life at the top landing. Hurry, Nicki, she thought; the others are growing impatient.

"I don't know why we should wait," Sarah Jane complained beside her. "Monique has kept us a full ten minutes as it is."

"She's saying goodbye to the children. Li'l Bit isn't happy about her going."

"Nor am I. This was to have been our excursion, Abbie. I don't know why *she* has to tag along."

Abbie knew why. Darcy had asked her.

Feeling that familiar pang, she risked a peek at him. He stood by the door, so tall and handsome in his uniform, but Abbie's heart sank as she saw how expectantly he too gazed up the stairs.

"We'll miss the steamboat," Sarah Jane went on. "Hark, don't I hear it coming now? You'd best call her, Abbie."

Darcy dropped his gaze to them. Embarrassed to be caught staring, Abbie looked away just as Nicki appeared on the stairs. She, too, must have heard the drone of approaching engines.

"You should arrange your skirts," Sarah Jane told Nicki as she joined them. "Though being you, you might prefer to have the men eye your petticoats."

Nicki looked at her hem. "The ties must have come undone. Oh, how I miss velcro."

"Belle Crow?" Sarah Jane gave her a funny look.

Seeing Nicki's discomfort, Abbie led her to the parlor. "Here, you can adjust your skirts in the petticoat mirror."

Nicki laughed. "So that's what these mirrors are for. I always thought it odd to have one on the bottom of a stand. You can't exactly comb your hair or brush your teeth lying on your side."

Watching Nicki reach into the waistband of her two piece dress to retie the petticoat, Abbie couldn't help but smile. Why was it, up close like this, she always seemed to fall victim to the woman's charm? Her quaint expressions and delighted wonder at things Abbie took for granted made it hard to believe Nicki was anything but what she claimed to be: A stranger, come to love them.

But then Darcy called out from the hallway, warning them to hurry, and she knew what prevented her from believing in Nicki—the way Darcy responded to her.

Letting Nicki join the others, Abbie stayed in the parlor, taking a moment to regain her poise. Jealousy was an ugly thing and she hated herself for it; but, truth to tell, she wished Nicki had chosen to stay home.

Drew was thinking much the same as the

steamboat neared the city dock later that morning. He'd been surprised to find her included in the outing though, lord knew, he shouldn't have been. Amnesia or not, it wasn't like Monique to miss a jaunt to town.

Eyeing the reticule she clutched close to her side, so bulky and heavy, he wondered what was in it. Had she packed items for an overnight stay? The last thing he needed now was scandal, to have their names bandied about town.

Looking out over New Orleans, he knew the day would be difficult enough. Outwardly, the city he loved hadn't been changed all that much by the war; but in the minds of her people, the Crescent City still battled Yankee oppression. It might have been a relatively bloodless occupation, but the lack of understanding between the victor and the vanquished had created battle scars that would long remain.

Drew understood both sides, belonging to one and serving the other; yet he knew neither fully accepted him. To the Yankee soldiers, he was a southern planter whose loyalty would always be suspect. To old acquaintances, well, they looked at him now and saw only the Union blue.

He wished he hadn't listened to Darcy. It would be demeaning, and no doubt useless, to go begging favors from Buck Stargell; but he needed those shovels and sandbags. Another good rain could burst the levee and flood his fields. He could then say goodbye to his sugar crop forever.

"Are you certain the children will be all right?" he heard Monique ask behind him. Startled, he looked over to where she stood with Abbie and Sarah Jane.

"Bertha has been serving my family all her life,"

Sarah Jane huffed. "Those children couldn't be safer than if I looked after them myself."

"I'm certain you're right." Monique forced a smile. "It's just, well, I'm finding it difficult to be so far away. I can't help but worry."

She should save her breath; she wasn't going to charm Sarah Jane. Miss Hawkins was a true Southerner, gracious and giving to a fault—until you betrayed her.

"If you were the least bit sincere about your worry," Sarah Jane said, taking Abbie's arm and flouncing off, "then you should have stayed home."

Monique bit her lip, clearly hurt, and unconsciously Drew took a step closer. In his mind, he saw her comforting Andrew after his nightmare, then bedding down on the floor beside Elizabeth, then—unbidden—her face after he'd kissed her in the hall.

Kissing her had left him with a warm afterglow, a haunting feeling he'd never known before—certainly not once they were out of bed. Wanting to kiss his wife had become more than a biological urge; he needed to melt into her, fuse with her, until she became part of him, too.

He stopped where he stood. Damn, she was weaving another of her spells around him, so subtly, so skillfully, he could almost believe she *was* a different person.

Monique had always made him want her; sex was never the problem between them. Couldn't he see that it was lust, not sympathy, that drew him toward her now?

He shook his head and shook himself, forcing his attention back to her reticule. Its bulging contents, he knew, held proof that she was up to her old mischief.

Monique didn't need comfort; she needed to be watched.

Yet who would keep an eye on her? Drew had to meet with Stargell, and then he must find a factor to sell what he hoped would one day be his sugar crop. Sarah Jane and Abbie didn't seem able, or even anxious, to stay with her; so that left Darcy.

Yes, it was a good idea, the ideal solution. But as he thought of his friend spending the day with his wife, all Drew could feel was a vague sense of loss.

Monica looked across the street, checking the address. She was certain it was the place Sarah Jane had mentioned.

She glanced around her, seeing no one she knew. As hurt as she'd been when Sarah Jane dragged Abbie off and then Darcy and Drew went in the other direction, Monica knew she was lucky to be left alone. Hers was not a mission that required a witness.

Crossing the street, she recognized the long, shuttered windows and ornate balcony grillwork above as a place she passed by often in her other life. Then, it had seemed old and tired and empty; but today, the pawn shop teemed with both customers and merchandise.

Perhaps Sarah Jane was right. Maybe the "adorable" Creole broker she raved about incessantly truly did treat his southern patrons well.

As she approached, the door opened with a merry tinkling bell and a gentleman emerged, clearly agitated as he rushed off down the street. The same bell heralded her own entry, but no one in the crowded shop offered a smile of welcome;

everyone seemed preoccupied with business of their own.

Making her way to the line at the counter, Monica was nearly run over by an elderly lady on her way out. Blinking back tears, her handkerchief pressed tight to her mouth, the woman was so distraught, she offered no apologies as she pushed past. The bell rang again, this time with an air of finality, as the woman fled from the shop.

Suddenly reluctant, Monica realized there were *too* many pieces of jewelry in that glass counter, a veritable swarm of watches and battle swords.

But then the pawnbroker smiled, showing the charm Sarah Jane had raved about, and Monica took her place in line. She might as well see what he had to say; the jewels weren't doing anyone any good in the closet.

When it was her turn, the broker introduced himself as Jacques Reynard and she offered her name. Hefting the bag out of her purse, she set her cache on the counter.

The man was handsome enough, she'd give him that, but the manner in which he eyed the jewels warned that his charm would stretch only as far as it made him a profit. With a "Forgive me, madame," delivered in a stilted French accent, he made an offer so low, Monica actually felt humiliated on Monique's behalf. No one deserved to have their life savings reduced to so paltry a sum. She began to see why the old woman had gone out crying.

Gathering up the jewels, Monica announced that she would take her treasure elsewhere.

He shrugged, that very Gallic gesture, and smiled at her sadly. "It is the times, Madame Sumner. I am a businessman, no? How do I make a profit when no one has interest in what you offer? Here, all wish to sell, sell, sell. Now if you had something rare, unique . . ."

He let the offer hang there, probing into her, until Monica remembered the ring she kept in her pocket.

Oh, she was sorely tempted. It would be such a relief to be rid of it. But then she thought of the unwary buyer, putting the snakes on a finger—what if they went through the same time displacement she had? Maybe they would be as lucky in their relocation; but, then again, maybe they would not.

In the end, she thanked Monsieur Reynard for his appraisal and walked away without a cent.

Outside, seeing the traffic trudge in and out of the shops, she realized everyone here was on a similar mission. It would take a miracle to get what this jewelry was worth.

Hard times. The war might be over but the uncertainty remained. Everywhere Monica looked from the cracks in the plaster, to the fear on the faces she passed, she saw the disintegration of hope. Reconstruction, she knew from her history books, would be a long and painful process. No, there would be no miracles for her today.

"Why the long face?"

Monica looked up to find Darcy grinning down at her. With a quick glance back at the pawnshop, she gave her own rendition of the Gallic shrug. "It's been a frustrating morning."

"Bad news seems to be the order of the day. I just left Drew. Stargell said no." Seeing her blank expression, he added. "Didn't he talk about this?"

"My husband barely speaks to me." There was no bitterness in the words; she was preoccupied by what might have happened to Drew. "Please, tell me."

Darcy shrugged. "It's no secret, I suppose. Drew came to town to ask a favor. Part of his levee has been weakened; and, if he doesn't soon get it shored up, a good rain will flood his cane. Drew's banking his future on that sugar. If it goes, so, too, will River's Edge."

Monica felt Drew's disappointment as if it were her own.

"The worst of it is," Darcy went on, "Drew came because I convinced him Stargell owed him a favor; but the good captain said, 'No money, no supplies.' I guess there's too great a profit to be made in this city to waste time on old friends. When Drew offered his battle sword as collateral, Stargell merely laughed, saying there's no value in a used blade. He conveniently forgot it's the same weapon Drew used to save his life."

How hard it must have been on Drew, offering up his pride only to be mocked. Feeling again the weight in her pocket, she told Darcy to please wait where he was, and she'd be back in a moment.

Inside the pawnshop, she watched Reynard's eyes widen as she presented the ring, his accent lapsing into Back Bay Boston when he asked where she had gotten it.

She could see he wanted the ring badly; so, using veiled references to New England—as well as her acquaintance with Sarah Jane—she haggled the man up to twice his original offer. It was a few dollars below her asking price, but she was willing to concede the extra amount, provided the man swore not to sell the ring before the end of next month. If she had to sell every gown in her closet to retrieve it, she was not about to let some unwitting innocent be transported off by that malevolent band.

In all, she felt rather proud of herself as she turned around with the money in her hands. Until she saw Darcy O'Brien in the doorway.

He said nothing to her, but his hand grasped her shoulder. Looking into his eyes, she saw him relax and lower his guard. With a half-smile, he let her go.

Monica continued outside, wondering just how much he had seen and how much she should tell him. She didn't want Darcy thinking badly of her, but what could she say—"Don't worry, I only sold what brought me here from the future?"

He, too, seemed to be struggling with words as he joined her. "Forgive what must seem presumption," he said at last, his gaze dropping to her purse, "but I'm glad you didn't pawn it all. Most of these merchants hope to take advantage of your desperation. And the rest, however compassionate and honest, can no longer afford to pay what you deserve."

"You know what they say about beggars not having much choice. Sometimes it's a matter of sell or starve."

"If you want the best price, take it to a reputable jeweler, not a pawnbroker. To be brutally frank, you haven't much hope of retrieving your things anyway."

"Oh, I don't want the jewelry. Just the cash."

He looked at her, clearly puzzled.

"It's a long story," she told him, thrusting the money into his hands. "For now, can you take this to Captain Stargell and see if it's collateral enough to get Drew what he needs?"

Given the time period, she'd guessed that sixty-five dollars was a reasonable amount, but Darcy's look of astonishment had her wondering. "If it's not enough—"

"Oh, no, it's more than enough," he said, looking around as he discreetly slid the cash into his pocket. "In fact, I hope no one saw how much. Let's hail a cab, and we can go talk to Stargell."

"Actually, I'd rather not be involved in this. It might be best for all concerned if he thinks the money came from Drew."

Though he looked at her oddly, he said nothing as he flagged down an open carriage. It wasn't until they drove off that he spoke what was so obviously on his mind. "I need to know about the ring you pawned. Is it Drew's?"

The clip clop of horseshoes was like a teacher's pointer, tapping against her conscience. *Be a good girl, and tell the truth,* it seemed to say to her. "No, I swear, it's mine. My aunt gave it to me."

"Then why not tell Drew where the money came from? Why were you so adamant the broker not sell it?"

No, she could never explain why she feared the ring's power. "Drew's too proud and stubborn to ever take money from me," she told him instead. "He'd rather starve than ever be beholden to his wife."

"Granted, but that doesn't answer my second question. What's so special about the ring that you feel this desperate need to reclaim it?"

Monica had a few questions herself. "How do you know I want to reclaim it?" she asked, wondering at his persistence.

He leaned back, feigning disinterest. "I heard you. Back there in the shop."

"I said nothing to show I was desperate. How

can you know how I felt?"

His gaze strayed to his hands; and then quickly, deliberately, he looked away. Thinking of the way he'd held her shoulder and the odd sensation she'd known the first time he took her hand, she spoke on impulse. "You're clairvoyant! You know by touching me with your hands."

From his startled expression, she might as easily have called him a mass murderer. "No!" he started to deny, but he seemed to reconsider. "Well, yes, actually, I suppose I do." He shrugged, as if embarrassed. "I seem to have an unwanted ability to see into other minds. Not clearly enough to read thoughts distinctly, but I can sense inner emotions."

"ESP." Seeing his blank expression, she added, "In my ti—where I come from, it's called Extra Sensory Perception. We have major clinics to study the phenomenon. You'd be surprised how many have the gift but refuse to use it."

He tilted his head, studying her. "You call it a gift. You might better call it a curse."

"I suppose it's all in how you use it. It certainly simplifies things for us, doesn't it? I mean, you must know by now that I have no intention of hurting Drew."

He gave her a slow grin. "Perhaps, but you still haven't answered my question. What's so special about that ring?"

"Not special. Dangerous."

He raised a brow.

And all at once, the urge to confide in him overwhelmed her. If he had psychic abilities, he must be more open to bizarre possibilities than the ordinary nineteenth-century man. "This is going to sound crazy . . ." she began; and then, sucking in a breath, she plunged in.

And confide in him she did, from her childhood longings for River's Edge to the deathbed scene with Judith, her nightmare marriage, and subsequent arrival in the swamp. She carefully omitted the ring's part in it; she reasoned her story was strange enough.

Through it all, Darcy nodded and raised an occasional brow, but at least he didn't snort with disbelief. "You're from the future," he said calmly when she was done, as if she'd just told him she'd come from Chicago.

"You don't think I've lost my mind?"

"Who am I to call anyone crazy?" He shook his head, grinning. "In a way, I suppose it even makes sense. Your radically changed behavior, Drew's confusion, the three different names."

"Please," she said with a nervous laugh. "Just call me Nicki."

"Well, Nicki, do you have any idea how you came to be here? Or why?"

She clasped her hands around the purse in her lap, still reluctant to talk about the ring. "At first, when everything was so new and frightening, I thought it some huge mistake. But then when I got to know the children and Abbie and . . . and Drew, I began to wonder if maybe I'm here for a reason. I mean, I can do so much for them all, if only they'd let me."

"What about your other life? Don't you ever wish you could return to it?"

Had that been a life? How drab it seemed in comparison—her teaching career, the awful marriage to Derek, a yawning, empty future. She shook her head. "As far back as I can remember, I've dreamed of being part of a family. My life is here, with the Sumners. If I have to die trying, I'm going to help Drew save River's Edge."

His smile broadened. "I take it by pawning those," he said, nodding at the purse in her lap, "you meant to take the first step? What changed your mind? Couldn't part with them after all?"

"I don't want the jewels. They're not mine anyway. I only held back because Monique would have been insulted by the pittance the man offered."

"Good for you. Because if you're willing to trust me, I might have another suggestion. My distant cousin, Samuel Weathers, is starting a jewelry business in New York. He might not be able to buy all you have, but he can probably direct me to where we can get the best price."

Weathers Jewelry, Monica thought with a start. She knew that name; it had been Judith's favorite shop, back when they'd both lived in New York. And then later, George Sumner had bought her aunt's birthday present there—a diamond pendant Judith had stored away after her husband's death. No wonder it had seemed familiar when she'd lifted it from Monique's hiding place in the closet.

Fingering her purse, Monica marvelled at the quirk of fate that had her selling the jewel she would one day inherit. Funny how often life seemed to move in full circle.

"I hate to impose on your generosity," she told Darcy as she lifted the bag of jewels from her purse, "but River's Edge could sure use the money."

He took the bag, clearly surprised by its weight. "My, this is quite a collection."

"It belongs to the estate," Monica said firmly. "Monique took it and now I'm giving it back." She hesitated. "If you don't mind, I'd rather Drew didn't know about the jewels either. You know how proud he can be, and I'd rather not risk that he won't accept the money. Maybe you could put the proceeds directly into his bank account."

"You don't want anything for yourself?"

"No. Well, maybe enough to reclaim the ring."

"Ah, yes, the ring. You still haven't explained its importance."

Nor did she wish to. Talking about the ring seemed to lend credence to its power. She didn't like to think of silver serpents lying in wait in that pawnshop for some unsuspecting victim. "It's just a family heirloom," she told him airily, glad he wasn't touching her hand.

"That must be some heirloom to be worth sixty-five dollars."

Some heirloom, indeed.

The carriage pulled to a stop; and, with a jolt, Monica realized they'd reached their destination. "I'd better get inside," Darcy said, climbing down. "I want to put your valuables in a safe place."

Looking up at the two-story building, its wooden walls plastered and scored to resemble stone, Monica felt as if she'd once again been transported in time. They were now in the American side of town, busier and far more ostentatious than the older *Vieux Carré*.

As if the change in scene had altered his mood, Darcy suddenly became a man of business. Helping her from the cab and showing her to a shaded bench, he patted his pocket and promised to be back shortly.

For the next half-hour, Monica sat on the bench watching the city go about its business and thinking how odd it was that she'd grown so accustomed to living in the past. She hardly missed the cars and buses and honking horns.

But then, there was something timeless about this city. As if underneath she could still feel the same, beating heart.

Looking at it from the perspective of the future, she realized then that she was watching the melting pot in action. European practicality warred with African legend, southern grace with Yankee brashness—all fighting for space, spilling together to become what the environment demanded. As in New York, each culture would eventually add to the underlying energy; but unlike its northern counterpart, here there was no sense of *hurry hurry, hurry*. Life flowed like the river it was built upon, content in knowing it would get to where it was meant to go, all in good time.

Perhaps she'd been wrong to see defeat in the cracking facade of the French Quarter. Be it Union occupation or a slumping oil economy, nothing could ever quite conquer this city. You just roll with the punches, New Orleans seemed to say with a perpetual chuckle. Just wait, and Ol' Man River will bring the good times rolling in.

Hearing a familiar voice, she looked up to notice Sarah Jane strolling by with Abbie. Neither seemed overly pleased to see her; they'd apparently come looking for someone else.

And the way their eyes lit as Darcy emerged from the building, it was clear who that "someone" must be.

"Colonel O'Brien," Sarah Jane gushed, snatching at this arm. "Do tell me Drew is still waiting inside."

So they didn't want Darcy either. Disappointed, for Monica wished Abbie would return his interest, she watched the girl ignore him, busy looking through her shopping bags.

"I'm afraid he's gone," Darcy explained, his attention focused on Abbie. "He was in a hurry to get back to River's Edge."

Monica looked toward the river, gleaming a few blocks away, and felt a need to join him. Now that her own errands were done, she remembered how Li'l Bit's wide eyes had filled with tears as she begged her to hurry home. "Is it far to the docks?" Monica asked Darcy, knowing she couldn't afford a cab. "Can I walk?"

"But we're not ready to leave yet," Sarah Jane protested. "We came to beg a few dollars from Drew."

"Sarah Jane, please."

Sarah Jane ignored Abbie's obvious embarrassment. "You deserve that dress, Abbie. You know you'll never find anything so lovely for so low a price."

"Let's just go home."

"I declare, Abigail Sumner, when will you ever stand up for yourself?" Sarah Jane turned to Monica. "We're not leaving yet, Monique. If you're in such a hurry, you just go on without us."

"Not by herself," Darcy protested.

"I'll be with Drew." That ought to be a fun trip, she thought. Three hours of her husband's forbidding silence. Still, in light of Darcy's reluctance to leave Abbie, Monica wasn't about to stand in the way of romance. "I'll be fine. Just point me in the right direction."

Darcy took her arm. "The docks are no place for a woman alone," he said firmly. "Coming, ladies?"

"Thank you, no. We mean to stay. We can find Papa's man of business to escort us to the docks later. Come, Abbie, I want you to meet Monsieur Reynard. Just wait until you see his shop."

Watching her flounce off, Monica had an uneasy moment, thinking about the ring. When she realized Darcy was watching her, she forced herself to smile. The Gem of Zombi would stay where it was, she told herself; Monsieur Reynard had promised to wait a month-and-a-half.

They walked to the docks in silence, each lost in their own worries. It wasn't until Darcy had booked her passage and they were strolling toward the steamboat that he asked, "Aren't you curious about what Stargell had to say?"

She blinked. "Oh. Oh, yes. Is he going to help Drew?"

"Cold hard cash seems to have perked up his altruistic side, if not his sense of urgency. Speed, apparently, costs an additional twenty dollars."

"Oh." She couldn't help but be disappointed. "Then it wasn't enough? Should I pawn some of the jewels?"

"I was being sarcastic. Stargell means to send the men and supplies—but not before the end of the week. It's a power struggle, you see. The man likes making his former commanding officer bow to his will. I could have offered a hundred or two, and it still wouldn't hurry him. That's why I kept out a little for you."

She waved away the small wad of bills he tried to hand her. "No, give it to Abbie when you go back to her. You can say Drew came up with a few extra dollars, after all."

"What makes you think I'm going back to Abbie?"

She smiled. "You're a gentleman. You can't leave two ladies wandering about on their own."

He nodded as he put the money in his pocket. "I must say, this is very generous. Pardon my saying so, but those two ladies haven't exactly been gracious to you."

"Who can blame them? They think I'm Monique."

"You're not about to change their mind by keeping them in the dark. They should know where the money comes from. For that matter, so should Drew."

"You know he'll resent my going behind his back to bail him out of trouble. Please promise you won't say anything."

Darcy shook his head; but from his rueful grin, she knew he understood.

"Besides," she added, "think what a hero you'll seem to Abbie."

He looked surprised, then his grin turned sheepish. "Am I that obvious?"

"I don't think she has a clue. You're one to talk about keeping people in the dark. You haven't given her so much as an inkling of how you feel."

His features darkened. "I can't. Drew is my best friend. He's finding it hard enough to re-establish his place in southern society without having a Yankee soldier courting his sister."

"Maybe, but do you mean to be a soldier forever? Why not move here, become a planter yourself? I've heard Bel Monde is up for sale."

"And have you also picked the clothes I will wear to my wedding?"

It was Monica's turn to be sheepish. "I'm sorry, I just want Abbie to be happy. Can you at least think about what I've said?"

"You drive a hard bargain, Mrs. Sumner. Perhaps you should have dealt with Stargell."

Monica sighed. "I just hope he sends his men in time. I couldn't bear it if Drew were to lose everything."

"Don't worry." He gave her hand a reassuring squeeze. "I'll be here in town soon, and I'll hound the good captain every day. In the meantime, though, you'd best get on board."

Looking to where he pointed, Monica felt the breath catch in her throat. Drew stood on the deck, handsome and proud, a gentle breeze ruffling the golden glints in his hair. Behind him, deckhands shouted as they rolled barrels and lifted crates, but neither they nor the milling passengers disturbed Drew's watchful stance. There was longing in his gaze as he stared out over the city. How lonely he seems, she thought with a pang. How troubled.

And as she thought this, their gazes met. For an instant, she lost all sense of the bustle about them. There was only Drew and she had to go to him.

With a quick thanks to Darcy, she hurried onto the boat. Approaching the man who was somehow her husband, she gave him a shy, tentative smile.

His own smile vanished and he looked pointedly away.

She stopped where she stood, embarrassed that she had read far too much into his gaze. It was clear he meant to snub her. He would rather be lonely than spend so much as a moment with her.

Biting her lip, looking only at the floor, she hurried to the opposite side of the boat.

It looked like it was going to be a long ride home.

Fourteen

The moment Drew realized he had been watching his wife, he forced himself to look away. He wasn't just watching—he'd been staring, unconsciously pleading with her to leave Darcy and come home with him now.

Though what he hoped that would accomplish, he couldn't guess. They'd only argue and end up wanting to strangle each other.

But then, there hadn't been any of those ugly scenes of late. Not since the day he'd found her in the swamp.

No, he told himself, no more of this. As it was, he'd been letting this woman haunt his thoughts day and night until he could no longer think straight.

I've been too long without a woman, he told himself as he gripped the rail. His was a physical need, easily appeased by spending a few hours in a brothel. He should have gone there instead of to Stargell.

Drew winced. Humiliating enough to go in begging, but far worse had been facing his former sergeant's indifference and scorn. They sat on opposite sides of the fence now, Stargell reminded, and who could be sticking his neck out for some down-and-out Johnny Reb farmer?

It was just one more disappointment, Drew told himself. He should add it to the list, take it in stride. Hell, he should be able to call out to his wife right now and not bat a lash when Monique ignored him.

Yet when he looked back to her, he saw only Darcy, waving. Monique was running onto the steamboat even as the crew readied to pull away.

She's coming home, Drew thought, a bit dazed.

He let go of the rail, turning to watch her, unable to stop himself. As she stepped on board, she seemed flustered, yet relieved, as if she'd been afraid the boat would sail without her.

She must be meeting someone. Monique would not mingle with the riff-raff here on the cheaper, less desirable main deck; she'd have found a lover wealthy enough to secure the comfort of an upper cabin. The thought made him angry, yet it had him wishing he could afford a cabin, too.

She saw him then; and, for a moment, her whole face brightened. *Maybe she is coming home,* some hidden part of him rejoiced, *and the only one she's searching for is me.*

As he realized that he must be grinning like a fool, he scowled and forced himself to look away.

But still, he watched her from the corner of an eye. Her own smile faded as she halted, glancing about her as if she just now realized where she stood. Reddening, clearly embarrassed, she drew up her skirts to step carefully past the crates, cages, and other passengers blocking her path to the opposite rail.

Turning, following her progress, Drew wondered why he had snubbed her. Did he truly feel the need to protect himself or had it just gotten to be a habit?

No, he told himself, he had to keep up his guard; yet the more he watched her, the less threatened he felt. She stood stiffly at the rail, reddening all the more as a pair of farmers and their homely wives stared at her openly, hiding whispers and giggles behind their hands.

Studying her lifted chin, her attempt to brazen it out, he felt a strange stirring in his chest. For the first time since he'd known her, he wondered if maybe it was Monique who needed the protection.

And before he knew it, he was at her side. "It's not you they're giggling at, you know," he said, leaning an elbow against the rail and pointing down. "It's your petticoat."

Looking at her hem, she grasped her midsection, shaking her head. "The ties must have come loose again. I don't suppose there's a ladies' room? Though by the time I found it, this stupid slip will probably be down around my ankles."

"Here, let me help."

As if it were the most natural thing in the world, Drew stepped up behind her, sliding his hands about her waist. "Just pretend this is a tender moment," he said in her ear. "I'll shield you from view."

She inhaled quickly as his hands touched her waist. So did he, for he'd just realized she wore no corset, no stays, nor very much more than her shift. Trying not to breathe in her faint floral scent, he worked to keep his hands steady. There was nothing to protect him from the warmth of her, the softness, and even after he'd found the damned strings and tied them, he found it hard to step away.

"Thank you," she said quietly when he moved back to the rail. She stood stiff, looking at the river as if determined not to show she'd been similarly affected.

"I've never been very good at this," she said suddenly. "I mean, the other girls always seemed to know what shoes go with what purse, when to wear pearls and how to fix their hair; but I always seem to get it wrong."

"It's just a petticoat."

"This time. Last night it was the wrong gown. Don't you think I realized how overdressed I was for dinner? Sarah Jane thinks I was showing off, but I thought that with guests there, well, I just didn't want to shame you."

"I thought you looked fine."

She gave him a weak smile. "Even now, when I should just politely say thank you and leave it at that, I find myself chattering. I do tend to run on when I'm feeling awkward. And I don't think you can get more awkward than this."

"I beg your pardon?"

She drew in another breath. "You, me, the hours we'll be thrown together. Tell me, must I spend the afternoon babbling or are you going to jump in here and say something?"

She was charming him, he realized, and doing a good job of it. "I'm not great with conversation," he said curtly.

"I see."

"Face it, Monique, what's the point? I just don't have the energy to fight with you today."

When she turned to him, she radiated sympathy. "I'm sorry, Drew. Darcy told me what happened with Captain Stargell."

"He had no right to discuss my private affairs with you."

She flinched, then quickly looked away. "He didn't have to tell me much. I saw your books, remember?"

"I remember."

"And I know you well enough to understand that you had to be desperate to spend a day away from the fields."

"Great. So you know everything."

"Not quite." She turned to him. Behind her, the paddlewheel churned the muddy water, the stacks belched smoke into the sky; but Drew saw only her concern. "Talk to me," she added softly. "Maybe I can help."

It was a poor choice of words. It brought him back to the day in his study when he'd caught her spying in his ledgers. "Help?" he barked, lowering his voice as heads turned to look at him. "Take a good look at the river, how high it is. If the slaves had spent as much time restoring the levee as in digging out that damned artificial lake of yours, I wouldn't have to worry about the next rain wiping me out."

Her lips tightened. "So you're conceding defeat?"

"I have one ancient shovel and a handful of bags to fill with clay. So unless you're prepared to start digging with those pampered hands, don't lecture me about giving up. I know when my back is against the wall."

"But is it? Maybe you're just being pessimistic."

"And where did you find such a rosy outlook? Can't you see it's not merely the economy that's dying? That our whole way of life is just about gone?"

"Then we'll start a new one." She looked up at him, her features gentle and pleading. "This isn't the first war you've fought—you know you don't have to win every battle to be victorious in the end. You can't give up now."

Deep down, he agreed with everything she said, but it annoyed him to hear her say it. "You gave me this speech once before, remember. 'Oh Drew,'" he mimicked, "'one day your brother's just got to appreciate what you're doing.' Silly of me, but I believed you. Until you turned around and married him instead and then made certain Robert went to his grave despising me."

"Drew—"

"I didn't become a soldier by choice, Monique. We both know I had to get out of that house to get away from you."

In the painful silence, Drew wished he had kept his mouth shut. It didn't feel better, letting his bitterness out in the open. Without the anger, he only felt empty.

"The war, prison, the fight with your brother—I know you have terrible memories," she said softly, looking up at him. "But don't you see? We've got to let the past go. It's the only way we can build a future."

"We?"

She drew in air as if it could brace her. "I'm not afraid of hard work. Neither is Abbie, nor even the children. We're a family—we should work together."

Why was he listening to this? he asked himself. Why did he wait, hoping she'd convince him to listen to more?

"You're right," she added, "things *have* changed. Why can't you accept that I might have changed along with them?"

"Overnight?"

She spoke slowly, seemed to weigh each word before she used it. "I understand your anger, truly I do, but can't you let me prove I'm not the woman you hate? For the time being, just stop thinking of me as Monique. If we have to spend the afternoon together, wouldn't it be more pleasant to pretend I'm someone else?"

"Like Monica Ryan of New York?"

"I'll compromise," she said with a half-grin. "You can call me Nicki."

Elizabeth's made-up name suited this new Monique. More, it transformed her. Studying her, Drew tried to figure out just what was different about her today. It could be the lack of a bonnet. It was unlike Monique to remove it; she'd never let the sun tint her cheeks that pretty pink. Nor would she let her hair escape from its well-controlled collection of ringlets. Though pulled back from her face as always, wisps of hair had escaped and now danced impishly in the breeze.

As if to reinforce the note of gaiety, the orchestra struck up a tune on the deck above. Drew didn't recognize the song, but its merry, lilting air matched her grin. Responding to it, his mood lightening, he decided to play along. "All right, *Nicki*. What should we talk about?"

"Nonsense." He must have shown surprise, for she went on hurriedly. "You know, the sort of thing you say when you first meet and are getting to know each other. I've never been flirted with, so I'd like to know how it feels."

"Come now, you were born flirting."

"*Monique* was. I've always been painfully shy and habitually overweight. No boy ever looked twice at me."

"You might be taking this playacting a bit too far."

She shook her head. "You don't know what I looked like in my other . . . when I was growing up. I was told it is one's inner beauty that matters; but now, when I look in the mirror and see this lovely new face. . . . Well, I know it's shallow, but I can't stop myself from smiling." She blushed. "I don't know why I'm telling you this. I guess I'm babbling again."

"No." And she wasn't. She could have drawn back and aimed, so skillfully had she hit her target. All Drew's life, everyone saw only his good looks. Robert was the one to achieve fame and fortune; Drew was expected to marry money, not earn it himself.

It had never been Monique's face or body that attracted him. He hadn't even noticed her until she drew him aside to talk. It was her apparent caring that lured him into her web, her ability to see down inside to the man he wanted to be.

And now here she was, doing it all over again; and, God help him, he didn't want her to stop.

"I guess it's hard to go back to mere flirting," she said with a grin. "Especially after we just had our 'tender moment.'"

"Are you suggesting I should slide my hands about your waist again?"

"No!" Her eyes went wide, then began to twinkle. "Oh, you were teasing, weren't you? I told you I wasn't very good at this. Let's see, maybe I should have said . . ." She put a finger on her chin and batted her lashes. ". . . I do declare, Mr. Sumner, you are far too bold."

"Leaving me to either prove you wrong . . ." He paused, inching closer. ". . . or prove you right."

Sidestepping, she moved farther away. "True, but then I would have to change the subject. After all, we've just met."

"More's the pity."

She shook her head, grinning. "Tell me, Mr. Sumner, are you this way with all the girls?"

He had been, Drew realized. There was a time when he'd indulged in idle chitchat with consummate ease. Life had seemed so grim of late he'd forgotten how much he'd enjoyed flirting. "Just the pretty ones," he told her, giving her the infamous Sumner smile. "And you, Miss Ryan, are one of the prettiest I've ever met."

"Nicki. Part of me wants to encourage you to go on with such bold-faced flattery, but that would hardly be proper, would it? So, tell me, just what is it you do up there at. . . . Where is it you live, Mr. Sumner?"

"Drew," he corrected, broadening his smile. "And I don't just live at River's Edge. I own it."

"My, you must be one of those planters I've heard so much about. I find the topic of sugar fascinating. Please, you must tell me all you know."

He chuckled. She might be manipulating him, but she wasn't trying to hide it. "I would bore you to tears."

"Oh, no. You couldn't." She looked like a child, all innocence and eagerness. "I mean, it's more than merely planting a crop. I can't think of anything more exciting than starting all over from nothing to carve yourself a life. A future. I more than admire that—I envy you."

"It's hardly an enviable position. Especially since I'm on the last year of my cane."

"I'm not sure what that means."

Once more, her aim had been true, for if there were one topic he could talk to exhaustion, it was sugar. Responding to her gentle probing, he explained how a chunk was cut from the existing stalk to replant for next year's crop. Though in this climate, good cane lasted only three to four years.

He went on to describe at length the problems with harvesting and processing. "Timing is vital," he summed up. "Any drop in temperature lowers the quality of the product. Most planters hire extra help when October rolls around, a worthwhile expense if you have the money. And that's the trouble with sugar planting," he added ruefully. "It takes ambition, hard work, and a *big* investment. I can take care of the first two, but cash is a serious problem."

"It does sound dire. But we have a saying where I come from. Each time it rains, check the clouds for a silver lining."

"I sure could use a little silver about now."

She smiled. "If you were suddenly to receive a lot of money, what would you do with it?"

He shrugged. "It's academic. There's no money to be had in Louisiana."

"We're playing pretend, remember? Let's say

you had this rich northern uncle who's secretly been admiring your attempts. If he left you a windfall, what would you do first?"

"That's easy. I'd buy more cane."

"Even though you don't have the tools or hired help to harvest it?"

He nodded. "Cane is like money in the bank."

"Oh. You'd use it as collateral."

It surprised him that she knew the term. "Exactly. It's amazing how eager banks are to loan money if they have something they can take away from you."

"But then, you wouldn't need a bank. Not with your silver lining."

He grinned. "In my experience, clouds just dump rain. I've never seen any silver."

"You never know," she said airily. "Life has a way of doling out surprises."

"Like you?"

She flushed then bit her bottom lip. "You're flirting again, aren't you? I wish you wouldn't smile at me like that. It does the strangest things to my insides."

"Maybe I want to do strange things to your insides." He barely knew what he said. Looking at her red, full lips, all he could think of was that night in the hall. "Maybe I want to do a whole lot more."

Her lips began to quiver, her eyes glittered with anticipation. She, too, remembered their kiss, he realized. And she wanted to repeat it as much as he.

He leaned closer, forgetting himself—forgetting everything but the need to taste her again. Wrapping her in his arms, he kissed her urgently, desperately, until with a tiny moan, she shook her head, broke free, and looked away.

Straightening, Drew clenched his fists. He didn't know if he was angrier at her for stopping the kiss or himself for trying it.

She laid a hand on his sleeve. "It's just so public," she said softly, glancing back at the farmers. "And they've laughed enough as it is."

Again, the arrow hit its mark. He hadn't been thinking about the social proprieties; hell, he hadn't been thinking at all. Maybe what they both needed was a nice, cool drink.

Offering to find them refreshment, he went to the bar. She seemed reluctant, but she made no protest, merely smiling feebly and urging him to hurry back.

And oddly enough, as he made his way upstairs to the bar, he found he was anxious to return to her. It wasn't until he was descending the stairs with her lemonade, anticipating her smile of welcome, that he realized his impatience stemmed from a need to see Nicki. Not Monique.

Just when had he begun thinking of them as two different women?

Annoyed, he hurried to the foredeck, only to find she was no longer alone. At her side, Reverend Byers wagged a finger, his features dark and ominous. Nicki seemed shaken; and, thinking to rescue her, Drew quickened his pace.

Byers was gone by the time Drew arrived. "What did that man want now?" he asked angrily. "Is he following you?"

"No. He's on his way upriver to visit in Baton Rouge. It was mere coincidence, bumping into him."

Drew noticed her pallor, her trembling. "Here,

take this," he said, thrusting the lemonade in her hands. "I'm going after him."

"No." She shook her head. "Please, just let it be."

"What did he say to you?"

She wouldn't look at him. "Oh, just—just more nonsense about my being an unfit mother. And he's probably right. I should never have left the children today."

Drew felt deflated. He'd wanted to dash off like some knight in rescue. Abashed as he realized this, he spoke more sharply than he intended. "They're not babies—the children can get by without you for a while. You can't be with them night and day."

"I know. Only I have this feeling . . ." She broke off, shrugging. "You're right, I'm being silly. *I'm* not the clairvoyant. It's just that I miss them, I guess."

"We're almost home. In another few minutes, you'll see for yourself they're alive and well."

She lapsed into silence, sipping her drink, while Drew scanned the deck for Byers. The worm had slithered out of his hole, thinking he had a clear path, only to go scurrying back underground the moment he saw opposition. One of these days, Drew swore, he would teach the good reverend not to bother his wife.

And just where had that fiercely protective emotion come from?

In all, Drew was glad to be distracted by their arrival at River's Edge. Just as he'd predicted, the children were waiting, waving frantically. Drew had to follow after Nicki, who was ready to disembark long before the engines slowed and was swallowed up by all three children the moment she stepped on the dock.

Drew felt like an interloper, standing to one side while they hugged and kissed. He had the feeling he could have fallen into the river and no one would ever have noticed.

"What's *he* doing here?" Elizabeth asked suddenly. Following her outstretched finger, Drew saw Byers, glaring down from the upper deck.

"He's not staying," Nicki told her, even as she clutched the child closer. "See? The boat is taking him away."

Even so, the children gathered near, closing ranks as if to shield her. Once more, Drew felt left out. "If anyone needs me," he said gruffly, "I'll be in the fields."

Nicki pulled her eyes from Byers to gaze at Drew with surprise. "But it's so late. Surely you can—"

"Playacting time is over. The real world beckons."

"I see."

God help him if she did indeed see, for then she'd know how much he wanted her to wrap him up again in her magic. Convince me to stay, he silently pleaded. Make me surrender to this need to feel your body pressed tight against my own.

But cursed with logic and good sense, he looked away before her huge, liquid eyes could unman him further. This was Monique, he must remember, the woman who'd made an art out of using his lust against him.

Angrily, he turned to march off, only to kick something in his path. Bending down to retrieve it, he saw it was her reticule. "What happened to it?" he asked, thinking aloud. "It was a good deal heavier this morning."

"Nothing happened," she said hastily, stepping up to snatch it back from his hands.

"It was bulging. You were clutching it to your side, though, come to think of it, you showed no such caution this afternoon." Of course not; she'd been too busy flirting, probing for information with her wide, guileless stare.

"Nothing happened to it," she repeated, refusing to look at him. "You must be mistaken."

She was hiding something, he knew, or she wouldn't be so flustered. Fighting off disappointment, drowning in a wave of self-disgust, Drew acknowledged that she'd done it again. And this time, he'd not only let her, he'd encouraged her to play him for a fool. The pleasant chatter, her offer of help—it was all just a game. Another illusion, designed to distract him.

"You're right," he said as he walked off. "I was very much mistaken."

Monica watched him go, sick at heart. She could see he didn't believe her, but how could she explain what she'd done with the jewels? Hearing him talk, she wanted more than ever to share his burden, but she knew he'd never accept a dime from Monique.

Especially after what Reverend Byers had just told her.

"Nicki?" Li'l Bit asked at her side. "Can Sadie come live at the house?"

Confused, having momentarily forgotten the children were there, Monica looked to Stephen for an explanation. "We went to visit the twins," he explained. "Li'l Bit was crazy to see the babies; and me and Andrew, well, we thought you'd want us along. It's a good thing we were. Rachel was there."

"She tried to steal the babies," Li'l Bit cried. "She said she'd hurt us if we didn't get out of the way."

"My God!"

"She'd never hurt us." Stephen, ever adult, tried to reassure her. "Rachel is scared of Uncle Drew. Besides, Jasper came and told Rachel to get out."

"Jasper can't always be there," Andrew piped in. "While he's helping Uncle Drew, Sadie has to be someplace safe."

Monica squared her shoulders. "You three go on up to the house. I'll see what I can do."

"We're going with you," Stephen announced.

"No." Monica gave a meaningful glance to his sister. "It's best that I do this alone."

"If we're there to tell Uncle Drew what she does, Rachel won't dare hurt you either." Stephen paused, lending menace to the words, making her acknowledge that Rachel just might relish hurting her. "We're going," he insisted forcefully. "Whether you say we can or not."

She looked at each child, seeing the same, stubborn glint. "You're going to need our help anyway," Stephen added. "Moving Sadie and her twins won't be easy."

He was probably right on all counts. "Very well then, but only if you promise to stay close."

All three nodded eagerly. Herding them through the woods to the slave quarters, she found Jasper standing on the infirmary porch, as if waiting for someone to relieve him.

"I was just going, Miz Nicki," he said quickly, reaching behind him for his straw hat. "Only came by for a moment. I'll be gettin' back to my chores now."

"I'm not here to reprimand you, Jasper. I came to make certain Sadie is safe. The children said Rachel was here."

He looked away, fiddling with the hat in his hand.

"What is this all about, Jasper? Why is she so interested in your sons?"

"Voodoo. Two babies make double magic."

Magic? How tame that sounded, but Rachel wasn't just pulling cute little bunnies out of a hat. "She isn't going to stop, is she?"

"No, ma'am, she's not."

"Then we'll have to bring your family up to the house."

"The Big House?" Plainly stunned, he nearly dropped his hat. "We can't be with you white folk."

Monica kept forgetting this was the rural South, that the Black Movement had not even been dreamed of yet. "Very well, the *garçonnière*. It's close; and of those six rooms, there must be one or two suitable for you and your family."

"But you have a guest there."

"Darcy won't mind; and, besides, he's leaving soon. Please, Jasper, let us move your family there. I'll sleep sounder knowing Sadie and her babies are safe."

He nodded, obviously feeling the same. "Truth to tell, I'd be beholden to you, Miz Nicki. That is, if you're sure Master Drew will approve."

She told him yes, of course he would, but even as

she did, she wondered if Drew might *dis*approve, merely because it was her idea.

As they moved Jasper's family, she thought over what had happened this afternoon. The way Drew smiled, even laughed, she'd begun to hope, to feel there was a chance for them. Until Reverend Byers happened along.

Happened? It might have been coincidence that they'd been on the same boat; but the odious man had been lying in wait for her, ready to pounce the second Drew left her alone.

She still shuddered as she thought of his claw-like hands closing around her wrist. "Drew Summer?" he'd hissed in her ear. "You belong with a real man."

She'd pulled away, not hiding her revulsion, blurting out that Drew was twice the man he would ever be.

He'd turned ugly then, ranting about what an unfit mother she was, loud enough to raise every eyebrow on the deck. And this time, he'd do more than have the children taken away. He would have her thrown in jail for murder.

She must have shaken her head in disbelief, for he'd wagged a finger angrily. "And don't think that husband of yours will save you," he'd thrown out. "Not when the victim was his brother."

And she hadn't said, *no, impossible.* All she had thought then—and all she could think now—was, *my God, what had Monique done?*

As she considered the ramifications, Monica swallowed painfully. What if Byers had proof, what if he went to the authorities?

It would certainly explain why Monique had abandoned this body. If Monica wasn't mistaken, the punishment for murder was hanging by the neck.

Though anxious to locate Abbie, Darcy looked at the sign above the pawnshop and gave in to an urge to step inside. As long as he was here, he might as well satisfy his curiosity about the ring Nicki had pawned. As he'd said, it had to be some heirloom to garner such a sum.

Introducing himself, he asked to view old heirlooms, especially rings, and he knew the minute he saw the twin snakes that this was the ring Nicki had pawned. Surprised by how dull and unremarkable the silver seemed, he saw there was no gem to lend sparkle—though granted, its design made it daunting in the extreme—nor anything else to make it worth sixty-five dollars.

"It's an ancient African talisman." The broker breathed the words, obviously excited. "If you've ever dabbled in voodoo, you might recognize this as the Gem of Zombi."

"Gem?"

The man leaned closer, speaking in a hushed tone as he pointed to the center of the ring. "See here? Beneath the snakes rests an ancient diamond, said to have mystical powers. According to legend, it glows with dazzling brightness when the god, Zombi, is near."

"How much?"

"Oh, *non.*" Straightening, the man seemed to remember his French accent. "The ring, it is not for sale. Not just yet. But later, perhaps I may be able to offer it. I do not see how the lady will ever reclaim her property."

Darcy touched the ring, meaning to study it closer, but a sudden vertigo had him jerking back his hand. Thanking the broker for his time, he turned and tried his best not to hurry out of the shop.

On the street, he took a deep breath, as if the air could cleanse him. It was a relief to know the broker would not sell the ring until the allotted time expired, but Darcy knew he must never let Nicki reclaim it.

As soon as he sold her jewels, he'd come back and make the man sell the Gem of Zombi to him. Darcy meant to toss it in the river, for he could not take the chance that Nicki, or anyone else, would ever wear the ring. Having touched the cold metal, he no longer wondered why she tensed whenever she talked about it.

He was still shaking inside, reacting to that instant he had brushed against the snakes.

Never had he felt such concentrated power.

Such evil.

Monique

June 18, 1862:

I feel like a prisoner of war.

Now that New Orleans is in northern hands, Robert insists I must stay at home. Night after boring night, he retires early to his study, leaving me to my own devices while he makes love to his decanter of brandy.

He's a fraud, my husband. For all his ranting about the Confederate cause, Robert mopes as if he can already taste the bitter tang of defeat. I would not mind this, if he did not blame everything on his brother. It frustrates me so, how Robert stubbornly refuses to let Drew visit.

What I am to do if I cannot have my revenge?

Damn this war. It's made life so dreary I am desperate for something, anything, to happen. Rachel hints that there are things I can learn, other worlds to explore.

I suppose I shall just have to go to Rachel.

Fifteen

Monica stood on the downstairs gallery, inhaling the soft evening breeze. It felt good to escape from the house; for the first time this evening, she felt she could breathe.

She'd been holding her breath all night, watching Drew for signs that he knew about Byers' accusation and wondering how she would ever change his opinion of her if he thought her a murderess.

No, she told herself firmly. He didn't think it; he couldn't. Otherwise, he would never let her near the children.

"Here you are." Pushing through the side door, Darcy smiled at her. "Why did you leave? Did you have enough of Sarah Jane's snide comments?"

Smiling, Monica turned to greet him. "I think she wants to see you and Abbie together as much as I do. If you're not careful, we just might have you wed by June."

His smile faded. "I won't be here. I'm leaving tomorrow at first light. I came to say good-bye."

"Oh." She'd known he meant to leave, but tomorrow? Life at River's Edge wouldn't be the same without his teasing and encouragement, and she sure was going to miss that grin. "It'll be quiet here without you."

"I wish I didn't need to go, but I've got to finish my work in New Orleans so I can head north to sell your jewels."

She looked up, suddenly eager. "I've decided I don't want the cash. Do you think you could buy cane with the profits? Drew could hardly refuse it if it were shipped here and dumped on his dock."

"Me? What do I know about sugar?"

"It's amazingly easy to get him to talk about it. Just ask the right questions as you're sipping your brandy, and I bet you'll come away knowing almost as much as Drew."

"Ah, the ever devious Mrs. Sumner. But you should know, it's bourbon we drink in the parlor. Do you think it will still do the trick?"

Impulsively, she reached out for his hands. "Drew is lucky to have you for a friend, Darcy O'Brien. I hope he knows that."

"No." He shook his head. "I'm the lucky one. When I was twelve—short, skinny and far too sheltered by my family—the bullies at school took one look at me and decided I was a victim. I would have been, too, if not for Drew Sumner. He got his nose bloodied standing up for me, and he's garnered a few more bruises since on my behalf. No, unlike Stargell, I know what I owe that man."

"Then help me help him."

Darcy shrugged. "Have you given thought to how he'll react?"

"He'll think we've been going behind his back, but what choice does he give us?"

"I suppose you're right. There is no other way."

She sighed, the sound heavy on the soft night

air. "You really can't be lingering out here with me. Drew will be asking where you've been."

"Yeah. I guess this is goodbye then." He dropped her hand. "At least for now. I've been thinking about what you said. Settling down here seems more attractive every day."

"Oh, Darcy, that would be wonderful."

He smiled, then drew her close for an affectionate squeeze. "Take care, Nicki." Releasing her, he went through the door, leaving Monica alone on the porch.

And suddenly it was too dark and quiet. She felt a tingling along her skin, as if she were being watched. Shaking herself, she, too, turned back into the house.

"See?" Sarah Jane hissed into Abbie's ear. "I told you it was an assignation."

"We don't know that for certain." Abbie wondered how often she'd repeated that phrase on this latest visit. Sarah Jane was a good neighbor, but there were times, especially after a full day of her harping, when Abbie was glad she had not married Robert after all.

"For heaven's sake, you heard her talk about going behind your brother's back."

Nicki had uttered this as she and Sarah Jane "happened by" in their stroll through the garden. She might as well have demanded they stop and eavesdrop.

"Open your eyes. You saw them embrace."

Abbie had, but she'd been too busy mentally pleading with Darcy. *Don't kiss her,* she'd chanted in her head. *If you do, I'll surely die of heartache.*

He didn't kiss Nicki, but he'd held her and then

looked at her with such warmth that a small part of Abbie died anyway.

"I want to know what you mean to do about it," Sarah Jane pressed.

Abbie shrugged. It had never occurred to her that she could do anything.

Sarah Jane eyed her with a schoolmarm's reproach. "The very least you must do is warn your brother. Unless you want a repeat of what happened to Robert."

"What are you saying?"

"Everyone knows how she cuckolded him. And quite a few of us question what really happened the night he died. She was, after all, alone in the room with him."

"That's absurd!" However jealous she might be, Abbie could not believe Nicki capable of what Sarah Jane implied. It was too impossible, too horrible to consider. "You can't really believe what you're saying."

"I believe enough to worry that when I go home to Bel Monde tomorrow, you will be here alone with her. You watch her carefully, Abbie. And make certain your brother does, too."

The next morning, waving Darcy off, Drew was surprised to find Abbie watching from the front doorway. She started when he looked at her, then turned back into the house, rapidly blinking her eyes.

He followed his sister to the kitchen, reaching it some steps behind her. She was breathing hard; she had run all the way. "What's going on, Abbie? Why are you crying?"

She reached for a skillet, setting it noisily on the

range. "I am not crying."

"I see. Are you going to tell me why you ran away?"

"I wasn't running away, either." She moved around the kitchen, grabbing a spoon, a knife, a big bowl. "I'm just—just very busy—is all."

"Breakfast can wait. The rest of the house won't be up for hours yet."

To his dismay, she set down the bowl and began to cry in earnest—big, gulping sobs he was at a loss to explain. He went to her, folding her in his arms in a brotherly hug. "Talk to me, Abbie. Maybe I can help." Ironically, those were the same words Nicki had used with him.

Abbie only cried more.

"Remember when you would hurt yourself and you'd ask Robert or me to kiss it and make it feel better? Maybe you're too grown up now for such soothing, but I am still your big brother."

"I know, and I love you." She gave his arms a squeeze and then pulled away. "I'll be fine. I just don't want to talk about it, all right?"

"No, it's not all right. I want to know why you're crying." He remembered her standing by the door, watching their friend ride away. "This doesn't have anything to do with Darcy, does it?"

He saw the fresh tears she tried valiantly to hide, the spoon she grabbed in a frantic attempt to keep busy. "Darcy? But you scarcely spoke to him the entire time he was . . ." Of course she wouldn't. Everyone had joked about her childhood infatuation; his proud, little sister couldn't bear being teased again. "Ah, Abbie, I wish I had realized. I'd have tried to help."

"You can't," she cried on a hysterical note. "No one can. The man's in love with Monique."

"No. That's not true."

"I know he's your best friend and all, but he can't help himself. Sarah Jane says no man can resist Monique once she puts our her lures."

"Sarah Jane is a bitter, old maid."

"I didn't want to believe it either. But you said yourself, Drew, that we should never trust Monique."

Her words annoyed him. "As I remember, you insisted I was being stubborn, that I *should* believe in her. Make up your mind, Abbie. You can't have it both ways."

She stood there biting her lip and gripping the spoon. "That was before she started asking about the jewels."

Jewels? A picture flashed into his mind—Monique clasping her reticule. No, his mind kept repeating. There must be some other explanation.

". . . and now Sarah Jane says I must warn you."

He looked at her blankly, realizing he hadn't been listening. "Warn me?"

"Yes, about Darcy and Monique. I told you, we heard him say he's planning on moving into the area to be near her."

Drew already knew Darcy meant to settle somewhere close; the man had quizzed him half the night about planting sugar. But that was in the vague future, and this was betrayal they were talking about. Maybe Monique would deceive him, but never Darcy.

Nor, he thought with a strange conviction, would Nicki. "Abbie, you're not making sense. One day you're defending Nicki and the next you're spouting accusations. What's gotten into you?"

"I don't know. But Sarah Jane says we should

watch her. To make sure what happened to Robert doesn't happen to you."

"And what's that supposed to mean?"

"I don't know," she repeated on a sob, tossing the spoon to the floor. "I swear, Drew, I just don't know any more."

Drew watched her run out of the room, feeling helpless. Picking up the spoon and setting it on the counter, he realized that in one thing he and his sister were in perfect agreement: He didn't know what was going on either.

Outside in the backyard, Stephen and Andrew led Monica to King Arthur's completed cage. She studied it, truly impressed. "You boys did this all by yourselves?"

Andrew nodded enthusiastically, but Stephen merely shrugged. The offhand manner was spoiled, though, by the stiffness with which he held himself. Tensed, he waited for her opinion, as if it mattered a great deal to him. Never had she wanted to hug him more.

"It's so clever," she went on. "I love the way you built two different sections."

"One's the throne room," Andrew piped in. "See that seat with the lily pad? That was Stephen's idea. Actually," he added with a sheepish grin, "he made the whole cage. I just brought him wood and nails."

"You did some hammering," his brother added quietly.

"You both did a fine job. I've never seen straighter nails." Monica smiled; Andrew beamed, and Stephen tried hard not to do either.

"Is it—is it as good as Andrew's cage?"

Stephen was so eager, Monica became effusive. "Every bit. Why, if I didn't know better, I would swear you and your Uncle Drew were cage-building partners. They'd call you Sumner and Sumner or, better yet, Drew Sumner and Son."

Andrew looked at her with mild suprise. "You know about that?"

"Know what?"

"About Stephen and Uncle Drew."

His tone was so matter-of-fact, it might have passed right over Monica's head, if not for his brother's sudden fierce expression. "Hush!" Stephen bit out.

"But it's only Nicki," Andrew protested, his features puzzled. "And you heard her. She already knows."

Monica hadn't known; but, thinking back, she wondered why not. Their looks, the way they held themselves—Stephen and Drew could have been cut from the same mold. "Andrew, why don't you put King Arthur inside?" she said slowly, gesturing to the cage. "Your brother and I are going for a walk." When Stephen tried to pull away, she added, "Please?"

Though none too happy, Stephen fell into step beside her. Letting the silence grow, giving him time to relax, Monica searched for the best way to start him talking. Funny, she never doubted Drew was Stephen's father. She only wondered how the boys had found out.

She stopped beneath a live oak, leaning against its thick trunk as she faced him and chose her words with care. "I know talking about it is personal and maybe even painful, but I need your help. With so many secrets in this house already, I live in fear of saying or doing the wrong thing.

The more I know, the less likely I am to hurt someone unintentionally. Do you understand?"

He nodded. "I guess I don't mind talking about it."

"Does your Uncle Drew know?"

"I don't think so."

What a terrible burden for a boy. No wonder he always seemed so solemn. "Can you tell me how you found out?"

"Mama."

"Your mother told you?" she asked, horrified.

He nodded again. "But I didn't believe her. Not until me and Andrew heard her say it to Papa. They were arguing about her locking us in her closet; and Mama said, 'What should it matter to you? He's not your son.' I still didn't want to believe, but I saw his face. If Papa believed it, then I knew I had to, too."

He paused, his voice cracking. "I don't know why I call him Papa. I should call him Uncle Robert, I guess."

"Oh, Stephen, no. He *was* your papa, in every way that counts."

"Not after that. He wouldn't even look at me."

Monica couldn't stop herself; she gathered him into her arms and held him close. The poor kid, suffering in silence, overlooked by the people he loved most. In that moment, she hated Monique. Of all the things the woman had done, by far her greatest crime had been robbing this child of his father.

Stroking his hair, she vowed to find some way to make it up to him. Stephen stood stiffly, but he made no move to break away. She hoped he was beginning to trust her.

"Your mother was a . . . troubled woman," she

went on carefully, "and your father had problems, too, but I don't think they ever meant to hurt you. They were just caught up in their own lives and couldn't see what they were doing."

"Mama knew."

She said nothing to correct him. He was probably right, and he was entitled to his bitterness. "Well, your mama's gone now; and, if you think about it, you're very lucky. You've had two papas, and one is still here. Drew loves you, Stephen. Maybe you should talk this over with him. I'll speak to him first, prepare him to lessen the shock—"

"No." Pulling back, Stephen shook his head. "It would just make him angrier, hearing it from you."

Sadly enough, he was probably right. After all this time, Drew still looked at her and saw Monique.

"Besides, I'd like to tell him myself. Man to man."

Staunch, independent Stephen—so like his father. If he insisted, she supposed she must let him do this alone, but she planned to be nearby, just in case he needed her support. "All right," she said with a sigh," but I want you to know: I may not be your real mother, but I'll be here for you—to talk, to listen—forever and always."

He hugged her then, so tightly it would have hurt if she were not hugging back.

"You are my real mama," he said, before breaking away and running off, "in every way that counts."

Staring after him, feeling ferociously protective, Monica knew he was right. She *was* his mother, a proverbial lioness, and she would kill rather than let Monique hurt that boy—or any of the children—ever again.

Mentally apologizing to Abbie, Drew set his plate in the washbasin. He was too exhausted to wash dishes tonight.

He made his way to the house, removing his boots before he climbed the outside stairs to the upper gallery. Hoping not to wake anyone on his way to his room, he moved quietly, quickly. He couldn't wait to throw himself on his bed.

Unbuttoning his shirt as he went, he had it pulled from his trousers and yanked off his arms as he turned the corner. He was not alone, he discovered.

Nicki stood not ten feet away, staring out over the railing. "Oh." She turned to him, startled. "I didn't hear you. I guess I was lost in thought."

Did she know how ethereal she seemed, wrapped up in that voluminous gown, the white cotton glowing in the moonlight? Yet it wasn't the ghostly aura that alarmed Drew; it was the jolt of desire shooting through him, drawing him forward. And the fact that he wasn't nearly as tired as he'd been mere moments ago.

"Let me guess your thoughts," he said stiffly, denying her effect on him. "Anything to do with missing Darcy?" Now why had he said that? It smacked of jealousy.

"I guess." She shrugged, then returned to her post at the railing.

Drew heard her hesitation and watched her carefully. "He tells me he'll be moving into the area. He plans to look for a plantation of his own."

"So he said."

Flinging his shirt over his shoulder, Drew moved closer, wanting to know just what could be so fascinating down below. Nothing he could see; she must be avoiding his gaze.

But why? Was she feeling guilty?

"I don't suppose you've talked to anyone else today?" Her probe was gentle; but, to Drew, it was about as subtle as the ballgowns she used to wear. Had she heard him talking to Abbie this morning and now wanted to know his reaction?

"Just my sister," he threw out.

"Oh." Her voice seemed flat, almost disappointed, as if she'd hoped instead to hear Drew and Darcy had been fighting over her.

Don't prove Abbie right, Drew wanted to shout. Be Nicki; make me believe. He nearly said, "My sister thinks you and Darcy are having an affair," but he stopped himself in time. If Nicki denied it, he'd still have his doubts; but if she did not, it was just liable to kill him.

He wanted to shake her. If she had to have an affair with anyone, why couldn't it be with him?

As if he'd voiced the question aloud, she turned to pin him with her large, soulful eyes. "What is it, Drew? What's wrong?"

He knew what was wrong—she'd become a fever in him, burning ever hotter until whatever slim control Drew owned suddenly snapped in the heat. Dropping his shirt, he swooped down to take her lips.

With a soft moan, she opened up to him, as eager as she'd ever been. Her hands moved across his bare chest, around to his back then up into his hair to pull him close.

Drew found himself moaning. His hands pulled at the nightdress, trying to lift it so he could feel her bare skin, but yards of cotton blocked his way. Muttering an oath against her mouth, he ripped at the gown, popping off buttons in his greed to have her naked and ready for his touch.

She broke free, pushing at his chest. Her eyes seemed huge now, frightened. "Drew, no."

"Don't tease me," he growled. "You can't back down now. Don't pretend you don't want me as much as I want you."

"No, I mean, yes, I do, but not here." She looked about them, pleading her case, before pointing to her bedroom. "Can't we go inside?"

Blinking to focus, he stared at the opened window. He remembered Monique once laughing at his suggestion they go indoors, saying that doing it in a bed made the act too tediously respectable. She had changed in so many other ways; did she now wish to be treated and wooed like a wife?

So be it. Sweeping her into his arms, he carried her over the threshold. Any protest she might have made was swallowed by his lips.

As he set her down, she held her arms up, urging him to join her in the bed; but first, he wanted to remove her gown. As he did, she seemed embarrassed to lie naked before him. Monique had always enjoyed flaunting her perfect body, revelling in the power it gave her, but maybe she'd learned the unexpected shyness was far more alluring.

Willingly entranced, Drew eased himself down beside her. Although he already knew each and every curve of her body, it was as if he were discovering her for the first time. She smelled faintly of roses; touching her was like running his hands over a bed of fragrant petals. Soft and giving, she enveloped him in a silky cocoon, spinning her delicate magic around him to shut out the outside world.

He'd been waiting so long for this, a lifetime it seemed, and though he meant to go slow, to savor the feel and sight and taste of her, each soft moan in his ears fueled his inner fever. Kissing her, tasting her, he lost all sense of who and where they were. He knew only that he had to take this woman beneath him, had to take her now!

She was warm, wet, and willing as he plunged inside her, and so tight and hot against every thrust he could not have stopped if she begged him.

But she didn't. Moaning with greater urgency now, she held onto him, meeting touch for touch, kiss for kiss, until Drew was swept up in a tide of emotion so strong, so encompassing, he might as well have been drowning.

Years of need and longing went into every move he made. Holding her close—kissing her neck, her face, her lips, he buried himself deeper and deeper within her until, with a surprised gasp, the years of deprivation proved too much.

He erupted, far too soon, inside her.

Hating himself, he pulled free and flopped back to the mattress. My God, he'd taken her like an animal, a madman. What had he been doing with all that frenzied thrusting? Planting himself, hoping a seed of love might sprout?

You need fertile ground for that, he thought bitterly. And the only one Monique would ever love was herself.

"Drew?" Her hand reached up to stroke his chest, her hoarse voice sensual, pleading for some declaration.

It served as a slap to the face. Sad, to realize that

he was no smarter now than he'd been when he'd first met her. Once more, she'd found what he wanted most and used it against him. So much for his vow that he would never again let this woman make him lose control.

"Don't read anything into this," he told her sharply, leaving the bed to jam his legs in his trousers. "I merely gave you what you've been begging for ever since I got home. What happened . . . Well, it changes nothing."

She lay stiff, the moonlight from the opened doorway making her skin glisten like white, polished marble. God help him, but he wanted to lie down beside her and stroke her flesh back to life.

"Believe me," he lashed out instead, "it won't ever happen again."

Still she said nothing as she reached for the sheet, pulling it up to cover her chin. Rolling over to face the wall, she might just as well have told him to go away.

He went, but he left with a bad taste in his mouth. He knew he was wrong to accuse her, that she hadn't been begging for it. If anything, it was his own needs and motives he should question.

But he didn't. Couldn't. Between the work on the plantation, the needs of the children, and the sins of the past, he had no business falling in love with his wife.

Monique

August 8, 1864:

I stare at my locked door, willing Rachel to come to me, for she is my only hope of escape.

Robert and I had an awful fight today. It disgusts me, the way he is when he drinks; and, unfortunately, I once more made the mistake of showing my contempt. He is so angry now I fear he will never again let me out of this room.

It is all that Stephen's fault. Willful child, I have told him again and again that he and his brother are never to play in my room. It was spite that made him defy me today. Defiance, that had him grab my arm to stop me from shoving Andrew in the closet. As loud as I screamed at Stephen, the boy would not bat a lash. Even when I hit his face with the hairbrush, he refused to shed a tear.

"You're as stubborn as your father," I raged at him. "Drew sneers at me in the same insulting fashion."

"Uncle Drew is not my father," he spat back.

"No? Look in the mirror. Count on your fingers. What do you think it means that you were born eight months after Robert and I married?"

Happily, I watched the doubt dawn on his face, but my pleasure was short-lived. Glancing up, I found Robert in the doorway, awesome in his anger.

Ordering the boys away, he came at me, so slowly my heart had time to rise to my throat. He wants to kill me, I thought; but then he staggered over my footstool, losing his balance, and I wondered why I had been afraid. He was naught but a clumsy, drunken fool.

"Look at yourself," I scoffed. "You can't even walk straight. Your precious Stephen should count himself lucky not to be sired by such a pathetic excuse for a man."

He picked himself up and came to me then, slapping me so hard it was I who was soon on the floor. "Whore!" he lashed out. "You betrayed me with my own brother?"

"He's more man than you'll ever be," I shouted back. "And what's more, you know it."

I had the pleasure of seeing how my words affected him, how the admission haunted his eyes. I don't think I've ever seen him look more defeated.

But he was not about to let me savor my victory. With a vicious smile, he informed that from now on, I'd be taking my meals in my room. In fact, I would be doing everything here. God alone knew how many more lives I could ruin if he allowed me out into the world.

At first, I thought he must be joking. The idea of keeping me locked in seemed too medieval, too barbaric. But I could not doubt his intentions when he slammed the door behind him and I heard the lock click into place.

Stunned as I was, I wasted ten minutes trying to

open the door. By the time I thought of the gallery windows, Jasper was standing guard outside while other slaves pounded the boards in place.

My first urge was to throw things about in a mindless rage; but these are my possessions and, if I must live in this prison, I intend to do so in comfort. Besides, sooner or later, I know Rachel will come to me. Not even Robert is so awful he will deny me my maid.

Ah, I hear the key turn in the door now; and, yes, it is Rachel being let in. From the way she smiles, I know all will be well.

August 12, 1864:

Poor Robert.

It's his own fault, really, for coming to taunt me each night. Fortified by brandy, relishing his power over me, he soon let me know the true reason he'd locked me in. He would not let me leave here, he threatened, until I told where I'd hidden my jewels.

I protested that they were mine, that I'd earned them well enough. Or did he think I enjoyed his pawing at me? that I could bear to have him touch me after I'd been with his brother?

So predictable, my Robert; I knew he would fly into a rage. As he came charging at me, I took full advantage of the opportunity to rip at his clothing and pull out his hair. There was anger in me as well, I discovered; and, frankly, I had been too long without a man. Robert might be an inept lover as a rule; but angry, he proved magnificent.

I enjoyed having sex again, and I especially savored his look of self-loathing as my husband left the room; but by far the most satisfying outcome was the articles I held in my hand.

With Rachel's help, I will use that cloth and hair.

August 15, 1864:

How can I describe my thrill of excitement as I lit the logs in the fireplace and stripped off my clothes? I knew why we had gathered, why Rachel was attaching the blond strands and white cotton to her primitive doll.

I see it still, etched upon my mind—the fire dancing in the grate, shadows leaping upon the wall, the doll becoming more and more like my husband as those deft, black fingers added each damning detail.

As she worked, Rachel chanted, the eerie, earthy music compelling her huge, black snake out of the basket she'd brought along. With a shiver, I felt its cool, rasping skin twine around my ankles. I perceived the darkness then, a world of secrets as mysterious as the source of life itself.

And deep inside, I could feel myself expand, letting some other force move within me, directing my limbs, my body. It seemed inevitable that I should give myself up to the serpent's touch, to welcome its slithering scales like the hands of some lover come to arouse me.

With every intonation, the snake moved closer, encircling me, stealing ever upward—over my hips, around my waist, between my bare breasts. I was panting and so wet and hot I moaned aloud. Up it crept, inch by inch, tantalizing, seducing, winding around my neck. It urged me closer to

Rachel; and, as my nipples grazed hers, the serpent passed from one throat to the other.

Holding its full weight, Rachel went rigid, her chanting ceased. Drawing back, she thrust out the hand holding the embodiment of Robert. I stared at it, transfixed.

The chanting resumed, taking on a feverish note as the snake wound down her arm. I watched it become an extension of her hand until, with a sudden, darting motion, it reached out to pierce its fangs into the chest of the doll.

I shuddered the entire length of my body, knowing a climax more deeply satisfying than any I've ever had from a man. I fell, limp and spent, to the floor.

Above me, Rachel smiled, while her serpent crawled back behind her to its basket. "It is done," she said to me. "The rest is up to you."

I felt a flicker of exultation again; the darkness had not left me entirely. "How?" I asked, my voice as high and rushed as a girl facing her first lover.

Rachel's smile was the one Eve must have given to Adam. Holding out the doll, she plunged a needle into the tiny holes the serpent had left behind.

She pulled it out immediately, her expression enigmatic as she handed both needle and doll to me. Each night at this time, she instructed, she would say the chants at the altar in her room, but it must be my hand that plied the needle.

I took the doll solemnly, a meek and obedient neophyte; but, inside, my mind whirled. The needle burned into my palm, branding it; I could feel its power seep slowly into my veins.

Ah, yes, I would have my revenge on Robert; but I had glimpsed that somewhere in that deep, mysterious darkness, I could have a good deal more.

September 5, 1864:

It is done.

In the three weeks since that ceremony with Rachel, each night as Robert fumbled with the key to my door, I've taken the doll out from under my bed. Secretly, I've stabbed it, feeling the power surge within me, my will merging with a force so dark and vibrant I know I can never be defeated.

For each time I gazed at my husband's increasingly drawn face, I knew I was killing him, this proud man who kept me prisoner, and there was nothing he could do to stop me.

Tonight, as Robert whined about the pains in his chest, about the doctor who could not cure them, I began to laugh. I could not stop, not even when his gaze went cold and hard.

Laugh, he told me, but I would get nothing at his death. River's Edge would go to Drew and the children; his brother would make a far better parent than I. He'd been wrong to blame and banish Drew; he meant to summon him home, where he belonged; and this time, I would not be there to come between them. Next week, he would send me back to my parents, stripped of all but what I'd owned when I first came to him.

I knew a black rage then. All I had suffered, all I had endured—all so he could take River's Edge away? Yanking the doll from under the bed, I jabbed the needle into its chest.

Robert staggered, pain becoming a mask over his features.

"How dare you tell me what I must do!" I screeched at him, hearing Rachel's chants in my mind as I plunged my needle again and again.

Robert sank to his knees, his eyes registering fear. He clutched at his chest, groaning as he fell face-first to the floor; but I stabbed another three times, each with a greater sense of pleasure, of power, until I saw nothing in his eyes and I was certain my husband would move no more.

Dropping the doll, I laughed in triumph. I could not help myself; I felt like a god. My will had been done.

But I heard a sound; and when I glanced up, I saw the children's tutor, that imbecile Anton Byers, staring from the door.

Sixteen

Heaving the mattress to the floor, Monica studied the frame. There must be some way to disconnect the ornate metal so she could move it out of the room. She was not about to spend one more night on Monique's bed.

It had nothing to do with Drew's rejection; she was sick and tired of living in the woman's shadow. Monica meant to strip the room clean, banish everything that even hinted of French Provincial, so if and when Drew ever came again, he would be coming to her alone.

But it wasn't her only reason for redoing the room. It was for the children, so they could come to her any time they wished and not be reminded of their mother's cruelty. She'd already taken the closet door off its hinges; from now on, she'd use an armoire like everyone else.

In her mind, she pictured Andrew, climbing up into the four-poster bed she'd bring down from the attic, talking over his nightmare as she crooned him back to sleep. Or perhaps Li'l Bit pretending a tummy ache, or maybe even . . .

There was no use denying it; no matter what she

did, her thoughts always snapped back to Drew.

She sat with a thud on the mattress. Trembling, burning inside, she told herself she was a fool. It had seemed a miracle when he came to her, and she'd wrapped him up in all the love her new body could give; yet in the end, as he so bluntly put it, "It didn't change a thing."

Maybe she should have held back. By showing her eagerness, her all-consuming need for him, had she frightened him off? Knowing his habit of believing the worst of her, he probably felt last night proved she *had* to be Monique.

"Nicki?" Abbie was at the door, clearly mystified by the disorganized room. "Uh, you've a visitor. Reverend Byers is here to see you."

Drew had been at the artificial lake, surveying the levee to determine how to strengthen it, when he heard the horse. Distracted from his study, he listened and realized its rider had stopped at the house. Curious, he crossed the road and went up the drive; but as he turned the last curve, he recognized the horse tied out in front. Byers, he thought with a burst of dislike. What did that prissy little busybody mean to do now?

Nothing good, Drew feared as he noticed the second horse. He knew that palomino.

Once again, Byers had not come alone. This time, he'd brought the sheriff.

Throat growing dryer by the moment, Monica moved down the stairs to greet her visitor. Visitor? If Reverend Byers had come, this was not likely to be a social call.

Below, Byers stood in his stuffy gray robe, seeming altogether too pleased with himself as he smiled at the man beside him. Her apprehension intensified with every step Monica took.

Seeing her on the stairs, the second man twisted the hat in his hands. "Name's Sheriff Sam Patterson," he offered hesitantly. "Hope you will pardon our imposition, Miz Sumner, but the reverend here insists some questions be asked. I'm hoping you can oblige us."

Monica hesitated on the last step. As polite as it sounded, he was not asking permission. He was warning her, in his calm southern drawl, that she could answer his questions now, nice and civilized-like, or she could face the interrogation in jail.

"I'm happy to help, Sheriff Patterson," she told him with far more poise than she felt. "But what is this about?"

"Don't play innocent," Byers interrupted, assuming control of the interview. "You know why we have come."

Patterson cleared his throat. "It's just an inquiry, ma'am. The reverend came to me with, er, some questions regarding your husband's death."

"My husband?" Sensing the sheriff had his doubts about Byers, Monica decided to play dumb. "But I just saw Drew, out working in the fields."

"We do not refer to your recent, hasty marriage," Byers snapped. "As you well know, we're here to question the death of *Robert* Sumner. And to ask just what were in those potions you were giving him before he died."

Monica nearly gasped. Had Monique poisoned the man? She shook her head to repudiate the knowledge as much as to protest her own innocence.

"There's no use denying it," Byers went on. "I caught you at it. You and your slave, that Rachel."

If Rachel were involved, it made the prospect of foul play more feasible.

Patterson cleared his throat. "Now, Reverend, we're just here to ask. No need to be tossing out accusations."

"I told you, others will back up my story. Do not waste time interrogating this woman. Ask her new husband instead."

Drew? Monica thought uneasily. God alone knew what he would tell them.

"Ask me what?" he said suddenly behind her.

She whirled, doubly nervous as she saw his stern and unforgiving face.

"Why are you here, Byers?" Drew surprised her by asking. "Have you come to bother my family again?"

Byers seemed twice as stunned. His lips pursed as Drew stepped up to place a supporting hand on Monica's shoulder.

"You know she did it," Byers snapped. "We talked about it at length when you first came home."

"*You* discussed it, Reverend. I was understandably confused. I have since spoken with my wife and I realize she could not possibly have hurt Robert."

Monica glanced up at Drew in utter amazement. He refused to look at her.

"You spoke with her?" Byers sputtered. "And on the basis of this, you retract your accusation?"

"It was your accusation, never mine. I've also spoken with my sister, who unlike myself, was here at the time. Isn't that right, Abbie?"

Abbie spoke from the doorway. "Yes, Drew, it is."

As if to cover her obvious reluctance, Drew went on quickly, "Abbie's convinced me you are quite wrong about my wife, Reverend."

"She has you all bewitched."

"This is not the first time he's been here to bother us." Drew smiled grimly at the sheriff. "Last month he brought Matron Harweather from the Children's Home to take the children away. Did he mention that?"

Patterson looked at Byers, obviously annoyed.

"I thought not," Drew went on. "Matron Harweather felt the children should stay where they were, in the excellent care of their mother."

"Bewitched, I tell you. She and that Rachel, they've been working their voodoo on you."

"Now wait a minute, Reverend," the sheriff broke in.

"Voodoo?" With a sad smile, Drew shook his head at the sheriff. "With all this crazy talk, I can't help but wonder if the good reverend is on some personal vendetta."

Byers puffed up, his spine as stiff as his collar. "I am only here to see justice done."

"Is that so? As I remember, didn't you entertain hopes of marrying my wife yourself? Monique tells me you were not pleasant when she refused you."

"How dare you imply—"

"I understand your position, Sheriff," Drew interrupted, "but while we are more than happy to answer your questions, I would prefer Reverend Byers not be included. I don't wish my wife unduly upset."

"He's lying," Byers cried out.

Drew stiffened, seeming more forbidding than ever. "I will try to forget I heard that. Dueling is against the law, and I know a man as religious as yourself has no wish to involve himself in anything illegal."

"I should say not!"

Drew cocked a brow. "One can only wonder where was such moral fiber when Robert died. It has been two years, after all. If you thought Monique murdered him, why not make your accusations then?"

"I—I needed proof."

"Do you have proof now? More than these ravings about voodoo? Let's face facts, Reverend. Unless you can produce a potion no one else ever saw, I'm afraid this looks like the petty spite of a rejected suitor."

Patterson struggled not to grin. "Forgive us for taking up your time, Mr. Sumner, but I was duty-bound to look into this."

"That's it?" Byers sputtered. "You're not going to investigate further?"

"No, I am not. And you might show more care where you go poking that nose of yours. A man in your position can't afford to be riling folk like the Sumners. I wouldn't blame them for asking your superiors to move you clear out of Louisiana. Keep bothering them, and I might do so myself."

This time when Byers glared at her, Monica saw something beneath the loathing. Fear.

Drew smiled at the sheriff as he showed both gentlemen to the door. "I mean what I say," Drew told Byers with a more strained expression. "I don't want you annoying my wife again."

Watching them leave, Monica shook her head in

wonder. If the man owned a tail, Byers would be walking with it between his legs.

Having wasted the night worrying about his threats, Monica couldn't help but indulge in a smile. Just like that, Drew had erased the problem.

"I'm only here because Drew asked me," Abbie said quietly as they stood alone in the hall. Then, lifting her skirts, the girl hurried back to the kitchen.

Stunned by all that had happened, she took a while to understand what the words meant. Drew had not only come to her rescue, he'd asked his sister to form a united front.

Monica went outside, meaning to ask him why, but their visitors were gone and Drew was hiking back to the fields. Pausing at the bottom porch step, she called out his name.

He, too, paused, looking back at her. There was no trust, or even liking in his gaze; he seemed as angry and resentful as Abbie.

"I just wanted to . . . to thank you," she called out, now reluctant to voice her questions.

For a moment as he stared at her, she thought he might explain, but he merely shrugged and turned away.

We get so close, she thought disconsolately; but in the end, he always turns his back to me.

She shook herself. It was foolish to be looking for miracles. She had needed Drew and he had come to the rescue. Why couldn't she be happy with that?

After all, heaven wasn't achieved in a day. She'd have to earn her way there, step by patient step.

Li'l Bit frowned as she studied the words. *M-O-*

N-D-I-E-U, she spelled out loud; but no matter how she tried, she couldn't make the words make sense.

Sighing with frustration, she tried again, but none so far were any of the words she'd learned in her lessons with Nicki. Sometimes Elizabeth feared she'd never be able to read this book. And she had to, for all their sakes.

Hearing a noise in the hallway, she crept to her door and saw Rachel sneaking out of Nicki's room. She knew she should go ask what the woman was doing there, but Li'l Bit was afraid. There was something about Rachel, something in her eyes, that was too much like her mother.

So she slid shut her door instead, running back to her bed to slip the little book under her pillow.

"There's nothing to do," Andrew complained from his bedroom doorway. "I hate it when it rains."

Monica looked up. Busy rearranging furniture, she hadn't realized it was raining. As she heard the drops hit the window panes now, she thought instantly of Drew.

The levee. Stargell had yet to send the tools or men.

"Can't you see we're busy?" Stephen snapped, shoving the last drawer into her new dresser. "If you have nothing to do, Andrew, help us put the room back together."

"We're just about done." Monica gave Stephen a quick smile to let him know how grateful she was for his help, but her gaze went distractedly to the window. With all this rain, the river must be rising. "As a matter of fact, I was thinking we should quit. I want to go outside for a while."

"Can we come?"

Gazing at Andrew's eager face, she thought it might not be a bad idea. If Drew needed extra hands, the boys were hard workers. "Change into old clothes," she told them, then realized all their clothing seemed worn. "At least wear shoes," she amended, going to her new armoire. "We're going outside to help your Uncle Drew."

"Help him? Oh boy, what are we going to do?"

Rummaging through her things, she realized she owned nothing appropriate. How she missed her jeans. "Well, to start off, Stephen, get an old shirt of your uncle's for me and a pair of trousers. Andrew, go ask Abbie to fix sandwiches and something hot to drink. I have a feeling we're going to need to keep our strength up."

The feeling intensified as, dressed and armed with food, they stepped out into the driving rain.

Hurrying to the river, they found Drew shouting orders to Jasper and the two other fieldhands working beside him. Beyond, the swelling river spilled into the cove, and Monica saw how much lower the levee around it was than at the other parts of the river. At the rate the water was rising, four men could not possibly work fast enough to avert disaster.

"What do you think you're doing?" Drew barked at her, eyeing his pilfered trousers.

"I'm here to get my pampered hands dirty," she told him defiantly as she and the boys neared. "What do you need us to do?"

"Go back to the house, that's what I need. When the flood breaks, I don't want the children anywhere near here."

"We want to help," Stephen told him solemnly.

"We're not babies anymore."

As harassed as he was, Drew took time to look at him. "I know you're not, but I won't risk your drowning."

"Don't worry about that," Andrew piped in. "Nicki's been teaching us to swim."

Drew raised an eyebrow at Monica and she quickly spoke up. "Swimming won't be of much use in a raging river, boys, but maybe we can help elsewhere. Someone has to fill the bags you're laying down, don't they?" she asked Drew. "Could we be doing that?"

"I've got but one shovel, and I'm running low on sacks."

"Then we'll dig with the shovel and scoop the dirt with our hands. As for bags, we can fill what you have and try to find more," she told him emphatically. "I warn you, I'm not giving up."

He ran a hand through his wet hair, then called to one of the fieldhands. "Jemmy, take Mrs. Sumner and the boys in the wagon up to the smokehouse. The clay floor there should be dry," he told Monica, "and therefore light enough for you to dig up. Jemmy can bring the filled sacks back down to us."

She nodded, her mind racing ahead, thinking of the sacks of flour, sugar, and beans in the storeroom. If they could find alternate containers, at least temporarily, they could fill the emptied sacks with clay.

As Drew went back to the levee, Monica went to the wagon. Watching him as they drove off, seeing how hard he pushed himself, she called him a fraud. Drew might play the pessimist to perfection; but he, too, had no intention of giving up. Swelling with a deep pride, she realized that man vas her husband.

At least one of them, she amended, remembering ıer other marriage for the first time in weeks. But ıs she thought of Derek, she saw how weak he ;eemed in comparison. Hard to imagine him out ıere fighting the elements to save his family home; Derek would have long since sold it off to land levelopers, letting them waste the fertile soil on ıpscale condos and a fancy golf course.

Reaching the smokehouse, more determined :han ever to help Drew, she sent Andrew back to ısk Abbie to empty the extra bags. As Jemmy dug :he clay soil, she and Stephen used their hands to ;coop it into the bags. Counting in her head, she reasoned that with the five they had here and the six or so in the storeroom, they would have eleven. As she pictured the swollen river, she feared it would never be enough.

Andrew returned within minutes, gleefully getting down in the dirt with them. Abbie, he told them, had already hurried off to the storeroom. Li'l Bit would be bringing the bags the moment her aunt emptied them.

When they had eight filled and set on the wagon, Monica volunteered to drive the load to the levee so Jemmy could keep shovelling. Abbie had already gone back to the house to see what else she could find. If worse came to worst, they'd agreed, they would start filling pillow slips.

Coming up on Drew and the others, Monica feared they might have already reached the "worst." As the men grabbed the bags, hoisting them onto their shoulders to run to the bank, she could see the knowledge of defeat in each face. The river was rising too rapidly; they hadn't enough bags or men to place them. Any moment, the water would crest over the top.

She looked at Drew, saw the rain battering against him, weighing down even his hair. "We can't give up," she started to say, but then she heard a sound. Perking her ears, she felt a budding excitement. "Listen, is that an engine?"

"Steamboat's coming," Jasper said beside them. "Looks to be dockin' here, too."

Peering through the rain, Monica said a silent prayer.

As if to answer it, Darcy O'Brien shouted and waved from the boat's foredeck. Without thinking, Monica ran to the dock.

It was no easy thing, securing a steamboat in that raging current; and the men were jumping off, tossing over supplies before the ropes could be tied. Disembarking first, Darcy was shouting orders as Monica rushed up to grab him in a fierce, grateful hug. "You sure cut this one close, Colonel O'Brien."

"Can't get a thing done in the military anymore." With a grin and a squeeze of his own, he held her away from him. "Tell me, how bad is it? Can the fields be saved?"

"If you hurry. We're down to our last sandbag."

"Well, I've brought plenty. As well as shovels and a dozen healthy soldiers."

"What is this?" Drew asked behind them.

As Darcy dropped his hands, Monica whirled to face her husband. "Darcy has come to save us," she said breathlessly.

Rain dripping down his face, Drew scowled at his friend.

"Stargell had a change of heart," Darcy told him with a shrug. "Let's get these supplies unloaded and you can tell me where you want the men."

"I'll take them up to the smokehouse," Monica offered. "We've been digging—"

"No!" Drew reached out to grab her hand. "I don't want you near those soldiers. Not dressed like that."

"I find your attire charming," Darcy said with a grin, "but Drew might be right."

There was a sudden shout behind them as the dock began to creak and totter. "It won't hold the steamboat in this current," Darcy shouted, turning to the soldiers. "Quick, make a line and pass the supplies to dry land."

Drew released her hand to join him, catching the cargo still being thrown from the deck. Despite the ropes and the power of its grinding engines, the vessel slowly drifted downriver, while beneath them, the dock continued its ominous creaking.

Finding a place in line, Monica helped pass shovels and sandbags to shore. It all became a blur of motion: Darcy unhitching the ropes, the steamboat edging away, Drew shouting orders through the wind and the rain.

Soldiers grabbed shovels and began to dig, while others ran to hoist filled bags onto the levee. Determined to do her part, Monica grabbed a shovel of her own.

"What are you still doing here?" she heard Drew ask quite a bit later.

"Don't be so stubborn," she snapped, stabbing her spade in the ground. "You need all the help you can get."

He blinked back the rain, looking at the levee. "It's not so bad now. There's a light at the end of the tunnel."

Wearily, Monica rested her arms on the spade.

"Are you sure it's a light you see? And not a silver lining?"

His sudden, fleeting grin went right to her heart, made a home there. "The men will need sleeping quarters. Could you see about securing them, perhaps in the old slave cabins? I'd suggest the *garconnière,* but I'm told you've already filled that up."

Why, he's teasing me, she thought. He knows I put Sadie and the babies there, and he's telling me he approves.

With a grin of her own, she straightened. "You needn't be so devious, Mr. Sumner. If you don't want me here, stop dreaming up things for me to do and just say so."

He took her hand, his fingers tracing the clay caked into her cracked fingernails. Thinking of other times he'd touched her, Monica held her breath, waiting for more.

"Very well," he said. "I don't want you here."

It was not the "more" she'd hoped for. "Okay, I'm going. With all these extra mouths to feed, Abbie will be needing my help in the kitchen anyway."

With the slightest tug, he let her hand drop. "Go on up and change into dry clothes."

"Don't worry," she told him as she stomped off. "I won't embarrass you by wearing your trousers again."

"Nicki?" he called out tentatively. Turning, she found him standing in the rain, staring at her with a strange expression. "I just—just want you safe."

He walked off; and, watching him go, Monica felt as dazed as if he had actually kissed her. *He wanted her safe.*

In that same daze, she changed into dry

clothes—a dress this time—and spent the afternoon setting up cabins. When she went to the kitchen, Abbie was stiff, discouraging conversation, but Monica barely noticed. She had enough else on her mind about Drew. Besides, having rearranged furniture for two days, she was too tired to talk. Every muscle in her body screamed in protest when she moved.

The men ate dinner in shifts, Drew coming in for the last one. The rain was letting up, she heard him tell his sister. Another hour or two and they could let up too.

Relieved, Monica went upstairs when the dishes were done. No sooner had she thrown herself on the bed than she heard Andrew at the door.

"I had a nightmare," he told her, rubbing his eyes.

"C'mon up and join me in bed," she invited, not caring that she still wore her dress. Wrapping an arm around him, crooning to him, she soon made them both so drowsy they fell off to sleep.

Drew went into the boys' room to check on them and was startled to find both beds empty. Concerned he made his way to Elizabeth, only to pause at his wife's open door. Maybe Nicki knew what had become of the boys.

In the bedroom, a candle still flickered. Drawn to it, he paused in the doorway. For there, cuddled close on either side of his wife, slept Andrew and Elizabeth, with Stephen curled up at the bottom of the bed.

His family, he thought with a rush of emotion, thinking of how they had hurried to help him today. All because of the woman now holding them in her arms.

Ah, Nicki, he thought as he noticed the speck of mud still dotting her face. Why hadn't he thanked her, washed the mud from her delicate cheek, made some attempt to show her how much it meant to him to have her at his side?

Was she his silver lining?

His smile faded as he saw her again, running to Darcy. That's why he'd said nothing, why the words had choked in his throat. Considering the way she'd embraced his best friend, it was far more likely she would one day take her sunshine away.

He indulged in one last look, then told himself this was Robert's family, not his. As much as he longed to stretch out on the bed beside them, he didn't belong here.

Blowing out the candle, he quietly quit the room.

Seventeen

Drew sat at his desk, staring out the window, looking at the new levee with a sense of accomplishment. It had been three weeks since the day of that near-disaster, during which he'd worked harder than he'd ever worked in his life.

And it had been three hours since he'd parked himself down at his desk, he thought with a frown. Half the morning was gone already and he still hadn't composed his letter.

It was like gulping down nails, penning this request; swallowing one's pride was a painful process. It wasn't easy asking a friend for a loan.

Especially after the farce with the levee. Drew knew full well Buck Stargell hadn't had a change of heart. Someone had paid him for those sandbags and shovels. And the only one with the means, money, and motivation was Darcy.

But since the day of the rains, Drew had discovered that he'd come as close as he ever wanted to be to losing his family home, and he would do anything, even beg on his knees, rather than put it in danger again. It had become far more than saving his heritage or even the means of proving himself to the world. River's Edge, he feared, was the one thing that kept Nicki near.

He'd seen how vigorously she'd worked on the place the past few weeks, how much pleasure and pride she derived from cleaning, restoring, and decorating the rooms with older, homier furniture from the attic.

Looking about him, he smiled at the improvements to his study. Gone were the ghastly velvet draperies; a green and beige pattern decorated the windows instead, letting in light but not heat. Dusted and rearranged, the shelves now sported a series of vases with flowers fresh from the garden. His desk sat in front of the window, making room for a plush settee in the corner, and a pair of comfortable chairs before the grate.

His mother would have called it "dressing the house for summer," but whatever the term, his study had gained a fresh outlook. All of River's Edge had, with its fresh, clean curtains and the newly polished, gleaming wood. For the first time in a long while, the house seemed like a home.

"Are you busy?" Stephen asked suddenly. He stood in the doorway, his thin frame poised for flight at the slightest hint of rejection.

"Nothing that can't wait." Drew tried not to look at the unfinished letter. The boy wouldn't be here if he wasn't disturbed about something.

Stephen stepped into the room. "Nicki and I . . . er, have been talking. We think I should discuss this with you."

Was it that time already? Drew thought, a bit alarmed. What would a boy his age need to know about sex?

"I-I don't know how to start," Stephen faltered. "It's a bit embarrassing."

Drew nodded solemnly. If Stephen needed to talk, they would talk. Rising from his desk, he gestured to the settee. Might as well get it over and done with, no matter how awkward it proved for them both. "I know what you mean," he told his nephew as they sat. "I felt the same at your age."

"You mean Grandfather wasn't your papa, either?"

Drew felt as if he'd just been punched in the gut. "Did I miss something?"

"I just thought . . ." Stephen wriggled on his side of the seat. ". . . I should tell you I know you're my real father."

All these years wondering, afraid to ask, and here was the boy himself making him face the truth. My *real* father, he'd said, so solemn, so adult, without the least indication of what he was feeling. Was Stephen happy about it? Or disappointed?

More to the point, Drew thought suddenly, how the hell had he found out? "Did Nicki tell you this?"

"No, it was Mama. My other mama."

It made Drew uneasy, the way the children persisted in thinking of her as two different people—especially when it reinforced his own tendency to do the same.

"She told me right before Papa . . ." Stephen hesitated, stumbling over the word. ". . . before Uncle Robert died."

Damn that Monique for placing such a burden on the boy. "You go right on calling him Papa," he told Stephen, reaching out to grasp his shoulder.

"That's what Nicki said. She told me I'm lucky to have two fathers, that I'm doubly loved."

"She's right."

Stephen shrugged. "Once he found out, Papa didn't want to look at me any more. Sometimes I think that's why his heart got sick and he died."

As Drew realized how his grip had tightened, he removed his hand. What had been wrong with Robert, taking out his hurt and anger on an innocent child?

But then, he knew what the problem was—Monique.

"You had nothing to do with his dying, Stephen." He paused, knowing his voice should be reassuring, not tight with strain. "Your papa had problems, serious problems."

Stephen shrugged. "I know. Sometimes, I also wonder if it was Mama who hurt his heart."

Uneasily, Drew thought back to Byers' accusations. So many times, he'd wanted to confront Nicki, have her explain what actually happened to Robert; but with their unspoken truce, he wasn't sure he wanted her remembering, didn't want to risk things returning to the way they'd been. Besides, each time he saw her smile or heard her laugh, he found it more and more impossible to consider Nicki capable of murder.

Or even being Monique.

But the boy had enough worries—he did not need his uncle's confusion on top of them.

He looked at Stephen—his son—and felt myriad emotions war within him. He felt guilt and remorse, for here sat the embodiment of how he'd betrayed his brother. He felt anger at Monique and self-loathing for himself. And there was the doubt, the wondering if Elizabeth, too, was a product of that frenzied, joyless passion.

Yet beneath it all, he knew a dawning wonder, a

pride that blossomed with each passing moment. Whatever their beginnings, no man could ask for finer children.

And right now, his son clearly needed reassurance. "Can we start all over, do you think? Forget the past and go on as if we've always known we're father and son?"

Stephen grinned sheepishly. "It's hard. I'm used to calling you Uncle Drew."

"What you call me doesn't much matter, I guess. But I want you to know, I couldn't be happier. I could search the world and never find a boy I'd rather call my son."

Stephen nodded, still too contained. Sensing he, too, struggled with mixed emotions, Drew pulled him close. "I guess you're too old for this, but I'm hugging you anyway. I figure we've got years to make up for."

Stephen not only hugged him back but did so with great enthusiasm, as if he also had a storehouse of hugs to give.

"I haven't been around for you much in the past, Son; but if you have any problems, anything you need to talk about, you will come to me, won't you?"

"I'd like to."

Looking down at the boy, Drew felt his chest swell with pride. This boy was his own flesh and blood, his legacy to the world, his hope for the future.

And all at once, it became more crucial than ever that he write that letter to Darcy.

Stephen must have caught his quick glance at the desk, for he excused himself suddenly.

"I *am* busy," Drew agreed, "but after dinner, maybe we could play a game of chess? Right here in the study, just us two men?"

Stephen's broad smile was a reward in itself. "I'd like that, Unc . . . Papa."

Tousling his hair, Drew saw Stephen to the door. Just outside, he found Nicki, standing guard with a dustrag in her hand. "I, uh, am on my way up to the attic," she said awkwardly, turning at once for the stairs. Watching her hurry up them, Drew saw the gentle smile curving her lips.

Stephen claimed she'd suggested this conversation. Nicki, always Nicki, everywhere he turned of late.

Odd, how comforting that thought had become.

Abbie heard the steamboat engine and forced herself to stay in the kitchen. It must be stopping at Bel Monde, for they certainly weren't expecting anything or anyone today.

It sure wouldn't be Darcy-to-the-rescue, like on the day of the heavy rain. No, by now he must be up north, sorting out his private affairs. Not that he'd spoken to her about any of this, mind you. All Abbie knew, she'd learned from her brother.

Granted, everyone had been busy that day, but she'd seen Darcy take time to embrace Nicki. All Abbie had gotten was a half-hearted smile as he trudged off to bed late that night and a brief salute when he left first thing in the morning.

He was now in New York, tidying up any loose ends that might prevent his return. And if and when he did come back, Darcy would be coming for Nicki.

Sometimes, the thought made her so angry Abbie despised the woman; but then Nicki would turn around and do or say something so disarming, she'd find herself softening again. Like this surprise party her sister-in-law was planning for Drew's birthday. How was Abbie supposed to hate someone who tried so hard to make her brother smile?

Sometimes she wondered if the woman truly were two different people. Nicki cared about Drew, Monique flirted with Darcy. Nicki was wonderful with the children; Monique meant to run off with . . .

Somehow, on the short side of the balance sheet, Abbie always came up with Darcy.

"Is it ready yet?"

Elizabeth stood beside her. Testing the cake batter had become a daily ritual, the child claiming only she could tell if it would turn out right. Afterward, Abbie would give her some chore, saying it was a good idea for Elizabeth to learn her way about a kitchen; but, in truth, she welcomed the company. It was lonely here now that she'd all but banished Nicki from the room.

But today, Elizabeth wasn't her only visitor.

She blinked, making sure it truly was Drew standing at the door. Hard to remember the last time he'd come to the kitchen during the day. "What's wrong?" she asked with a touch of panic.

"No, no." He waved a hand, answering distractedly. "Nothing's wrong. It's just . . . I'm confused. You didn't order sugar cane in New Orleans, did you?"

"Cane?" Wiping her hands on her apron, she went to the door, surprise making her forget Elizabeth was there.

"There's a shipment of it, down by the river. I thought maybe you—"

"Where would I get money to go ordering cane?"

"I don't know, Abbie. I sure don't have money. They're not giving the cane away, so how the devil did that shipment get here?"

They looked at each other. "Darcy," she said at last. "He knows you need new stock. And he's the only one with the funds to get it for you."

"But I haven't finished the letter." He looked behind him, preoccupied by something outside.

"What letter?"

He didn't answer. As he stared off into the distance, Abbie followed his gaze. Seeing Nicki beating a rug on the washline, she felt her anger return and grow. Her brother was no better than Darcy; must she become invisible every time that woman was near? "Who do you think bought it?" she snapped. "Your wife?"

He looked at her, surprised.

"Wake up, Drew. Did you never stop to wonder why Darcy is leaving the army and moving down here? I think maybe he sent that cane in atonement. So when Nicki leaves you and goes to him, you won't be left with nothing."

"You think so?" He seemed more puzzled than hurt or even angry.

His lack of outrage fueled Abbie's own. "Ask her about it, why don't you? I bet Nicki knows more about where that cane came from than you or I ever will."

But he merely nodded and walked away, as distracted as ever. At first, she thought he meant to confront his wife, but he veered off and headed toward the dock.

With a huff, Abbie turned back to the kitchen, ready to hurl the batter at the nearest wall. Until she saw her niece.

Pale and clearly shaken, Elizabeth had heard every word.

"Uncle Drew?" Tugging at the skirt of her nightgown, Li'l Bit waited beside his chair. More than anything, she wanted to climb in his lap and cuddle close, but she was scared she'd startle him if she touched so much as a hair. He was so deep in thought she wondered if he'd even heard. She gently repeated his name.

Though he started, he didn't yell like Mama would have. Instead, he smiled slowly, holding out his arms to help her scramble into his lap. "And what brings you to my study at this hour?" he asked softly. "Shouldn't you be in bed?"

"I couldn't sleep." She'd been waiting for Uncle Drew to finish his chess game with Stephen, but she didn't tell him that. There was too much else on her mind. "Is it true?" she blurted out, unable to keep the worry inside any more. "Is Nicki going away with that man, that Darcy?"

"Is that what she told you?"

He sounded impatient, almost mad, and Li'l Bit rapidly shook her head. "Nuh-uh, no one told me. I heard you and Abbie. Today, in the kitchen."

He made a face, as if he'd eaten something nasty, and then got the look that parents use when they want to make things seem better than they are. "Honey, we—"

"Nicki promised me," she interrupted, too worried to be soothed. "She said she and that Darcy were just friends. That she'd be my mama now and she'd never go away."

"If she promised, then I imagine she meant

what she said." He sounded so certain, she let herself be soothed after all.

But just a li'l bit soothed. "Yeah. I s'pose. It's just she wasn't here for supper, and then . . . well, the jewels."

His grip tightened. "Jewels?"

"When I went to the closet, they were gone. If Nicki isn't going away, what did she do with them?"

"I don't know." As if he'd just realized he was holding her too tight, he lifted Li'l Bit off his lap and set her down. "There's but one way to find out. We'll have to ask her."

Elizabeth smiled. That's what was good about Uncle Drew. He always knew how to get to the bottom of things, how to fix them and make them right. For the first time all day, she had the feeling it might all work out fine. Reaching up, she grabbed his hand. "C'mon, let's go."

"Whoa, young lady, it's past your bedtime. Suppose you let me do the asking and I'll come share whatever I learn, first thing in the morning."

"Promise?"

He held his free hand over his heart. "I swear."

Nodding solemnly, she released his hand and went to the door, hesitating a moment when she got there. "Talk nice," she advised. "Make her want to stay."

He nodded, but Elizabeth feared he hadn't heard. He was too busy thinking; she could see it in his eyes.

Worried again, she vowed she would stay up all night. For how could she sleep, until she was certain Nicki would stay and be her mama?

* * *

Monica pulled off the tent-like panties, letting the white cotton float to the pile by her bare feet. How blessedly free she felt without all that clothing; how cool. Busy reorganizing the attic, not even breaking for supper, she'd been dying for this cleansing dip all day.

Moving toward the water, she gazed gratefully up at the full moon. Not only did it light her way, but it lent a certain magic to the cove. Moonlight trailed across its surface, making an enchanted path for her to follow. Stepping into it, she watched the beams scatter, dancing like a thousand tiny fairies around her.

Easing her way through the water, she was reluctant to disturb the tranquility with so much as a ripple. It felt warm and silky, and she could imagine cloaking herself in it, using the moonbeams for buttons. Wading to her waist, she felt the soft breeze blow in from the river, caressing her bare shoulders, filling each breath she drew with the whiff of late spring blooms. The night truly was all moonlight and magnolias.

Stroking quietly toward the dock, she thought of the children and hoped they weren't upset that she'd skipped dinner. The moment she was done here, she'd go upstairs to tuck them in and explain that she hadn't wanted to intrude on Drew and Stephen's first night together as father and son.

Floating on her back, gazing up at a star-studded sky, she smiled as she thought of Drew's expression this morning. How proud he'd seemed staring after his son. How happy.

When his gaze had drifted to her, the smile might have slipped a bit, but at least he hadn't been scowling.

"He's beginning to accept me," she whispered

to the stars. "Maybe even trust me."

One of these nights when he came home for supper, before he buried himself in his study, she was going to screw up her courage and talk to him, heart to heart.

She'd start with telling him what had been in her purse that day. He must still be wondering, maybe even guessing it was the jewels, so why not explain? To Drew, avoiding the truth would seem as devious as outright lying.

And she really should warn him about the sugar cane that would soon arrive. Presenting a *fait accompli* had seemed a good idea at the time, but the more she learned about Drew, the more she understood how he valued honesty. He'd probably get mad, maybe even stubbornly refuse the shipment, but he'd respect her more for telling the truth.

It was just a matter of timing. If she picked her moment right, used the right words, surely this new, almost-smiling Drew would understand. She need only be honest with him and, somehow, they could work things out.

Or so she thought until she turned to swim back and found him waiting on the shore.

He wore no shirt or shoes, only his rolled-up trousers. Hands on hips, legs stretched and planted, he towered over the water like some pagan god. He was utterly beautiful, yet as unattainable as the moon shining above.

Stiff, wary, he watched her. With a gulp, she wondered how long he'd been there.

Swimming slowly, she prayed he hadn't heard her whispers. What could she say to him? Before we have our little heart-to-heart, would you mind handing me my . . .

Twenty feet away from her clothes, she remembered she'd taken them off.

"Hi." Squatting in waist-high water, she felt awkward and silly. She almost added, "What's a nice guy like you doing in a place like this?" but it was as well she resisted the urge. Clearly, Drew was in no mood for levity.

Eyes probing her, he spoke with clipped precision. "We have to talk."

Ominous words, the kind men use as a prelude to, "I'm seeing someone else," or "I want a divorce." The emotionless tone didn't help, nor did his penetrating gaze. Trapped in the water, Monica felt the slow, throbbing pressure of doom.

"I've been talking to Abbie."

She couldn't guess the content of their conversation, but the way his sister had been acting lately, whatever she might have told Drew couldn't be good. "Abbie?" Monica repeated stupidly.

"She thinks you know where the jewels are."

Oh, yes, not good at all. "I-I don't have them."

"Please. Don't lie to me. Elizabeth says you found them. And now they're gone."

Monica's dream world crashed down around her shoulders. She'd always had a lousy sense of timing. Why had she waited so long to explain? It was too late now to stop him from jumping to all the wrong conclusions.

Forgetting her nakedness, she waded closer, pleading with him anyway. "I found the jewels, yes, but I didn't tell you because I didn't want you thinking I was Monique. You're always ready to believe the worst of me; and, well, who else but Monique could know where to find them? But I swear, I never meant to take them for myself. Trust me, they're in a safe place now. I—"

"Dammit, Nicki, just tell me the truth."

She didn't know if it was the pleading note or the fact that he called her Nicki, but the panic suddenly left her. "I am telling the truth," she said evenly. "I gave them to Darcy to sell. He has a relative in New York who can get the best price for them."

"Is that how he bought the cane?"

So the sugar had already come. "Believe it or not, I meant to tell you," she told him quietly, "but I didn't want you thinking I didn't believe in you or that you could save River's Edge. I'm a coward—I could never quite work up the courage to explain."

Looking up into eyes so guarded they could have belonged to a stranger, she grew conscious of her nakedness, her vulnerability. Longingly, she thought of her abandoned pile of clothes.

"Why?" he demanded, taking hold of her arms.

"The jewels never belonged to me," she tried to explain. "They're part of the estate—it's only right that they be used to keep it going."

His grip tightened. "No, I mean why did you pay Stargell? Why buy the cane?"

Even dressed, she realized, she could never hide from him. It was more than her body he saw when he gazed at her like this; he was looking down into her soul. "That day on the steamboat . . . I saw your face . . . and, well, I know how much this place means to you. I . . ."

Looking into his eyes, she could not say another word. She could only drown in the longing and need and desire.

"You're not Monique." Husky now, his quiet tone rang with conviction. And wonder. "My God, you actually *are* this Monica Ryan."

And then he was sweeping her into his arms, alternately kissing her and whispering in her ear. "Ah, Nicki, I did want to believe the worst, but you never let me. Listening to Abbie, then Elizabeth, I kept thinking, no, there's some explanation. God, woman, have you any idea how much you mean to me?"

Throwing her arms around his neck, she was kissing him, too—on his face, his neck, his chest. "Tell me."

"You're so soft. So warm. I want to wrap myself inside you." He pulled her against him, hoisting her up until her legs straddled his waist. Moving, he eased them both into the water. "I've been going crazy since that night in your room—aching to touch you, hold you. It's hard accepting a miracle. I don't know how to act."

"Kiss me, Drew. That'll do fine for now."

And he did, cradling her head with his hands, letting the water support her weight as he waded into its languorous warmth. Moonbeams danced around them; the river whispered along the shore, but all Monica knew was that her dreams had at last come true.

Reaching down, helping him loosen and then kick out of his trousers, she remembered once wanting him to take her like this, pushed up against a wall; but, oh, how more seductive it was here in the warm, silky water. Nestled in a soft cocoon of sensation, her body came alive to his sure, yet gentle touch.

And as Drew kissed her breasts, drew them into his hot mouth, it was *her* body he aroused. Gone was the insane urgency, the blind greed to possess his flesh. With her love and his recongition of it, they had banished Monique for good. Together.

Making love became a wondrous discovery. Touching him, tasting him, she knew a slow, building need to please this one man alone, to hold him forever close to her heart. And as she opened herself, she felt Drew fill all the empty places inside. It was incredible, so perfect, so . . .

She stopped thinking then, losing herself in sensation. The water caressed her skin as Drew turned them slowly, pulsing to life deep inside her. Waves of pleasure coursed throughout her body; and he began to move faster, thrust deeper, and she was crying into his ear, "Yes, yes," yet still he kept kissing her, filling her, swirling his agile tongue around her own. "Oh, yes, more, more," until with a burst of incredible joy, she seemed to shatter into a million shimmering pieces.

A shattering that somehow made her whole.

And then Drew was groaning, "Yes, oh, God, Nicki, yes!" as he clasped her tight and shuddered the length of his wonderful body.

Drew held her close to him, savoring the wonder of their joining, feeling strong and utterly invincible. "Oh, Nicki," he sighed, unable to put his emotions into words. For all the times he'd ever loved a woman, never once had he felt this complete.

Reluctantly easing himself out of her body, he set his wife gently on her feet. She leaned against him, resting her head on his chest with a quick little sniff.

She was crying? "God, Nicki, I lost track . . . I got so . . ." He lifted up her chin, making her look at him. "The last thing I wanted was to hurt you."

"No." She sniffed again and swiped at her eyes. "Oh, Drew, do I look like I'm hurt? I told you I'm hopeless. I always cry when things are too beautiful to bear."

He found himself grinning. "Then maybe I should be crying, too, because I've never seen anything more beautiful than the way you're looking at me right now."

"I love you."

Yes, she did. It had always been there, staring out from her extraordinary eyes, but he'd been too blind to see it. There had been no need to ask about the cane; deep down, he'd known all along only Nicki could have bought it.

He leaned down to kiss her, to try to begin expressing the love—the outright gratitude—brimming inside him, but he should have realized what the taste of her lips would do.

Pulling back reluctantly, he smiled down at her. "You do know we're liable to be caught. They may be asleep at the house, but there could still be boats on the river."

"You could see me from the house? Is that why you were so stern?"

It was hard to see, even in the moonlight; but, knowing her as he did, he guessed she was blushing. "From halfway down the drive at least. And if I seemed stern, it was me I was angry at. I was half-undressed before I realized why I was charging into the water after you."

Yes, definitely blushing. "Come on," he said gently, taking her hand to lead her to shore. "Let's go back to the house."

"What you said before," she asked tentatively, "does it mean you believe me now? You know I'm not Monique?"

Leaning down for her clothes, he shook his head. "It's crazy. I can't begin to guess how it happened, but I do know you can't possibly be. What you did, buying that cane . . ."

"I-I just wanted to help."

"I know." Sliding the dress over her shoulders, he turned her around to fasten the buttons. "But that's just it. Monique would have found a hundred ways to use the money on herself, but you chose to invest in me, in our future."

"Then you're not angry?"

He reached for her, holding her close. "If anything, I feel humbled. No one has ever put such trust in me. I thank God for sending you here, Monica Ryan."

"Sumner. It's Monica Sumner now."

"Ah, yes, my wife. My lovely, loving wife." Tilting her chin, he kissed her again.

"But I'm not lovely. I'm nothing like what you see now. In my other life, I'm overweight and plain."

"I don't want to hear it," he told her sternly. "It isn't your face or body that draws me—it's what I find when I look in your eyes. You could hide in a hundred other forms, but I'd still see the woman inside. Don't you see? It's Nicki I want, Nicki I love."

"Stop, or you'll start me crying again."

"Can't have that," he said, sweeping her up into his arms. "I have other plans for you, most of which involve my bedroom. Let's go home, Mrs. Sumner."

"But you can't carry me all the way. She wriggled in his arms. "I'm too heavy, you'll break your back."

Reluctantly, with a long kiss, he set her down.

"All right, but only because I have all that cane yet to plant. It might have been nice to use your skirts to hide the fact that I'm buck naked, though."

"Oh, that's right," she said with a grin. "Your pants are still in the water."

He looked at the cove. "Maybe we can come back tomorrow night to get them."

"Maybe." Her grin turned adorably shy as she bent down for his shirt. "Here, we'll just wrap this around you," she said, tucking the sleeves at his waist. "It should take care of the vital parts, but I do suggest you run."

Giggling, she took off for the house. Chasing after her, laughing himself, Drew realized how little fun he'd had of late. It was like being reborn, having this woman tease him, love him. With Nicki at his side, maybe he could believe in miracles after all.

Making love to her throughout the night, in the big, pine bed that had been too long empty, that *maybe* evolved into a definite conviction. She was his miracle, this incredibly giving person; Nicki was indeed his silver lining.

As they lay together afterward, he longed to ask about every single detail of her other life, but she was already dozing off, looking so serene and happy he contented himself with holding her close. There would be time to talk later; they'd have years to discover each other. Drifting off to sleep, he smiled, thinking of the long, happy days ahead.

Early the next morning, Elizabeth poked her head through the door of her uncle's room. He was still sleeping but she could not bear to wait a moment more. "Uncle Drew?" she asked as she neared the bedside. "Tell me, please. What did you find out about Nicki?"

It was then that she noticed he wasn't alone. "I talked real nice," he said with a grin, placing a kiss on the top of Nicki's head. "And I do believe she's staying."

Monique

March 15, 1866:

Widowhood, I've found, is not all that convenient.

For two years, I was on my own—an eternity of fending off offers of marriage from every fool in Louisiana. Could they not see that if I had to find a man to take care of me, it would not be anyone here in the South, where the air of defeat still clung to the air? Far better to ally myself with one of the Union soldiers I'd been entertaining—a wealthy one, with the means of getting me what I want.

Even Anton Byers had the gall to propose, after the obligatory, oh-so-proper period of mourning. I very nearly asked what made him think I would spend my life with as loathsome a creature as he; but, in time, I remembered that I must humor him, stall him, until I could learn what he saw the night of Robert's death.

It was uneasy time, sidestepping Byers so as not to show my derision and trying to live on what little remained of the estate. The more I learned of how my fool of a husband mismanaged his plantation, the more I wanted to scream. Abbie insisted we must scrimp and save to keep the place from falling down about our ears, but I soon grew sick of her long faces and dire predictions. Why should I suffer, after all, when River's Edge would go to the children?

With Robert gone, I had thought, ah, at last I can be with Drew, but a letter came from Washington, reporting him missing in battle. Damn the man, I'd thought as I read that missive; what use is he to me dead, or even crippled?

For months I wandered about, distraught and undecided; but I'd come to the conclusion that I must marry a Yankee, one rich enough to buy River's Edge for me before it was sold for taxes, when I saw Drew coming up the River Road.

Oh, what joy I felt as I watched him ride over the hill. One glance, seeing him sit so tall and erect in his saddle, and I was aching again, burning to feel his naked body next to mine. He is my weakness, that man, a beckoning light on a dark horizon; and for a helpless moment, I let myself forget how deeply I'd travelled into Rachel's world. Trembling with need, I ran to him.

But as it had been the first time we met, it was not me he saw as he neared. All his yearning, all his love, was aimed at the damned house. It hit me then, like a slap to the face, that I would never hold a place in his life.

I am ashamed to say I wanted him still.

Though my infatuation cooled as he went on his rampage of reform. Appalled by the condition of the plantation, Drew changed everything, from the time of our meals to who would or would not be welcomed there. First to go were my Yankees, but next was Anton Byers. Drew said we could ill-afford to pay a man who spent more time chasing after me than giving the children lessons. That was one decision I applauded.

But then, one day, Byers demanded I run off with him. I needed a husband, he insisted; I couldn't stay alone at River's Edge. He hoped I wasn't fool enough to think Drew Sumner would marry me.

When I asked why not, he went as stiff as his collar, no doubt guessing this was why I'd refused him. "Because I shall talk to him," he said righteously. "That is why not."

And so he did. I cannot know precisely what they talked about, closeted in the study for two long hours, but I did learn later that Byers questioned Robert's death. When Drew demanded proof, Byers grew nasty. He could prove I was an unfit mother, he threatened. Indeed, perhaps it was his duty to have the children taken away.

I was told this when Drew called me into his study after the man left. "I will ask you once," he said icily. "Did you or did you not poison my brother?"

I almost sighed in relief. The toad had seen nothing if he thought I'd *poisoned* Robert. I told Drew no—how could he think such a thing?—without having to tell a single lie.

Still, Drew did not seem relieved. Looking at me with disgust, he swore that if I ever gave him reason to think otherwise, he would not hesitate to put me behind bars.

He then informed me we would be married, but only to protect the children—not out of any desire on his part. Make no mistake, he warned. Ours would be a marriage of convenience, for he meant never to touch me again.

Angered by his attitude, I almost told him the truth about Stephen and Elizabeth, just for spite; but I saw I might better use such ammunition later. I wanted to make certain he suffered the proper amount of guilt and remorse. And once he got to know and love the brats, perhaps I could use the children against him.

Moments after our quick and businesslike wedding, Drew was back to giving orders. Rachel was banished from the plantation: He'd learned of her magic and wanted her nowhere near the children. There was no reason to contact my "acquaintances" in the city either. Now that my townhouse must be sold to pay off my debts, I would have nowhere to entertain in New Orleans anyway.

In short, I was to become the ideal wife and mother—staying at home, learning to perform my duties from Abbie. When I asked what he'd do if I refused, he told me I had two choices—I could do things his way or I could go to jail.

I doubt he meant his threat. If he suspected I had anything to do with his brother's death, he'd never let me near the precious children.

Still, I feared the power of the Sumner name. It was one thing to dismiss the ravings of a fool like Anton Byers; but should the victim's brother begin speaking of foul play, others would listen. I might as well have poisoned my husband for all the good my protests would do.

An intolerable situation. I cannot live as a prisoner again, not even for Drew; nor can I live out my days as a nun.

This is why I crept out of the house last night to visit Rachel's cabin in the swamp. I told her how life is strangling me, how my husband is driving me mad.

She smiled her secret smile and asked if I wished her to make another doll. Yet as angry as I was at him, I found I could not bear to imagine Drew, crumpled and broken like Robert, all by my hand.

When I said no, she nodded; but I could see she was displeased. She hates Drew, perhaps even fears him; and she no doubt hoped I would get rid of him for her.

Turning away, she reached for a small brown pouch from her altar. Composed as she faced me, she said she had a talisman, a source of power far greater than any other charm or spell.

Her smile was sly, as if she knew I held my breath, that my heart beat three times its normal rate. I didn't care what she saw. I knew my destiny waited inside that bag.

Sighing dramatically, she withdrew a ring, a band of two twining silver serpents. The Gem of Zombi, she explained, holding it in her outstretched palm. A priceless token passed down from mother to daughter long before her family was taken from Africa. Inside it dwelt the powers of the awesome snake-god, Le Gran Zombi Himself.

If I were prepared to study and learn and to perform whatever He might ask of me, one day Zombi would show me the means to escape my stifling life.

She spoke these words with a hushed reverence, an awe I understood for I had felt the power of that snake-god of hers. As I reached out to stroke the contours of the ring, a dark, pulsing energy flowed through my veins. There was a hissing, as if the writhing serpents spoke to me, offering vistas of a world beyond my comprehension.

Throbbing with a black, mystical force, it calls to me, that immortal serpent, compelling me to join it.

I must seize the power it offers. And once I do, I shall never let go.

Eighteen

John Foxworth, lately known as Jacques Reynard, looked up at the pale southern beauty gazing at him with such admiration. He rose to his feet, swelling with pride. When Sarah Jane Hawkins walked into his shop, he no longer saw himself as a mere pawnbroker, scraping and clawing to make his fortune. He became a man of business, a gentleman, every bit the cultured Creole he tried so hard to be.

One day soon, he meant to ask for her hand in marriage. He'd heard the rumors, knew her daddy was one step shy of the poorhouse, and it made him grateful that she might just turn to him. It wasn't money he wanted, nor beauty, nor any other superficial measure of a woman's worth. To Jacques, Miss Sarah was the epitome of gentility and good breeding, eons removed from the Boston slum in which he'd been raised.

And because of this, he would happily slave dawn to dusk to earn their fortune, just to have a lady like Sarah Jane to grace his house.

"A good friend is celebrating his birthday," she explained in a slow, cultural drawl, "and I need something special to wear to the occasion. Nothing too expensive, mind you. Papa would have absolute apoplexy if he knew I was in here looking at jewelry."

"Then please, if I may be so bold, let me present a gift. A way of thanking you for adding such light to this humble shop. And perhaps, if I may be bolder still, to express my hopes for the future?"

She blushed, demurred prettily, but Jacques could see her delight. "With your permission, I shall be calling upon your papa later this week; but please, you must choose some token in the meantime. Anything that strikes your fancy. Nothing could give me greater pleasure than to know my gift adorns your delicate beauty."

"That ring! It can't be. Where did you get it?"

Thinking more of pearls, Jacques was shocked when she pointed to the Gem of Zombi. "A woman, a neighbor of yours, in fact. Mrs. Sumner begged me to hold it until the end of the month."

"I want it," she said, stabbing at the ring. "That is the gift I want."

"But, no! Anything but that." Jacques was genuinely distressed. A symbol of an ancient African culture, as well as the subject of a curious legend, the ring could prove to be worth a small fortune.

She looked at him with hurt surprise. "But you said I could have anything. This ring is what strikes my fancy."

He could not bear to see her disappointment. What did it matter? he told himself firmly. Soon they'd be wed and the ring would revert to him anyway. He had not meant to sell it just yet; and its owner, well, he knew the signs of poverty. He'd never truly believed Mrs. Sumner would return.

"Very well," he said reluctantly, lifting it out and threading it on a chain. "As long as you promise never to set it on your finger."

"Why ever not?"

He felt foolish explaining the legend; surely it was mere superstition. "The metal is old," he told her instead, "and might discolor your exquisite skin. Promise me, *ma chérie,* you will wear it only upon this chain."

Laughing daintily, she took the gift from his hand. "Very well, if you insist. Thank you so much, Mr. Reynard."

"Please, you must call me Jacques."

Thanking him again by name, she turned to dance out the door. Bemused by the picture she made, he did not think to add the reminder that it might be best if she did not show the ring to anyone, at least not until the end of the month.

It will be fine, he told himself; Mrs. Sumner would not be back. There was no need to worry.

Or so he believed until the next day, when Colonel Darcy O'Brien stood glaring at him from across the counter. "You what?" the man demanded in a low, forceful growl.

"I told you, I gave it as a gift."

"To whom?" The words were shot at him, as if bursting from the pistol at Colonel O'Brien's side.

"My financée," he blustered, trying not to feel defensive. "Miss Hawkins."

"Sarah Jane Hawkins?"

Jacques had barely nodded before O'Brien turned away. "God help you," the man tossed over his shoulder as he strode out of the shop, "if something should happen to any one of those women."

*   *   *

Monica hurried into her room with a ewer of water, intent upon making herself look respectable. It would be some work after a morning spent cleaning the grates in the upstairs bedrooms. Filling the basin with tepid water, she tried not to frown. Oh, what she wouldn't give for a long, soaking bath!

Each time she mentioned indoor plumbing, Abbie argued, no doubt seeing the suggestion as just another snobbish renovation. Still, Monica was determined to have the pipes installed the minute the plantation began to see a profit again. She could never hope for Judith's ultra-modern bathrooms, but other houses of this period had hot and cold running water. Some even had a decent tub.

Not that she objected to the nightly trips to the cove, she thought dreamily. For the past few weeks, they might do their separate chores by day—Drew planted; she worked in the house—but every night they met at the cove, each joining more magical than the last. Amazing, the things he could make her body do, make it feel. At long last, she understood what the fuss was all about, how loving could bring so much joy to a woman. Each time Drew touched her, or even looked at her, he made her feel beautiful—inside and out.

And later, in bed, nestled in each other's arms, they would talk—about the past and about the future they would build together. When he spoke about war's deprivations and the cruelties of prison, Drew swore his children would be spared such horrors. Monica explained about her parents, how all she'd had after their deaths was Judith and how she'd make certain Stephen, Andrew, and Elizabeth never suffered such a lonely, unhappy childhood.

Yet somehow, she could never bring herself to mention the ring. Better that Drew never knew what it was that had brought her here, for the silver serpents seemed to cast a shadow over her happiness, an ugliness she must find a way to banish. The moment she received the money from Darcy, she meant to retrieve that awful band and toss it into the river.

Washing herself, scrubbing as if she could wash away such unpleasant thoughts, she concentrated on what she would say to Sarah Jane on her visit this afternoon. Somehow, she must charm the woman, make her see that Monique was now *Nicki,* who was not, nor ever would be, her enemy.

Not that she'd confide the truth—she and Drew agreed that most would regard such claims of time travel as outright lunacy—but she had to put a stop to the constant barbs and the way Sarah Jane influenced Abbie against her.

More than anything, Monica wanted to reestablish the easy comraderie with her sister-in-law. It hurt that she remained stiff and wary. Maybe if Sarah Jane would unbend a bit, Abbie would come to accept Nicki as her friend.

Dressing in a plain skirt and blouse, she told herself that, above all, she must be patient with both women. Patience had paid off with the children. And Drew.

As they did at least three thousand times a day, her thoughts went instantly to her husband. Hugging herself, she marvelled at how he had moved into this room—and her heart—with such ease. It was as if he had always been there.

She smiled at his comb and brush, nestled up close to hers on the dresser. Stroking the gold handle, wanting to feel the warmth of Drew's touch, she happened to glance at her own brush. Uneasily, she noticed that once more, the hair was missing.

It didn't make sense. If Abbie had come in to tidy up, why clean her brush and not Drew's?

As if called, she whirled to face the long window. Her feet started forward. Before she could think what she was doing, she was lifting the window to step out to the gallery.

Even before she looked down to the road, she knew she would find Rachel.

Staring up at her, the woman clutched something in her hand. It was too far away to see what it was, nor could she make out Rachel's indistinct features, yet Monica could still sense her hateful, triumphant smile.

She felt pulled by the malevolent gaze, tugged closer, and once again her feet began to move on their own.

Rachel turned suddenly to look up the River Road. Sound rushed into Monica's mind, the rapid thud of an approaching horse, filling the vacuum she hadn't realized was there. As if waking, she found herself poised at the top of the gallery steps. Looking back over her shoulder, she could no longer see Rachel, but she could still feel the malice.

She fled to her room, knowing on some subconscious level that it was Rachel who had been in her room.

The only question was why.

*   *   *

Cursing the nag, the sad remains of her papa's once-fine stable, Sarah Jane badgered the animal to pick up its pace. At this rate, she would never reach River's Edge.

Sometimes it felt as if everything conspired against her. First it was papa's post-bourbon maladies, then the agent arriving to negotiate the sale of Bel Monde. Did no one care that this was her one chance to gloat? That she could scarcely wait to see Monique's reaction when she learned just who had her ring?

Sarah Jane saw the slave, Rachel, standing in the middle of the road as if to block her way. What was that dreadful woman doing, lurking about Abbie's house?

Armed with self-righteous indignation, Sarah Jane stopped the cart and secured the nag to a fence post. As she marched toward the black woman, she heard Rachel chuckle softly. Following her gaze, Sarah Jane noticed Monique on the upstairs gallery, scurrying back into her room.

Incensed, she became convinced that those two were plotting again. "What are you doing here?" she lashed out, holding her riding crop in both hands. "I believe Mr. Sumner told you to stay away from this house."

Rachel merely smiled in her slow, insolent fashion. "It's a free country now." She spoke more like a haughty queen than a slave. "And this is a public road."

Sarah Jane's grip tightened on the riding crop. Ever since the war, these people had been getting more and more above themselves. "You go on, now," she said, using the crop in a shooing motion.

Rachel raised a brow. "Do you forget who

makes the gris-gris to lure your Creole into proposing marriage?"

Looking quickly around, Sarah Jane hoped no one could hear. Few would understand why she'd resorted to Rachel's nonsense, but it didn't bear thinking on—the prospect of spending the rest of her days catering to Papa's demands in some ramshackle cottage in town.

"You should not threaten me," Rachel went on, "when the man has not yet declared himself."

"But he has!" Reaching under her dress, Sarah Jane pulled out the chain. As she watched the woman's eyes widen at the sight of the ring, she puffed up with pride. "See? He gave me this as a token of his intentions." At least she hoped he had.

Seeing her doubt, Rachel pounced. "Did he ask you? Or talk to your papa?"

"Well, no, but—"

Rachel shook her head sadly. "It takes powerful magic to bring a man to the altar."

In her heart, Sarah Jane knew the woman was right. How else could Monique steal Robert away, if not for Rachel's voodoo? "What must I do?"

"To have your Creole, you must give me the ring."

Sarah Jane shook her head. No, she had to gloat. She'd been living for the moment when she could finally say, "Here, Monique, now I have something *you* want."

But Rachel clearly had other plans. Her dark eyes settled on Sarah Jane, pinned her.

"I can't." Sarah Jane tried to protest, but she felt swallowed by a stronger will. "It was a present," she went on feebly, her resolve melting the more she looked into those eyes. "You don't understand—Jacques will be . . . he'll be . . ."

Rachel held out her hand. "Give me the ring, Miz Sarah," she said in a cadence both soft and soothing to the ear. "Give me the ring now."

Her words flowed around Sarah Jane like a dream, hypnotic and compelling, until she was unclasping the chain and placing it in Rachel's hand.

In less than a blink, the black hand closed over the ring and concealed it from view.

Jolted awake, Sarah Jane reached out for it, but Rachel was already gone. Sarah Jane pulled back her hand, appalled by how it was shaking. She had just made a dreadful mistake.

She stumbled to the house, seeing it as a refuge, until she saw Monique hurry down the porch steps.

"You!" she cried out. "It's all your fault!"

Abbie was hard put not to smile as she watched her brother with the children. How adorable the four of them looked, covered head to foot in flour as they struggled to fix their surprise. None of them really knew what this *pizza* should look like; but since Nicki mentioned longing for the taste, they were determined to make it for her.

It was meant as a surprise, to celebrate the second full month Nicki had been with them. Ironically, while Drew planned his surprise, Nicki set up the last details of *his* party. Bless those youngsters for being consummate actors—Drew hadn't a clue that they would also be celebrating his birthday tonight.

Abbie sighed as she returned to her own work, the elaborate cake she'd promised both conspirators she'd bake. As she stirred the batter, she sneaked glances at her brother. She hated to admit it, but she had never seen him happier. Drew was madly in love.

Nor was he alone in this. She'd seen the way Nicki's eyes sought her husband in the distance, how they softened whenever they found him. Anyone who looked at the pair could see they shared a quiet, yet deep understanding.

Yet as envious as this made her, Abbie knew Nicki had put the smile back on her brother's face. For that alone, she supposed she could forgive the woman anything.

Though Drew was not smiling now; he was frowning at the dough he and the children were kneading. "I think we've pushed this around long enough, Abbie. What's next?"

Laughing, she told them to set the dough back in the bowl and let it be for an hour or so. Drew, with an eye to his fields, promised he'd return as soon as she called for him. The children scampered off to play.

Alone in her kitchen, Abbie put the cake in the oven and gathered the items she'd need to decorate it. She wanted everything perfect. It was time, she'd decided, for her and Nicki to be friends. The devil with what Sarah Jane said. Anyone who could love Drew like Nicki did couldn't be that much a monster.

As if to deny this, Sarah Jane's screech broke through the still, afternoon air. Alarmed, Abbie rushed outside to the front of the house. "It was you and her, conspiring together," she heard her neighbor shout. "You are to blame."

Nicki shook her head, seeming as confused as Abbie by the woman's behavior. "I think you should come in and sit down, Sarah Jane," she soothed. "You look terribly pale."

"And no wonder. I'll wager you set her on me. You knew I had it and you wanted to get it back. I-I . . ." To everyone's amazement and dismay, Sarah Jane broke into tears.

"Come, let's just get you into the house." Nicki held out her hands, only to have them slapped away.

"Let me." Stepping up to support Sarah Jane, Abbie realized it was Nicki's aid she'd come to, not her friend's. "Nicki's right, you know. You should be sitting down."

Leading Sarah Jane into the parlor, feeling her trembling, Abbie sat them on the huge, old sofa. As she rubbed the woman's icy hands, she was surprised to find they were alone in the room, that Nicki hadn't followed.

"What happened?" Abbie prompted, knowing Sarah Jane was more apt to confide in her without Nicki there.

"It-it was as if I couldn't help myself—she made me give it to her."

"What did Nicki make you give?"

"Not her. That—that Rachel. She made me give back Monique's ring."

Abbie heard the gasp. Looking up, she saw Nicki had returned with a glass of water. "Ring?" Nicki asked in a strange voice as she offered the glass to their guest.

Sipping, Sarah Jane began to recover. "That snake ring. Jacques—Monsieur Reynard—gave it to me as a token of his . . . his regard."

"No." It was Nicki's turn to go pale. "He promised."

"Not all men are your devoted slaves, Monique. With your vanity, it wouldn't occur to you that

Jacques actually prefers me."

"You gave the ring to Rachel?" Nicki asked with an urgency that was fast becoming contagious.

"You heard me. I already said that I did."

"Do you know if she put it on her hand?"

"Why?" Sarah Jane looked at Nicki queerly. "Jacques said something against wearing it. Why shouldn't we?"

Nicki grabbed Sarah Jane by the shoulders. "I have to know," she pressed, her voice tight with strain. "Did Rachel put the ring on her hand?"

"How am I to know? She took it and ran off."

Nicki backed away, her expression both frightened and frightening.

"What is it?" Abbie asked, catching her fear.

"I don't know. I have to think. I-I'll be upstairs."

When Abbie would have gone after her, Sarah Jane clutched her arm. "It will be all right now," the woman said bitterly. "Thanks to Rachel, Monique will soon have what she wants and she'll leave us alone."

Listening, Abbie heard her sister-in-law hurry up the stairs, each step making her heart beat faster. She'd seen the look on Nicki's face. Deep down, she feared Sarah Jane was wrong. Things were far from all right.

Li'l Bit reached under her pillow, feeling the cool black leather. It always unsettled her to touch it, this legacy from her mother; but after hearing Nicki and Sarah Jane, she figured there were scarier things to be faced.

Maybe it was time she took Mama's book to Nicki.

Li'l Bit could hear her down the hall, pacing across her room. Going to the door, easing it open a crack, she heard Nicki ask, "Maybe Monique's spirit is inside Rachel. That could be why she hates me so."

Li'l Bit blinked, confused. Who was Nicki speaking to and what was she talking about?

"I have to find out," she went on, and Li'l Bit realized she was talking to herself. "With the ring, Monique can reclaim her body whenever she wants. I have to stop her."

Glancing back at her pillow, Li'l Bit made her decision. Nicki was upset and the black book would probably upset her more; but Nicki needed to know about Mama as much as she did. And unlike herself, Nicki could read.

While she might not know what or why or how, Li'l Bit sensed there was something in the book that would help Nicki stop Mama from ever coming back to hurt them.

Running to the bed, she snatched the book out from under her pillow. She hurried out into the hallway and down to Mama's room.

But when she got there, Nicki was already gone.

Monique

March 29, 1867:

Tonight will be the night.

It is strange, when I think of all the time I've wasted, turning and twisting in my empty bed, aching to feel Drew pulsing within me. I should have known no man could ever satisfy me completely. What I need, what I seek, is to be possessed by a god. To be one with Le Gran Zombi.

Some might say I have been seduced away from the world of the living; but, ah, they cannot have felt the ecstasy the serpent offers.

And in truth, what does Drew offer but a lifetime of drudgery? Rejection.

With Zombi's help, I can have another life, in another time.

For this is the secret of the Gem of Zombi, Rachel confided last night, pleased at how I have given myself to her rituals. Watching her black snake twine about my naked limbs, she pronounced me ready, that Zombi Himself has granted His blessing.

And tonight, she promises, I shall ride the serpent to wherever He wishes me to go.

There is, she warns, a price to pay. He is a hungry god, her Zombi; His appetite must be assuaged. He will find me new life, yes; but in exchange, I must give Him the soul that now dwells inside the body I take.

I said "Yes, of course, anything," and with a maddening lack of speed, she reached into her pocket. I gaped at her, for she held a second, duplicate ring, one she would pass down to a Sumner bride in the future.

According to legend, she explained, the rings would form a link between the present and the future, a conduit through which two souls could pass. My job was to make certain no soul ever found its way to my current body. There could be serious consequences if Zombi's hunger was never appeased.

Once more, I said "Yes, of course," but I barely heard her. Rachel is a good slave and an able teacher, but I am ready to strike out on my own.

Tonight, all alone, I shall travel through time.

Nineteen

Abbie stood at the foot of the stairs, wondering if she should go up and talk to Nicki. Sarah Jane had insisted she "Leave well enough alone," but with their neighbor gone, Abbie became more and more convinced Nicki needed her.

As she took the first step, she heard the thunder of an approaching horse. Wondering what could have upset Sarah Jane now, she went to the door.

It wasn't Sarah Jane; it was Darcy.

Her heart did flip-flops as she hurried to greet him. Visibly upset, he jumped from his horse, barely managing to stop it. Before she could soothe him, though, he called out, "Where's Nicki?"

Abbie nodded at the door, feeling like she'd been tossed in an icy lake. She didn't trust herself to speak, knowing her envy and resentment would spill out in torrents.

"Got to . . . find out . . . about the Gem . . . of Zombi." He huffed out the words, trying to catch his breath.

"Gem?" It was no use; the bad feelings came rushing out anyway. "Darcy O'Brien, how could you buy her jewelry? Drew is your best friend!"

"Buy her . . . Abbie, what are you talking about?"

"She makes every man buy her things and then tosses them over for someone richer and more exciting. Can't you see she's using you to get back at Drew?"

"Is that what you think?" He grabbed her by the arms, gazing down at her like no one had ever looked at her before. Then to her utter amazement, he kissed her so thoroughly she couldn't think at all. "That," he said hoarsely as he pulled away, "should show you how wrong you are."

She stood there, gaping at him, touching her tender lips with her fingers.

"This is one hell of a time for a declaration; but if I'm going to make a fool of myself over a woman, Abbie, it'll be over you. I love you, and I mean to make you my wife; but right this moment, would you please tie up my horse so I can go talk to Nicki?"

"She's upstairs. In her room." Still dazed, she watched him stride to the front door. "But Darcy, what is this all about? What's wrong?"

"I'll explain later," he threw over his shoulder as he went into the house. "But I have a feeling Nicki is in grave danger."

Monique

March 14, 1980:

My first words in this journal were that the name Monique de Vereaux would someday be known in every salon in New Orleans. Isn't it ironic that I shall gain my fame and recognition as Judith Sumner instead?

I look down at my ring, the symbol of Zombi's power, and for the first time here in the future, mine is a genuine smile. Ever efficient Rachel. As promised, she must have passed the ring down to the day when poor unsuspecting *Judy* set the Gem of Zombi on her finger.

And when she did, Judy created the conduit, charting the course I could then follow into her body.

Ah, but my journey was incredible. Even now, I shudder with pleasure to think of that wild, sensual ride. It was hard to leave the serpent's grasp, harder still to send Judy's soul into it, but I was ever conscious of the need to reach my new life.

Still, I screamed when I first arrived in this

alarming new world of the future. Its noise, its strange machines and contrivances, all combined to stagger my mind. Like a baby ripped from its mother's womb, I took months to understand I had no need to shriek in protest, that I am right where I was always meant to be.

Today, I went to River's Edge.

Oh, the memories it brought back, standing before the house my third husband has now inherited. Gazing upon its weathered boards, I knew with a burst of revelation why the serpent sent me into this body.

My husband George might not have inherited the Sumner looks or charm, but he will, however unwittingly, hand River's Edge over to me.

Leaving him with the lawyers this afternoon, I went upstairs to my old bedroom, straight to the cubbyhole in my closet. To my joy, my jewels waited there, sparkling in all their splendor. I left them, my safeguard for the future, but I did take my journal.

I needed to recapture the Monique I'd once been, so the Judith I've become can gain her knowledge and strength. Together, body and spirit merged as one, Monique-Judith shall make certain George Sumner never puts his family home up for sale.

River's Edge is mine; I will share it with no one.

Li'l Bit heard footsteps on the stairs—heavy steps—and swiftly hid Mama's book behind her back. This was for Nicki to read and no one else.

She was glad she'd hidden it. Seconds later, that man, that Darcy, came charging into the room. "Where is she?" he barked at her.

Li'l Bit shook her head. He wanted Nicki—she knew it without being told—but he was the last person she'd confide in.

"It's important, Elizabeth. I must talk to her."

Again, she shook her head; but he didn't give up and go away. Instead, he came closer, hunkering down so he looked her in the eye. "I'm not here to hurt Nicki. I'm a friend who's concerned about her."

"You're from New . . . New, that place she's from. You want to take her back there."

"Don't you know by now Nicki loves you all too much to ever leave? Besides, I'm not going back to New York, either. I'm going to stay here and marry your Aunt Abbie."

Him and Abbie? Yes, that would be good. So good it made her smile.

"But right now," the man went on, "something is wrong with Nicki and I need your help finding her. Can you tell me where she went?"

Once more, she shook her head, but not in stubborn defiance. "I dunno. She was here a minute ago, talking about Rachel."

"Your mama's Rachel?"

The way he asked it, sharp and urgently, Li'l Bit got scared again. She remembered the day Rachel had come up to them and grabbed Nicki's wrist. Nicki had just stood there, not fighting, staring into Rachel's eyes.

No, she told herself. Nicki was scared of Rachel, and she hated the swamp. She'd never go to that ugly, old shack.

Would she?

In truth, Monica didn't know where she was

going. She'd been told Rachel lived in the swamp, and she assumed it must be somewhere near where she'd first arrived; but she couldn't remember the route Drew used to get back to the house.

She moved on instinct, as if an invisible string tugged her along. It felt like her destiny was mapped out before her and she need only follow the predetermined path.

Sure of her mission, relaxed about its successful outcome, she waved at Jasper as she passed by. In the distance, she could see Drew, shirtless as he worked in his fields, pausing to wipe the sweat from his brow.

For a moment, Monica felt so drawn to him, she nearly abandoned her mission. How could she have ever thought him Derek, when the physical resemblance was as superficial as her first husband? Drew exuded strength, honesty, caring; Derek had only an oily charm. Drew was right—it *was* the person underneath who made true beauty. It was hard, now, to imagine what she had ever seen in Derek.

Yet oddly enough, it was his voice she heard, a whistling whisper on the breeze faintly calling "Cuz?" Part of her responded to the scared-little-boy plea, yet a bigger part became frightened herself.

She felt cold suddenly and flooded by a gaping sense of loss. Drew, she thought, needing his warmth, longing for the sound of his voice; but when she glanced over her shoulder, neither he, nor even the fields, were in sight. She stood ankle-deep in the brackish water of the swamp.

Frozen, barely blinking, she wondered how she had gotten here. Overhead, the cypress branches twined so tightly she could no longer see or feel the sun. As if responding to the chill, or perhaps breeding out of it, a slow, curling fog wound like a snake about her feet. An awesome quiet closed around her, a silence so deep and muted she could have been standing in a tomb.

She had no idea how she had come to this awful place; and, worse, she didn't know how to get out.

Yet while a soft, dulled panic simmered inside her, outwardly, she remained serene and calm. Her mind might scream, "Run!" but her body was content to patiently wait there until whoever had summoned her came to lead her away.

She did not wait long. Rising up out of the haze, Rachel materialized on the high, dry ground before her. "You are here at last," she uttered, reaching out with a helping hand. "Come, it is time."

The calm part grasped the hand; but, deep inside Monica, a tiny, frantic voice was calling her husband's name.

"Drew!"

Straightening, Drew almost dropped the plow as he glanced around him. He felt foolish as he realized it wasn't his wife he heard; it must have been the breeze whistling through the cane.

Yet for a moment the sound had been so real he could have sworn Nicki stood at his side.

Must be all those nights they spent together, he thought with a grin. Loving, talking, holding each other close; no wonder they often knew what the other was about to say. It had gotten so he wondered how he'd ever existed without her.

In his mind, he saw Nicki as she'd looked the night they'd fought the rains. Half-drowned and covered with mud, she might not fit many descriptions of beauty, but she couldn't have looked lovelier to him. "We'll work together," she'd told him stubbornly. It was then, he now realized, that he'd first felt the load lift from his shoulders. For the first time, he had seen there was no need to struggle alone.

He dropped the plow. He had no wish to be by himself today, either. Wasn't getting much accomplished, mooning over his wife; he might as well go collect Nicki and sweep her up to their bedroom.

He'd tell Abbie and the kids he was distracting her while they finished the surprise, but he aimed to do far more than just divert Nicki. He wanted to fill her up so full of him they became one person. God, he wondered if he would ever get enough of that woman.

He grinned, this time a bit sheepishly. A few months back, he'd have been horrified to hear himself carrying on like a boy in the throes of first love; but what the hell, he *was* in love, for the first time in his life.

"Nicki," he whispered to her, the word soft and loaded with promise. "Wait for me, I'm coming."

Monique

March 19, 1993:

What a helpless feeling, facing death. For all my money, my power, and influence, the ugly, encroaching cancer might yet win. Unless, of course, I am right about the ring.

At this moment, the thieves I've hired are breaking into the Sumner crypt, opening the casket that holds the remains of Monique Sumner. If I am right, if my body was entombed with the Gem of Zombi on my finger, I shall soon have the matching pair.

I wish now that I had not destroyed my original journal, that I had more than its black leather cover to remind me of the past. At the time, though, it seemed my wisest choice. After George's death, then that of my sister and her husband, I could ill-afford to let such incriminating words fall into the wrong hands. As I told the handsome lieutenant who came nosing around with questions, their deaths were terrible accidents I want my niece to forget.

I could wish, however, that in my panic to cover

my tracks, I had not destroyed the last few pages. On them, I'd scribbled the chants Rachel taught me, the means of summoning Zombi to carry me away.

What if I don't remember them correctly? Or worse, what if the serpent chooses not to help me again?

No, it is my illness talking, clouding my judgment and sapping my confidence. Of course Zombi will come to my aid. He is hungry, is he not? And I have the soul he craves, carefully set in place.

Foolish Monica. Each time I see her chubby body or call her at that dreadful school, I know she means to defy me. But I did not dispose of her parents and play the dutiful guardian to be thwarted now. If it takes being cruel, or loving, or even a blend of both, I shall bring her around. After all, she wants a family; and I am all that she has left.

She will come, to please me; but I must offer more to keep her at River's Edge. As much as I have enjoyed seducing her suitors away, like I did with Abbie, it is now time to dangle the ideal husband before her. A man to give her children—a man who looks enough like Drew to be his twin.

My fingers grow numb and my arm is weak, and I can no longer write for any length of time. Another woman would rant and rave and curse the death that lingers round the corner, but I secretly smile with satisfaction.

I have my Monica, you see, and I have the ring.

Monica hesitated, looking at the ramshackle dwelling with a start. Confused, disoriented, she felt pulled in two different directions. Hazily, she could hear someone call her name, but she could not make herself turn and leave. Though she knew she must go—go now—she sensed it was somehow her destiny to enter the shack.

Boards warped and weathered, its roof sagging and porch posts ready to buckle, it seemed a sad, neglected structure. Little stirred in the dark trees or stagnant water around it, save for the large, black snake curving in and out of the splintered railing.

Monica might have stood there, staring and shivering indefinitely, had Rachel's cold and insistent hand not pulled her inside the squeaking door.

It was no more welcoming indoors; its single room was dark and dank, the feeble fire in the hearth merely deepening the shadows. Along the back wall, a black curtain fluttered eerily as if someone moved behind it; but, judging by the temperature of the room, it was more likely the chilly air seeping in the cracks of the walls.

The room was sparsely furnished: A straw mattress in the corner, a table and two chairs, a shelf filled with jars and unfamiliar implements on the near side of the curtain. Children did not play here; couples did not whisper love chants in the night. It was less a home and more a place for work to be done.

I'm here for a reason, she thought, trying to remember what it was. I must get what I came for and go. Quickly.

"You are chilled," Rachel said beside her. "I will make tea."

"Tea?" Monica repeated, her brain reacting slowly. "But we don't have any. Abbie says it's too expensive."

"I make my own. From herbs."

Herbal tea, Monica thought—warm, bracing, and good for your health. Though the way she felt now, she could probably use some caffeine.

Rachel crossed the dirt floor to the black pot simmering on a tripod in the hearth. As the woman lifted the lid, Monica caught a whiff of a wonderful fragrance. It brought home memories of rainy days in her childhood, the rare occasions Judith had time for her. Whenever they'd shared a pot of herbal tea, Judith seemed to become more the loving aunt Monica wished her.

An image flashed across her mind—Judith, screeching, her claw-like fingers reaching out with the ring. Cursing her, damning her . . .

Rachel appeared at her shoulder with the steaming cup and Monica reached for it gladly. She wanted to regain the good feelings, needed to erase the ugly deathbed scene from her mind. Shuddering, she gulped down the liquid, letting the warmth spill into her body.

As it filled her, becoming heat, Monica half-recognized the sensation. There was something familiar about it, almost unsettling; but she felt too relaxed to worry over it now. If the thought were important, it would catch up to her. If not, she'd enjoy the feeling, content to drift.

For that's how she felt as she wandered about the cabin, as if she lay on a raft in the river, lazing in the sun while the current pulled her along. Touching the crude furniture, running her fingers over the jars and odd-shaped tools, she floated toward her destiny.

Pulling back the curtain to face an elaborate altar, she knew she had arrived.

Her fingers trembled as she reached out for the

primitive doll lying prone among the many flickering candles. Jutting out of the doll's head was a long, piercing needle, attached to several yards of white thread. It, too, held an air of familiarity; but this time, she had no need to wait for the memory to find her.

Recognition filled her with an eerie, icy chill. The dress was made of her missing pink satin; the hair, so real, so alive, had come from her brush.

Repulsed, she almost dropped the doll, but perhaps her wits were not totally dulled. Reaching for the string, she yanked with all her might.

As it broke free, Rachel laughed behind her. "It is too late. The doll has already summoned you. The potion will keep you here now."

"No." In her mind, Monica said the word forcefully; but with her muscles losing strength by the moment, she could manage little more than a squeak. What had Rachel put in the tea?

Monica wanted to run, but her legs felt heavy. So did her arms, which dropped to her sides, letting the doll fall to the floor. Looking down at it, she noticed the snake. Coming in from the porch, it stealthily approached, its scales rasping across the packed dirt floor.

"I told you," Rachel said, closer now. "You do not belong here. You belong to the god."

"No," Monica repeated in a whisper, trying to plead her case, fighting the dark wall closing around her. The snake inched closer, hissing softly, as if urging Rachel to hurry.

"She is yours, oh Great Zombi," the black woman intoned, dropping to her knees before Monica. "He calls," she whispered. "You must go to him now."

Falling limply beside the doll, Monica remembered now why the warmth seemed so familiar. She'd felt the same dizzy detachment the night in Judith's room when she'd first put the ring on her finger.

Far off, she could hear Rachel chanting, the sound growing dimmer and dimmer. Unable to move, she watched the snake slither down her outstretched arm.

"No," Monica protested again as Rachel took her hand and slid the Gem Of Zombi on her finger. With horror, she thought of the Sumners, how she'd promised never to leave them. Li'l Bit would be devastated, not knowing why. And the boys, especially Stephen, would never trust a female again. She had to stay, had to finish teaching Li'l Bit to read, show the boys how to have fun, help Darcy win Abbie . . . and Drew, oh God, how could she bear to leave Drew?

But it was already too late. With an ugly, sickening surge, she could feel herself being lifted up and away.

Monique

June 17, 1993:

Something is wrong.

Each day, it seems increasingly difficult to control the life I have taken from Monica. There are times, late at night, when I fear my serpent has deserted me forever.

If only I could remember what happened on my last journey. I seemed to ride the pleasure wave forever, and I was most reluctant about being yanked away; but I can't remember seeing Monica. I know I must have dealt with her—she has never posed much of a challenge—else, how could I be here in her body?

But it makes me uneasy, for each day it seems more of my power is being drained away. The Sumner fortune has dwindled, though I can't discover why or how; the IRS is showing untoward interest in my tax returns; and last week, when in desperation I went to my closet to pick a jewel to sell, I found the entire cache missing.

I would accuse Derek of the theft—if I thought him capable. He is my greatest disappointment of all, for I have found that, despite the superficial resemblance, he is nothing at all like Drew. All looks and little substance, he's an utter disaster in bed. He will tell you this is because he must make love to his mistress; but from her tight lips and angry glances, I can see Amy Piersoll is no more content than I. Derek's one passion, I fear, is pampering himself.

I would get rid of Derek, even as I did Robert and George before him, if I did not so desperately want his baby.

For it is through his child, that heir to the Sumner name, that I shall achieve both my destiny and revenge. On the day my daughter turns twenty-one, when she is considered legally able to run her own affairs, I will make certain she places the ring on her finger. Her body shall be mine.

And at long last, I shall not only own the Sumners; I shall be one of them. The only one left.

But, alas, I am not yet pregnant; and more and more lately, I wonder if I can afford to wait. The way Amy studies me, I can imagine what she must be plotting. One day soon, she just might goad the unimaginative Derek into murder.

Perhaps Amy can be my stepping-stone, like Judith and Monica before her, a place to roost until my baby can grow into a woman. I've always coveted her looks. Even with the forty pounds I've shed, Monica's body makes me feel like an Amazon. I want to be petite and blond, and there is every possibility that Amy's womb will prove more fertile.

I've seen the way she eyes the Gem of Zombi. If anything should happen to me, Amy will not let my body chill before the ring is on her hand. She cannot know, of course, that I have its mate, taken from Judith's lifeless finger. But then, it is only fitting that such greed should cost the treacherous female her soul.

A perfect plan, though I could wish I were more certain of the chants. If only Rachel were here to help me.

Looking down at the ring, I wonder about the passage of time, so fluid as I rode the serpent through it. In that river of minutes and hours, could it be that Rachel is this very moment saying the chants that first sent me into the future? Could I call out to her, *help me,* and she would hear me across the years?

Yet even as I write this, my door opens. Standing before me is my husband, urged forward by his avaricious mistress. From the looks on their faces, I imagine they've learned about the restrictions I've placed upon his bank account.

I try to ignore them for the last thing I want tonight is a domestic squabble, but it would seem Derek means business this time. There is a gun in his hand.

Rachel, help me . . .

Twenty

When Monique opened her eyes, she found she was no longer in her lavish bedroom facing an angry Derek and Amy, but rather in a dingy shack, staring up at her old slave Rachel. Looking down, she saw the diamond within the ring, still glowing with a fading white fire.

"I am back?" she asked, touching herself to make certain she was solid and real. Somehow, she seemed to have returned to her old body, but the exchange had happened so quickly she could not remember riding the serpent.

Rachel eyed her warily. "It is you?"

"Of course it's me," Monique said irritably, sitting up to look around her. "But how did this happen? I took no potion. I said no chants."

Rachel sat back on her heels, continuing to study her. "The potion is merely to lull the unwilling or to make the transition easier. The chants I said myself."

"So you did hear." Monique smiled to herself. She should have known Rachel would rescue her mistress from harm. "Thank heavens. The bastard was about to shoot me."

Rachel stood abruptly, muttering under her breath as she turned away. Her long, black snake slithered across the floor beside her.

Monique paid little heed as she too rose and noticed the bedraggled skirt and dirty, torn blouse she wore. "I forgot how tedious it is to drag around these heavy skirts. What am I doing in such rags anyway? I could swear I was wearing my blue muslin." With a deepening frown, Monique leaned down to pick up the doll. "And what is this? It looks like me."

"There is much you do not understand."

Impatiently, Monique tossed the doll aside to pace about the room, consumed by a restless energy. "I'd love to learn, but I haven't time. I must get back before that imbecile squanders away my estate. Quick, say the chants again."

"No," Rachel said quietly. She stood at the altar, presenting her back, the snake moving slowly up her outstretched arm.

Monique stared at her, incredulous. "No? What does that mean? You've got to help me; I've set it all up. The minute Amy thinks I'm dead, she'll have the ring on her finger. Stop playing games, Rachel. Say the damn chants."

Rachel continued to stand there, faced away, saying and doing nothing.

"You are my slave," Monique said. "Obey me!"

"I am a free woman now. It is no longer you I must serve."

Monique felt an inhuman fury. She could not believe this. First Derek and Amy dared threaten her, and now Rachel—her Rachel—showed open defiance?

"You have angered Zombi," Rachel said as she

turned, her snake twining around her neck. "I can no longer help you."

"*He* is angry? You might better worry about my rage. I issue the orders here, Rachel, and don't you forget it. Your precious Zombi can do nothing without me for an outlet."

"You promised him souls."

"I will get them. And don't fret about where or how. I don't need you to get what I want, Rachel. I have the ring."

She held up her finger; but they just stared at her, black woman and black snake, their gazes unblinking. Furious, Monique left the shack.

She didn't need Rachel, she swore as she made her way out of the swamp. If this were the past, she could go to her closet and get the chants from her journal.

Li'l Bit could hear Darcy downstairs talking with Abbie. Now that he was going to marry her aunt, he'd seemed a whole lot nicer.

He sure seemed worried, too. Looking at the black book, Li'l Bit wondered if maybe she should give it to him. If he read Mama's words, he might find some way to help Nicki.

The thing was, could she trust him? After Mama, it was hard to trust anyone.

The book felt heavy in her hands. If only Nicki would walk in the door with her in-the-eyes-smile. She always seemed to know how to make everything all better.

I'll wait for Nicki, Li'l Bit decided, but not here with the book in plain sight. She'd have to hide it someplace safe.

Clutching it to her chest, she realized there was

one place, somewhere only she and Nicki knew about. Turning, she looked at the closet.

As Drew approached the house, he saw his sister by the porch steps, gazing up at the door, expectant and tense. He felt the stirrings of apprehension.

But then Darcy burst onto the porch, and Drew relaxed. He knew now why Abbie had seemed nervous. Bless you, Darce, he thought as he watched his best friend take her by the arms. It was clear he had eyes only for Abbie.

"Hate to interrupt," Drew called out before this could become embarrassing for them all, "but have you seen Nicki?"

They looked at him, then at each other; and something in the silent communication revived his sense of unease.

"We've been looking for her, too," Darcy started slowly. "She's not here."

The uneasiness mushroomed into alarm. "Where is she?"

"As I was just telling Abbie, Elizabeth heard her mention going to Rachel."

Rachel? Drew felt outright dread. He shouldn't have stopped at banishing the slave from the plantation; he should have driven Rachel out of the country. "I'm going after her," he said, knowing he must not leave Nicki alone with that woman.

"I'll come with you."

He paused for a moment. "No, Darce. Stay with Abbie and the kids. Keep them all safe."

"Safe?" Abbie's face drained of color.

Drew didn't stay to reassure her. He was

consumed by the need to see Nicki, untouched and unharmed.

As Monique approached the house, she sneered at how shabby it seemed without the new siding, how seedy the grounds were without the landscaping and her kidney-shaped pool. She'd been a naïve seventeen, coming here the first time and thinking this was the very best there could be.

Oh, how she longed to go back, to the River's Edge she'd resurrected and recreated in the future.

Intent upon her mission, it took a while to realize why she felt uneasy. She could have sworn the cane had been barely sprouts the night she'd left, yet it now reached up to her chest. And hadn't the levee around her artificial lake been a good five feet lower?

She shrugged it off. She'd been Judith Sumner for twenty years and Monica for few months after that, so she couldn't really trust her memory. It felt odd, knowing she'd lived all those years, yet here she was the same age as when she'd first gone into the future.

Hearing someone speak, she shrank back against the side of the house. Time lapse or not, she'd know that voice anywhere. Drew had threatened her often enough.

He was talking to Abbie and some male Monique didn't know. Nor did she care to; the last thing she wanted now was to make small talk. Her memory was not so distorted she could forget Drew's angry words before he left for the city. She was not, he had warned, to step foot out of the house.

Edging backwards, she made her way to the

gallery stairs, choosing the outside route to her bedroom.

As she opened the window and stepped inside, she caught her daughter, Elizabeth, at the door of the closet.

"Nicki!" the child gushed with obvious relief. "I knew if I waited you'd come back to help me."

Monique barely heard. For a moment, she thought she'd stepped into the wrong room, for her beautiful French furnishings had been replaced by local cypress junk. Who'd put that awful armoire in the corner?

Pressing a hand to her temple, she tried to orient herself. It was her room, she knew that, but why had it changed? In travelling through time, could she have slipped into another dimension? Outwardly, things seemed similar, but she kept finding more and more odd little discrepancies.

She marched to the closet, wondering what had become of the door. Her hiding place was still here, she was relieved to note, but when she flung up the floorboard, she found the niche empty.

She rounded on Elizabeth, standing behind her. "You did this, didn't you? Always spying on me, wanting to get your hands on my jewels. I'll bet anything you've been playing with them in your room."

"No."

The child looked hurt, then frightened. "There was a book in here, dammit." Monique grew angrier by the moment. "What did you do with it?" She despised children who cowered and cried. That her own should cross her arms protectively over her chest was more than an embarrassment—her weakness was an insult.

Before Elizabeth could edge backward, Monique

snared her arm. "Do you want me to paddle your backside? Or lock you in the closet?" Damn, the door was gone. No matter; she could stuff this little bean pole in the armoire.

Elizabeth shook her head, surprisingly stubborn. "I'm not telling you anything. You're Mama!"

"Of course I am. Who else would I be?"

The child bit her lip as if regretting her outburst.

"You called me Nicki," Monique pounced, remembering how Elizabeth had first greeted her; and as she did, she began to consider things she hadn't before.

Why had she woken in the shack and not in the ground where Rachel had put her? The cane, the levee—did all the discrepancies add up to more than distorted perception?

In her eagerness to escape, she'd never stopped to wonder what would happen to her body. If her spirit could so easily enter Judith and Monica, what was to stop another soul from taking over her own abandoned shell?

"This Nicki," she asked Elizabeth, tightening her grip on the skinny arm, "did she take my journal?"

"No."

"Don't lie to me. What did she do with it?"

Elizabeth thrust out her chin. "She-she ripped it up in a hundred-hundred pieces, and then she burned it."

Monique believed her. In Nicki's place, she'd destroy such incriminating words, too. Come to think of it, she had . . . in the future.

She became overwhelmed by the intricacies of time travel. Could a change in the past alter the future? Uneasily, she thought of the dwindling

Sumner fortune, the disappearance of the jewels from her closet. In assuming her life, had this Nicki taken more than just her body?

"You helped her, didn't you?" she lashed out, digging her nails into Elizabeth's arm. "Traitor! I bet you did everything she asked."

"I love Nicki."

Monique was furious. Without the journal, she'd have to go grovelling to Rachel for the chants. She'd need some way to force the woman into helping, but what would intimidate Rachel? Nothing, she realized—except maybe Drew.

Maybe she could tell him that Rachel had long ago cast a spell on her and she now needed his help to break free. It should work, if she handled him right and this brat wasn't there to mess things up.

"Little girls should love their mamas," she snapped at Elizabeth, dragging her across the room. "To teach you what loyalty means, I'm going to lock you in this armoire. And here you'll stay until you remember just what you owe me."

"No! Mama, please, no!"

Monique ignored her, dragging her by the arm to the armoire. "Keep quiet about this and maybe I'll let you out," she told her daughter as she shut and locked the door. "You will learn to never again betray me. Don't forget I'm family, the only family you have."

She half-grinned, remembering how well that taunt had worked on wimpy Monica. Hopefully, Elizabeth would be too scared to speak out if and when anyone discovered her. Considering the look on her face as the door closed, her daughter would probably be catatonic anyway.

Leaving the room, Monique glanced at her ragged clothes. She wished she could be better dressed, but she could hardly go back to the armoire. Then, too, her pleas might be more effective if she looked pathetic. Drew always had been a sucker for anyone in need.

But it was not her husband she found in his study.

Staring out the window was a stranger—an incredibly good-looking one. "Nicki! Thank God," he said, whirling to face her. "I thought . . . never mind, you're here. That's all that matters."

He started toward her, hands extended, but Monique stayed at the door. Did everyone think she was this Nicki? Maybe she should play along, pretend to be her, so she'd know how to coax Drew.

"We heard you'd gone to Rachel's shack. Drew went after you, thinking you might need him." He stopped, studying her face. "What happened? You look—"

"I'm all right now," she said with just the right touch of weariness. "I had to run from Rachel. She put a spell on me. Drew—"

"I'll go get him."

"No." She smiled, moving closer. "Drew will be fine. Rachel fears him too much to ever hurt him. It's just . . ." Placing her hands on her temples, she tried her best to look confused and frightened. "Rachel has something, a doll I think, that keeps pulling me to her. Only Drew can stop it. He alone can save me."

"Then I should get him."

The last thing she wanted was to have this decisive man helping Drew. "He has to go there, see for himself what Rachel means to do. Don't you see? I need him to believe me; and, well, he's refused to in the past."

"But I thought you two had worked things out."

He seemed genuinely confused. "Abbie thinks Drew's finally learned to trust you."

Who was this woman, Monique wondered resentfully, that she could bring a cynic like Drew Sumner to trust her? "I hope so," she said evenly. "But what if he hasn't?"

"Then we'll show him his new bank balance. I managed to sell your jewels. Even subtracting the money for the sugar cane, there's still a healthy sum."

The woman had stolen her collection and had this man sell it? Worse, she had given the money to Drew?

Ill with rage, it was all Monique could do not to throw things about the room. Everything was ruined. If she stayed here, she'd be a virtual pauper—and her husband's slave.

She had to get to Rachel's shack before Drew left it. And without this handsome stranger.

Strolling up to him, putting just the right sway in her hips, she posed mere inches away. If there was one thing Monique knew how to do it was to disarm the opposite sex. "You're right," she said, giving him her Mona Lisa smile. "I think I'll go on up now and make myself more presentable. You will call me the very instant Drew arrives?"

"Of course."

"You're a darling," she said, putting her fingers to her lips, then gently placing them on his. She let them linger, making her message clear, before turning to glide away.

Abbie stood in the doorway. Monique recognized the look; she'd seen it on dozens of jealous women. Her sister-in-law wanted this man, wanted him badly.

What a shame she couldn't stay to stir things up

a bit. It would have been great fun, seducing him away.

Brushing past, Monique grinned. She couldn't have asked for a better distraction. Abbie would keep the man busy with accusations while she herself escaped to the swamp.

"Darcy, are you all right?"

Looking down at Abbie, Darcy shook his head, striving to recover his wits. How could he express what he'd felt as those evil fingers rested upon his lips?

"You're like ice," Abbie went on, taking his hand. "Talk to me. What is it?"

"Elizabeth." As if forced out of him, the word became a floodgate, letting loose the knowledge he'd gained by that touch. "She has something for us, but she's in trouble. We've got to find her. And then we've got to help Nicki."

Still holding his hand, her feet stubbornly planted where they were, Abbie stopped his forward motion, "Will it always be like this? The woman calls and you follow?"

It hit him then, what she must be thinking. Again, he shook his head. "You don't understand," he said, staring at the door. "That wasn't Nicki."

Drew stomped through the mud, barely feeling the damp seep through his boots in his concern for his wife. Damn, where the hell was that Rachel?

Unable to find either woman in the shack, he'd gone searching in the swamp, his worry building with each step. Not that he feared being lost; he'd mapped out every trail in his youth. But it would soon be getting dark and he hated to think of Nicki in such alien surroundings, cowering in some dark, lonely corner and shivering with fright.

"Call to me," he pleaded silently. "Just call, with your mind, and I swear I will find you."

He turned, feeling more than hearing. Rachel's shack. For some reason, he knew he had to return there.

Lifting up the snake, Monique glared into its dark eyes. "I know you're nearby, Rachel," she said to it. "So you might as well come, before I cut off this reptile's head."

"What do you want?"

Monique spun, startled to find her slave standing before the kettle at the hearth. As her grasp relaxed, the snake wriggled free and slithered across the floor.

Damn, she could have used it as hostage, but perhaps Drew would be threat enough. "You know why I'm here," she blustered. "Let's get it over with."

"I am having tea." Rachel turned, offering a cup of steaming liquid. "Would you like some?"

"This is not a social call. I want the damned chants."

"We have a few moments." With a sad smile, Rachel handed her the cup. "And we must talk."

Monique, realizing that she'd had nothing to eat or drink for some time, began to sip distractedly. "I told you, I haven't the time. You should know, Rachel, any moment—"

"Your husband will come through that door?"

It unnerved her, how the woman often knew what she was thinking. "I thought you were afraid of Drew?"

"Not of him. Of his power over you." Rachel flashed her most enigmatic smile. "But then, he will be too late."

"Dammit, Rachel, you must help me."

"Must I? To the end, you will remain vain and selfish. Sit," Rachel added, nodding at the chairs by the table.

Monique bristled, for she did not like the slave giving *her* orders; but all at once, she felt incredibly weary and sitting seemed a good idea.

"Were you not so concerned with yourself," Rachel began as they both sat, "you'd have long since asked why, if I had both rings, I did not use them myself. My life," she said as she gestured about the shack, "is no less stifling than yours."

Monique had wondered, briefly, but she'd always believed it was Rachel's place to serve her mistress, to get her the things she wanted. She thought Rachel believed it as well.

"I knew the legend of the rings," the woman went on, leaning across the table. "I was insanely curious and eager to test them, but I knew the consequences when a soul is allowed to escape Zombi's clutches. My people would not be slaves today if one spirit had not broken free to live among us, to change the past and rewrite our future."

Monique blinked, trying to focus. "So? Why are you telling me this?"

"Because, according to legend, the woman who let that spirit escape died a hideous death. Not wanting such for myself, I decided to use you, as you had always used me."

"I never—"

"Did you ask if I wished to come to this country?

No, you took me from my family, and demanded I stay here to be treated like a freak."

"You're not a slave now. If *home* is so blessed wonderful, you could go back any time you wish."

"How? I have nothing to show for my years of service. You let your husband exile me here without even a crust of bread. Only by giving you the ring could I win true freedom. I knew Zombi would shower me with blessings if I gave you to Him." She looked Monique in the eye. "But you have angered Zombi. I must send you back. He must have His soul."

"Me?" Monique set down the empty cup, confused. "But I gave him souls. First Judith, and then . . ."

Was that why she could not remember the exchange with Monica? The botched-up wedding, when she'd refused to take the ring; had Monica somehow slipped by and . . .

Of course. She should have recognized the goody-goody Nicki was her niece, but it had never occurred to Monique that anyone could love Monica. She was just so . . . so plain.

Oh, how she must have loved waking up in this body.

Too bad for her, Monique thought, for they'd apparently made the switch again. And by now, Monica was no doubt learning just what Derek intended to do with that gun.

Not that her own situation wasn't equally grave. All at once, she knew why she felt so groggy, so tired. That damned potion. Rachel must have put it in her tea.

Staring into her slave's cold, unrelenting gaze, Monique faced the prospect of her own mortality. "If you want to please Zombi," she pleaded, "you've got to let me try again. It's Monica's soul he wants."

She tried to stand, to lend strength to the protest, but her knees buckled and she dropped to the floor. She sat there, her supporting arm losing strength by the minute. "I'll get her this time. I swear it. I know how to deal with that girl."

Rachel stood over her, regal and proud as she smiled her secret smile. "Zombi has lost patience. He will not treat you kindly if you fail."

"I won't fail," Monique swore, even as she fell over onto her side. "I swear it," she added feebly.

"See that you do not. Or yours, too, shall be a hideous death."

In the back of her mind, Monique could hear Rachel's steady droning, could sense Drew's steady approach; but none of it truly mattered. With a rush of relief, she was stretching, reaching out for the serpent, for that slow, sensual ride through time.

Rachel smiled, looking down at the woman who'd kept her in bondage all these years. Foolish Monique. It mattered little if she won her battle with Nicki or not. Without Rachel to finish the chants, both would go to Zombi.

"Are you doubly pleased?" she asked the snake.

Zombi slithered away into His basket—a timely reminder. Lifting the basket, she left the shack, knowing she must be gone before the man, Drew, came with his questions.

It was time to leave anyway; her work here was done.

* * *

Monica woke slowly, hearing voices whispering above.

"Do you think she really fainted?"

"Wake up, Derek; it's just another game. You know how she loves to play with your mind."

"I hope she's not pregnant."

Monica could sense things were not right, but she felt too groggy to figure out where they were wrong.

"Great," hissed the other voice. "Just what we need, an heir in the way."

Recognition flickered. Not because of the harsh whisper, but more the attitude. A soft, pink package wrapped up in greed. Amy Piersoll.

Oh God, no! Somehow, she had returned to her old body. All at once she remembered Rachel sliding the ring into place. Reacting instinctively, she yanked it from her hand.

It went skittering to the floor. Diving for it, Amy snatched it up, smiling as she slid it on her finger.

Monica watched her, growing sicker by the moment. What could have happened that she could be back in her old life, here with Derek and Amy? Had Monique found the way to retrieve her body?

It was all gone, she thought on a wave of desolation. Her home, the children, Drew. She could never go back to them; more than a hundred years stood in the way.

"I'm warning you, cuz," Derek said sharply. "Either sign this paper or I'll shoot you."

Horrified, Monica noticed his gloved hands, the gun. "What is this, Derek?" she asked, backing away from him. "Have you lost your mind?"

"I'm sick of your bullying, your using my father's money to get me to toe your line. I've had it up to here. I mean it. If you don't sign this paper, I'll kill you."

Monica shook her head. She should be in the kitchen cooking supper with Abbie or upstairs teaching Li'l Bit to read. Fighting despair, she pleaded with Derek. "Stop this. You can't get away with murder."

"No? Right this moment, Hartley's having a party. He and a good twenty others will swear I've been with them the entire evening."

Hartley Buford, Monica thought, Derek's best man and lifetime crony. No wonder she'd always disliked him.

"Us," Amy corrected, stepping up to stand beside Derek. "That alibi was set up for us both."

"Of course." Derek gestured at Monica with the gun. "So you see, darlin', a burglar must have shot you with your own gun. Or maybe it was a ticked-off servant. The way you treat the poor folks, who could blame them?"

Amy parroted his smile. "If you had stayed sweet, old biddable Monica, someone might have questioned your death; but ever since you turned into the wicked witch of the South, all anyone will say is, 'Ding, dong, the bitch is dead.' Go on, shoot her Derek. We have to get back to the party."

"That's cold, Amy. Even for you." Holding out a sheaf of papers, Derek flashed his most endearing grin. "We can at least give her the chance to sign the new will."

"And what good will that do? She'll just bring back her lawyer to draw up a new one, and we still won't have the money. Don't be a wimp, Derek. Shoot her."

At the insult, a sudden determination blazed in his eyes. Before she could protest, Monica heard the blast and felt the white hot pain rip into her chest.

Stunned, she dropped like a brick to the floor, to watch the spreading stain on the cold, white carpet.

"You idiot," she heard Amy snap. "Where's the silencer? With the noise you made, someone will call the cops."

"They don't make silencers for a stupid little lady's pistol. Besides, who cares? We won't be here. Let's go."

"We can't leave. Not until we're sure she's gone. I told you to shoot her in the head to set up the question of suicide. Can't you do anything right?"

Monica, gripping onto life, focused on the ring on Amy's hand. Was it her imagination, or was it beginning to glow? "I want my ring," she gasped, knowing it was her link to the past. Ironic, that it should prove her only hope of rescue.

"Not on your life." Amy covered it with her other hand. "It's mine now. Everything will be."

"Fine." Monica gritted her teeth, trying to ignore the agony in her chest. "I don't imagine anyone will question why you have a dead woman's wedding band on your finger."

The words were directed at Derek, who responded at once. "She's right. You have to put it back," he told Amy. "You can have it later, after the stink's blown over. C'mon, hurry up. I want to get out of here."

Amy muttered under her breath but she stooped down to put the ring on Monica's finger.

And none too soon. As the life ebbed from her body, the ring glowed brighter. It was happening again, that lifting, swirling, roller-coaster ride through time.

"Drew," she cried out in her mind, as if he were the guiding star to lead her way.

Drew threw open the door, ready to threaten Rachel, only to find his wife's pale, motionless body on the floor.

Alarmed, he dropped to his knees beside her, for she was *too* pale. He took her hand in his, as if by squeezing it he could somehow transfer his warmth into her cold and lifeless form.

Numb with fear, he kept rubbing her hands, her face and arms. She was his miracle, his silver lining; God, he loved this woman more than life itself.

But still she did not stir. There had to be something he could do. Casting about in his mind, he remembered her breathing into Elizabeth. Her CP—something. Taking her chin in his hands, he tried to force his own life into that motionless body.

"Drew?" Darcy burst into the shack, carrying Elizabeth on his hip. "Oh, God, are we too late?"

The words *too late* echoed across the room. Drew breathed all the more urgently into her mouth.

As a hand settled on his shoulder, Drew looked up. Darcy had set Elizabeth down and they were both now kneeling on the other side of his wife. "We've come to help," he said softly. "Abbie and the boys will be along any moment. There's no time to explain everything but we just found Elizabeth locked in a closet. This woman isn't Nicki, Drew. From what Elizabeth tells me and what I have sensed, I have to assume this is Monique."

Feeling as if he'd been singed, Drew let go of the chin.

"Can I have the book?" Darcy asked the child.

Nodding, she reached inside her apron bib to hand him a small, black diary. As Darcy opened it, Abbie and the boys came into the room. "I only had time to read the last few entries," Darcy explained to them all, "but from what I gather, Monique has somehow taken Nicki's spirit and has her trapped somewhere in time."

With a wrench in his gut, Drew knew this was far worse than being lost in the swamp. Nicki must be terrified. She was so alone. "What must I do?" he snapped at Darcy.

With a grim smile, Darcy pointed at the ring, glowing faintly on her other hand. "It's all somehow connected with the Gem of Zombi, so I suggest you hold onto it. Everyone else, come form a circle, touching Drew on both sides."

"But, Darcy," Abbie asked, her own face devoid of color, "how can you know all this?"

"I promise, I'll explain later, but we haven't a moment to lose. Try to trust me. While I say these chants, you're all going to have to reach out with your minds for Nicki. I know it sounds bizarre, and it may mean our sanity; but if we want to save her, we're going to have to reach in wherever she is and pull her free of Monique."

The obvious whats and whys and hows whirled through his mind; but deep at his core, Drew knew questions weren't going to save his wife. "Start saying those chants, Darce."

As his friend began his intonations, Drew tightened his grip on the hand. "Hold on," he thought, remembering how he had said the words earlier. "Wait for me, Nicki. I'm coming."

* * *

Spinning crazily, it took Monica some moments to realize she was no longer alone on her ride through time. Someone was holding her, pulling her.

"Go to him," a voice whispered in her ear, the sound soft and seductive. "He's waiting for you."

She shook her head, resisting. She could see nothing in the spiralling void. She could hear and feel, and what she felt filled her with dread.

"Do as I say, darling. This is your Aunt Judith and you promised me."

Monica hesitated, for the voice summoned up old hurts and rejections, her longing for love.

"Do this for me," the voice continued to coax. "I'm your family, the only family you have."

And all at once, a wave of sheer joy flowed into her, buoying her in a strengthening flood. She had a real family now, and she had to get home to them.

"I'm not the scared, lonely girl you once bullied," she cried out, determined this once to stand up to her aunt. "I have something to fight for now."

"Ha! You can't fight Zombi."

"No? Watch me."

A wind began to howl at her ears, pulling at her as if it meant to suck the very life out of her limbs; but as if they were her anchor, Monica held tight to her image of Drew and the children. She pictured them surrounding her, cuddled up close in her four-poster bed. And as she did, the wind began to lessen.

"Go to him, damn you," the voice said in a

frenzy. "Do as I say or . . . or . . ."

"Or you'll lock me in a closet?" As she said the words and remembered all the other little cruelties, Monica realized why her Aunt Judy had changed so much when she put on George Sumner's ring. It wasn't Judith anymore; it was Monique.

The monster she'd vowed never to let near the children.

She felt a superhuman strength then, as if she had swelled to ten times her size. If she had to fight a dozen Moniques she was not going to bend to the will of an evil spirit. She had her own power, the power of love; and, whatever it took, Monica meant to protect her family.

"You must obey me," Judith-Monique demanded, the wind around them dwindling to a pathetic whine. "Zombi must have his soul."

"Then *you* go to him. Better yet, go to hell!"

She heard Monique's scream of rage; but then with a whoosh of air, Monica was stretched like a piece of taffy, until she was spiralling off through time.

Monique felt herself settle, and she thought, *See, I knew Zombi would not fail me.*

A strange noise intruded on her triumph, dulling it; and, with dismay, she felt the spreading agony in her chest. Opening her eyes, she saw Amy Piersoll playing with the ring on her finger. The sound, they both seemed to realize at once, was the rapid approach of a siren.

"The police," Derek shouted, tossing the gun on the floor. It skittered tauntingly close, but just beyond reach. "Sorry, darlin', but I'm out of here."

Amy tried to go after him, but Monique grabbed

her wrist. She was weak, losing strength by the moment, but she could not let go until she had the other ring on her finger.

Damn, she was so weak and her pocket seemed miles away. All her strength went into holding tight to the startled Amy. Monique heard the siren suddenly cut off and then the footsteps on the stairs before she gathered the resources to reach in her pocket.

To her disbelief, the second ring was no longer there. Damn that Monica, had she tampered with that in the past, too?

As Monique lost her grasp on the wrist, Amy sprang to her feet, seconds too late. Standing over the body as the policemen entered the room, she was the perfect picture of guilt.

"It wasn't me," she tried to protest. "It was Derek."

Good, Monique thought, the pair would convict each other.

Realizing that it was time to let go of Monica's useless body, she drifted up and out of it in search of a place to roost. In a growing panic, she knew there would be no Rachel to help her, no serpent to serve as escort—from now on, she would be completely alone. All that remained was a dark swelling void that threatened to swallow her whole.

With abject terror, she remembered Rachel's warning. Was this, then, the start of her hideous death?

Screaming, she felt herself sucked off into the wasteland, knowing this time, she would die forever.

* * *

"It's Nicki," Monica heard Li'l Bit cry. "See, she's smiling with her eyes."

Looking around her, seeing each member of her family staring anxiously down at her, Monica knew an overwhelming sense of rightness.

"Welcome home, Mrs. Sumner," Drew told her hoarsely as he slid the ring from her finger. "And this time, you're home to stay."

Epilogue

Monica stood on the porch, watching Abbie and Darcy stroll off through the live oaks toward the river. Grinning, she wondered if they, too, had discovered the magic of the cove. If so, they'd better hurry along their wedding.

"Gotcha," Li'l Bit cried out, and Monica looked to the railing where the girl had a strangehold on her brother's leg. "I did it, Nicki. I finally caught Andrew."

Monica smiled, remembering the first day she'd come, how they'd been playing the same game. Watching them then, she'd sensed how close to heaven her life could one day be. "Good for you, sweetie," she told the girl. "Now maybe he won't tease you so."

"Ah, Nicki, you always take her side."

"Is that right? Then who was it that made her give back your slingshot yesterday morning? Come here, both of you. And you too, Stephen. I think it's past time you three gave me my hug for today."

The boys grumbled and complained; but they'd been there beside Drew to pull her to safety and for the present, at least, they were willing enough to indulge her with hugs.

"I've been thinking," Li'l Bit said as she squeezed her. "I don't want to call you Nicki anymore."

Surprised and a little hurt, Monica looked at her. "Why not?"

Li'l Bit shrugged. "I don't need to. I want to call you Mama."

As she looked expectantly to her brothers, Stephen said, "Us, too," while Andrew gave a distracted nod. "That is," Stephen added, "if you don't mind."

Overwhelmed by emotion, Monica shook her head. "No. No, I don't mind."

"Good." With that taken care of, Andrew pointed to the drive. "Last one up the oak tree is a silly baby."

With a trio of whoops, they were running off to climb the tree. Watching them, feeling happy enough to burst, she heard the door open behind her. She knew without turning around it was Drew; after that awful night in Rachel's shack, a link had been forged between them.

He came up behind her, settling his warm hands about her waist. Later, when she had better control of her emotions and they could talk alone in bed, she would tell him about yet another child, growing steadily inside her.

"Is it done?" she asked instead.

"It's done." Resting his chin on her head, he pulled her closer to his chest. "We can rest easy now. The journal has joined the ring on its way downriver."

They'd gotten rid of the ring immediately, but they had both felt a need to read Monique's diary.

They had to know the full extent of her evil and how it might affect the future, but it wasn't something they wished the children ever to learn.

It bothered Drew that they'd never found Rachel, but Monica knew they would never see her again. She was glad of it, for something had been purged by getting rid of all traces of Monique; even the air seemed fresher.

Not that there weren't questions left unresolved. It made her head spin each time she thought about souls switching bodies, about how she might have come here and unwittingly changed the future. At first, it made her uneasy to think she might be tampering with the past, but being here felt so right and everything was working out well. Lately, she'd begun to believe she was meant to be part of Drew's life all along. That she'd been right, that long ago day, when she'd seen herself at the edge of heaven.

"The children say they are going to call me Mama," she told him, her voice unsteady.

He turned her to face him. "Don't tell me you're going to cry again. I declare, Mrs. Sumner, sometimes I think you turn into a waterspout just to get me to kiss you."

"Whatever works."

Grinning, he pulled her into his arms to kiss her breathless.

They might never be rich and she could forget about all modern conveniences; but she had this house, her children, and a fine man to love her.

And as she melted into Drew's warmth, she knew she was no longer on the edge looking in—she had found her way to the very heart of heaven.